## Praise for *The List*

"A biting, hilarious send-up of D.C.'s

—*People*

"Hildy Johnson would recognize a kindred spirit in twenty-eight-year-old Adrienne Brown, a Beltway-bred, New York–trained reporter who sacrifices sleep, sanity, and sex to feed the wonky digital/paper beast the *Capitolist*—or "The List" as its rabidly ambitious scribes call it . . . . Former *Politico* reporter Tanabe's roman-a-clef is a hilarious skewering of digital journalism—and how news is tweeted and blogged at a dizzying pace by armies of underpaid and overworked twentysomething journos—as well as smartly paced and dishy debut, part political thriller, part surprisingly sweet coming-of-age tale, and part timeless ode to dogged reporters with good instincts and guts of steel. Hildy would be proud."

—*Publishers Weekly* (starred review)

"A contemporary, politically astute novel that is both wickedly humorous and enticing . . . [with] complex characters, an intriguing plot, and tightly brilliant execution. When word gets around about *The List*, readers will clamor for their copy and devour this book."

—*New York Journal of Books*

"Tanabe gleefully skewers digital media sweatshops . . . [but] despite its breezy, chick-lit tone, *The List* has more in common with newsroom satires."

—*The Washington Post*

"Appealing . . . everything a die-hard chick-lit fan could want: plenty of fluff, sibling rivalry, deceit and intrigue, and a spunky heroine."

—*Kirkus Reviews*

"*The List* is mandatory reading for anyone who wonders about the impact of new media on Washington's political culture. Tanabe has written a novel that is delicious fun and incredibly revealing about life at the intersection of politics and journalism."

—Nicolle Wallace, *New York Times* bestselling author of *Eighteen Acres*

"A gorgeous book—I loved it. Funny, intriguing, and utterly unputdownable."

—Penny Vincenzi, international bestselling author

"Karin Tanabe's energetic, humorous debut is narrated by a young reporter trying to prove herself by chasing the biggest story of the year. *The List* perfectly captures the frenetic, all-consuming pace of political reporting, with a healthy dose of scandal, glamour, and intrigue thrown in. Think *The Devil Wears Prada* meets Capitol Hill."

—Sarah Pekkanen, author of *Catching Air*

"*The List* is a wonderfully witty insider's romp through Washington. Karin Tanabe has as sharp a tongue as she does an eye for detail, about everything from political scandal to office politics. And I thought New York was a tough town!"

—Cristina Alger, author of *The Darlings*

"*The List* is a breezy, dishy romp through Washington, DC, politics, journalism, and scandal—a witty and caffeinated glimpse into a world few of us ever see, let alone know as intimately as Karin Tanabe surely does. But underneath the considerable pleasures of its glimmering surface, it's a surprisingly moving coming-of-age story about a young woman navigating the bumpy terrain between ambition and ethics, between her hunger for professional success and the quiet truth of her own heart."

—Lauren Fox, author of *Friends Like Us*
and *Still Life with Husband*

"Part coming of age, part political thriller, Karin Tanabe's *The List* is a mordantly funny send-up of quadruple espresso–fueled journalism in the Internet age, with the most irresistible heroine since Bridget Jones at its center. This is Evelyn Waugh's *Scoop* for the twenty-first century."

—Susan Fales-Hill, author of *Imperfect Bliss*

**ALSO BY KARIN TANABE**

*The List*

# THE PRICE

## *of*

# INHERITANCE

*A Novel*

## KARIN TANABE

WASHINGTON SQUARE PRESS

NEW YORK   LONDON   TORONTO   SYDNEY   NEW DELHI

Washington Square Press
A Division of Simon & Schuster, Inc.
1230 Avenue of the Americas
New York, NY 10020

First Washington Square Press trade paperback edition August 2014

WASHINGTON SQUARE PRESS and colophon are registered trademarks of Simon & Schuster, Inc.

For information about special discounts for bulk purchases, please contact Simon & Schuster Special Sales at 1-866-506-1949 or business@simonandschuster.com.

The Simon & Schuster Speakers Bureau can bring authors to your live event. For more information or to book an event contact the Simon & Schuster Speakers Bureau at 1-866-248-3049 or visit our website at www.simonspeakers.com.

Interior design by Kyoko Watanabe
Cover design by Min Choi
Cover photograph by Arcangel

Manufactured in the United States of America

10 9 8 7 6 5 4 3 2 1

Library of Congress Cataloging-in-Publication Data

Tanabe, Karin.
    The price of inheritance : a novel / Karin Tanabe.—First Washington Square Press trade paperback edition.
        pages cm
    1. Single women—Fiction. 2. Antique dealers—Fiction. 3. Man-woman relationships—Fiction. 4. Archaeological thefts—Iraq—Fiction. I. Title.
PS3620.A6837P85 2014
813'.6—dc23
                                                                        2013046055

ISBN 978-1-4767-5860-2
ISBN 978-1-4767-5861-9 (ebook)

*For my husband*

"Anyone who lives within their means suffers from a lack of imagination."

—OSCAR WILDE

# THE PRICE
*of*
# INHERITANCE

# CHAPTER 1

It starts in my ears. A slight ringing that fades in and out like a faint Morse code signal. Then my heart takes off. It beats and thumps and pounds so loudly I'm sure the people next to me can hear it. I smile and laugh nervously. I think about reassuring the worried-looking man to my right that I'm sane; it's just a little heart murmur and I'm not in need of a Xanax or an EKG. But nothing can stop the rush of adrenaline, anxiety, and animal-like sweating. My palms start to clam up, from the tips of my fingernails to my wrists. They become damp, soaking even, as the bids in the auction room start low—low in billionaire-speak—and soar up in minutes. I want to join them, calmly dishing out seven figures for that Chippendale armoire handmade by craftsmen in the eighteenth century, like it's as routine as buying a latte. But that's not why I'm here. I'm here to get the super-rich to buy, and as the room buzzes with the sound of moneyed voices, I know my job is almost done. But that doesn't calm me down.

The bids rise as a waterfall of sweat swims down my back. I'm so sticky I could keep a fish alive in my shirt. I'm sure I look crazy, but I try to smile through my adventures in perspiration. The auctioneer's sophisticated voice works its way rhythmically through the crowd and hands go up and down like a rich person's version of Whac-A-Mole. Then, finally, only the most determined bidders wave their paddles in the air—some tentative, some powerful, others unnaturally relaxed as they bid with someone else's money. Then, a pause. A single hand rises in the crowd, the auctioneer acknowledges the final bidder, and the hammer hesitates, then firmly falls. The mahogany hits the podium. And just like that, someone very rich and rather sentimental has spent millions of dollars, dirhams, yuan, or pounds on a painting, a table, a coin collection, dueling pistols, or an old pair of Kennedy underwear.

After ten years of the money-fueled adrenaline fest, I knew what to expect when I walked into the Christie's saleroom in New York on September 13 at 6:30 P.M. As soon as my leather soles squeaked through the institution's glass doors on the periphery of Rockefeller Center as a nineteen-year-old intern, I vowed to never leave Christie's, and I hadn't. For the last decade I'd been assisting, and then appraising and finally acquiring lamps in the shape of boats, clocks in the shape of birds, and desks made by men who loved powdered wigs. And all that—along with a few good connections—had led me to today.

The last time the famed Nicholas Brown Chippendale Mahogany Block-and-Shell Carved Desk-and-Bookcase sold at auction was in 1989 and it went for $12.1 million, a world auction record for American furniture. All the art journalists wrote about it. And everyone agreed that the desk, crafted by the Townsend-Goddard School of cabinetmaking in Newport, Rhode Island, was worth the astronomical price. There was plenty of buzz around the sale, and no one thought it would sell again for decades. But they were wrong.

Thanks to a tip about a family's failed investments from

a collector whom I'd worked with for years, I'd made two trips to the Cayman Islands in six months and one to Boston to convince Jack Davidson, the fickle heir of an old Massachusetts family, that yes indeed he should sell his prized desk to help pad his bank account. And I convinced him that only my distinguished place of employment, Christie's, could get him a higher price than the eight figures he'd paid five years ago.

To keep Jack from contacting rival Sotheby's while we wined and dined him, I'd immediately made a $12 million guarantee. Every dollar above $12 million that the piece brought in would be split by Jack, the seller, and us, the auction house. I'd also promised him prime placement on the cover of our September auction catalogue, skybox tickets to the Boston Red Sox, and a ninetieth birthday party for his father at the Christie's headquarters in New York. I assured him that he and his third wife would be put up at the Plaza in the F. Scott Fitzgerald suite for the weekend, and that I'd personally take his youngest daughter to the American Girl store and to lunch at Delmonico's. "Around strangers, she only eats condiments," he'd warned, pushing back his dapper mop of brown hair and giving his diabolical seven-year-old daughter a wink and several packets of ketchup before heading back to the hotel.

Before I showed Jack the mockup of our catalogue—which I'd had the graphics department put together in twenty-four hours—I tied it with a linen bow handmade in Nantucket and spent thirty minutes starching and ironing it until it could barely be knotted. American furniture is mostly bought and sold by Americans. But this cabinet was a record breaker. I knew collectors in Russia, Asia, and the Middle East would be interested; it was something we had to have.

The courting we did in the American furniture department to woo estates was nothing compared to what went on in the bigger departments—Old Masters, Impressionist, Contemporary. I wanted Jack Davidson to build a relationship with Christie's, and as soon as his beloved father, Paul Davidson, died, I wanted him to think of no one but Christie's when he sold his estate. So a big-dollar promise was made and now I had to deliver on it. We both knew there was no guarantee I could keep my word. Worst-case scenario, it wouldn't sell for $12 million and Christie's would own the piece. I would be branded a failure and the next decade would see me selling plastic chairs in church parking lots.

I woke up on auction day in my tiny apartment on East Fifty-Ninth Street and pushed back the covers an hour before sunrise. I went through the same ritualistic motions on every big auction day as I tried to steady my racing mind. I picked up the *New York Times* and the front-page headline read: "Economy in shambles. Never spend another dime! Move to burgeoning New Delhi," or something like that. But I was ignoring the pessimists. Those grizzly economists always saw the champagne glass half empty and there were lots of rich people left counting Bentleys and Picassos between their spoonfuls of fish eggs. I knew it was wrong to ask God for large sums of money to be spent on ludicrously expensive furniture, so I didn't pray. Audibly, anyway. Instead, I walked. It was the same every time my department had an auction. My alarm went off at 5:30 A.M., I ate an entire bar of dark chocolate and three organic breath mints, and then I hit the pavement for an hour.

The morning of the desk auction, or Chippendale Day, as I'd been calling it during nervous phone calls to my therapist, I headed toward the park. I would start by strolling around the edge, the empty streets full of historic buildings inhabited by the extremely wealthy, and then, when the sun started to rise, I would turn into the park, watch the orange rays cover Manhattan, and sweat out a tiny portion of my nerves in the city's cloud of green.

I walked twenty-three blocks, watched the yellow cabs race by, and climbed up and down the steps of the Metropolitan Museum of Art. All I could think about was money. Specifically, $12.2 million. I'd be happy with that. Not thrilled, but happy. I sat down on the steps, letting the morning wind slap my pale face, and stretched out my arms. In the next hour, I would wash, dry, brush, powder, and paint myself into someone who looked like she knew what she was doing. I'd appear polished and intelligent. Someone who deserved to have the job title Senior Specialist, American Furniture and Decorative Arts; someone Christie's was proud to have associated with their venerable name.

I thought back on the first full day I worked at Christie's as an employee instead of an intern. I was twenty-one, I was terrified, but I knew much more about American furniture than your average college student. I was a little obsessed. I thought about getting a tattoo of a Chippendale drop-leaf dining table on my inner forearm. To me it said, Passion, Old World, Awesome. To my parents, it said Lunatic, Criminal, Antiquities Freak, so I never did it. But I was ready to. That's how much I loved what I was doing. And maybe Christie's had seen my obsession, which, combined with the fact that my grandparents were once a pretty big deal, led them to slap a secure entrance card in my hand and give me a desk and access to very expensive things.

In the nearly 250-year history of Christie's, I was the youngest senior specialist ever to be employed by the American furniture department. And as much as my parents were disconcerted by the way I wanted to express my passion, it was a job that was in my bones.

All through my childhood, my mother, Laura Everett, taught American art history at Salve Regina University in Newport, and my father was an architect specializing in nineteenth-century restoration. My family liked old things. Most of the time we liked old things more than we liked each other. But no one was in Newport anymore. We were just three, my parents and me. My grandmother, Virginia Everett, lived with us until I was thirteen years old. My parents had me far too young, when they were just getting ready to devote their lives to PhDs and academia, and quickly concluded that they weren't kid people. So my grandmother beckoned us from Boston to Newport and raised me while my parents focused on what really mattered to them—things without a pulse. It was clear to all of us by the time I could walk that I was happiest when I was in my grandmother's arms. When she passed away from liver cancer the void she left was something even teenage freedom couldn't fill. Our house, once booming with the sound of her thick Rhode Island accent and determined matronly ways, became very quiet. At thirteen, I was considered an adult by my parents, and they didn't bother to fill the silence.

When I finished boarding school and was about to become a very nervous college freshman, my parents shipped back to Boston, home to a whole host of nineteenth-century buildings for them to have fits over. They abandoned our history and our little house with the green glass roof.

My heartbreak pushed me swiftly into studying nineteenth-century American architecture and decorative arts, which turned into my first job at Christie's as a summer intern in the Valuations department. I got to handle not only American furniture but Renaissance art, Chinese scroll paintings, South American and Asian pottery, Middle Eastern artifacts, and a lot of massive diamonds. Before I had my Princeton diploma, Christie's officially hired me in April of my senior year. As I was allowed to become more of an expert, everything else faded away until I was surrounded only with what I loved most, American history. I became a junior and eventually senior specialist in the American Furniture and Decorative Arts department. I loved old things, but I really loved old American things. And if they had been pieced together in Newport, I went into joyous cardiac arrest.

On the unseasonably chilly morning of the auction, the wind ripped through my thin jacket as I watched the vendors set up their carts. The summer's ice cream and soda stands were slowly turning into New York's fall street food— roasted nuts, salted pretzels—but everything else was the same: the *I Love New York* T-shirts, the mass-produced wall art, the mini plastic versions of the city's iconic buildings. Mementos for normal people to enjoy.

I took in the five-dollar price tags as I thought about the hours in front of me. Was having an auction this close to the summer holidays a good thing or a terrible idea? Terrible idea. Was the senior director of my department going to have me done away with if I didn't keep my $12 million promise? Absolutely. Death by old-world hands and an antique butcher knife was predicted. But I had to give a price guarantee to lure the cabinet out of a handsome house in Boston and onto our showroom floor. Everything we sold had a reserve price—we were never going to let Édouard Manets sell for a nickel—but pieces or collections we really wanted to acquire and keep away from Sotheby's we gave a guaranteed price to. That's just how it was done. Sometimes we even gave half the guarantee in advance so the seller could buy more porcelain dogs or whatever oddity they were coveting. My department knew that the $12 million I had given was very high, but collectors liked records, and it wasn't going to break a record again unless it went past $12.1. There was money in the world and people wanted to spend it on well-crafted mahogany, I was sure. Funds from blood diamond sales, arms dealers, drug cartels—surely someone wanted to own the most expensive piece of American furniture in the world. And we weren't picky! Money was money.

I needed to rope up some confidence. This was not doomsday, even if my central nervous system seemed to think so. This was a day I had worked very hard for. At one time, my family had an astronomical amount of money. When I was born, most of it was gone, but I grew up around enough millionaires to feel comfortable with wealth. That was the key to working with the extremely rich. They couldn't intimidate you, scare you, or disgust you. You had to sit down to dinner with them and declare, "You paid eight hundred dollars for that haircut (*that looks like it was done with a fork and gardening shears*)? What a bargain! Your (*pot dealer*) child is taking seven years to graduate from Choate? There's no hurry! You have a Queen Anne Carved Mahogany Armchair and want fifty thousand for it? Of course, totally possible, more than happy to discuss."

It wasn't normal life. The people were rich and crazy, the men were pompous, the women were vain, and everyone wanted to win in front of an audience. If no one was watching then it wasn't worth it at all, which is why the filthy rich always bought at auction. I absolutely loved it.

I had reached my salary high at Christie's this year: $85,000. Many of our buyers made that in a day, but I would have done my job for much less. When I started at the auction house, thanks to connections and solid grades at an Ivy, I made $20,000 a year and had to live in a friend's home office. My bed was so close to her power shredder that

I slept with shoes on, just in case. But I'd moved up quickly by consigning the right collections. During non-auction weeks, I spent my workdays putting together catalogues, researching provenance and doing appraisals, sourcing pieces, working on client relationships, and trying to stay on the winning side of our duopoly with Sotheby's.

Now, even when the art market, especially American decorative arts, was shaky, I was still managing to bring in big collections, and that was partially because my late grandfather was Marlin Everett, whose grandfather first came to Newport for the summers after *his* father made a pretty penny in New York working in steel manufacturing. He, along with Andrew Carnegie, was a key investor in the mass production of American steel through the Bessemer process, brought over from Britain. My grandmother, Virginia Everett, served as chair of the Red Cross Ball three times in a row. I liked to think it wasn't the only reason I was at Christie's, but I knew it helped. At all the major auction houses, your relationships mattered enormously. They cared about your last name, your mother's maiden name, your parents' bank accounts, how many millions your grandparents had, and where your biological tentacles reached all over the country. They asked you about private club memberships, university club memberships, and when they were done grilling you, they did it all again in French, and maybe Italian or Mandarin, too.

Just before my first day of work, when I was deciding on which black dress out of fifteen nearly identical black dresses to wear, a family friend who had worked at Christie's but had left to run a gallery put her hand on my shoulder, pointed to the plainest one, and said, "It's not *Vogue*. It's brain wars." She sat down on my bed—thin, polished, a patrician profile and professionally straightened hair—and kicked off her Prada loafers. "People don't collect bags; they collect foreign languages, dialects, degrees, and academic papers. They know everything about their collectors—their favorite foods, their birthdays, what perfume they wear, how their parents died, any diseases in the family that might kill them off and when. I can tell you the projected life expectancy for every cancer diagnosis. You have to know which collection could move when and be in front of it. At Princeton you were very smart, but at Christie's you'll feel awfully stupid. Good luck." I had eaten three Sprinkles cupcakes and cried that night. And she had been right, in a way. Every person at Christie's had gray matter for days. They argued in Russian, coaxed clients in Japanese, and did interviews for *Le Monde* while walking around the Met with former spies who were now premier experts on Fabergé eggs. But that wasn't all. Your academic knowledge of art was important, but equally important was your ability to get close to the right people and schmooze. Some hated that reality, but I thrived on it. Except for right now.

On my way home, I tried counting how many auctions I'd attended since I started at Christie's. My department, American Furniture and Decorative Arts, was small, but going to auctions of any kind—numismatics, weaponry, wine, ceramics—was encouraged and I'd been slipping in and out of them for a decade. Auction day should no longer be intimidating, but when it was mine, it was—every single time.

My professional integrity, and possibly my career, was on the line. If the desk didn't make the guarantee, the sale would become known as the greatest missed opportunity our department had ever had. If it went past $12.1 million, it would be our most important sale in the past twenty years. I felt strangled by the pressure but there was nothing I could do now but chew handfuls of Klonopin, freebase espresso, and cry in the fetal position. The catalogues were printed, we'd shown the works, the sellers were ready to buy, and all I had to do was carry on getting dressed, dry my hair, finish putting on makeup, and pray for my anxiety to fade away. Holding on to the towel rack, I looked at myself in the mirror and flashed a big fake smile. Why were my teeth so small? I looked like someone who only ate candy and had rotted away her bicuspids. And my eyes were *very* brown, a unique shade of polluted swamp brown. I picked up my brush and straightener and ironed my blond hair to near perfection. My hair was long and extremely light, which was good for being spotted in a crowd or attracting men with a love of Renaissance fairs or the Pre-Raphaelite Brotherhood. I once went out with a photographer who loved to take my picture and yell, "You're so elfin! A woodland sprite goddess!" He didn't seem to mind that my coloring was *Children of the Corn*, and neither did anyone at Christie's. I did everything that I could to stand out, to be memorable, the one people called when they wanted to break records. I'd even had a perfume mixed by the most famous nose in Grasse, which was partially made from ground money in several global currencies. "You will actually be wearing the smell of money," he'd announced, and I'd been spraying it on religiously for a decade. Some might call it over-the-top; my boss deemed it ingenious.

Twenty Rockefeller Plaza: the intimidating address where Christie's has ruled the auction world since it moved out of its smaller Park Avenue offices in 1997. My workday, getting ready for the evening sale, was going to be hell. But at least hell was located in a very nice building. At first, I had trouble associating Rockefeller Plaza with anything but ice-skating in December and the country's best Christmas tree, but after I first walked into the Christie's office in 2004, a nervous college intern, Rockefeller Plaza would mean nothing to me but Christie's. I was destined to become one of those high-powered, brilliant women who threw out words like "figural marquetry techniques" before heading off with my fellow artistic geniuses to the Waldorf Astoria to drink highballs and discuss the ongoing crisis in the Middle East. "It's awfully awful!" I'd say before handfuls of millionaires stopped by our table for fashionable tête-à-têtes.

"Good evening, Carolyn. Happy Chippendale Day," John, the building's head of security, whispered to me with a smile as I finally made my way from our offices to the auction room, checked in, and tried not to faint directly into his arms.

"Yes! It's going to be exciting," I said, unbuttoning my blazer.

"You'll be fine and it *will* be exciting," John replied, and I tried to smile in agreement. He was right, it would be exciting, because I was going to die. "It was art that killed her," they'd declare before speedily donating all my organs to people with apartments full of West Elm bookcases.

Deciding not to check in with our chairman, but go straight to the auction, I walked inside and headed for the very back, where it was standing room only. My colleague Nicole Grant, a direct descendant of Ulysses S. Grant and junior specialist in American furniture, was already there, leaning nervously against the wall. She waved me over with a polite twist of her thin wrist.

"Carolyn, it's time," she whispered as I made my way through the crowd. "Your crowning moment! You look beautiful. Like you're made of snowflakes. Are you nervous? Don't be nervous, because I'm nervous for you. I've been scoping the crowd for half an hour and there are some major players here. Victor Wong. Peter Rensselaer from the Museum of Fine Arts, Boston. I think I saw Bridget Donahue, too. How come you didn't come down early?"

"Because I would have marched up to every single person and demanded to know their net worth. I am not sane right now. I can't be trusted in a public place."

Nicole smiled supportively.

"I think you'll at least match. Twelve-point-one million."

"You know I can't have it just match," I said, trying to keep from shrieking. Nicole was the most junior person in our small department but she understood the stakes. If the price for the Chippendale didn't exceed its previous selling price of $12.1 million, my brilliant moment would be stained forever with the words "Americana worth nothing. Sell immediately. Economic downturn proves fatal. Carolyn Everett to blame. Will be beheaded at dawn." And all those trips trying to rationalize with a very eccentric seller would be for naught. Though we'd been preparing this auction for months, each lot would get only thirty seconds to five minutes of bidding time—an exceptionally short amount of time for someone to spend $12.2 million—and the whole evening sale would last just over two hours.

I stood motionless next to Nicole as the remaining potential bidders filed into the room. The noise of the crowd swelled as we approached the start of the auction—the chatter and air kisses, the adrenaline increasing everyone's pulse. The first lot of the day, a sideboard built in Newport by the school of Thomas Howard Jr., went on the auction block and Nicole and I listened as the lower-dollar bids rose past the reserve and then finally neared an end. We always packed the front of an auction with some of the more valuable pieces, then moved to lower-priced objects before the high-dollar pieces. The prices rose and fell like a heart monitor, but you had to warm people up and get them ready to empty their wallets with a little help from the civilized thrill of the chase.

One more sideboard, an end table, three desks, and two sets of priceless side chairs, which suddenly had prices, were sold. Eight lots down, twenty-one left, but suddenly no one cared about anything except the Super Bowl of American decorative arts, Lot 30.

The esteemed Olivier Burnell was calling the auction, something he'd been doing for Christie's for the last twenty-three years. I half listened to him as he finished Lot 29, and then I sucked in my breath and held on to Nicole's wrist for support as he announced either the apex or downfall of my career, lot number 30.

"Lot number thirty is the Nicholas Brown Chippendale. The Mahogany Block-and-Shell Carved Desk-and-Bookcase," he said calmly, his perfect British accent pronouncing each word as precisely as a translator. "Showing on your far right and as described and illustrated in your catalogues. Lot thirty," he repeated. Without pausing for breath, he started the bidding.

"Now five million dollars to start. Five million. Five million dollars." I crossed my legs so tight that my right ankle started to seize and I accidentally kicked a bald man in front of me so hard that he jumped up like he'd been launched out of a cannon. Olivier almost mistook him for a bidder. "So sorry," I muttered quietly just as the auctioneer's voice rose and sped up like a posh version of a man selling a pig at a county fair.

"Five million five hundred thousand . . . six million now. Six million dollars . . . six million five hundred thousand. Against you here at six million five hundred thousand . . . now seven million dollars. In a new place with Michael now."

Olivier pointed to one of the Christie's employees taking phone bids on the far right-hand side of the room.

"The gentleman in the center. Now on this telephone here. Now in the room, this side," said Olivier, pointing. "New bidder now in the room at eight million five hundred thousand, against the telephones now, gentleman's bid here," he said, moving his eyes expertly across the crowd.

"Against you Agnes now," he said, looking toward the phones at one of our Russian speakers, who was covering her mouth with paper to make her conversation totally anonymous.

"In the saleroom, and against you here," said Olivier as Agnes's bidder kept going against the room. "Now yours here up front at eight million five hundred thousand," said Olivier as the bids sailed past $9 million.

Olivier swept his arm across the space where two different men in the center left of the room were bidding. Another phone bidder went up with a colleague who spoke Mandarin, and then the bids moved quickly back to the crowd. While some governments had strict laws about keeping their country's heirlooms at home, the United States didn't care. If you had money, you could buy our stuff and take it out of the country, even if you lived in Sichuan Province.

"In the room now at nine million five hundred thousand dollars," Olivier declared quickly, scanning for new hands. I needed just three million more. A tiny, paltry little three million. I closed my eyes, praying that when I opened them a passionate billionaire with five black AmEx cards and tears of joy in his eyes would appear and announce his love for eighteenth-century American furniture. Instead, I opened my eyes and felt like I'd developed cataracts. Nicole looked at me like I was taking my final breaths.

"Are you okay?" she said, leaning over and gripping my right hand. "Are you always this hot?"

"Oh, don't worry about it. Poor circulation due to childhood illness. Polio," I whispered back.

"You had polio?" she said, clearly imagining my painful childhood spent as a clone of FDR.

"Sorry, not polio, I meant pox. Like chicken. Chicken pox."

My tongue now had a mind of its own. Next I was going to declare myself the illegitimate ruler of France. I felt one step away from a supersonic meltdown. And, as Nicole soon pointed out, a real problem with hives.

"You look like you have enormous hickeys all over your face," she said, physically recoiling.

"I know, I know," I said, reaching in my bag and taking out my foundation. "It will go down as soon as this auction's over." I opened my purse again and popped three Benadryl and did a few of the breathing exercises that I'd learned in my Virgin Airlines Flying Without Fear class during a work weekend in London. When I'd paid the £300, the teacher said I would learn lessons to carry me through all the stages of life, and he was right. Now was I supposed to hold my breath and puff up like a bird? Or was it slow and rhythmic stomach breathing? I tried both and the result made me gasp for air like a scuba diver with the bends. Nicole grabbed my hand again and I began to calm down and itch less, but it all started again when Olivier reached $10 million, and there was silence in the room.

I held my breath until Michael's phone bidder bit on the bid.

"Raise your hands, raise your hands!" I quietly pleaded to everyone in the room as the bids went just past $11 million. I needed to shatter records. I wanted my name in the papers and on the pages of *Art in America*. I'd even had a new head shot taken last week by one of Annie Leibovitz's minions.

The Chippendale had to break $12.1 million, a sum so insanely high that I didn't actually grasp what it meant. Except that at minimum wage, you had to work for more than 1,600,000 hours to have enough money to buy it, which is about sixteen lifetimes.

Olivier's voice coming from his elegant form behind the rostrum snapped me back into the present and I touched my face to make sure my hives were still covered by my industrial-strength foundation. I heard $11 million from the phones, then $11.3 million in the room. When $11.5 million rose to $11.9 million, I froze.

Without showing any trace of emotion, Olivier said, "Did I hear twelve million?"

Did he? Was someone bidding twelve? It was Michael's phone bidder. I wanted to leap over to him, steal the phone, and pledge all my white blood cells, future children, and savings bonds to that person. But I still needed it to climb.

"Twelve-point-one, please," I silently begged. Someone! Bill Gates! The Zuckerberg man-child. A corrupt Vatican official. Kanye West. Anyone! I needed some heavy testosterone and ego proving to start pumping through the air.

And then, as the sweat from my palm actually dripped onto my gray dress, someone did. I saw it, from the left corner of my eye. Paddle 79 went up and no one gasped.

"Twelve million one hundred thousand from the gentleman in the middle," said Olivier, looking at a man who had dropped out until now. Michael flicked his hand up, the arm of his suit falling ever so slightly.

"Michael, yours now on the phones for twelve million two hundred thousand," said Olivier. He quickly took the bid up by another one hundred thousand. The man in the center of the room in the navy suit with silver hair lifted his paddle again and Olivier declared, "Here in the room at twelve million three hundred thousand."

The bidding had just hit $12.3 million, then $12.4 million, and a second later, $12.5 million. I looked out at the sea of white hair, the bald spots, and the slightly hunched shoulders in yards of Madison Avenue tailoring, and got ready for my heart to explode. Olivier looked to the phones again but Michael's bidder had backed off. Olivier scanned the room quickly and then declared to the former bidders, "Not yours, or yours, Michael, but here in the room at twelve million five hundred thousand dollars." Olivier pointed again at the phones for one last second and declared, "Selling this time at twelve million five hundred thousand."

The gavel went down and Olivier repeated, with a flick of his pen scribbling the bidder number on the thick Christie's embossed paper in front of him, "Hammer price of twelve million five hundred thousand." The crowd clapped, the price flashed on the large screen to his left in several different currencies, and Olivier got ready for the next sale, making no indication that he, with a lot of help from me, had just completed the highest sale for a piece of American furniture ever.

Nicole put her hand on my shoulder and squeezed as tightly as she could and we didn't say a word, which was good because I didn't know what to say. I was barely twenty-nine years old and professionally I would never top this moment. Everything I'd done to make this happen was suddenly worth it.

I stood through the last lots with Nicole, unable to react, unable to do more than smile and watch Olivier do his job, until the last table sold and Nicole steered me out the door to the auction prep room, where I was greeted with dignified cheers, hugs from everyone in our department, and a handshake from Christie's CEO, Dominick Swansea.

"We have to celebrate," declared Nicole as we walked out of the room an hour later with our two American Furniture and Decorative Arts colleagues. It was just past 8 P.M. and I had never been happier. Not when I lost my virginity to the cutest sixteen-year-old in Newport, when I graduated summa cum laude from Princeton, or when I'd been asked to do an appraisal on *Antiques Roadshow*. This was my moment. I had antihistamines coursing through my veins, burn victim makeup on my face, and beads of sweat evaporating on my neck, but none of that mattered now.

"You just changed the course of the entire auction world," Nicole continued. "No one ever thought a piece of American furniture could hit the twelve and a half million mark, even the Nicholas Brown, but it just happened. And you helped make it happen. Everyone thinks you're the best and you just proved them right. It's time to raise a glass, or five, to your success."

It was? Of course it was. We walked outside, through Rockefeller Center, taking in the fresh night breeze. It was September in New York and the air was filled with the last traces of summer. I inhaled deeply, something I hadn't done for six months, and felt like everything in my life was going right. Better than right, it was perfect. Sure, I was technically single but occasionally sleeping with Alex, my ex-boyfriend from boarding school who was only balding on his left side, and both my parents had actually called me by the wrong name last week, even though I'm an only child, but all that seemed completely irrelevant now. I'd get Alex some Rogaine and buy my parents a few bottles of ginkgo biloba. I, with a little help from a 250-year-old company, had just gotten someone to spend $12,500,000 on a desk.

# CHAPTER 2

I didn't head home after celebrating that night. Instead, I went downtown to Alex's apartment on Lafayette Street. He had one of those super-fancy elevators that drops you in the middle of the living room and his doorman knew me, so he didn't have to come to the door to let me in. I walked into his place, took off my shoes, and let my cold feet touch the shaggy white rug that sat like a docile animal under his coffee table.

I was about to wrap it around myself when my phone started to buzz in my pocket. I reached into my coat and smiled when I saw Jane Dalby's name on my screen. Of course she was the first to call and congratulate me, because the Dalbys were first at everything.

During my childhood in Newport, the Dalby family lived in the much larger house, the parent house to my family's carriage house, on Bellevue Avenue, Newport's most famous street. "Dalby in miniature," my grandmother used to say of our house, but it was more like Dalby in minuscule. Like most of Newport, they spent much of the year outside of Rhode Island (in the Dalbys' case it was in Boston, overlooking the Charles), but from June to August and many weekends on either end, they were in Newport. There were two Dalby girls, very pretty and smart, with thick brown hair with blond streaks framing their faces and Irish Catholic roots. I went to Princeton with Jane, though she was a year above me, and her sister, Brittan, was a freshman when I was a junior. I told my parents I went to Princeton because they were alumni, but it was really because Jane was there. I could leave Rhode Island, but there was no way I was leaving the Dalbys.

I pressed accept on my phone and Jane's voice pulled me out of my reminiscing.

"You did it, Carolyn! I just heard!" Jane screamed into the phone from her palatial house in Newport. This year, she was spending the winter there with her husband, Carter, and a partially blind Labrador who won best in breed at Westminster a decade ago.

"You were so worried, but I was right, of course."

I smiled. She was right. Just like she'd been right when she said I should dump that prick Chris Walters at Princeton because he was cheating on me with a slutty cross-country runner who ate breakfast in a sports bra and when she said I shouldn't dye my hair red because I would look like a lost Irish dancer.

"Are you thrilled? You better be."

"I am happy," I said, laughing. And I was.

"What did Alex say?" Jane asked. She had gone to high school with us, too, and we'd boarded in the same dorm for the three years we had overlapped at St. George's. I was one of two kids who lived in Newport year-round who boarded. Alex was the other.

"I haven't told him yet," I admitted, not disclosing that I was currently doing snow angels on his rug.

"But I did have a big celebratory dinner with my colleagues and I even got a text from my mom that was three whole sentences long."

"Amazing!" said Jane, knowing full well that from my mother, not exactly a verbose or supportive woman, that was equivalent to a ten-page letter, salty tears, and a dozen roses.

"Now go wake up Alex and tell him the news. He'll flip. Love you, and congrats," Jane said before hanging up the phone. I missed having a house full of Dalbys next door.

I put my phone and keys on the table, took my blazer off, hung it in the hall closet, and walked over to the bedroom. Alex was covered in blankets and I could only see a few strands of hair sticking up from under the quilt, refusing to be hidden with the rest of him.

I took my clothes off, folded them, put them on the leather armchair next to the bed, and got in next to him. He didn't budge. It wasn't until I put my arms around him and started tugging at his thick chest hair that he woke up.

"Alex. Alex . . . ," I whispered, trying to get him to look at me. "It sold for twelve million five hundred thousand dollars. We broke the record for a single piece of American furniture. I'm so relieved. I can't even explain it. I can finally take a deep breath again. There is oxygen left despite what I kept telling you about fraudulent science and our impending doom. All those nights chewing my nails—my hands really—until my fingers looked like strips of bacon. It was all worth it. I was terrified, but it actually happened. Twelve five. I'm in shock. But happy shock."

Without turning around, Alex kept his eyes closed and mumbled, "I'm so happy for you," then fell immediately back to sleep. I wasn't going to try to wake him up again. His snores, which sounded a little fake, signaled he was in deep hibernation, but I wasn't about to sleep. So he didn't have a marching band to congratulate me. Or even a hug. Anything really except some garbled sleep talk, which I forced out of him. I wasn't the kind of person who needed her ego stroked and handed enormous gold trophies and mono-grammed cakes. But still, a little congratulatory screaming and fainting with pride would have been nice. I grabbed his iPad from his nightstand and googled "Nicholas Brown Chippendale." It was already on Twitter and the important art blogs. I knew that on Sunday, it would be somewhere in the *New York Times* Arts section. I would scrapbook it, laminate it, and possibly sleep with it under my pillow for the next decade.

The next evening was Saturday, and quickly notic-ing that I was a tad pissed by his nonreaction to my big life-changing news the night before, Alex promised to take me to a celebratory dinner at my favorite restaurant in New York, Daniel, on East Sixty-Fifth Street.

During our first few years in New York, Alex and I tried hard not to be together. He had dated a series of emaciated blondes who worked in marketing or magazines and he found them all fascinating. Or so he would always tell me when I'd run into him with someone I was considering dating. But no one ever really stuck besides me, and vice versa. We'd try dating the right people, spending a few months imagining them as our better halves, and then call each other after we realized they weren't up for the chal-lenge. Even when we weren't officially together, Alex was always there for me as the essential New York plus-one, or if I just wanted a warm bed to sleep in, with clothes on or off. Were we crazy about each other, or were we just used to each other? It was a question I thought about a lot, but it didn't keep me from calling him in the middle of the night, wandering to his house when I'd had too much to drink, or opening my door for him when one of his dates got a little too excited about his parents' money. "State school gold digger," he'd say pouring himself a scotch, which he'd brought with him. Sometimes I chided him, sometimes I ignored him, and other times I went to bed with him because it was what I'd been doing since high school. We had ease, and that often mattered more to me than romance.

When Alex came up, he gave me a kiss and an Edible Arrangement, which I much prefer to flowers because flowers are just elegant vessels for bugs to enter your home and stay forever. I once had giant red ants invade my kitchen and I swear they rode in on a large, comfortable sunflower.

I was happy. Happier than I'd been in months, years maybe. When we were outside, I started to do an adult version of skipping down the sidewalk. I had energy, life, joie de vivre.

"What are you doing?" said Alex, speeding up to keep up with me, his stiff brown leather dress shoes creasing slightly at the toe.

"I'm walk jumping," I explained between bops along the sidewalk.

"Good Lord," said Alex, clearly still entrenched in his conservative New England ways. "Isn't there some ADD medicine you can take?"

The thing about Alex was that he wasn't exactly comedian funny. Or funny at all. Actually, I once presented him with a drawing of a funny bone and suggested that he have it inserted by a doctor. He did not heed my advice. But he was very successful, was kind when no one was looking, and was incredibly sexy. Take-your-underwear-off-with-his-teeth sexy. We'd met when we were fourteen, when we were both at freshman orientation for boarders at St. George's. Though we'd grown up in Newport, we didn't know each other until we went to school together. Alex had kissed me three weeks into the year and declared that

I looked like a fragile rose. That won me over a little and when he whispered in my ear that his mission in life was to give me an orgasm, that won me over entirely.

It's not that Alex didn't like going a little bit crazy. He did. We were once reprimanded in Vegas for jumping into a lazy river while wearing wooden shoes after a "going Dutch" party. But sometimes he didn't like my extremes. My nerves around auction time, my need to be very successful at everything I gave a morsel of energy to. I knew he wanted me to be steadier, more stable, just like him and his emotionless family.

I looked at Alex, still so perfectly handsome. His skin and his hair and his eyes all matched, almost an identical golden taupe, which didn't make him striking, but he was very good-looking without the shock value. He was a bulky six feet tall with muscles that refused to be well defined but were somewhere under there. He ran track in high school and college and told me he always liked sports better when you didn't have to rely on idiots. "I'm not a team player," he'd once said after he won the 400-meter dash. "That's why I always win." He was pleased with the way he looked, and the haughty way he acted, and so was everyone else, including me.

When we got to Daniel we both forgot that he actually wanted a different version of me, the me that existed before I had my dream job, before I understood what real pressure was. Instead we ate, talked about people we knew from home, and kept floating down the line of shared experiences. We would always be connected because of school, because of Newport and falling in love there when we were very young, and for now, that was good enough.

After dinner, Alex suggested that we go back to his apartment, take off our underwear, and drink heavily. I thought that sounded like an exceedingly good idea. It took us a few minutes to grab a cab and I hid my face in Alex's navy blue blazer, letting the soft material rub against my made-up face.

"After you, star of the art world," he said, opening the cab door for me; I swooned just a little as the air caught his brown curls and they fell across his forehead. Well, on the right side of his face, anyway.

"Star, you say?" I asked him, trying to keep the conversation on the topic of my life-changing accomplishment. "So you're proud of me, then?"

"You sold a twelve-and-a-half-million-dollar table," said Alex, whistling under his breath. "And frankly, it's not even attractive. I'm impressed. You should be a criminal. People will buy and sell anything when they see that angelic face," he said, squeezing my cheeks like a lemon.

Maybe he could tell I was annoyed by his comment and he wanted me to calm down, or maybe he just knew how to turn me on after fifteen years of turning me on, but he put his lips next to my ear and said, "You're the most beautiful woman I've ever seen. I want you naked for the next twelve hours." The cabdriver was thrilled to get rid of us.

When I woke up for work that Monday, I was ready for compliments and cheers at the office, but instead I got a call from Louise DeWitt, department head of American Furniture and Decorative Arts, at 6 A.M. sharp. She demanded that I meet her for coffee in thirty-five minutes and that I better have a bag packed because her assistant had just booked me a flight to Texas and I might have to stay for a few days. I didn't ask any questions. I assumed that someone very rich who had important pieces of American furniture had just died. I packed a bag full of completely impractical items and jumped in a cab to the Starbucks on Lexington Avenue.

Louise had on a brown, asymmetrically cut blazer and

so much jewelry I was surprised her head wasn't weighed down. She looked like a beautiful giraffe wearing necklaces. "Carolyn, here I am!" she called out, waving both her hands, though it was perfectly clear to both of us that I could see her. Louise was in her late fifties, but she carried her age beautifully, like a woman who had always been told she was attractive, and always would be, even when the words "for your age" were tacked on to the end of the compliment.

"Thank goodness you found me," she said, patting the seat next to her. "This place! It's so crowded." I had an odd feeling that this was Louise's first trip to Starbucks, but I just smiled and murmured something about the chain being somewhat popular with New Yorkers between the ages of .001 and 110.

"I took the liberty of ordering you three coffees." Louise informed me that none of them were decaf because decaf was for people who lived in California and ate grass. "I like what you're wearing," she said, eyeing me approvingly. I was wearing an outfit that I called "expensive shades of beige." Every ensemble in my closet bore a descriptive label: "deal-making black dress tailored in Rome, the Chanel that New Englanders like, the St. John for deals with southerners, backless shirt to wear with clients under forty." I made a mental note that Louise liked the beige.

"Carolyn Everett. A beautiful blade of wheat. That's what you look like." She took a sip of her coffee and looked at me with her deep-set eyes. "Did you get the plane ticket emailed to you?" She started flipping through a leather file that she'd placed in the middle of the table.

"Yes, a few minutes ago. Houston, eleven A.M. I got it, it looks great, but I'd love to know why exactly I'm going to Texas today." I didn't ask why there wasn't a return flight booked.

"I figured you might!" said Louise, snapping her fingers rhythmically. "Two words. And try not to faint when I say them."

She paused for what seemed like a full year of my life before eventually whispering a name I thought I'd never hear.

"Elizabeth Tumlinson."

Elizabeth Tumlinson. I immediately felt faint.

"Elizabeth Tumlinson is thinking about selling her estate? Through us?" I asked incredulously.

"Right you are!" said Louise, lifting her espresso in triumph.

Elizabeth and her late husband, Adam Tumlinson, had the best collection of seventeenth-, eighteenth-, and nineteenth-century American furniture in the country. Adam had made most of his money by being born to the right parents, early real estate moguls on Maryland's eastern shore, and he'd padded it out nicely by being one of the first to see the potential in Baltimore's many dilapidated warehouses. He flipped the old buildings into ultramodern lofts bought up by Johns Hopkins doctors. The Tumlinsons lived for many years between St. Michaels, Maryland, and the Roland Park historic district of Baltimore, then moved to Texas, where they solidified their status as the top Americana collectors. When Adam Tumlinson died last fall, my department started courting Elizabeth like she was debutante of the year. But she told us, and we knew she'd told Sotheby's, too, that she wouldn't think about selling even a sliver of her collection while she was still breathing and we'd have to move on from courting her to wooing her children after she passed away.

"Wait. Are you sending me to value the estate of Elizabeth Tumlinson?" I asked in disbelief. Louise couldn't just be sending me. She never sent just one person from our team to assess an important estate. I was sure she must be coming, too. Unless Louise was having open-heart surgery at the Starbucks, there was no way she would send someone in her stead to meet with Elizabeth Tumlinson.

"I'm not sending you just to value it. I'm sending you to acquire it as fast as you can. Nicole will be going, too," she said, reading my mind, and noting that Nicole would meet me in Houston since she was currently in Washington, D.C., looking at an early nineteenth-century Hugh Finlay table. Why would Louise send Nicole and me? We were the two most junior members and she was the department head. Surely she wanted to meet with Elizabeth and explain that Sotheby's was a bunch of cocaine addicts who would take a 99 percent commission.

"You need to work on your poker face," said Louise as I pulled my hand away from my mouth.

"You want to know why I'm sending you and Nicole and why I'm not going myself," Louise offered up, pushing another coffee in my direction. Heat and speed were the last things I needed, but I drank it anyway, afraid that Louise would change her mind about my trip if I couldn't drink two grande coffees in ten minutes.

"I suppose I'm wondering a little." What a lie. This was more interesting than Bigfoot or the Shroud of Turin.

"She requested you. She somehow knew—and liked—your grandmother. She knew her in Baltimore, I believe. Did your grandmother live in Baltimore?"

She knew my grandmother? How had I not figured that out? I had gone through my grandmother's address book eight times when I first started at Christie's, contacting everyone who might have some American-made object to sell, but I had never seen the Tumlinsons' name. I took immense pride in always knowing a connection before Louise did. When Adam Tumlinson died, I was aware of his death before the obits were written, before the body was even cold, thanks to a doctor I knew in Texas. Louise had been the one who contacted Elizabeth, but she had been mighty impressed by my ability to hear about the death even before close family members.

"My grandmother did live in Baltimore, but not for long," I explained to Louise. "It was for a year in the early sixties. My grandfather was having some health problems and was being treated at Johns Hopkins."

"I mentioned your name and the Nicholas Brown Chippendale and Elizabeth asked if you were related to Virginia Everett. When I said you were, she said she wanted to work with you, so there you go. I also put Nicole on there because everyone knows Nicole's family and I have a lot of faith that you, with some help from her, will handle yourself just fine. You're the smartest person I've ever had in the department, and I don't say that lightly. Sometimes you're even smarter than me."

I smiled in thanks at Louise and thought about what she said. Elizabeth Tumlinson was friends with my dead grandmother? While she was living, of course. I doubt she'd developed a close relationship with the late Virginia Everett via voodoo. I was mad at myself for missing that connection and was glad Louise didn't seem upset by my oversight. The name Elizabeth Tumlinson meant nothing to me until college and by then my grandmother had passed away, but my parents were American furniture freaks, too. Had she never felt compelled during one of our solemn family dinners to drop the fact that she was friends with the grande dame of American decorative arts collecting?

"I don't know how to say this without just saying it directly, but we need this sale," Louise acknowledged, her left hand over mine. "I don't want her to meet with any art dealers. If she hasn't met with Sotheby's yet, I don't want her to set something up. We need this estate and we need it . . . well, I don't want to say desperately, but it would be an appropriate word. Last year, Sotheby's American furniture department outsold ours for the first time in nine years. Nine years! Dominick is putting so much pressure on us to reverse that damage."

She looked at my face, my embarrassment, and patted my hand. "You know that, of course, and you know that that's not happening again this year. Your historic sale. The Nicholas Brown Chippendale. It did so much for the department, but I still worry it's not enough. But if you could get this estate—"

"Louise," I said, interrupting her. "If I need to slice open my arm and give the woman my bone marrow with a teaspoon, I'll do it. I will not leave Texas without a signed contract, I swear to you."

"Good, good," Louise repeated. "Her collection will determine the American furniture market for the next few years. If it sells well, there will be no more talk of a flat market . . . and Sotheby's, they would just . . . it would be amazing. I can't take another year like last year. I can't. Just get it signed."


I really felt the weight of what I'd been asked to do as my plane started its descent over the dry plains of eastern Texas. This wasn't just me going to chat with someone about one table. I was doing an estimation of an entire estate and making an immediate offer. I was taking on the operation of wooing then selling the very charmed life of Elizabeth Tumlinson, and I had to be successful.

When I saw Nicole at the baggage carousel waiting for me, I ran up to her and gave her a huge hug. I was suddenly so appreciative of her friendship, her expertise, and her ability to keep a level head.

"I am so, so glad you're here," I said as I finally let her go, untangling her softly curled dark hair from my watch.

"You're going to kill it," she said, hugging me back. "I'm just happy to observe your genius." I let her comment flood me with confidence and smoothed the tiny wrinkle in my fitted blazer. I wasn't free of nerves, but I knew how to look and live the part.

I'd spent the whole plane ride reading a biography of Elizabeth, sent from the same Houston contact who had told me about her husband's death. She had grown up in the quaint coastal town of St. Michaels, Maryland, and had met her very rich husband through a mutual friend during a political fund-raiser in Washington, D.C. They hadn't moved to Texas until he was semiretired and she was in her mid-fifties. Now Elizabeth was heavily involved in everything a very rich older woman was expected to be involved in: the Houston Ballet; the Museum of Fine Arts, Houston; Texas Children's Hospital; the other children's hospital; and the Houston Historical Society—her money was sprinkled all over the city. Nicole and I wondered why the Tumlinsons had abandoned the life they had built in Maryland for sprawling Houston, but none of our contacts had been able to give us a hint, so we assumed better weather and less crime.

As I turned away from the traffic on Texas Avenue, I kept my foot steadily on the gas pedal and headed toward Willowick Road in the very wealthy River Oaks area of the city.

Before we went to Elizabeth's, Nicole and I stopped in

the country club near her house, which one of Nicole's sellers had gotten us access to, and went over the final details of our proposal.

"Well, this isn't Baltimore, now, is it," said Nicole, looking out at the nearly fluorescent green golf course and women in tennis whites.

"I would meet that woman in a back alley in Newark if she wanted to. I just hope she hasn't contacted Sotheby's," I said, sitting down at a somewhat secluded table overlooking the golf course. "Or if she has, that we're going first."

"I know," said Nicole, looking at the women next to us eating what looked like heaven in a breadbasket. "Christie's is almost always first, but I'm still terrified. I actually dreamt last night that she had us do a Hashiyama."

I sucked in my breath and nodded understandingly. It was one of those stories that was legendary in the auction world. In 2005, Takashi Hashiyama, the president of a big Japanese company, couldn't decide if he wanted to sell the company's eight-figure art collection with the help of Sotheby's or Christie's. So instead of going with his gut or flipping a coin, he had the head of Christie's Tokyo and the head of Sotheby's Tokyo play rock, paper, scissors. Christie's won and we suddenly all started practicing playground games in the office.

"Of course, in this day and age, she'd probably make us play something more timely, like Angry Birds." Nicole stared at me, checked her high score, and then we both laughed nervously.

"Okay, so if she doesn't make us have some sort of video game contest with Sotheby's, we stick with our twelve percent buyer's premium."

"Yeah, we probably have to," I said, making little check marks next to the proposal I had typed up on the plane.

"And we waive seller's commission and we give our guarantee, half of which can be paid out to her upon signing."

"Thirty million."

"Yes, thirty million. That's high, but it's doable."

"I've made a list of possible extras," said Nicole, looking at her list. "Her oldest son, Gordon, he's the one who spent a little time in rehab, he's a huge Ravens fan. I can get him a meet-and-greet in the locker room."

"You can? How?"

"Don't ask, but I can. As for Elizabeth, I can't pinpoint anything she might want that she can't already buy, so we'll just feel it out."

I could see the words "American Ballet Theatre, Clydesdale horses, space aviation, and Duke of Gloucester" on her list but didn't ask any questions.

"I also looked and saw that Olivier Burnell was at the rostrum for every New York sale her husband attended in the past fifteen years. We can put it in her contract that he will conduct the auction and if he can't, she can withdraw."

"Olivier has never missed an auction. Even that time when he sliced open his thumb with a steak knife . . ."

"And just wore cashmere gloves," Nicole said, finishing my sentence. "I know he never misses an auction, but she doesn't. Let's write it in. I think she'll appreciate it."

"Okay," I said, mentally preparing the baskets of Airborne and vitamin C that I was going to start bringing Olivier on a weekly basis.

"Louise said she wants high estimates."

"They all want high estimates," I replied, rolling the corner of the piece of Christie's embossed paper in front of me. "It can backfire, but sellers never seem to care."

"I know, I know, the reserve prices can go too high and then there's the risk it won't sell. But if we don't go high, you know Sotheby's will give her the high estimates she wants."

"You're right." I sat on my hands so I would stop fidgeting and looked at our papers—our talking points, the proposal, everything we had laid out before even seeing any of her collection in person. We typed up our final proposal, used the club's business center to print it out, and paused in front of a wall-to-wall window overlooking a manicured lawn.

"I feel ready," said Nicole, standing up.

"Me too," I replied, placing the new contract in a leather Christie's folder.

Elizabeth's house was roughly the size of Belgium and got bigger as we noticed a back wing and then a separate guesthouse. I pressed the button on the loudspeaker next to the gate of her ivory brick mansion, it clicked open, and Nicole motioned to an area on the stone driveway where I should park.

The first thing that surprised me was that Elizabeth opened her own door. I was absolutely sure she would have a dozen *Downton Abbey*–style footmen who called her "your grace" and brushed her hair with boar bristles, but no. And the next thing that surprised me was how beautiful and healthy she was at seventy-six years, five months, and seventeen days old. I expected her to be in declining health if she was thinking of selling a large part of her estate. But here she was, ready to compete in the Mrs. Grandmother of the Universe pageant.

"You must be the women from Christie's," she said, her cream bouclé suit resisting a crease as she reached her thin hand out to us. "Louise warned me that you were young." She moved out of the way and let us through the heavy, wooden, double French doors.

"As you both know, *youth* is not the word of the day. We're dealing with old things here, including me."

Nicole and I started gushing—she looked amazing, sensational, her house was stunning, her collection unparalleled, we were thrilled, no, elated, to get a chance to see it, to meet her, we were bursting at the seams, what an honor—and through our gushing, she just kept a tight smile on her face and ushered us inside her house.

She led us to what looked like the first of eight living rooms. She pointed to a beige high-backed sofa for us to sit on, which was placed next to a beautiful piece, which I recognized as the work of eighteenth-century Annapolis cabinetmaker John Shaw.

We spent the first hour at Elizabeth's not up to our elbows in mahogany looking for signatures and hidden drawers in precise places to authenticate the pieces, but listening to Elizabeth tell us about her late husband, Adam.

"You can't imagine how lonely it is to be a widow," Elizabeth said, bowing her head slightly, her tight gray chignon unmoving.

Really? But didn't she have six children?

"Death is terrible," I said, solemnly bowing my head to match hers. What was I saying? How did I know death was terrible? I had never died.

"Loneliness is terrible," I said, backtracking.

"It is," she agreed, patting her eyes with a handkerchief she seemed to have pulled from the couch cushions.

"Loneliness is killing me. My bones are shaking. I need a change."

She needed a change, did she? Well! I had a change for her. Minimalism! Was it time for me to pull up pictures of Le Corbusier buildings on my iPad? Tell her that stark white walls with nothing on them were this decade's Thomas

Eakins paintings? Or maybe I'd suggest the naturalist route. This woman should kiss all this Texas gaudiness away and move to Walden Pond. Really find herself in her final years. She needed to shed the shackles of wealth and make like a Buddhist.

"There are, of course, my six children. I always thought I would leave it in their hands."

Heartless worms! All children were. They didn't even come visit her, by the sounds of things. They didn't deserve her furniture. What was I supposed to say? Screw your children? Yes, that's what I was supposed to say, just not in so many words.

"It's possible, if they're not passionate about American antiques, that they would immediately sell your collection and spend the money on other things," I said, talking about how so many young wealthy people wanted private jets and private islands.

"The values are different," I continued. "They don't want Chippendale and Queen Anne; they want fast money, fast cars, Swedish furniture made of metal." She physically recoiled when I strung that last phrase together. I could tell she was having visions of her huge house filled with IKEA furniture with impossible-to-pronounce names covered in umlauts.

I wanted to tell her that Bjøoïrniger sofas were sure to be the downfall of the next generation of Americans, but I didn't want to push it.

"I know they don't really care about all these things," she said, motioning to her end tables and armoires. "But my children aside," she said, sighing, "sometimes the thought of selling everything, watching my collection, Adam's collection, being torn apart and sold off bit by bit . . . well, it might just send me to an early grave."

Was seventy-six an early grave? It wasn't my place to ask. And I didn't want this elegant woman to actually die. It's just that I wasn't allowed to walk away with nothing.

"We have a very good offer for you," said Nicole, cutting the small talk. "We'll of course need to take a look at everything, but I know that the number we are willing to put on the table will exceed your expectations."

"I need a guarantee," said Elizabeth, her voice suddenly turning firmer.

"Of course," we both said in unison.

"And I'd like you to set up a trip for my children to attend the auction. They quite like the St. Regis."

"Will you want to attend?" I asked, writing notes and knowing that Louise would put her entire extended family and their pets up at the hotel if we could sign Elizabeth.

Just as I was about to stand up and start gently flipping over furniture to find signatures, she shook her head and declared, "All this talk is rattling me. I feel like I'm at a car dealership with Slick Rick and I don't like it."

What? How was this like a car dealership? We were trying to get her to sell, not buy, and who in this scenario was Slick Rick? I caught Nicole's eye and she mouthed, "You."

"Maybe I'll just donate everything to my alma mater, the University of Maryland," Elizabeth said, starting to smile as she reached for her soda water.

The University of Maryland! Why? So that frat boys could puke on cushions that once held the posteriors of the American settlers? While I was thinking about our next move, Nicole was playing the friendship angle, telling Elizabeth all about her recent trip to Maryland. She was also peppering her stories with ten good reasons why Elizabeth should sell her estate.

"The Baltimore Museum of Art has expressed a lot of

interest," said Nicole. "Think about how much of your furniture would return to Maryland if you sold it through us.
We have a very high percentage of buyers from museums in
the mid-Atlantic."

Elizabeth smiled and declared, "Good people come from
Baltimore."

What did she mean good people came from Baltimore?
Had she never seen *The Wire?* And Edgar Allan Poe was
from Baltimore. The original Goth!

"Everything I'm considering selling is in these eleven
rooms," she said, making a dramatic motion with her arm.
"Now, I said 'considering,' so don't start mentally writing
up your catalogue yet. And no fast talk and shouting out
numbers. I like to live a civilized life."

Well, it was a good thing I hadn't done my usual routine
of appraising things in a loincloth.

There were one hundred twenty-seven pieces in the
eleven rooms and we started in the very last drawing
room, taking pictures of each piece from every angle, including inside the drawers and underneath the legs. We
looked at the inlays, the mother-of-pearl detail on some,
the tongue-and-groove joinery, ran our hands across the
claw-and-ball feet of the Chippendale works, inspected
the scallop shell mounts on the Queen Anne pieces, made
sure the cabriole legs had no splits in them, same for
the pierced back splats on the side chairs. We looked for
visible saw marks on eighteenth-century pieces and then
almost lost it when we found a companion piece to a side
table already owned by one of New York's most prominent
collectors of Newport-built eighteenth-century furniture.

"We didn't know you had this," I said to Elizabeth, running my hand across the wood.

"Well, one's life can't be totally public," she replied. "It was one of Adam's last purchases. It came from a dealer in New York. I have the papers."

Tracing furniture was very straightforward. We could easily determine the precise time period when a piece was made, the region where it was constructed, and the creator, just by looking at the wood. Certain woods were in vogue at different times and the handmade screws of the past centuries and the oxidation they left behind on the wood helped a great deal. It was possible to forge a clay pot, and at a certain level, it was possible to fake furniture, and could be lucrative, but it was extremely difficult and expensive to do it well.

When it was nearly nine o'clock and Elizabeth seemed rather sick of us manhandling her possessions, she suggested we pick it up again the next day.

"I appreciate you ladies coming, and you've made excellent arguments for why I should sell with Christie's, but all this . . . I don't know. As you're aware, Adam was always the one who did all the actual buying and selling. Maybe I should just wait until I'm older to sell, because right now, it still means a lot."

"We understand how difficult the selling process can be, but the wonderful thing about selling your estate instead of letting your children handle it later on is that you have control. If you work with Christie's you will have the right individual collectors, museums, universities all bidding on the wonderful collection that you and Adam procured. And if you would like to use the financial returns to build another collection, we would be thrilled to assist you. Maybe you would like to start your own collection. Something you can be known for alone, without Adam."

"What do you suggest I collect, Miss Everett? Gold boxes? Sporting art? Islamic artifacts? Maybe musical instruments. Do you think this house would look nice lined with rusty tubas?"

"We try to avoid selling rust," I answered with a smile that was getting very strained.

"Will I see you both tomorrow?" she asked.

She would indeed.

I wanted to remind her that she was the one who contacted Louise. We hadn't shown up at her doorstep unannounced with a contract.

"She'll sell," said Nicole after we walked outside. "She asked if we were coming back tomorrow and no mention of any other auction house. She's ready. But she certainly doesn't need the money. I can't figure out why she wants to sell now."

"You never know about people's private lives. Maybe she has some loose ends to tie up."

Nicole laughed and got in the little rental car. "Loose ends" was a term many sellers used instead of "I'm strapped for cash, I've got debts, my son gambled away all our money in Monaco, we were victims of a Ponzi scheme, Wall Street screwed us, or our daughter is addicted to the devil's sugar, and we need to pay the rehab bills."

Elizabeth had said that if she were to sell, she wanted to lead the January sale. Usually, it took us a full year to get an estate of her size ready for auction. We certainly didn't want to rush it, and four months was beyond rushing it, but if that was one of her stipulations, I knew Christie's would do it. Our department was not a big one and we never said no to estates like Elizabeth's even if we had to work night and day to get it ready for January 18. We only had sales twice a year: September and January. The rest of the time we lived in fear of getting enough to wow the world in September and January.

I had texted Alex three times since I'd been gone to tell him I was in Houston, potentially working on a huge deal, and he had only written back, "cool." Really? "Cool?" Did that mean he was chilly? Or that my job was awesome? Or maybe he was screwing someone else and had only been able to pound out "cool" with one of his thumbs while he twisted her into a Boy Scout knot? I couldn't stop thinking about it. Alex and Elizabeth Tumlinson were flooding my brain.

The next day, Nicole and I were ready to turn our attention to old auction records, historical records, and previous sales from each of the craftsmen. When we went back to Elizabeth's at 9 A.M., she told us that she had a meeting with "a few others" that evening so it was good we were planning to wrap it all up that morning.

"By a few others she means David Marcham from Sotheby's, you know. Maybe Valerie Hemmet, too," said Nicole as we inspected an end table on the other side of the house. "Louise is not going to be pleased they're here."

We had thought that with the time Elizabeth was allotting us, David wasn't coming at all, but we were clearly wrong. David Marcham was a legend in the American furniture industry. He had hair that smelled exactly like fine leather and was on *Antiques Roadshow* twice a month. He had once made a woman cry when he told her that her antique baby chair was a fake and looked like dog feces molded into the shape of a rocker. His brother was the preeminent expert on American numismatics and had once shot himself in the foot on live television to prove a point about the Civil War era Whitworth rifle.

It took two hours of talking to Elizabeth to get a thing out of her about Sotheby's. Nicole didn't want to ask, I didn't want to ask, but we had to know if they were definitely coming that night, as we might lift our guarantee a little if they were.

After we rephotographed a few pieces because the morning light was better than what we had the day before, Elizabeth decided to get chatty, but not about what we were hoping she'd talk about—her transfer of assets from her living room to our New York showroom. Instead she talked about herself. And we listened.

Sitting tall on a muted blue settee and pulling her hands into her lap, she smiled and looked at us smiling back at her like desperate idiots. She knew she could talk to us about pig intestines for fourteen hours straight and we would have to continue nodding enthusiastically and gasping over the complexities of swine innards.

"I've always been a collector," she said, pointing out the obvious. "Even before I met Adam. I didn't have the money to buy the really important things—the Lannuiers, Thomas Afflecks, Duncan Phyfes—like I do now, but I've always been taken with collections. Not only did I like to acquire things; I could never get rid of anything, either. My mother, Janet Tivoli, died Christmas Day of 1963, and, well, she was the same way. She once said that throwing out a sweater was like ripping the wings off an angel. That really stuck with me."

Holy God. If I took one hundred twenty-seven pieces from her, would I be killing 63.5 angels? Or would that be one hundred twenty-seven angels?

"I'm just like you," I told her. "I can't get rid of anything. I have every letter I've ever received, every photo I've ever taken. I don't use digital because I can't bear the thought of deleting things."

Nicole raised her eyebrows at me, sure that I must be lying. She probably took nothing but iPhone photos and had a posh, perfect, clutter-free existence.

"Your grandmother was the same way, wasn't she," said Elizabeth, looking at me.

"Yes, she really was."

"We met at a dinner in Baltimore, you know," she offered up.

"I didn't know. But I'm sure she was very fond of you," I suggested. Of course, my grandmother had never mentioned knowing Elizabeth, but I was going to ignore that. Just like I was going to ignore the fact that my butt was completely asleep because I had been sitting on this very attractive, very expensive, and very uncomfortable chair for two hours. I felt like a geisha. Soon I would be asked to do a tea ceremony.

It was somewhere between talking about how she had first collected Revolutionary War era lamps (because she didn't like to be kept in the dark) and how she then decided to move on to silver soup tureens that she mentioned Sotheby's.

"David is very interested in my estate," she announced, as if we had no idea. "We spoke last night and he's convinced me it wouldn't be in my best interest to give everything to Maryland, because real collectors, real lovers of the finest Americana, should have a chance to own history just like I did. He made a very good point."

Yes, he had. It was one both Nicole and I had made about five times the day before.

"We agree wholeheartedly with that point, as we voiced yesterday," Nicole said politely. "I can promise you that Christie's will put the best deal on the table. Along with the thirty-million-dollar guarantee, half of it paid to you upon signing, Christie's is very willing to lower our commissions, to waive certain fees, and to commit ourselves to really showcasing your work in the best way for it to sell." I took out a rendering of Elizabeth's estate displayed in our showrooms along with a note from our graphic designer that was faxed to us just hours before.

"Your collection would have its own catalogue, which would go out to thousands of very important buyers," I added.

"I like you both," said Elizabeth, looking at us like we were rabid dogs about to chomp off her ankles. "And I know my husband was very fond of Louise, but Sotheby's has given some very good preliminary numbers, too, without even seeing the collection. So you'll understand why I gave them a loose verbal agreement last night."

Had Sotheby's given over a $30 million guarantee? There was no way.

Nicole scribbled something on her notepad and I looked over and saw the word *bluffing*, scrawled in her tiny handwriting. She scratched it out while we kept talking.

Was Elizabeth bluffing? She could definitely be bluffing. She knew I couldn't just call up David and casually ask.

"We don't think that's the right decision," I said firmly.

"We just made history with the Nicholas Brown. We also made history with the Richard Edwards Chippendale pier table when it went for four-point-six-two in 1990," said Nicole.

"Yes, but that was 1990," Elizabeth replied.

"But the Nicholas Brown was four days ago," I pointed out. "I arranged that sale. Our record in American art is unquestionably superior to any of our competitors. We have the resources and the buyers and we will get you the dollar amount you deserve."

Elizabeth stood up, so we both followed her lead and stood up in front of her. I was only five foot three but in the grand room, I felt even smaller, like a garden gnome.

Maybe Elizabeth had no intention of going with Chris-

tie's in the first place. Perhaps David was her best friend
and he was actually in some guesthouse suite watching us
writhe in our failure on a CCTV feed. He was probably
screaming, "Another martini, Jeeves, and some unemployment forms for the girls! This is simply rich!" as he
watched me try to control my urges to throw myself on
my stomach in front of Elizabeth and beg her to go with
Christie's because she knew my grandmother, because
we both loved the great, strangely shaped state of Maryland, because C came before S in the alphabet. Anything!
Perhaps it was time for me to fabricate some story about
David Marcham being a closet pyromaniac who couldn't
control himself and his little match collection around
two-centuries-old mahogany?

Maybe it was because Nicole seemed to have thrown in
her hand and was already talking to Elizabeth about people they knew in common in Maryland, but I blurted out,
"Thirty-seven-million-dollar guarantee and a four-percent
commission. Anything we make over thirty-seven, we keep.
That's the best offer I can give you and it's an extremely
good one."

Elizabeth looked at me startled, her glassy green eyes
not quite registering what I had just said.

"I'll also waive all fees. The insurance fee, the illustration fee. Everything. You and I both know David won't put
that offer on the table even if you say we did. I shouldn't
be putting that offer out. But I am. You'll lead the January
sales. It's a very fast turnaround to get your estate ready by
January but it seems very important to you—"

"It's a deal breaker," Elizabeth interrupted me.

"Right, we will have everything ready for January, then.
Absolutely guaranteed."

Nicole was doing the math in her head as she looked at

me looking at Elizabeth. She had clearly figured out how many million I had overpromised by and started to turn very pale and shook her head no at me. I ignored her and repeated the numbers.

An hour later, as I knew she would, Elizabeth signed our offer.

# CHAPTER 3

When Alex didn't return my calls for five days I started to worry. We had always been able to go days, sometimes weeks, without speaking to each other, but we never ignored each other's big life moments. This was the second time in twenty-two days that he had taken my happiness and shredded it with his silence.

He finally called me during the last week of September, but didn't apologize for the time lapse, for ignoring me, or for yet again letting me down when I needed support. He talked to me the way he'd always talked to me and we drifted back to laughing about summers in high school. When everyone we boarded with headed home and we were left to be wild teenagers in Newport. So I forgave him. I wanted familiarity and Alex always delivered that. I didn't have time to think about why I tolerated the rest of him because I, along with Nicole, Louise, and Erik Wagner, deputy chairman of Christie's America, had three months to get ready for the January sales.

My job became my everything. I stopped going out. I ate lunch and dinner at my desk. I talked to Jane Dalby only occasionally and very late at night, when I couldn't fall asleep. I sent the occasional text to my parents that said,

"I'm alive, not to worry." The rest of the time, I was at work. It was a very cold fall, even for someone used to six months of cold, and my walk to and from the subway became the only time I spent outside. The leaves turned from beautiful to brown, the number of tourists packed into Rockefeller Center thinned out a little before the holiday storm, and my world shrank to my apartment, my office, the deli where I bought coffee, and the occasional inside of a cab when I was too tired or too cold to wait for a train.

Elizabeth's estate, or the estate of Mrs. Adam R. Tumlinson as it was called in the catalogue and in the press, was poised to bring in 70 percent of the January sale's revenue.

"I thought as much," said Elizabeth when I called to tell her at 9 A.M. sharp on the first Monday in December.

"I did, too," I replied. After all the red tape had been peeled away, Elizabeth had told me more about her friendship with my grandmother. They'd spent time on a museum committee together and had formed a bond that Elizabeth seemed to regret losing.

"She was a fair bit older than me, you know," she said as we changed topics from the upcoming auction to the familiar thread that linked us together. "But she was the kind of woman everybody wanted to know. She'd had a child just a few years before."

"My father," I pointed out. "He's an only child, so that's how I'm sure," I explained.

"Is he now? That's too bad. Only children tend to develop a mild case of the crazies later in life."

I had to agree. At times I felt like I already had an acute case of the crazies. The next time I went to the doctor he'd glance at my pupils and say, "It's the crazies! And you'll have them for life. Here's a pill, it will do nothing for you."

"Is it true that by the time you were born, all the family

money was gone?" asked Elizabeth, touching on a subject I tried very hard to avoid.

It was true, I told her. The Everett steel money was nearly depleted. My grandfather had lost a lot of it in his final years, when he was trying to make good business decisions with a mind that wouldn't allow them. And when my father married my mother, "a penniless academic," according to my grandmother, she refused to give him what was left, since he had killed her hope of his marrying some heiress who could keep them living the life she had raised him in. She lived with us for thirteen years, promising my father would inherit what remained, but she gave it away instead, changing her will at the very end of her life and leaving half a million for my education and a little less for my parents, who, she stated, "were smart-asses enough to not need any more education." I gave Elizabeth the very short version of the story.

For the last couple of weeks, talking to Elizabeth—who almost always spoke to me, rather than to Louise, Nicole, or Erik—I had started to think that she had known about me before Louise mentioned me. My name was in bold under Louise's and Erik's on our department website and I had been in the auction room in New York with her husband before. We all knew Adam Tumlinson, but Elizabeth had never been present at a New York auction. I started to wonder if her familiarity came from research rather than name recognition. If it did, it didn't really matter. Maybe it swayed her decision to go with Christie's, and if so, I was just lucky to have the right name.

By the end of the first week in January, I felt like the world was releasing its grip a little. The auction was catalogued and organized and generating great buzz and Louise and Erik were absolutely fine with the guarantee we'd given Elizabeth. Even Nicole had forgiven me for the way I'd handled things in Houston, mostly because *Art in America* had valued the Tumlinson estate at $39 million, but speculated that it could hit $40 million.

So when I received a call on my office phone from an unknown number that afternoon, I answered it with a sprightly hello instead of letting it roll over to voicemail.

"Is this Carolyn Everett?" a man with a deep voice asked, mispronouncing my last name. He sounded very hesitant.

"Yes, it is," I replied. He explained that he'd been transferred to both Louise and Erik but neither had answered their phone and he wanted to speak to someone in the American furniture department.

"Well, you can talk to me," I said cheerfully. "How can I help you?"

"I don't know that you can, but I'll tell you what's what and then you can tell me if you can help me."

"Okay . . . ," I said, starting to regret that I'd picked up the call.

"My name is Richard Jones. I live down in Baltimore and I've got no real interest in American furniture."

Wonderful. Thank goodness he called the American furniture department at Christie's then. Perhaps I should call up a butcher, introduce myself, and tell him I'm a vegetarian.

"But here's the thing. My sister Nina Caine, Nina Jones Caine, she's a librarian at Three Rivers High, that's here in Baltimore . . . and . . . well, she's very interested in American furniture. Has been since the sixties. She pays attention to all the buying and selling and stuff like that and she came around last night and showed me the magazine for your upcoming sale—"

"Is that one of our January catalogues, you mean? Your sister has a catalogue?"

I knew everyone our catalogues went out to and I was not familiar with the name Nina Caine, but they were for sale online and found in university libraries.

"Right, your catalogue. I don't know all the lingo, but what I do know is that Nina showed me the catalogue, the Property from the Collection of Mrs. Adam R. Tumlinson catalogue, and she was very upset because right there on page seventy-three was a picture of a table she owns. Well, we own it because it was our mother's, but it's on page seventy-three of your catalogue and it's also in Nina's living room."

It wasn't rare for Christie's to receive phone calls when catalogues came out about something being inauthentic, but the calls were usually nothing to be alarmed by, just people wanting to make a quick buck off the Picasso they had just "found" in their grandmother's attic. But it didn't happen in the furniture department.

"Could you send me a picture of your table?" I asked. "It's hard to take anything to the next step if we don't have a photo," I explained.

"Trust me. You should take this seriously because Nina has that table."

"Can you please just start by sending me a photo?" I asked, giving him my email address.

"Yes, I can send you a photo but don't you want to come down here to Baltimore and see it? You're about to sell a fake."

I was less than two weeks away from our sale. I was working fourteen hours a day and I still felt like I was three months from being ready. The last thing I was going to do was take a train down to Baltimore to see some flea market table someone was trying to pass off as a Hugh Finlay, a furniture maker that rarely fetched prices higher than the low six figures.

"If you could just send me a photo . . . that's how we start everything in the auction world," I repeated. "If we can't see it, we can't do much with it."

I let Richard go and spent the rest of the day and evening refreshing my email, but nothing from Baltimore came through. I happily let the call go as some petty, highly original criminal trying to make a buck and I set my mind back on Elizabeth's sale. When I helped consign the Nicholas Brown I had a little bit of luck thanks to the tip. Jack had changed his mind a few times as the American economy continued to rapidly tank, but I'd paced him through that. He was a seller who was ready to sell. Elizabeth was different. Elizabeth's estate was a very tough get but presented one hundred twenty-seven chances for historic sales.

It wasn't until three days later that I got the picture that Richard from Baltimore had promised me. It came to my Christie's email address from his sister Nina along with a message saying she was absolutely positive that the one in the collection of Mrs. Adam R. Tumlinson must be a replica or a fake. But she was wrong. It wasn't a piece that we'd known Elizabeth had for years, but we had inspected it in Texas and it was no mistake.

We were now ten days from the sale, and it had taken them seventy-two hours to send me a photo. I refused to pay attention to these people. It was without question a Hugh Finlay stenciled pier table made in Baltimore in the early nineteenth century. There was no hole in the provenance on that piece. It had been in the Tumlinson family for generations and they had two other Finlay pieces, which could be traced to the same decade. One was a Federal mahogany sofa, which had been reupholstered. It was bought at auction in 2006 from a prominent family who had been in South Carolina since the early eighteenth century. It had never been owned by anyone else besides them and the Tumlinsons and was estimated between $190,000 and $200,000. The other was a round tea table built around 1790, which had been in the Tumlinson family since it was bought by Adam's great-grandfather, James Tumlinson, in 1817. Adam's family came to Baltimore aboard the *Dove* in 1634 and just shy of 30 percent of Adam and Elizabeth's collection had been passed down exclusively from family. They'd even had pieces sell, through Christie's, that had the exact same provenance as the pier table. Three of those Hugh Finlay pieces all sold in the early nineties. Hugh Finlay kept meticulous records. And James Tumlinson appeared in his records. That was as good as it got.

I shouldn't have been anxious. I knew the Impressionist and Modern Art department received calls like this frequently. The only thing that was worrying me was that we didn't. I had never gotten a call about a fake and it was something I thought I was immune to in my department. When I got into bed that Thursday night, I knew sleep was not in my immediate future. My nerves were shaky and I couldn't stop thinking about Baltimore. After two hours of restlessness, I got out of bed and sat on the small Queen Anne walnut side chair that I had spent three months' salary on during my first year at Christie's. It was the only thing I had ever bought at auction and it only made me love the world of buying and selling and bidding and winning and losing even more.

I pulled open the metal window next to the chair and let the freezing night air in. I didn't have a very good view, but I liked my bad view best at night, when everything, includ-

ing the insides of the buildings, was still. It was in that chair
that I eventually fell asleep with my feet propped up on my
bed, and when I woke up that morning at six, I was clinging
to my quilt, which I had managed to rip off the bed, and my
nose felt like a Popsicle screwed onto my face. I'd probably
contracted seven different strands of the cold virus and even
an hour-long shower couldn't warm me up.

It was while sitting on a bar stool, eating a green pepper
and cheese omelet as the sun rose, that I first felt real anxiety about the phone call from Baltimore. The thing about
the Hugh Finlay table was it had such a unique look. It was
marbleized, grained, and stenciled. It had gold leaf inlay and
stood out because of the level of detail. I pulled a Christie's
folder toward me and opened it, taking out a color print of
the picture the woman in Baltimore had sent me. It looked
a lot like Elizabeth's. I stared at it with a brass magnifying
glass. It looked exactly like Elizabeth's.

I turned the piece of paper upside down and looked at the
legs. The photo looked old, but the table appeared to be in
great condition, just like Elizabeth's was. I pushed it across
the counter and swirled my eggs around the plate. Why was
I so worked up? There were dozens of ways to doctor an
image. It had to be inauthentic. This was just another crazy
person trying to make a buck. I tried to convince myself of
that as I finished my cold, runny eggs and all I could come
up with was, why this piece of furniture? It was not where
the money was. Why wasn't this woman trying to scam
the Impressionist department? Or if she was furniture obsessed, why not pick something that was worth a lot more?
Something with less detail yet more value? If someone were
skilled enough to fake early nineteenth-century furniture,
why would they waste their efforts on a small pier table?
This was ridiculous. I threw my plate in the sink, not caring

if the egg remained solidified there for a year. I hated myself for picking up that call.

On Saturday, more than a week after I had drunk in my office with Nicole on New Year's Eve while we worked, and only eight days away from the January sale, I emailed Nina and told her I would meet her and her brother to look at the table the following day. It would take all day to go to Baltimore and back, but the certainty with which Richard Jones had spoken was haunting me. In 2000, Christie's and Sotheby's pleaded guilty to fixing sellers' commissions and integrity was something we were all trying to push to the forefront. I had to make sure nothing from under the surface was going to boil up and ruin the auction.

I hadn't spent much time in Baltimore. I focused more on New York and New England when it came to acquisitions, but Nicole had a real interest in mid-Atlantic and southern furniture. I thought about showing her the picture. She knew Hugh Finlay better than anyone in the department. But she had been leaving the office at midnight and was more stressed than I had seen her in the past five years. I couldn't pile on the panic, especially for something as small as this. So I headed to Penn Station alone and boarded the regional train south.

The train flew by Newark, central New Jersey, and northern Maryland and I sat with my piles of provenance documents for all the Hugh Finlay pieces that the Tumlinsons had ever bought or sold. I read them over. When I went bleary-eyed, I turned to the latest issues of *Baer Faxt* and *Kovels'*, and then went back to the papers. There was no way, I concluded. No way that Elizabeth's table had any provenance issues.

I exited the train at Baltimore's Penn Station and took a cab toward the Inner Harbor. Baltimore, it turned out, was charming in the way that things without the sheen of money can be. It had life, if not wealth. There were pockets of affluence, I imagined—all those Hopkins doctors, and people like the Tumlinsons—but they weren't on the beaten path. One of the things I loved about American furniture was that it was beautiful without being showy and the people who collected it liked solid, traditional things, not the gild and the glitz of furnishings from France, Austria, and Italy.

A few minutes too early to meet Nina and Richard, I watched men and women in thick coats walk their children in the direction of the Science Center and looked out across the redbrick plaza. I was meeting them at a restaurant called the Rusty Scupper, which sounded like a place that served canned worms with a side of fish heads, but it was actually very nice. I wasn't going to go to a stranger's home, because it was already unorthodox for me to meet them in Baltimore, rather than having them come to the Christie's office or at the very least New York. Instead, they assured me they'd bring the table in their car and I could take a look at it. I sat down at an elevated bar table by the window, which looked out toward the boats docked just a few feet in front of it and the rectangular, squat office buildings on the other side of the harbor. Two minutes later I ordered a bottle of water and the waiter barely had it poured when a stout African-American man in khakis and a black down parka and a petite woman in a red wool coat approached me.

"Are you Carolyn?" asked the man, without even a hint of a smile.

"I am," I said, trying to look equally unhappy. I put out my hand and shook his and his sister's. They sat down across from me, and without opening their menus, thanked me for coming down.

"It's my pleasure," I replied, urging them to order something. "We always take any concerns of provenance or authenticity very seriously."

"Oh, this is not a question of authenticity," said Nina. She had smooth skin, despite her age, and just a swipe of red matte lipstick on her downturned lips. She must have been in her late fifties or early sixties, but because of her skin, small frame, freckles, and the way she carried herself—like a teacher whose class you never dared mouth off in—she looked younger. She took off her red coat, folded it neatly behind her, and adjusted her perfectly pressed gray wool dress, which looked like something she'd been wearing to important lunches for years. "This is a question about ownership," she said firmly. "And that table, the Hugh Finlay table on page seventy-three in this auction catalogue"—she moved down and took the Tumlinson catalogue out of her black laptop bag—"well, that's not Mrs. Adam R. Tumlinson's. That table belonged to my mother. Would you like to see a picture of that table?"

Why was she showing me a picture of the table when she was about to show me the actual table?

"Here it is," she said, pushing a grainy photo in my direction, the same one I had in my email. "Here is the picture of that table. Not Elizabeth or Adam Tumlinson's table, but my mother's table. My table. I have a few other pictures, too."

She reached back into the bag as her brother looked on, and brought out a small manila envelope with a piece of cardboard inside to keep it from bending. She emptied the contents and showed two black-and-white photos of an attractive woman in a cotton dress with a small hat pinned to her head, sitting at a table. Though not zoomed in and slightly out of focus, the table did look a lot like the Tumlinsons', which was printed in our catalogue right next to the photograph.

Nina pointed to the picture again.

"Look here, right here," she said. "Even in black-and-white you can see it. Look at the decoration on the sides and on the legs and that thick marble top; it's all clear in these photos: the pattern, almost like a double-sided arrow. That's the same as the one you have here in the catalogue. It's the same table!"

"So are you saying that yours is the real table and Elizabeth Tumlinson's is not what it purports to be? Because I can assure you that we have done our research on her table and we have no reason to question its provenance. James Tumlinson, Adam Tumlinson's great-grandfather, his name appears in Hugh Finlay's sales records."

"Well, then it had to be for something else," said Nina, clearly winning our staring contest. "Because this table here, this is the table that was in my mother's shop until April seventh, 1968. She didn't know it was worth a thing, which is why she had it in the store all covered in hats, but just before April of '68 a woman, and I was there so I remember this very well, a woman who taught at Johns Hopkins came in because she was lost and she asked for directions. My mother gave them to her but the woman didn't leave. She picked up several hats off the table, looked at the top of it and underneath, and asked my mother if she knew that she had a very expensive table in her store. My mom said she didn't know too much about it, and the woman showed her the signature and explained that it was made by Hugh Finlay and the reason she knew this was because she had worked for the Baltimore Historical Society and studied that kind of thing. She offered to buy it, but I think my mother was pretty proud of herself for having something someone of that stature would recognize so she kept it. Turns out that was the wrong decision because just about two weeks later, on April seventh, it was gone."

"What do you mean by April seventh?" I asked. "April seventh, 1968? You wrote and said you would be bringing the table in the back of your brother's car." I looked at Richard, who looked at his sister.

"Well, we don't have the table anymore," she said matter-of-factly.

"You don't have the table? But you told me you did. The only reason I am here is because you said you had the table!" My knee hit the underside of the much less expensive table we were sitting at and rattled my water glass.

"Well, my guess was that if I told you I only had a picture of it, you would not have come down," replied Nina.

All of a sudden, I got it. I understood why I was in a restaurant and not in a parking lot looking at the table. Their mother could have been to the Tumlinsons' at one point or another when they were in Baltimore and posed for a picture with their table. It was possible. I had come all the way down here, ignoring the million things I had to do before the January sale, just to look at a picture that I had already looked at sitting at my desk in New York.

"Listen. Lying to someone is probably not the best way to conduct business, or whatever this is," I said, starting to lose my patience.

"Just hear me out, though," said Nina. "I don't have the table, but I do have a few things to show you. Will you give us five more minutes?"

I had left New York four hours ago. What was five more minutes.

"This table," said Nina, holding her picture next to the catalogue, "was in my mother's store for years, right at the front entrance. She and my father owned a women's clothing shop on the fourteen hundred block of North Milton Street, though she really ran the place. And when he died in 1965, she did run the place. North Milton, now, I don't know how much you know about that time, but that's the street where the fires started during the Baltimore riots of 1968."

Looking me over and deciding I was too young to know the details of what she was talking about, she said, "Those were the riots that took place all over the country after Martin Luther King was shot."

I nodded, listening, aware of the riots, but not much about them.

"My parents, they kept that table near the entrance of the store, close to the cash register, because it had such a nice look about it. Like I said, there were usually a few of the most expensive hats we sold and other small items on it. And even after they knew the table was worth something, they kept it there. In fact, they cleared it off, cleaned it better than ever, and inched it a little toward the front. They hoped it would attract people to the store and they planned to eventually sell it to that woman to put us through college. But neither of us ended up going to college because on that day in April, part of the store burned. Not the whole place, like some of the other businesses on North Milton. Well, all over town really. But part of it did. And the store and our business never recovered. That riot, it was devastation."

"And the table," I said, interrupting her.

"Well, it didn't burn, because we never found any trace of it. It must have been looted. So much of the area was and people took everything during those riots. They stole clothes from the dry cleaners next door. Just filled up bags and took them. And they did the same thing at our place. They took everything that wasn't charred by the fire."

"If you don't mind me asking, how old were you during the riots?"

"I was fourteen years old, but trust me, I remember that table. And I'm sure, and I mean sure, that it is the exact table that you have up for auction."

There were tables out there, which were "most likely" Hugh Finlay but were not certainly Finlay. The more I looked at Nina's table, and heard her story, I started to think it could be real. But if it was, that certainly did not mean Elizabeth's was inauthentic; it just meant this was a companion piece to the Finlay we had. Or maybe it was just a copy of a Finlay. The thing about Finlay, which I explained to Nina and Richard, was that he not only built furniture from mahogany; he also sold mahogany. He was also not the only person making Federal-style furniture in Baltimore in the early 1800s.

"I take it your mother is no longer alive?" I asked them.

"I'm afraid not," replied Richard.

"Are there any identifying marks on the table? Any chips or defects?"

"Not that I remember."

"Do you know how she got the table?"

"I don't," said Nina. "I remember her always having it in the store. It could have come with the store."

"I think your table was possibly a companion piece, which would mean that it looked exactly like this one in the catalogue. That's the most probable explanation, and I'd like to help if I can. It's just that we're a little busy in New York right now, as you might assume, but maybe I can after the sale."

"What do you mean about companion piece?" said Richard.

"Companion piece, it just means that the maker made

two of the exact same table, to go on either end of a sofa or chaise. This, on page seventy-three is a pier table, it's possible that he made two, but no one knew about it because the table was never bought or sold publicly and it wasn't in his records."

Nina and Richard looked unconvinced.

"Tell me about your family," I asked. "Has your family been in Baltimore a long time?" What I was more interested in now was how a Hugh Finlay table could have ended up in a women's clothing shop in a lower-income African-American neighborhood in Baltimore in the late sixties.

"We've been here for just about ever," said Richard. "As far as we know, and I've done plenty of research, our great-great-great-grandmother was born in the Cape Verde Islands and was brought in a boat, a Spanish ship we think, but one originally built in Baltimore, in 1820."

"A lot of the boats in the international slave trade were built right here in the early eighteen hundreds," said Nina. "Even though it was illegal. But no one really did a thing about it."

"Do you have a family tree? Or some other record of your family? Who was born when, who lived where, their places of employment, that kind of thing?"

"We don't have a family tree. Like an actual tree on paper with names and all that," said Nina. "But we've got a lot written down."

"Your brother," I said, motioning to Richard. "He said that you're interested in American furniture and that's why you have our catalogues. Is that because of this table? The one your mother had?"

"You mean this table?" she said, pointing to the picture in the catalogue. "My table? Absolutely. I was there when that woman said it was worth a lot of money, and frankly, there have been many times in the past couple of decades where I could have really used the money. And now I see it, estimated here between two hundred and twenty and two hundred and thirty thousand dollars. That's a lot of money."

She flipped open the catalogue with her slightly chapped hands and ran her index finger over the picture.

"I never believed it burned. I always thought it got taken. If you walked into that store it was clearly the nicest thing in there. Anyone could have seen that. And I loved it. When I would help my mom in the shop, she used to let me dust it and place the hats back on it. That was the best part of my day back then."

I did not have time for this, whatever *this* was, and no one else in the department did, either. I was in no position to pass this all along to Louise. We were in the middle of previews. We had buyers all over the world requesting condition reports. And we had a lot of interest. It was only panic time when you didn't have interest, but that wasn't the case with the estate of Mrs. Adam R. Tumlinson. Why should I stop what I was doing and listen to these people who may or may not have owned a companion piece forty-five years ago? What weight did they have? She worked in a library and he worked in shipping—they weren't art experts. All they had were some old photos and memories. That wasn't enough to do anything with and it certainly wasn't enough to convince me to pull Elizabeth's table from the auction. I thought it would sell for around $240,000—it wasn't a lot, but it wasn't nothing, either. Plus, they had already lied to me.

I shivered as I tried to hail a cab and muttered the time of my train to the driver, asking him to hurry. The city still had Christmas decorations up, but in the wet snow, they looked sad. Why had these people bothered me with their story when they knew how close we were to the January auction? The catalogue had been out for weeks. It was January 11 and I had a week left before the auction. I had met them, I had listened to them and looked at their pictures, I had offered to help them when the auction was over, and I would. But right now, there was nothing else I could do.

## CHAPTER 4

The morning of our January auction brought sheets of freezing rain, the kind of rain where you feel wet even if you're just watching it from indoors. Five degrees colder and it would have been snow. Instead, New York was being forcefully flooded: the cars, buildings, streets, and people bathed in freezing rain. Like every evening sale since Nicole and I had worked together, she got there first and I joined her on the later side in the back of the room. Maybe I'd left my nerves in Baltimore, or maybe I had just gained a little faith between September and January, but when I moved through the already packed auction room and stood in the back with Nicole, my heart felt steady and my sweat glands were behaving.

"Did you see Nick Marshall-Smith in the second row?" said Nicole, nodding very subtly in the direction of one of the country's biggest collectors of mid-Atlantic eighteenth-century furniture. "And Harriet Traymore is three down from him. Michael Floyd is sitting far left, sixth row back. Marvin Levine and his new wife, there, right side, by the phones."

"This crowd . . . ," I said, scanning the room and recognizing many of the faces. For some auctions—Impressionists, contemporary art—reservations were required to attend. We had an open-door policy, as we had enough low-dollar items to appeal to a wide audience, and we had enough high-dollar items to bring energy and adrenaline to the room.

As always, Olivier Burnell was calling the auction, and as always, he packed the front with some of the best items, brought the dollar amounts down for a few lots, and kept the very best for smack in the middle. Nicole looked at me again, pushing one of her curled strands of hair out of her eyes, and smiled. "No hives today?" she said, looking at my smooth face. I had about a pound of pancake makeup with me, but so far, I had no need for it.

My short nails dug into my clenched fist as Olivier transitioned to Lot 29. The rotating wall to his right turned and on a small platform anchored against it was the Hugh Finlay.

"Lot number twenty-nine is the Hugh Finlay pier table, inlaid with gold leaf and marble." Olivier lifted his arms and started the bidding at $75,000. "Seventy-five thousand dollars on the floor, seventy-five thousand," said Olivier, looking at the crowd.

It was times like these when I cursed my short stature, but try as I might, I did not see Nina or her brother in the room. Thank God. Thank almighty God. I would not have to hurl myself across the podium as they reached for the table screaming their mother's name.

The bids moved quickly past $170,000 and Olivier said, "I can sell at one hundred ninety thousand," revealing the reserve to the buyers. "The lady's bid here at one hundred ninety thousand," said Olivier, pointing to a woman seated on the left side of the room. "Two hundred thousand here in the room," he said, switching sides. When it moved past two hundred and ten, I let myself exhale. The woman on the left finally dropped out, there were no phone bids, and it stood at $260,000. "Are you all done in the saleroom?" asked Olivier with his hands up. "I'm going to sell it." He hit the podium and announced, "Sold at two hundred and sixty thousand dollars." And like that, the Hugh Finlay table sold to another collector, who had nothing to do with the city of Baltimore.

When Elizabeth's estate had finished and we were an hour and fifty-five minutes into the auction, Nicole pressed the total key on her phone calculator and put it in my hand. The estate had gone for $40,900,000, including buyer's premium.

"Didn't I tell you thirty-seven million was way too low for a guarantee," she said with a grin.

The auction wrapped up twenty minutes after nine o'clock and Nicole and I agreed that if there was ever a time for celebratory drinks, this was it. Elizabeth, our trip to Texas, pulling it all together for January when we should have had nine months more—it was crazy, and I hadn't come down from all of it yet, and this time I didn't want to.

"Let me just see Louise before we go," I told Nicole when the auction room was nearly empty. "I'll meet you and Erik at the bar."

I found Louise in the narrow hallway leading back toward our offices on the fifth floor. She was leaning against the frame of her office door, not quite inside and not quite outside. When she saw me, she motioned for me to come closer and pointed toward the phone she had against her ear.

I loitered a few feet away as she wrapped up. I was about to do a very restrained and respectable celebratory dance involving a backflip, but Louise's face stopped me. She finished the call, put her phone in the pocket of her dress, and looked at me.

"I need to talk to you, and here you are."

She motioned to a chair in her office and closed the door. She put her hands in her lap and stared blankly at me across her desk. It had a little paperweight on it made from a Japanese cherry tree branch that I had bought her for her fiftieth birthday. Louise always used the things you gave her, and I always noticed.

"I just got the strangest call from the newspaper in Baltimore, the *Baltimore Sun*. They asked me for a quote regarding a human interest piece they're running tomorrow about a family whose store was looted during the Baltimore riots of 1968 and somehow their table ended up in our auction catalogue and just sold for two hundred and sixty thousand dollars."

Maybe it was the fact that my body had just gone rigid, but Louise asked, "Would you know anything about this? Because that reporter who just called me said you did."

"I should have told you, I mean, now that I have the stress of the auction off my shoulders and I'm thinking a little more clearly, I realize I should have told you." My words poured out of me, my voice starting to crack. Louise looked at me trying, and failing, to steady myself. There was no compassion in her face. "This brother and sister, about fifty-five, sixty years old, they called me," I explained. "They said the table was their mother's and that it was with them in Baltimore. I went to see it—which I know I shouldn't have—but I did. I just wanted to be sure there was nothing to their story because I cared so much about Elizabeth's estate. And when I got there they didn't have the table. They lied. All they had were some blurry pictures and a story that didn't add up. I thought, if anything, it was a companion piece that was now lost. What was I supposed to do with that? Pull the piece? Pull the whole collection? Seventy percent of our January sale?"

"What you were supposed to do is to ask me what I would do because I am your boss!" Louise screamed, pushing the desk with her hands.

"Of course I should have. I'm sorry, Louise. I'm so embarrassed. It's just that you were under so much pressure from Dominick. You said your hair was falling out from stress. I didn't want to be the source of—"

"Those people are black, Carolyn. And poor! We're going to look like we steal from poor black people!"

I didn't interrupt her again.

"That reporter said the table, that very low-, low-dollar table, was their mother's. And that their mother got it from their grandmother and that she got it from some family that she worked as a maid for in the early nineteen hundreds. This reporter found that family, the Smarts or the Smarths or something, and they confirmed she worked for them. They even have pictures of her! So they're now claiming that the grandmother got it as a gift from the children of this family who were very attached to her and she gave it to her daughter who owned it until it was stolen and the Tumlinsons bought it from a dealer and we sold it thirty-five minutes ago."

"What!" I screamed through panic. "I didn't know any of that. Nothing! They didn't say a thing about another family or their grandmother or anything. If they had mentioned any of those details I would have told you immediately. All I saw were some old pictures of a table they hadn't seen since 1968." I was paralyzed with fear. This could not happen. This absolutely would be the death of me. I wasn't the only one involved in the estate of Mrs. Adam R. Tumlinson, but in Christie's eyes, I was.

"I didn't know about any of that, Louise!" I repeated. "They didn't tell me anything."

"I need to talk to our general counsel," she said, still

holding the edge of the desk. "We need to contact the buyers, the media. We need to suspend all of the sales in the
Tumlinson collection until they are verified. Do you know
what this will do to the department? We're going to be
shoved with the instrument sales! Numismatics and armor!
I'm already selling chairs with lamps, Carolyn. I don't know
if you understand the gravity of what you've done. And it
all could have been avoided. We would have pulled one lot."

"I'm so sorry, Louise. I don't know what to do. Tell me
what to do." I glanced up at her desperately.

"Carolyn, I'm sorry, but . . ."

There is nothing more terrifying than the silence of
your own heart. I knew it was just a few seconds before I
opened my mouth to respond, but in that long moment, I
couldn't hear anything but a stillness of where my heartbeat
should have been and the cold shock of my promise, my
potential blowing away.

"I know," I said weakly, trying to dry the tears from my
face. "I understand. I'll get my things."

I ran to my office, looked at Nicole's empty chair with
the gray cashmere cardigan on it, pulled out my phone, and
called the number I had for Nina Jones Caine. She answered
after one ring.

"Who did you tell about your table? What did you do!" I
screamed into the phone.

"I didn't *do* anything. I just told my story to a reporter
over lunch. I've known his mother for years; we were just
eating as family friends. It wasn't even meant to be on the
record."

"Really? Well, when we don't want something to be on
the record, we start with the words 'off the record,' which
you clearly forgot! Nina, I just lost my job because of what
you did."

"No . . . not really . . . did you?"

"Yes I did!" I said, unable to hold back the tears. "You have ruined my life! I tried to help you. But these things don't happen overnight. Why couldn't you have talked to me first? I went down to Baltimore. I listened to your story. I did everything you asked. I was going to help you."

"I'm so sorry. I didn't mean to hurt you, to get you fired! I just thought it was time to increase public interest in our story, with the auction about to happen. And Jeffrey, the reporter, he was able to find out so much in such a short period of time. I showed him an album of my grandmother and he recognized the house she was standing in front of. He knows the people who live there now. We were shocked. But still, maybe that wasn't the right thing to do. Is there someone I can talk to? Can I try to fix this?" When I had met Nina, she had spoken in a firm, self-assured way. But now her voice had flown up in pitch. She sounded worried, almost repentant, but I didn't care.

"Your talking just caused Christie's to potentially lose millions, for me to lose my job, for my boss to get in major trouble. All the Tumlinsons' pieces from Baltimore will take years to recover their value. Elizabeth Tumlinson is seventy-six years old. She'll probably die before that happens!"

"I'm so sorry. I didn't know that our story had so much more story to it. Jeffrey just traced it faster than we ever could. He found this family we didn't even know about, thanks to that photo and some black-and-white picture in the *Baltimore Sun* archive, and the whole thing unraveled. But he couldn't have written anything yet; I just talked to him."

"Well, now you know that in this world, that's all it takes. One conversation!"

I slammed down the phone. I wanted to stay in my office forever. Maybe no one would notice me. I could climb into the comfortable oblong metal trash can, lean back against piles of crumpled paper, and stay there until I died. How long did it take a person to starve to death? A few days? Weeks?

At quarter to ten, Louise opened my door and watched me empty the contents of my first desk drawer into a paper bag. "I can always bring you the rest tomorrow," she said, watching me. My purse wasn't much bigger than an envelope.

"No, it's fine, I can manage tonight," I said. "I don't need much. I'm sorry I'm still here."

When I walked out the doors of the almost empty building and into the night air, crisp and cold, I knew I would never step foot inside Christie's again.

# CHAPTER 5

I barely remember the hours after I left Christie's that night. I wanted to sprint, to get away from everything that had been jarringly stripped from my life, but my heels were too high and my body was too tired to do anything but move slowly and sadly. This couldn't be happening to me. This sort of thing happened to other people. The men or women whom I read about very quickly in the *Art Newspaper*, I'd purse my lips at their gaffes and announce to Nicole how I was "embarrassed for them." We'd whisper something kind, like "morons," and continue our dominance of all things American and made of wood. When word got out about Elizabeth's sale, some girl, just like me, would do the same thing, but it would be my name she was reading.

Somehow my feet turned in the right direction and took me home. I found my keys under a thick stack of embossed and letter-pressed business cards that I'd shoved in my purse, let everything I was holding drop to the ground right inside my front door, threw my clothes in the direction of the bathroom, and cried. I felt pathetic, but I didn't know what else to do but mourn the person I had been only two hours ago. Had it all been my fault? Would Nicole, Erik, or

Louise really have acted differently in my situation? Was it terrible judgment or terrible luck? It didn't matter now. I couldn't undo it.

My apartment was freezing so I turned the heat up to 85 and then remembered that I was no longer employed and turned it down to 50, adding another blanket to my bed instead. The blanket smelled like wet dog, and I didn't have a dog. But who cared. So I would smell. So I would become a shut-in who resembled Jodie Foster in *Nell*. I'd forget the English language. I would sleep on a bed of moss. I'd be like *Lord of the Flies* without the other flies. "The lone fly," I said, crying. "Piggy."

I heard my phone ring repeatedly that night but didn't stir to turn off the ringer or answer it. When I woke up the next day at noon, all I did was open my metal apartment door to take out the keys I had left in the lock, close the door, put the chain on, and pretend that the world outside was something that no longer applied to me. I didn't turn on my computer to see if the article had run in the *Baltimore Sun*. I didn't check to see if it had gained traction or if someone had made a GIF of my head with the words EPIC FAIL flashing on it. I didn't want to know. I ignored voicemails from Nicole and text messages from Alex. I just let my phone battery blink in warning and die.

After seventy-two hours with the curtains drawn I lost track of day and night. When I wasn't hiding from the outside world, I alternated between sleeping in my bed and sleeping in the wooden chair I had spent the night in before everything happened, before Christie's became a place I was no longer welcome. And then, suddenly it was Monday. It was January 22, four days since the auction. I had almost no food left and I didn't want to order any. Instead of eating, I drank tap water with the occasional shot of vodka chucked

in. I just wanted to sit, and stare, get wildly drunk, and ignore my newly acquired life crisis.

But I wasn't that lucky. Only one person had the key
to my apartment besides my landlord: my mother. On
Wednesday night, she decided to use it. I was facedown on
my bed, naked, covered in sheets and blankets, which were
starting to get pungent from sweat, when I heard the lock
snap open. I should have immediately turned around to
make sure it wasn't some zombie-eyed killer who liked to
bludgeon women who'd already lost the will to live, but I
didn't. It wasn't until I heard my mother's monotone voice
imploring me to remove the chain that I turned my head to
look at her. I could just make out a thin strip of her body
between the wall and the door and her left eye. She put two
fingers on the chain motioning for me to come open it.

"Carolyn. Now, please," she said, rattling the paint-
coated old chain.

I looked up from my bed, registered that it was her,
and lay back down, not planning on moving again. Maybe
she would give up and go away. My parents were fond of
abandoning me. They'd forgotten me in the Uffizi Gallery
in Florence once for seven hours. I'd been found napping
under Caravaggio's *Bacchus*, which could explain my pen-
chant for alcohol and men with questionable morals.

"Nicole called me. She told me everything," my mother
said from the hallway. "We were worried when we didn't
hear from you after the auction, but you can be very distant.
So we weren't all that worried. Actually your father won an
indoor tennis tournament last weekend, men's senior sin-
gles. They gave him a laurel wreath, which I thought was
odd . . . but I'm off topic. Nicole, she called and explained
everything that happened, she sent the link to the *Baltimore
Sun* article. And understandably, now we're very worried."

So there had been an article. Was I mentioned by name? Was Louise? Or did they just use the general Christie's American Furniture and Decorative Arts department label? I wanted to ask. But I didn't want to know the answer. My mom was the very last person I wanted to see. She, who never failed.

I remember when I was little and brought home report cards full of A's, she would smile and say, "Good job, kiddo. You're just like me. Smart as a flea." She'd blow a kiss in the general direction of my face and go straight back to her work. But I remember living for that praise, hence my lifetime of near-perfect grades.

I heard her fiddling with the chain again, trying to break her way inside. She raised her voice and demanded to be let in or she would "find an ax and chop, chop, chop," so finally I got out of bed completely naked, removed the chain, and went straight back under the covers. The TV was still on and she immediately turned it off, cracked a window open muttering something about "a retirement-home-strength stench," and sat on the edge of my bed. She smelled like wool sweaters and parental disappointment.

"What happened?" Her hand grazed my calf and then moved on to my foot. She wrapped her hand around it, not exactly stroking it or massaging it, just holding it. My mother was only twenty years older than me and she barely looked it. When she turned forty-nine at Christmastime, she shrugged, glanced at herself in the mirror, and announced that everything was just fine. That's the way it was in my family; everything was always supposed to be just fine.

"I don't know what happened," I replied, not lifting my head from the pillow. She could probably barely hear me, but I didn't care. I hadn't asked her to come.

"And is it as bad as Nicole said?" she asked, still awkwardly holding my foot, which probably smelled like a fish at this point. "Have you disgraced yourself, your family, and your future offspring?"

Is that what Nicole said? How wonderful. I was so glad to have acquired such loyal friends during my decade at Christie's.

"I'm sure it's much worse," I replied, lifting my head slightly. "You read the *Sun*?" I asked, finally looking up at her.

Her face looked smooth and distinguished, the kind of face that never wrinkles very much because it never moves very much. Her light blue eyes looked at the wall next to my bed and fell on the chair by the window.

"Is that chair broken?" she asked, looking at it and ignoring the question.

"The arms fell off," I replied.

And by *fell off* I meant that the night before she knocked on my door uninvited I ripped them off with the help of my foot.

"That's too bad; such a pretty chair." She turned her face and looked at me. My mother's presence was making it feel more real. She was here to bail me out and I knew that it took a lot to get her to that point. She unbuttoned her cardigan and put it on the broken chair. She looked nothing like me. She was tall, with willowy limbs, an air of ambivalence, and a perpetual tan. I, on the other hand, was regularly described as petite, pale, and intense.

"What am I going to do?" I asked sadly.

"You're a very smart girl, Carolyn. You're my girl. And you're not going to worry about it now. In a few days, you'll fix it."

I ignored the second half of her sentence and concentrated on the first. My mother wrapped her thin arms around me and mumbled something about my flair for the dramatic. It wasn't the kind of hug that warmed your bones with love and compassion. It was the kind of hug that came from a woman who shuddered at the thought of professional ruin. But she'd called me her girl. And she was here, helping me.

She changed my sheets and blankets, pointed to the center of the bed, and told me to wait there while she went out to get us food. And I did. I sat still until I started to slink down, deeper and deeper until I was lying flat again, drifting off to sleep. I faintly heard her come back in, but I barely stirred. Then I could sense her getting into bed next to me. I had never been a kid who curled up in her parents' bed. There were very firm lines drawn in my house of where I could and could not be. But here was my mother sharing my bed. Watching me. Taking care of me. And for a second, between all the self-pitying I was doing, I felt lucky. I felt loved.

"I have a plan," my mother said as soon as my eyelids fluttered the next morning. She smiled at me as if she were about to announce that I was going to have all my teeth removed with rusty pliers by children playing doctor.

"Nothing in life is worth mourning like this, Carolyn. You need to make a few of the right moves now, and then you'll see, everything will turn out just fine. You are allowed to mourn your loss for twenty-four hours and then you have to let it go and get your life back. Like I said yesterday, you're my girl, and this"—she pointed at me slumped over in bed, a jar of peanut butter and a baking spatula on the floor next to me—"is not my girl." I looked at her with my recently perfected sad face. With her shiny brown hair and flawless makeup, we didn't even look related. She even smelled like success.

"I think I'm the horse who jumped off the track and now the owner has to shoot it."

"Oh Carolyn, stop it. Where did I find you? Universal

Studios? You're being ridiculous. You're going to go out and get a haircut. Getting haircuts always makes a person feel better."

"I just got a haircut."

"Well, then get it cut again!" my mother screamed without really looking at me.

"After you have a day of relaxation, we are going to go to the Vollinger Gallery at seven P.M. sharp for the opening of the Pennsylvania Furniture Show. I know you already RSVP'd to it. I asked Nicole this morning. She plans on being there, too. She was instructed not to speak to you by Louise but she's going to blink at you across the room three times to show she cares." My mother paused and listened to me say the word *no* about fifteen times.

"The thing you do not understand, Carolyn, is how important it is to get back out there immediately. You put on a brave face and show the world that none of this affected you. You're above this and too smart for their petty gossip. Tell the art world that this was just an inconsequential misunderstanding. If you act that way, they'll see it your way. Trust me. I know about these things." She sighed and stared at me like I was some rent-a-kid she still couldn't believe she got stuck with.

"No," I said again. "No way, not happening, not even entertaining the idea."

"You will go, or I will not leave your apartment. Ever," my mother said firmly. "If you go with me tonight, I will leave tomorrow morning and let you make your own decisions. Now, doesn't that sound appealing. How to get rid of your mother." I knew I should have emancipated myself at sixteen like Macaulay Culkin.

I left the apartment, but only because my mom was in it and I wanted to be far away from her. But I was not getting a haircut. What I needed to do was read. I had to suck it up and open the *Sun* article. I had to check my email, listen to my voicemail, and tell Nicole, Alex, and Jane that I wasn't dead. I turned on my now-charged phone and sent three texts, all of which said, "I am not dead. Just trying to figure things out. I'm sorry I've been out of touch. I appreciate your concern and I'll call you soon." My hand was shaking so I stood up and bought two Rice Krispies treats, sat at a table in the back, and tried not to hyperventilate. It didn't work. I was hyperventilating. Next I'd be sweating, and based on the last few days, tears would follow. But what choice did I have. I couldn't exactly go to some party at the Vollinger Gallery and not know what shape my career was in.

The *Baltimore Sun.* I had to start with the *Sun.* Or maybe I should just google myself. No. The *Baltimore Sun.* It was a warm and friendly paper. Meg Ryan's character worked there in *Sleepless in Seattle.* There was no way they were going to trash an innocent person like me. I loaded the home page on my phone. "Triple homicide, all children, bludgeoned by masked man." Great. That was a swell headline. Was this paper printed at the penitentiary? I searched for my name in the paper's archives and exactly one article came up. "Christie's big Baltimore boo-boo." I dropped my phone on the table and stuffed one of the cellulite bars in my mouth.

The article followed just what Louise had said. This enterprising reporter, whom I now wished great harm upon, had managed to find the family that Nina's grandmother worked for and that family had produced photos of the table in their house. They'd also found some bankbook or record where their great-grandfather had noted that the table had been given to "the negro maid" when she retired as a thank-you gift. There was no concrete theory on how it had gotten from the Joneses' shop into the Tumlinsons' house, first in

Baltimore and then in Texas, but some unnamed source said Adam Tumlinson had dealt with art dealers who had been in trouble before and another said that Adam Tumlinson himself employed several personal aides who were less than ethical in helping him build the perfect collection. Where exactly was this information when we were working with the Tumlinson estate? Had I not checked enough? Could I have found all this? Christie's had been helping Adam buy and sell for decades and nothing like this had ever come up. I felt sick. The provenance of all of the Tumlinsons' Baltimore furniture was now in question, and the whole estate felt shaky. The paper called it "a grave embarrassment for the small, yet respected, American Furniture and Decorative Arts Department, led by Louise DeWitt." Some art expert who they probably found selling chalk art to tourists on the Inner Harbor said it would take the department "years to recover. Maybe a decade." But I knew that. I knew that as soon as I had heard Louise utter the word *stolen.*

My stomach was churning. It was all here, in front of me, the demise of my career. Louise was mentioned by name and so was I, along with Nicole and Erik. It made us out to all be at fault, not just me, which meant that they wrote the article before they knew I had been exiled from Christie's. Had there been a follow-up? Not in the *Baltimore Sun.* The story hadn't been picked up by the *Times* but the *Washington Post* gave it a few inches and every inside art publication had run it or linked to it, which meant everyone in my industry knew about it. And unfortunately, those were the only people I cared about and the only ones who could give me a job.

There was no way my department, my former department, was going to recover from this quickly. It wasn't just the one piece; the Hugh Finlay table was poison to the whole estate. And still my mother was convinced that someone from Sotheby's or Bonhams was going to sprint to me at the Vollinger Gallery, hand me a big fat contract to sign on the line, and say, "Welcome to the family, little one."

I slowly wove through the city blocks home and my mother opened my door before I reached it. She had on her navy blue shift dress, a Chanel copy she'd had custom made in the Garment District, which she'd been wearing with sensible kitten heels and a double strand of pearls for the last decade. Her dark hair was arranged in her perfect helmet of success. She looked at me and said, "Vollinger Gallery. You have no choice. Please get ready." So I would die in public. I'd probably be stoned. Louise surely had Nicole pushing around a wheelbarrow full of boulders just in case she ran into me and had to kill me like in "The Lottery." I put on a black sleeveless dress, which I'd found in a ball on the floor, no makeup, and motorcycle boots. I looked unpolished, unkempt, un-Christie's, which is what I was. I was accepting my fate.

The Vollinger Gallery was the best American furniture gallery in New York City. If you weren't buying American furniture at auction or from a private dealer, you were buying it from Vollinger. I sat against the leather seat of the cab and mentally went through a checklist of who could be there. Louise could definitely be there, if she wasn't too busy wading through the mess I'd left her. David Marcham could be there, too. He might slap me on the back and thank me in front of everyone for taking out his competition so publicly and swiftly.

We arrived on the early side, which was good and terrible. It was good because there were fewer people milling through the five floors of the nineteenth-century town house on East Eighty-Fourth Street, and bad because the few people who were there were all looking at the door anticipating who might arrive next.

None of them was expecting me.

Rebecca Wall was the manager of the gallery and was so tall you almost wanted to ask her what the air was like up there. She also had one of those pan-British accents that made you think she was raised between London and some former British African colony like Malawi. She had a perpetual tan and always wore her hair in a topknot like she wanted to conduct electricity. She saw me when I walked in and actually put her hand on her heart.

Marisa Irving, another gallerina and the manager of the well-known Steiner Gallery, moved briskly toward Rebecca in her over-the-knee Louis Vuitton boots to talk about one thing: the ignoramus that was I.

"This is really fun, Mom. What's next, lethal injection?" She shut me up with a flick of her wrist and gave the room her best academic smile, a little sincere, a lot more menacing.

I stood in the corner with her and watched everyone who dealt with American furniture walk in except Louise, Nicole, and Erik.

I knew that normally one of them would have made it. Probably Louise. But they were surely still at work dealing with the aftermath of the auction. Within the next five minutes, they would know that I was there. Someone would text them and preface it with "Guess the buffoon who just walked in??!!"

I leaned over to my mother and whispered, "I need to leave. Where is the door? I can't be here."

"You are a very smart woman. Just persevere. Smile. Let them see that what happened is no big deal. Nothing to gawk at. People will take cues from the way you present yourself."

It was at that moment that my own mother abandoned

me. Without warning, she beelined out the door and left me standing there, exposed. Within seconds, a group of five women, the dreaded gallerinas, rushed over to me.

The gallery girls of New York are like starving attack dogs in really nice clothes. All have legs for days and glasses so edgy you wondered why they didn't just strap two paperweights to their faces with some hooks. I knew most of them, I was friends with a few of them, and I didn't want to see any of them. But as these girls appeared next to me with dinner-plate eyes and their fingers poised to text everyone my reaction, it was clear that I had no choice. They were going to stone me.

"Carolyn Everett! I can't believe you're here! I'm going to blog about this immediately," said one named Jacqueline, grabbing me by the elbow and pouting like a model who eats only baby carrots and laxatives.

"Bold. Extremely bold move, Carolyn," said her friend Kira.

I hated my mother. Hated. How could she leave me like this? She knew this was going to happen. She was probably standing outside watching me from a window in some form of sadistic parenting.

"How much Xanax are you on? Can you see me? Do I look like a cartoon character?" said Kira.

"I wouldn't be able to walk," said Jacqueline. "I'd be too distraught. Someone would have to push me in a delicate chair. Not like a wheelchair but maybe a Chippendale fauteuil with small sliding disks on the bottom."

"Are you thinking about rehab?" Kira asked. "I know a few places that will let you in to rest even if you don't have a valid addiction. But if you play your hand right, you could just convince everyone that your mistake was due to an innocent little meth problem."

Wait, a meth addiction was better than making a mistake? The girls waited for me to reply and all I could say was, "I hate my mother."

They shook their heads in agreement and started swapping stories of their crazy childhoods. Who needed a family? I could be like Mowgli the jungle boy and live in the forest and befriend ants. I did not need to be exposed to this slow, female torture.

"You really picked *the* party to come to," said Kira. "Everyone's here. Lots of nonfurniture people. Do you know Michael Ando from Christie's Tokyo? He's upstairs. And Max Sebastian from Sotheby's London. Do you know him? He's very good-looking, for someone so terribly old. He's right over there with that thief of an art dealer Greta Merch." She waved her wrist toward the windows.

"How old is he?" I asked, looking at the man regularly called the silver fox of the art world.

"Fifty. Halfway dead."

Max Sebastian looked very much alive. He was a pleasant-looking fifty, wearing age in a way that caused people to say, "If that's what fifty looks like . . ." But despite the comfort of his looks, he had a standoffish quality that made him just right to be a department head.

"Miller McCarthy is here, too. Sotheby's. Impressionism," said Kira, pointing at a wisp of a woman in a cape and riding boots.

"Why is she here?"

"She's here because Max is here. Oxbridge connection. Max is here because Francie Aldridge is here. Francie is here because Louise was supposed to be here and you're here to show all these people that you're a real tough cookie, right?"

I wanted to punch her.

The girls finally left me to fight back my rage, which I

had to do with twice as much strength when I spied David Marcham walk through the door. Instead of ignoring me, as he should have done, he walked right over with a big, expensive smile.

"Hi, Carolyn. How are you?"

"I've been better," I said, deadpan.

My mother might not understand my level of mortification, but David did.

"Pretty brave of you to come out here. Especially to this," he said, motioning to all the women in the room. "It's full of hawks."

What was I going to say to that? My mother made me? I was planning on throwing myself off a building but this seemed like a more uncomfortable way to die?

"Well, I guess I used to be one of them."

"A hawk," he said, smiling. "Yes, you were. Ruthless even. And very good at your job. One of the best I've seen in that department at Christie's, maybe ever."

"Thanks," I said, genuinely appreciative of his compliment. The only nice thing I had heard lately was when I walked out of the shower and my mother said, "You stink less than you did fifteen minutes ago."

"Why are you here?" he asked.

That was a very good question.

"I don't know," I said, biting my bottom lip. Why was I there. "I guess I'm hoping that eventually I can do something else. Find another job."

"Ah, I see," he said, cutting me off before I could embarrass myself even more. "I doubt you want my advice but I'll give it to you anyway."

I looked at him expectantly. Hopefully his advice was "Run, don't walk to Sotheby's; there's a desk waiting for you."

He smiled at me and put his hand on my shoulder, not condescendingly but more as a person who didn't want me to end my life on a cold gray night in January in New York.

"Go do something else for a while. Take a break. The art world can be very unforgiving."

Yes, it could be. It was being unforgiving right now in the form of a slightly balding man in a very expensive suit. But what else could I do?

I let my evening finish on that note and left the gallery without another word. By the time I reached my apartment I was crying again. My mother walked up to me and apologized.

"I was only trying to help, Carolyn. I call it modern parenting for the unconventional child. I'm sorry. I didn't mean to embarrass you."

"It's okay," I said, running my hand across my tears and smearing them across my face. "I wish you hadn't left me there."

"I know. But no one was going to talk to you if I was standing there."

"That would have been nice."

"Did you speak to anyone interesting?"

"David Marcham." I put my hand up to caution her from doing leaps in celebration. "It went terribly. He suggested I leave the auction world altogether."

"He's an imbecile."

"Not exactly. Though I've never liked him very much. All that showboating on *Antiques Roadshow*. It's weird."

The next morning, my mom packed her things, made sure my cabinets were well stocked with food, poured the rest of my vodka down the sink, and gave me a hug.

"You don't need me anymore, do you?"

"It's not that I don't need you, it's just that I don't need this right now. My old life is not mine anymore."

"Don't you want it back?"

"I don't know. Maybe. I mean yes, but not today. Not right now. I tried to get back on the same track and I just can't. No one wants me right now."

"Well then, they're idiots! Pea-brained fools," said my mom, giving me a stiff hug before she reached for her bag.

"Don't be a stranger," she said, doing her walk-away-and-wave move. I heard her soft steps down the carpeted stairs. Soon she would be at Penn Station on a train back to Boston and she'd think about how different the two of us were after all.

I'd only been rid of my mother for ten minutes when Alex called. She'd probably called him on her way out and told him to contact me immediately so I didn't run out to buy more vodka to mix with my tap water.

"I'm worried about you," said Alex. "I'm very, very worried about you. But I figured you needed your space. So I gave it to you. And then your mother called and said you have had all the space you can handle, so I called. Are you feeling better now?"

"A little," I said, lying.

"Would you like to see me?"

Did I want to see Alex? That was a very good question.

"I'll take your silence as a 'not right now,'" said Alex diplomatically.

"Carolyn?"

"Yes," I said, apologizing for the long, awkward pause.

"I'm sorry that happened to you."

"Do you know everything?"

"Well, not everything, but I read the papers and Nicole called me and your mother called me, so I guess I have a pretty good picture of it all."

"I'm so sorry," I said, trying to fight back the distinct sound of shame in my voice. "I know how much you care about our shining careers. How much we both do. We always planned to be such big New York success stories and now I've written that other kind of story. The kind where the heroine dies penniless and forgotten." I was crying again.

"Carolyn, stop. You made a mistake. Big deal. It was about time you made a mistake."

"Time I made a mistake? Do you take some perverse enjoyment in watching me fail?"

"No, but you never fail. You didn't fail now. I think it's good for people sometimes, for things to go wrong. It builds character. And you, you've just never really done anything wrong. You graduated summa cum laude from Princeton. You were in Ivy Club, you got a job at Christie's before you even graduated, and you were the youngest person to ever hold your job there. You're a wunderkind. It was time for you to mess up."

"What should I do, Alex?" I said, my voice tired and gravelly.

"Why don't you try something else? You've only done one thing your entire professional life. Even when we were in high school you wanted to work for an auction house. There are millions of other jobs in the world. Try one."

"'Try one.' You make it sound awfully easy. Which one should I try?"

"I don't know. Stockbroker, tightrope walker, teacher, parachutist, lawyer, cosmonaut. You're a smart girl, Carolyn, and you need a break right now. From me, from New York, from art and auctions, and frankly, from yourself."

"I hate how well you know me."

"No, you don't. That's part of the reason you love me."

I let the word *love* sit there between us and didn't reply.

"You need a break, Carolyn. That's obvious, maybe not to your mother or the Dalbys, but to me."

"Yeah, I know."

"So take one."

When I hung up the phone with Alex, I regretted not asking him to come over. I wanted two big, strong arms around my waist. I wanted him in bed with me. I knew that seeing him naked and moving on top of me was not the way to solve all my problems. It might cause me to scream the words *Jesus* and *Christ* while digging my nails into his back, but that wasn't a long-term solution. So instead of calling him back I turned on my computer and logged on to the real estate section on Craigslist. I listed my apartment as a monthlong sublet. I wrote what I paid a month and then subtracted seven hundred dollars from it. I wanted to leave quickly. Alex was right, and even David was right in a way. I needed a change.

There was just one person I wanted to call before I started figuring out exactly what that change was.

Nicole was already crying when she picked up the phone. I apologized over and over again as she cried, and she told me to stop apologizing while I cried.

"I need to get out of this city, Nicole," I said after she told me about how Christie's was handling the Tumlinson estate. She'd been completely taken off it and Louise and Erik were dealing with everything. She wasn't allowed to contact Elizabeth or Nina at all. Or me. Especially not me.

"Leave New York? I think that's a good idea."

"Do you?"

"I actually do. Sometimes this city can suffocate you. Go to the Hamptons. Go to Block Island."

"It's January."

"Right. Go skiing. Go meditate in an igloo. Find yourself at Canyon Ranch. Just do something to begin anew."

"Can I ask you something?"

"Of course."

"Do you think, in a few . . . years. Do you think I could work at another auction house again? Not Christie's but maybe Sotheby's or Phillips?"

She hesitated before saying, "I do. But I think, like you said, it could take years rather than months."

"So if you were me . . ."

"I think if I were you, I'd become a dealer. Work for yourself. Do what you love. Make some money. Christie's and Sotheby's may be off the table for . . . well . . . a decade, but you're not dead in the art world. You have clients who trust you. You're very smart. Branch out on your own."

"Maybe."

"Maybe? What else are you going to do?"

"I'm going to go to Newport," I said suddenly. "I'm going home."

## CHAPTER 6

It was exactly three days before Valentine's Day when I drove a rented car from the Providence train station to Newport. The man at Hertz asked if I wanted to upgrade my vehicle from tin can to slightly larger tin can; I said I was tempted to downgrade it to the bus. I'd subletted a small apartment in Newport close to the tennis club but not close to the water for twelve hundred dollars a month—a third of what I paid in New York—and packed two suitcases full of winter clothes and my laptop. Despite two phone calls to Houston, I still hadn't spoken to Elizabeth about what had happened and Nina hadn't called me. I promised myself not to harass anyone having to do with the Tumlinson estate so I could have four weeks of peace. In a month, my tear ducts would be functioning properly and I'd head back to New York, maybe still a pariah, but one with self-control.

Before I drove to my rented apartment, I went to the Dalbys' house. Jane and her husband were staying there while her parents spent the winter traveling. I'd had no communication with her since I texted her to let her know I was alive, but Jane wouldn't be mad because of my silence; she would just be worried. I turned my car down to the southern coastline of Aquidneck Island toward Bellevue

Avenue. There are roads and there are roads, but there are few pieces of pavement in America quite like Bellevue Avenue. If you're a tourist in Newport, you go there. And if you're the original old money in Newport, you live there.

The Dalbys—not just old money, but among the founders of Gilded Age Newport—had lived on Bellevue Avenue since 1875, when the family had built the A. H. Oxmoore house, better known as Morning Star. It was named for the École des Beaux-Arts–trained architect who designed it, then renamed by the Dalby matriarch. Once it was up, the Dalbys never left. Jane was the fifth generation of Dalby to summer in the house, but Jane and her husband now made it a base along with a $10 million house in Boston while her semiretired parents traveled between Newport, New York, Boston, and the other nicest corners of planet earth. The house I grew up in was on the other side of the expansive green lawn on the east side of the Dalbys' house. My family had lived there, thanks to my grandmother's very close friendship to Jane and Brittan Dalby's grandmother, and the two matriarchs had decided that we were all going to grow up together in one big garden. I looked up at the French neoclassical exterior and already felt lighter. All I wanted to do was spend time inside 6460 Bellevue, where I had lived the happiest days of my life. The street, also home to the Marble House and the Elms, carved its way through town, north to south on Aquidneck Island, but as soon as it hit fabled Rough Point, the smell of money turned west onto Ocean Avenue. On Ocean, part of the famous drive, the Atlantic held the huge houses in on the south side, and on the north side were Almy Pond, Lily Pond, and Goose Neck Cove. Holding court on the winding road, built by and for generations of old money, was the very private Bailey's Beach, where the prosperous and thin scions of the town's oldest families sipped cocktails before noon, glided through the salty air, and checked up on the goings-on of each other's tribes.

I turned toward the water in the tiny red Ford hatchback I had rented, entered the gate code, drove down the long driveway, past the fountain that worked through the winter, and parked outside the sprawling house. It had every Gilded Age comfort one could ask for, including twenty-seven bedrooms. The Dalbys had later added a lawn tennis court, an indoor swimming pool, manicured gardens fashioned after Chatsworth (inspiration for Pemberley in *Pride and Prejudice*), and a maze of hedges, and had expanded the rows and rows of big bay windows that the sun always seemed to hit just right. In the summer, they were left wide-open and you could call someone's name and they would put their head out and look at you in the yard. I used to run from my little house toward the Dalbys', screaming, "Jane! Brittan!" and wait for their heads to peer out the windows, thick brown hair flying in the wind, their laughter bouncing off the 140-year-old walls. In winter, the windows were closed to the freezing air, but the curtains were always pulled open as if to prove to the world that wealth and privilege didn't always mean one was standoffish, not that the world saw very much of the house other than what they could photograph through the gates. For those scurrying on Newport's famed Cliff Walk, the back of the house was visible, which was why most of the life that was lived outside was lived in front.

The Dalbys may have inhabited a $20 million summerhouse, one of the most expensive single-family homes in New England, but Jane didn't treat it like a family estate. That afternoon, just like every other, I knew their front door would be unlocked. I walked up the path, pulling a wool hat tight onto my head, turned the heavy brass doorknob, and shouted, "Hello?" into the foyer.

A few seconds later, I heard a musical "Hello?" respond.

It wasn't Jane's voice, or her mother's; it was the Dalbys' housekeeper, Florentine's, which was warmer and a little older sounding than I remembered.

"Carolyn! What a surprise!" She walked up to me and hugged me, just like she had on my visits for the last twenty-nine years.

"Are you on vacation? Do you take vacation? Jane said the other day that you haven't gone on a vacation in seven years. Is that true? You shouldn't do that because your bones will start to cry. And who wants that?"

"My bones will start to cry?" I asked as she put her arms around me. Florentine and I were the same height, so hugging her meant the warmest, most welcoming hug imaginable. Not like hugging a Dalby, where your head went directly into their muscular shoulders.

"Oh yes. You should be very careful."

She hugged me again and brushed my hair behind my ears. Florentine had been brushing the hair of the Dalby girls and their friends since I could remember. She was a fixture in their house and would always remain so.

"But you're here now, and on vacation!" she exclaimed. "Good for you."

She thought I was on vacation. Seven years without a real vacation—just Christmas with my parents in Boston for thirty-six hours, year after year—and here was Florentine celebrating the fact that I had some mirth flowing through my body. My instinct was to start wailing and explain to her that I was a failure, but instead I just said, "Nope. It's not vacation. I was fired. No more job. It's a long story but I was and, well, I guess that's just what happened. Now I'm here because I need a break. I rented a little apartment on Memorial but I just wanted to see if anyone was home here before I drove over."

"On Memorial? Why aren't you staying here? You know Jane will be very mad at you."

"I know," I said, looking through the house toward the beautiful water lapping to the east of us. "But I can't live off the Dalbys my entire life, Florentine."

"You don't live off anyone, and neither did your parents. Hardworking people. You all work too hard."

"So do you," I said, giving her a kiss on the cheek and holding her hand in mine. It was soft and wrinkled from years of looking after a family that liked being looked after.

"Carolyn, poor baby," she said smoothing my hair. "Who was stupid enough to fire a nice, smart girl like you?"

"Well, I guess a nice, smart girl very much like me fired me."

Florentine took my left hand in hers, too, so that we were facing each other like we were about to start doing the minuet. It was just then that Jane showed up behind her and screamed.

"Carolyn! What are you doing here!" she said, putting her hands on her mouth and looking at me all wrapped up for a blizzard.

"This is the best surprise ever. You scared me!"

Jane looked perfect, just like always. No matter what age she turned, or what she was wearing, Jane looked breezy, beautiful, and very rich. It wasn't because she was dripping in money; it was just the light around her, her carefree attitude, like she knew that at the end of every day, everything would be all right because she had the millions from past generations shrouding her in safety. Jane had a law degree from Yale and ran the very large Dalby family foundation. She worked from whatever home she felt like, but had a huge office in Boston waiting for her when she wanted to put in the hours. For now, she was happy to dole out Dalby money from Newport while her sister, Brittan, helped make more of it in New York working on the finance side of her father's company. She came to the door barefoot—Grace Kelly with dark hair and triceps muscles. She gave me a hug, put her head on mine, and didn't let me go right away. When she did, she declared, "You look like hell. Really, terrible. What have you been doing?"

"Not that much. Getting fired, crying, drinking, wallowing in self-pity, fighting with my mother."

Jane pouted and opened the door wider. Her hands were tan even in winter with a burgundy manicure and a diamond engagement ring that was eight carats and had belonged to her grandmother. I heard the clink of three thin gold bangles, which she always wore on her right wrist, even when she was swimming.

"Yeah, your mother told me that. She said you've been abrasive and that you only drink vodka and tap water and that we should all be very concerned."

"Oh yeah? That's nice. She's so concerned she's called me not once since she threw me out to the wolves in New York."

Jane didn't say anything else about my mother. We had been having the same conversation for decades. My mother didn't show up, or didn't call. She forgot to do this or that. But she was always very worried, very concerned.

"How long are you back for?" Jane asked after chiding me for not staying with her.

"A month. Just a month."

"Then it will be a wonderful month," she replied, leaning her tall body against the door frame, too.

I turned down Jane's multiple invitations to come inside, to stay for dinner, to stay for a month, a year, however long I wanted, and headed away from the mansions and the water to move into the apartment I had paid for, sight unseen.

It was a second floor walk-up in a town house fifteen blocks from the ocean. It was musty. The windows were dirty, so dirty that you could barely tell it had begun to snow outside. The couch was heavy velvet and the color of split pea soup and the dining room table was oak and looked like it had doubled as a butcher block for the last five decades. None of the chairs at the table matched and the plates in the cabinets were plastic. There was nothing antique, nothing charming, but I didn't care. I liked that it didn't feel like me, or my life. This was a stranger's apartment. Plus, I couldn't afford anything else if I didn't want to squander my savings. Who knew how long I would be unemployed. I threw my bags in the bedroom, peeked around for lung-destroying black mold or termites, and fell onto the couch, which immediately made me cough. I took a Zyrtec and listened to the booming silence around me. I was definitely no longer in New York. I was in New England, in February, and I had absolutely nothing to do.

When I was in high school, and for the part of the summers in college, when I wasn't interning at Christie's I used to work for $8.25 an hour in an antique store in Newport called William Miller Antiques. It was a very small but quaint store that sold "architectural antiques, furniture, clocks, silver, nautical pieces, jewelry, militaria, textiles, lighting and general ephemera." I had loved working there. I remember thinking that what we were selling was exquisite and that was mostly because William Miller found almost everything that had once belonged to someone dead and gone very important. Even if he would only pay me the same $8.25 that I made in high school, I was going to ask William if he would let me work with him for a month. I needed something to do and if someone was going to help me remember why I loved antiques and collecting in the first place, it was him.

On Tuesday, after a weekend of wandering around my hometown, I gave William the same shock I'd given Jane. I knocked on the door of his little store an hour before it officially opened at 10 A.M. and William came straight to the door. He had turned sixty last year but still had a brown beard without a glint of gray, as well groomed as a topiary. He always wore suits, even when lounging on weekends, and told me that his secret wish was for blue jeans to be declared illegal and that bowler hats would come back in fashion with a vengeance. "Think of it, Carolyn, bowler hats. Would anything be more splendid than that?" he'd always say after a few glasses of wine. I had nodded enthusiastically and agreed, though I could think of a few thousand things that might be even nicer than looking like Magritte-obsessed Surrealists. William was convinced that if the world looked nice, it would help wrinkle out the peskier problems, like rape, murder, and disease.

"Carolyn. I'm very happy to see you," he said, shaking my hand after he had opened the door. William didn't hug people; I had even seen him shake his own wife's hand. He was, as always, wearing a suit that looked tailor-made for him, right down to his socks. If he could have worn a morning coat to do his books without being labeled an eccentric, he would have.

"What brings you back to Newport in February?" he asked as he opened the door for me. He pointed to two William and Mary–style chairs in the middle of the gallery.

"Really?" I asked before I sat down. They were definitely from the late seventeenth or early eighteenth centuries.

"Sure," he replied. "We've got to make sure they work before we sell them. If yours breaks, let me know."

I laughed and sat down with a firm thud. "Feels just fine to me." I rubbed my hands down the thick ash-wood arms and closed my eyes. "I love William and Mary furniture. It feels like the beginning of America."

"Yes!" said William enthusiastically. "What a great way to put it. The beginning of America. It really does. And it is. It was made by the hands of the earliest Americans. Men who weren't even born here, but came here looking for a better life. That's exactly what these are." He smiled his appreciation for our shared love and he asked me again why I was in Newport in the dead of winter. "Were you hungry for frostbite?" he asked, gesturing for my coat.

"But don't you know why, William? You read the art press. I'm sure you know."

"Well, I was hoping it was for another reason," he said, turning away from me and putting my coat on a less expensive chair.

"Did you really lose your job over that thing? I mean, how do they know these Baltimore people are telling the truth?"

"I don't know," I said fidgeting in the chair. "But everyone seems to be buying their story, and I hate to say it but after all this new information that's come out, it sounds accurate. I just wish I'd known about it sooner. I mean the details."

"But you didn't get—"

"Fired?" I interrupted him, saving him the embarrassment of having to say the word. "I definitely got fired. I tried to shop around for something new in New York. Save face and all that. But it's not realistic right now. So I came home."

He eyed me and I knew he knew what I was looking for.

"You were overwhelmed, Carolyn. That's all. Just over-whelmed. I've known you for years and it takes a lot to get you overwhelmed. They shouldn't have let you get there. Louise DeWitt could have helped you."

"I don't know about that. I should have told her about Baltimore."

"Maybe, but I don't think I would have, either."

"Really?"

"Really."

"What do you think I should do while I'm in Newport for a month?"

"Well, work here, of course. That's why you came by, isn't it?" he said, winking at me.

"It is. But I wouldn't fault you for not hiring me."

"Nonsense. But I'm paying you what I paid you in high school, plus commission. Sound fair?"

Eight twenty-five an hour plus commission? It sounded like I would be eating a lot of macaroni and cheese. I'd go back to New York looking like an orange, rotund noodle.

William stood up from his chair and dabbed his brown eyes with a handkerchief. Years of being around musty fur-niture and memorabilia made his eyes water like a puppy with a sinus infection.

"You know what I want you to do?" he said, heading to his computer to print something. "I want you to buy for me. Scout and buy. I trust you to do that. You know more than I do at this point so you don't even have to check in with me first. I'll give you a budget for the month and you spend it. I'll split commission with you any time it's over two hun-dred dollars. How's that sound?"

"That sounds pretty fair," I said, taking an address from him.

"There have been some very good local auctions down in an old converted fire station in Narragansett put on by a retired fisherman named Hook Durant." He pointed to the address he had just given me. "You know him?"

William looked at my face and laughed. "Not the crowd you've been hanging out with at Christie's, I guess."

"Let's just say they have a particular clientele."

"I bet they do," he replied. "But that's too bad. I think everyone deserves to own a bit of history and that history can cost five dollars or fifty million."

"Right. That's why I always liked working here."

"Oh yeah?" he asked, looking over his reading glasses. "Go after many five-dollar lots over there at Christie's?"

He laughed at himself and kept talking. Before I left the store that day, he wrote down my new working hours on a scrap of paper and handed me a check for ten thousand dollars. I looked up at him, said, "Seriously?" and he gave me a little slap on the back.

"Find me things! Wonderful things. Go, go!"

"Your happiness scares me, William."

"Carolyn," he said sternly. "You are a very happy person underneath all this. I'm glad you left New York with all those . . . people."

Narragansett was a coastal town about a thirty-minute drive southwest from Newport. It was wealthy, but not like Newport, and it was one of those places I was always driving through rather than stopping in. Their old firehouse had been bought and sold a half dozen times since it was built. It was part of a hotel, and then used as a gym, was donated to a church group, bought back by the hotel, used as a lawyer's office, and now, I guessed, was empty and being used as a type of auction house, though it was styled more like a high school gymnasium than any auction house I had ever set foot in.

The first thing that surprised me about Hook Durant's was how casual it was. And then really, how strange it was. To kick things off, they were serving alcohol. Tons of it. I could see what looked like a barrel of oddly colored red wine near the door. Second, the auction was at ten o'clock in the morning and it was full of women. I was expecting around ten people to be in attendance, but at 9:45 in mid-February, there were already thirty people in the room. Some women looked affluent, some looked much less so, and some just looked a little eccentric and curious. There were a few men, too, mostly older, but they seemed to be accompanying the women, not leading the show. At Christie's, it was almost always the opposite.

I spotted Hook right away. He looked like a weight lifter wearing a navy blue sweater. He was chewing on a pipe instead of smoking it and his roving eyes seemed to take in everything in the room, even what was going on behind him. Everything about Hook was big. He was broadly built and had large features and wild, unkempt black hair. He must have electrocuted himself every morning to get it to stand up the way it did. And though he seemed the kind of man who would be far more comfortable in a pair of carpenter pants and a flannel shirt, he was wearing plaid dress pants.

I sat on the back row of the metal bleachers holding my paddle. I was the only person on the row when the auction started, so I quickly slid down to the next row and placed my paddle square on my lap. I was wearing jeans, because the only piece of advice William had given me for the auction was "Wear an old pair of jeans. Hook loves to swindle the rich." I flipped the paddle over between my fingers, fanning myself even though it was about fifty degrees inside the building. The paddle was nothing more than a thick tongue depressor with a printed cardboard square on it. Inside that square was my red number, drawn in marker, number 37.

At exactly 10 A.M., with the room filled with forty-five women who clearly didn't care a thing about indoor voices, Hook started things off with the first lot. I didn't know if the former fisherman knew anything about antiques, though I liked many of his first lots. And the man could definitely call an auction. He sounded like a gypsy who had gotten hold of fifty years of Christie's auction recordings and learned to emulate them adding a thick dose of home-spun rhetoric. His voice rose, he scanned the room expertly, never missed a hand, and moved lots for much more than I thought they were worth. I did not plan to pay that kind of money, so I waited. The first thing I bid on was a wooden carved American eagle for $160. Then I bid on a side table of questionable provenance, a nineteenth-century copper weather vane, and an old Amoco gas station sign, but was outbid by a woman in my row who was clearly on the road to getting completely wasted.

"I don't recognize you, do I," she asked me after she slapped me five across the laps of two other women when she won.

"I don't think so," I said, introducing myself.

She eyed me and lifted her glass. "Merlot makes every-thing better, don't you think?"

"Well, maybe not auctions," I replied. "Level head and all that. I've actually never seen it served at an auction. I think it's illegal."

"Illegal? I love it. You're a crackerjack! Come on, keep bidding. It's Valentine's Day and I want to beat you again." She wrapped her plump hand around her paddle and prac-ticed shooting it up skyward.

"Hey, time me! How long does it take me to get my paddle up?"

She waited for me to look at my watch before doing it again.

"Less than a second," I replied.

"I knew it, I knew it. I'm like a human rocket ship. Kaboom! Bid again, Everett."

So I kept bidding. And I let her beat me again.

The following Tuesday, I was back at Hook Durant's auction. William had sold the copper weather vane for six times what I paid, the side table was Thomas Molesworth and would certainly make back more than double, and the eagle had previously sold at Christie's for a hair above thirty thousand dollars.

"Did you recognize this eagle, Carolyn?" William said, stroking the head of the painted, gilded object. He gave it a hug and ran his hand down the wing. It was gripping a wooden American flag and a red, white, and blue shield with its claws.

"I thought I recognized it from a 1992 Christie's catalogue. The position of the feet looked familiar."

"Thought you recognized it. And from 1992! Let's not belittle this accomplishment. You're an absolute genius. You were when you were young and you're even smarter today. Christie's is going to seriously regret letting you go." We stood together and admired the expensive piece of Americana. "I'm going to try to sell it for thirty-one thousand. That should net you enough of a commission to stay in Newport for another couple of months. You have to stay. I knew you would do well at Hook's. Everyone else there is drunk. Don't drink. Don't even look at that poison Merlot he serves. He makes it in the backyard," William advised me. "And don't let those old heiresses bid you up too much. They're just there for the game. It's like gambling to them, without the blue-collar reputation or the hookers. I don't know how Hook got such a great eye, but he has one. Luckily yours is better. He can tell if something is beautiful, but you can tell what it's worth. I want you to spend every Tuesday at Hook Durant's. How many Tuesdays do you have left?"

"Four, counting today," I answered, surprised that I'd already been in Newport more than a week.

On that next Tuesday, feeling very optimistic and hungry after last week's buys, I sat on the top bleacher in Narragansett again. Unlike houses that had auctions by department, Hook Durant ran his little auction like he was putting his hand in a magic suitcase and selling whatever he found. He would sell a gun, followed by an oil painting, and then some antique children's toys, collectible wine, a Chinese vase, whatever he had in his arsenal. And the best part about it was that in Rhode Island, in the winter, when the population around Newport was reduced by half, there was still a buyer for almost everything.

I had passed on the first twenty-three lots that Tuesday, but Lot 24 piqued my interest as soon as Hook set it on the card table next to him.

"Next up we've got this little bowl! Who doesn't love a bowl. This bowl is about a foot across and definitely from the Middle East. Arabic origins. Yemen or Egypt perhaps. There's Arabic writing inside. And look at that detail. This looks like it took fifty years to paint." He flipped it on its side so we could see the beautiful, intricately detailed vegetal motif. "It's small, but it packs some historic punch! Of course, I have no idea what that is, but I'll leave it to the lucky buyer to find out. Could be very old, could have been made yesterday. Let's all have a big swig of Merlot and then we'll get the bidding started at five dollars."

Hook actually waited for people to drink, singing part of a drinking song that involved a pirate, a girl named Sue, and another girl named Sue, which sounded very perverted. Then he was off.

"Who's got five dollars for me?" He scanned the crowd and pointed his finger at a woman with short red curly hair and purple glasses sitting in the front row.

"Crazy Annie! You've always got a fiver for me. How about it?"

Crazy Annie? And he was telling her to bid? Insisting that she bid? I was obsessed with this place. There were plenty of Christie's customers I would have loved to tell Olivier to call Crazy Annie.

Crazy Annie started the bidding at five dollars.

Middle Eastern art history was my weakest field, and there was nothing noticeably ornate about the bowl, but it was uncharacteristically attractive for a piece that didn't have an original shape or any gilding so I bid on it, too. I wanted to let Crazy Annie off the hook and I was hoping the bowl might be a hidden five-figure gem like the wooden eagle. For a few bucks, it was worth a gamble.

"New girl, give me more money," said Hook, pointing at me. "You got twenty for me?"

"Sure, why not," I said raising my paddle.

No one bid me up, and like that, I had my first purchase of the day. I finished the auction with ten Italian coins, the bowl from the Middle East, a Japanese stoneware drinking vessel, a stained-glass lamp, a Windsor chair, a colonial era American flag, and a vintage Dior evening gown. I was definitely going to have to ask William for more money.

When I was walking down the bleachers to leave, Hook stopped me and commented on my purchases.

"You're buying all over the map. I like that. And you've been here two weeks in a row. I like that, too."

"Yes, I have," I said, reaching my hand out to introduce myself. "I'm working for William Miller for a little while."

Hook scowled and then barked like a dog. He actually barked like he'd eaten a St. Bernard for lunch. "You're working for that crook? Well then, I'm going to start demanding more money from you."

"He's not a crook at all," I said, a little peeved. No one was allowed to insult William except for me. And that was only when he bought things because he thought they would be lonely without a good home.

"Yeah, yeah, I know, lighten up," said Hook. "How about a drink?"

I declined his homemade chuck and he lowered his eyes until he was looking at me through his squinted eyelids.

"Are you boring or something? What's your story?"

"Yes. I probably am boring. I'm not in the habit of drinking at auctions. Though I have been drinking a lot in the morning lately."

"Good! I knew it. You're not boring. You're very pretty. Pretty women are never boring. In my opinion anyway," he said grinning. "You single?"

"Um, no. I'm not. I'm dating a convicted felon. He also makes poison in his spare time."

"You are not. You're a liar!" Hook brought his hands up like he was going to punch me in the face. He was terrifying.

"Fine, I'm not," I said, taking a step back. "I'm in a complicated relationship with my ex-boyfriend from St. George's."

"Yeah, that's what I figured. You look like you spent a lot more time in prep school than prison."

"I didn't have much of a choice in the prep school matter. The boyfriend, well, I'm pretty good at making bad choices."

"I'll drink to that," said Hook, raising his mason jar full of wine. "Please make many poor choices while you're inside these walls."

"Maybe I'll drink next time," I offered. "If you can tell me one thing."

"What's that?"

"Where did you get this?" I lifted the bowl I had just bought. It was very heavy for being only a foot across. "I'm pretty good at provenance, but I'm not knowledgeable when it comes to pottery, especially from the Middle East."

"Wonderful, I'll try to sell you more things from that region since you refuse to drink the Merlot. I've got a perfume bottle from Yemen for next week. You gonna buy it?"

"Do you really know if this stuff is from Yemen?" I asked.

"Not really. A friend told me that. He's from Yemen. I guess that might make him a little biased."

I refrained from telling him that he couldn't legally call his backyard hooch Merlot. The French wouldn't like it. And that he couldn't make up provenances, even in an unsanctioned auction.

"What was it you asked me? Where did I get that bowl?"

"Yeah."

"Some of my regulars won't buy that stuff, you know. Middle Eastern art with that Arabic writing, bad connotations."

"That seems pretty ridiculous."

"Well, some of my customers are ridiculous. But they love to buy. I mean, this may be the smallest state but there's plenty of cash here. Especially right where you're from. Are you a billionaire?"

"I work for William. You think I'm a billionaire?"

"Nah, I don't," he said, eyeing me again. "You're too serious. Billionaires are more laid-back. Know any billionaires?"

"I know the Dalbys. They're right up there."

"I know them, too. I'm in love with Jane Dalby."

"So is everyone. About that bowl?"

"You know," he said, pausing just to piss me off a little bit, "I can tell you, but if you don't like the story, you're not getting your money back. Agreed?"

"Sure, agreed."

"Well, I'm a bit of a picker when it comes to the stuff I sell," said Hook with pride. "I'm trying to get my own show. I have a real face for television."

I didn't argue with him.

"You were saying about the bowl?"

"Oh right, that white and green bowl. Like I said, I'm a picker. And one place I always go is . . . well . . . you promise you're not going to go screaming for your money back?"

"Yes, I promise. And you promise you're not going to lie to me?"

"Why should I lie to you, girlie? I'll tell you exactly where I bought that bowl. I bought it at a Goodwill."

"Did you really? You bought this from Goodwill?" I eyed the bowl again and turned it over in my hands to look for some sort of marker or stamp. The bottom was slightly ridged with some sort of pattern, but there was no other identifier.

"Yeah, I did, for a dollar seventy-five. What did you just pay?"

"Twenty."

"I guess it was a pretty good day for me, then." He looked at me with a content smile. He definitely seemed like a man who loved the buying and selling of objects more than he actually liked the objects themselves. And if you liked your men sort of overbearing, hairy, and rude, then he did have a good face for TV.

"Do you remember when the Salvador Dali etching was found at the Goodwill in Tacoma, Washington?" I asked.

"I do," he said grinning. "I might not look like it, but I read some of that art crap. When was that now, last year?"

"No, it was two years ago. And it ended up selling for just shy of twelve thousand dollars. Is that what has you heading to Goodwill?"

"Nah. I was doing that long before that dead Spaniard squirmed his way in there. Just, after the Dali was found, I started going a little more often. But there's only one in Rhode Island. It's in North Kingstown. If I'm on the road picking then I'll stop by the Goodwills in Massachusetts, New York, and Connecticut, too. 'Cause for every five-figure painting found, there has to be one that was missed, don't you think?"

"I don't know," I said honestly. "I don't think I've ever been inside a Goodwill. I hate to say it. It sounds pretty snobby, doesn't it?"

"Not really. Why would you go to Goodwill? You're a Newport girl. You go to cocktail parties and debutante balls and cruise on yachts."

"Girls don't really have debutante balls anymore. They're a little sexist and archaic, don't you think?"

"I don't think nothing about nothing like that. Just don't know what all you rich people do with your time if you're not getting all dressed up for something or other."

"As I said, I'm not that rich."

"You look rich. That's enough for me."

I tried not to sigh with frustration right in his face.

"Well it's probably time I go. To Goodwill."

"Fine then. Go. Like I said, North Kingstown. Just don't go buying all the good stuff. I need to dupe women like you to make a living."

"Women like me?"

"Yeah, the cute naïve ones. My favorite kind."

I very rarely bought something that I couldn't pin down to a time period of a hundred years, especially if it wasn't furniture, and with the bowl, I couldn't peg it to a period of five hundred years. Still, it was only twenty dollars. It was in extremely good shape, which made me think it wasn't very old, and it was made of ceramic, but looked inspired by Chinese porcelain. The first layer was glazed white and there were two tones of very detailed green vegetal motifs along with a calligraphic design in the center in the darker tone. The color alone made it really stand out among the Arabic pottery I had been in contact with but it was the detail of the patterns that made it so striking. There were no date markings or signatures and no expensive ornamentation, but it still felt like something. I needed to find someone who read Arabic, but my guess was that the writing inside was religious. Besides just being attracted to the look of it, I was at a loss. I was a little better with Asian ceramics, which is why I bought the Japanese stoneware bottle. I knew Christie's in London had recently sold a similar one from the nineteenth century for eight hundred dollars. I had paid two hundred seventy-five. It had a band of phoenix in flight, which was what made me think of the Meiji era. Or at least I hoped. That was the thing with these backyard auctions: they were a guessing game.

When I got back to William's store I told him all about the drunks at the auction and how Hook had called him a crook and then barked like a dog.

"He's a little eccentric," said William, looking at everything I bought and taking notes in his brown leather Moleskine notebook with his sterling silver pen.

"And this," he said, lifting the bowl. He turned it around in his palm and inspected the glaze.

"Honestly, that one was a bit of a guess. I paid twenty bucks for it and then Hook admitted that he bought it at the Goodwill in North Kingstown for a dollar seventy-five so I felt a little duped. But I don't know, I still think it's very striking. Look at the detail. That vegetal pattern, I've never seen a motif that small and intricate on pottery from the Middle East. It's very heavy, though, so probably not that old. I bet we can get a couple hundred for it, just because it's pretty and in good condition."

"I think we can get more than that. This could be another wooden eagle. Maybe you can turn this into five figures with your Carolyn Everett magic. That design is too unique to just be something quickly fired in the neighborhood kiln in Kabul. It sure would help if we knew something about it, though," he said turning it around in his hands. "A thousand maybe, without any provenance. This is not my forte, I'm afraid. Any idea what the writing says?"

"I didn't learn Arabic in my spare time. But I can ask someone."

William took the bowl in his hand and turned it around slowly. "Look at the slant of the calligraphy, how it bends so far right. I've never seen that before."

"Me neither," I said, peering inside the bowl. "Do you really think it's worth over a thousand?"

"Maybe. Maybe way over. Why don't you go to the Goodwill and ask them if they know where they got this?"

"There's just one more thing," I said, turning it around and getting a magnifying glass from William's desk. "Do you see that on the bottom there? There's some sort of very faint pattern. It almost looks like—"

"Like Hebrew," said William, looking closely. He held it under a desk light and looked at it again.

"Hebrew? Is it?"

"I really think it's Hebrew. But it's so faint."

"Why would there be Hebrew letters on the bottom of a bowl with Arabic writing inside?" I asked.

"I don't know. Could be some very good copy. Like those designer clothes they rip off but accidentally print both Prada and Gucci on them."

"So now you think it's a knockoff? Something really worth a buck seventy-five?"

"My gut says no, even after seeing the writing. I think it's something important. It's a beautiful piece. Look at these windswept palmettes. The motif is so detailed. And the white glaze mimicking Chinese porcelain, that was popular during the Abbasid dynasty."

"Abbasid dynasty? The eighth to the thirteenth century? It can't be that old. Look at it, it barely shows any age. And that style was used much later, too."

"True," said William. "But I can see why you reacted to it, and I'm sure others would, too." He took his magnifying glass and looked at the Hebrew writing again.

"Honestly, Carolyn, I have no idea."

"I'm going to send a few pictures to Max Sebastian," I said to William, grabbing his Canon camera from the back, where we photographed items for the Web. Max, whom I had glimpsed during my forty-five minutes of hell at the Vollinger Gallery in New York, was unarguably the premier expert on Middle Eastern art and he was with Sotheby's in London, not Christie's, so I stood a chance of hearing back from him. He was the son of a British diplomat and had spent much of his life in the Middle East. He'd studied Middle Eastern art and history at Cambridge and had been at Sotheby's for twenty-five years. He spoke and was literate in Arabic, Hebrew, and Aramaic and was pretty much the be-all and end-all when it came to appraising Middle Eastern stoneware and pottery.

"You're just going to email Max Sebastian?" said William.

"Why not? What do I have to lose? My reputation? I'll spin it that we have a seller that has a much larger collection and wants to sell with Sotheby's but we're just not sure about this one thing. Plus, he has no idea I'm in Newport. He could think I'm a dealer in New York now."

"And what if this bowl is worth twenty-seven cents and he laughs you all the way to the Piggly Wiggly?"

"Well then, he can just join the rest of my hecklers."

I sent Max a quick email from my personal account along with pictures of every angle of the bowl.

"You should forget Max," said William. "He only gets back to billionaires and archaeologists. You should just go straight to the source and then walk backwards. I can finish up here today. I don't think we'll have many customers pounding down the door this afternoon; it looks like it's going to snow again. Why don't you drive to North Kingstown and ask around. I bet you've never even been to a Goodwill before."

I took William's four-wheel drive, as he said he didn't trust my "electric sled" in the snow. I drove past the towering mansions on Bellevue, and headed toward the highway just as the first snowflakes started to fall from the dark gray sky. The drive to North Kingstown was only about twenty minutes but halfway there the flurries turned into real snow. Not the kind of snow that makes everything look clean and wintery; this was in-your-face, it's-almost-impossible-to-drive snow. March was only a week away, but in Newport, winter was making itself comfortable.

Goodwill was a one-story brick building in a strip mall. When I ran in, pulled off my hat, and opened the glass door, three bells tied to the handle chimed and the two people working as cashiers in the front of the room looked up at me and smiled. They were both over seventy and probably volunteers. I wanted to walk the aisles and look for the next Salvador Dali Goodwill find, but William had ordered me to find out about the bowl. I brought it to the counter and smiled.

"Hello!" I said far too enthusiastically. "I was wondering if you could help me with something," I asked the man who was right in front of the register. He had thinning silver hair slicked back with pomade and deep wrinkles on his small hands. One of his nails was bruised and another was yellowing and cracked.

I held the bowl up and handed it to him.

"This was purchased a few weeks ago from this store and I was just wondering if you had any information about it. Like how long it was in the store, or even if you knew who dropped it off."

"Well, now let me see, what is this. A bowl?" he asked, looking inside of it with interest.

"Um, yes, it's a bowl. I think it's from the Middle East."

"What a nice bowl. That's one of the nicest I've ever seen. Now why do you want to know who donated this bowl? Is it your bowl?"

"It is now. I bought it. But I'd like to know more about it, because I won't be able to sell it if I don't know anything about it. So I'm hoping that I can find the person who do-nated it to you and they can tell me about it."

"You're a bowl salesman!"

"Not exactly."

"You're a soup maker?"

"Not at all."

This nice man was trying to help me and it would be wrong to slam my head against the counter in frustration while screaming obscenities about pureed vegetables.

"Yes, I guess in a way I am a bowl salesman," I said calmly. "I work in an antique store in Newport and I would like to sell this bowl."

"But you bought the bowl here."

"Well, I didn't, but someone did."

The man was quiet. He looked at his colleague, slightly confused.

"Yes," I lied. "I bought the bowl here."

"So you want to know who donated this bowl."

"That's right."

"Okay, let me ask around."

"Oh, the bowl was actually bought by Hook Durant, by the way," I added.

"Hook Durant."

"Yes. Do you know him? He runs an auction out in Narragansett."

"Course I know him. He buys a lot of things here. He's a treasure hunter."

"That's a nice way to put it."

"One man's trash is another man's treasure, right?"

"I suppose it can be."

"But you said you bought the bowl here," he reminded me.

"I was confused," I said loudly. "I meant my friend bought the bowl here. Hook Durant."

"Feel free to look around the store," he said as he walked off toward the back, to the donation area.

"It's okay, I'll wait here."

"Don't you like buying things?" he asked, concerned. "I mean we don't have the fanciest things in the world but you might find something that's nice to look at."

"That sounds great, actually," I said with more grace than I'd been showing in my frustrated state. "That's kind of why I bought the bowl. I just thought it was pretty."

"Well, we've got hundreds of bowls. You look and I'll ask a few people if they know about this," he said, carrying it away. I thanked him, and started slowly walking up the aisles.

There were five shelves to my right, all packed with tiny porcelain and earthenware knickknacks. There were candleholders with wax drips down the sides, a pair of angel bookends, and a wooden carving of a fox that looked like it was carved by someone whose eyesight was nearly gone. In fact, the fox looked more like a rabbit but he happened to be wearing a plasticine T-shirt that said "Fox." I walked to the back of the china and cutlery aisle and almost backed directly into a woman with a good one hundred extra pounds on her. She had a pleasant face and smiled when she saw me. I apologized and started to walk away.

"What are you looking for, dear?" she asked me as she placed a ceramic teapot back on the shelf.

I looked behind my shoulder because I didn't feel like a person whom someone would call "dear." But I was the dear.

"Me? Oh no, nothing in particular. Just, you know, looking."

"Oh, me too. I love to just look. But I always look for the same thing."

"What's that?"

"Teapots. I'm crazy about teapots. But the funny thing is, I don't drink tea. I only like to drink lemonade."

We both looked at a slightly cracked teapot in front of us and she swept it up into her arms before I could get to it.

"A teapot made of purple clay sold for two million dollars in 2010. And it wasn't even old. It was made in 1948. Just a year later a pair of melon-shaped teapots sold for two-point-one million," I said, smiling at her and taking a teapot off the shelf.

She looked at the price tag of the one in her hands.

"This one's a little cheaper."

"Oh, that's good. I thought two million was a bit of a rip-off anyway."

"Really? Two million dollars on a pot?"

"Really," I confirmed.

I smiled as I turned the corner and moved on to another shelf, where I found an old chess set. The pieces were strange. They looked almost like teeth. Was this some sort of serial killer's chess set? Was the board made out of pelvic bones? I wrapped my index finger in a tissue dabbed in Purell and attempted to touch it.

Before I had time to dry-heave at the thought, the teapot collector was back. She gave me a tap on the shoulder, though I was already quite aware that she was right behind me.

"You seem to know a lot about how much things cost. Why is that? Are you one of those people who are obsessed with numbers? Or maybe you're a mathematician?"

"I used to work at Christie's, the auction house," I explained.

The past tense on that phrase was biting.

"Christie's! That's beyond my reach, but that's fascinating. Just fascinating. Tell me some other facts. You must know a whole lot. I love facts and figures."

"Well . . . ," I said, thinking back on all the Christie's and Sotheby's milestones.

"Winston Churchill's dentures went for twenty-three thousand dollars. Not even his real teeth. Just his dentures. And Edward Scissorhands's scissorhands went for sixteen thousand dollars. Oh, and this is one of my favorites. In Japan two cantaloupes once sold for twenty-three thousand five hundred dollars."

"The kind you can eat?" she said, almost giddy.

"Yes. The kind you can eat."

"Well, I hope they were good."

"Me too."

Some people shopped at Goodwill because the very low price point was right for them, while others clearly just loved a bargain. Some seemed to be devoted to supporting a good cause and others, like my new pal Mrs. Potts, appeared to be really into the hunt, probably a hoarder trying to find another good thing to add to her collection.

"Discovering anything interesting?" she asked, peering over my shoulder to look at the chess set.

"I kind of like this chess set. But . . . what do you think the pieces are made out of? Kind of look like teeth to me."

"Teeth? Let me see. . . ." She took the queen in her hand and rolled it around. She was definitely holding a human molar.

"This isn't a human tooth. It's a canine tooth."

So much better.

Just as I was about to gag and weep, the man who was helping me walked my way with a pleasant smile.

"It's your lucky day. One of the guys taking deliveries today remembered this nice bowl."

He handed it to me and I put it back in my bag.

We smiled at each other but he didn't give me any information. The woman who identified the dog teeth was also there, smiling, too. We were like three Cheshire cats with nothing to do.

"Did he say who dropped it off?" I asked, when I realized the information was not going to be forthcoming.

"Oh yes," said the man. "He did. A Marine captain from the base dropped it off. He drops things off pretty often, so we know his car and all that. It's a Jeep Wrangler. Dark orange, like a pumpkin color, with a black roof. Not that kind you can fold down, one of the solid ones."

"And do you know his name? What he looks like? Or could I talk to the guy in the back who knows him?" I motioned to the south side of the building.

"No need," said the man, still smiling. "I've got all the information. His name is Greg LaPorte and he's on base. I don't know what he looks like really, but the guy out back, Bill, he said he's got brown eyes and a shaved head and is about yay big." He held his hand out until the measurement seemed about six feet tall. Well, a man with a shaved head and brown eyes who was about six feet tall on a naval base. This wasn't going to be like finding a zebra in a pack of horses. But I had a name. That was all I needed. I thanked the man, wished the woman with the teapots luck, and bought the dogtooth chessboard just because. I would send it to Alex and he would write me and say I had the sense of humor of a mortician.

Naval Station Newport was on the western side of the city, on Peary Street, and when I was growing up it had always seemed like a world completely outside mine. My father had never served, and neither had either of my grandfathers. The military, though I appreciated living in a country that had a good one, wasn't something I gave much thought to. I would see navy men walking around town and though we both called Newport home, they had nothing to do with the Newport I knew.

I could have gone to base and asked for Greg LaPorte,

but the idea of doing that intimidated me. It wasn't exactly a place you just skipped on over to and poked around in, unless you wanted to get shot. Thankfully, I knew I had just as good a chance of running into him at a bar on Thames Street called the Blue Hen. It was always packed with the men, and a few women, from base and we used to get in there with fake IDs when we were home for the summer in college because the staff were desperate to fill the place with girls. I asked Jane to go with me that Friday night but she said there was no way she was going to "that semen factory," so I was on my own.

It was pretty busy considering it was February. I took off my coat and put it on the rack by the door, hoping no one would steal it. I had given up the cashmere coats with the thick fur collars I wore in New York for my old black ski parka.

"What can I get you?" the bartender asked me.

"A vodka soda. And can I ask you a question?" I said, leaning on the wooden bar.

"Sure. No lime?"

"What? No. Yes, lime. No, I have a question. Do you know who Greg LaPorte is?" I shouted. "He's from base."

"Yeah, sure, he's here all the time. He's a Marine captain. Been here in Newport about six years I think. He's here tonight, if that's what you're asking."

"Yeah, it is. Can you point him out to me?"

"That one. There," said the bartender, pointing to a table in the back where five guys with telltale military haircuts were drinking beer. Above them a Bruins game played on a flat-screen TV and there was a red plastic basket of soggy ripple-cut chips and hot dogs on their table.

I thanked him and walked over. It was when I was standing there, staring at them, that all the men at the table looked up at me, a little eagerly, a little surprised. I had no choice but to talk.

"I'm sorry to bother you, but I'm looking for Greg LaPorte. Is one of you him?"

"Yeah," said one with very short reddish hair and brown eyes. He smiled at me and put his hand out. "I definitely am Greg LaPorte."

"Oh great."

"It is great. I love being me."

I laughed and tried to ignore the fact that his friend on my right had just tipped his chair back to get a better view of my ass. I instantly regretted taking off my coat.

"Can I help you with something? I'm happy to help you however I can," said Greg, offering me a beer from the table.

"I'm good," I said holding up my drink.

His friend who had just let out a low whistle when he admired my posterior joined in.

"And if he can't help you, I am happy to help. I'd love to help you."

"I work over at William Miller's Antiques on Spring Street and I bought something at auction the other day, which I think belongs to you," I said, ignoring Greg's friends. I reached into my bag and took out the heavy bowl. "Is this yours?"

Greg took it from me, turned it around in his hands, turned it over, looked at the base, and shook his head.

"It's not mine, but I did drop off a huge load of old stuff at the Goodwill in North Kingstown about a month ago. It wasn't just my stuff, though. I do a collection on base and I take it in because I'm just that kind of guy. I'm a really, really nice guy. You should get to know me."

"I think that's Ford's," said one of his friends. I looked at him, surprised to see how young he was.

"I remember I saw him drop it off one night with some other junk he was giving away. I went through it because sometimes Ford has really good shit. I got this shirt once, it's like this really thick cotton. I wear it all the time."

"You steal Ford's Goodwill donations? That's sad," said one of the other guys laughing.

"Shut the fuck up," said the Goodwill pincher. "I saw it in there," he said to me. "I'm sure. It's pretty cool-looking. I should have taken it. He's got all sorts of weird old crap from Iraq. He's been there four times."

"He's a sandman," said another one of the guys, waving his hands around and laughing. "He even speaks sand."

"The rest of us call that Arabic," said Greg.

"Stay far, far away," his friend continued, still moving his fingers like a drunk sorcerer.

"It's Ford's," said Greg, looking up and smiling at me.

"Ford's . . . his name is Ford?"

"It's Tyler Ford," said the friend. "Why do you care?"

Why exactly did I care? Because both William and I thought it could be our ticket to another five-figure sale. Because it was beautiful and had potential. I wanted it to do even better than the last lots I'd turned a huge profit on from Hook's. I had William treating me like I was the auction whisperer and there was no way I was going to miss something about it, some telling detail, the way I'd done in Baltimore. That was never going to happen again.

"I want to sell it, so I need to know something about it. I was hoping that the person who dropped it off—Ford—might be able to fill me in on a little history. It could be worth a few thousand."

"A couple grand? Oh, well it's mine then," said Greg, reaching out his hand again. "My name's Ford, Tyler Ford."

"This guy's clueless. It must be mine," said another one of his friends. "I'm Tyler Ford. My memory's going. You understand. I did just turn twenty-six."

He looked a lot younger than that.

"So, Greg," I said, looking at the one whose name I knew. "Where would I find Ford?"

"Oh, you can't find Ford. He'll find you. We'll tell him you're looking for him."

The butt pervert laughed.

"No really, ignore him. We'll tell him you're looking for him, like in the normal way," said Greg. "Though lots of girls are looking for him for the other reason. You looking for anyone like that?"

"Never mind," I said, backing away.

"Sorry. Sorry. Don't go. We'll tell him, I promise," said Greg. "William Miller Antiques on Spring Street. The pretty blond girl."

"Yeah, you'll like Ford," said one of the guys who had been silent until now. "He's the best-looking guy you've ever seen. And you haven't even met him yet."

That must have been saying a lot, since the guy who said it was pretty good-looking, too. He had bright green eyes and dark skin that I would happily have seen more of. But that was the thing with military guys. They were all very neat. Clean-shaven, trim hair, uniforms. If you weren't attractive, you still looked pretty good in a uniform. If you were attractive, you looked half divine.

The guy with green eyes looked at me as I stood there confused.

"I'm not all gay or don't ask, don't tell or anything," he said. "Tyler's just got that reputation, you'll see."

"Yeah, he does," said Greg. "He's a bastard, though. He'll break your heart. Trust me. I'm a much nicer guy. You should go out with me. Greg LaPorte. *Captain* Greg LaPorte. Naval Station Newport. Come say hi."

"I'll try," I said, finally backing away.

From that moment on, I looked up every time the door at William Miller's opened. I was waiting for He-man to walk in, shirtless in February, maybe toting a gun and a dozen roses. But it was always our usual clientele, mostly older rich people or tourists. Jane came one day to buy two iron sconces for her backyard and accused me of having a nervous tic.

"You keep looking at the door," she said as William kissed her hand and she gave him three thousand dollars in cash.

"I have a muscle spasm," I lied. "From too much heavy lifting. They work me to the bone here."

William laughed and I promised Jane I would stop being an antique store recluse and visit her soon.

I began to think that I would never meet Tyler Ford. I doubted those guys at the bar had taken me seriously. Why would they bother?

By the time I finally got up the courage to look for Tyler myself, he came looking for me.

Greg was right. Tyler Ford was the best-looking guy I'd ever seen. As soon as he had one foot in the door, I knew it was him, and I was paralyzed. The smile I had practiced every time the door opened since I'd been waiting to meet Tyler failed me. Suddenly the room felt very hot, like I was being forced to sell furniture in Dante's inferno while wearing a turtleneck. This was not how I wanted to look when being approached by the most handsome man I'd ever seen. I stood there and tried to move my mouth in an upward motion while he walked straight to me.

"I'm Tyler Ford," he said. He was a good foot taller than me. "A friend of mine, Greg LaPorte . . ." He switched gears, smiled, and said, "I heard you're looking for me."

"Oh, yes. Greg LaPorte," I said. "He mentioned . . . that . . . I am. I am looking for you." I moved out from behind my desk, toward him.

Tyler didn't look anything like I thought he would. He was very tall and muscular with a symmetrical face, a strong, square jaw, and perfect skin—all those superficial things that make a person extremely handsome. But that wasn't what surprised me. It was his air of seriousness that took me aback. His aloofness, almost like he was talking to you but not very present, wasn't something I expected from a twenty-something guy in the military. I was used to men like Greg and his friends, who wore their masculine bravado like a shield and stared at your ass. But Tyler had the kind of mystique not found in most men. And as a result, he was the most attractive human being I had ever seen in my entire life. Man, woman, child, animal. He had dark brown hair, cut in typical military fashion. He had perfectly even skin, not quite olive, but nothing like my extremely fair complexion, and bright blue eyes, very light in the middle but rimmed in darker blue, that leapt at you before you even saw the entire person, just like my parents. He looked more like their child than I did.

"I think I have something of yours," I said, moving back to the desk to take the bowl out of the drawer where I was keeping it.

I unwrapped the thin pieces of muslin around it and placed it on the desk. He leaned down, took it in both his hands, and held it for a long time, rubbing his fingers over the light green glazed pattern. He didn't say anything.

"Are you in the navy?" I asked, breaking the silence. Of

course he was in the navy. He wasn't like some wandering magician who just took refuge on a naval base.

"Actually, I'm a marine," he said correcting me, and finally looking up. "I'm with Mardet. Marine aviation."

A Marine aviator at a navy base? I felt like he was the military equivalent of a turducken but what did I know. My knowledge of the military was pretty much completely created by Hollywood and fiction.

"Oh, a marine," I replied.

After another minute of just looking at the bowl, he looked up and smiled. "This is mine. Or it used to be."

"Oh! Oh good. I had to ask a few people so I'm really glad it's yours."

"Did you want to give it back to me?"

Did I want to return it to him? No, I wanted to sell it. I wasn't in the business of regifting Goodwill items to their original owners.

"Actually, no. I bought it at auction because I was hoping to sell it. I'm very interested in antiquities, but—"

"Yeah, I can see that, working in a place like this," he said, looking around. "You must really like all this old stuff."

"Old stuff? Like priceless antiques that represent the changing face of our nation?" I said. I hadn't meant to sound offended, but Alex had called me an eighty-year-old trapped in the body of a teenager all through high school and I was a little sensitive about the word *old* when it was applied to what I loved.

"Yeah sure, old stuff," he said, cracking a mischievous smile. He looked at me trying to maintain my composure, as he poked fun at my lifelong passion. Under his big winter coat, he was wearing a black sweater and jeans; the only thing giving away his career in the military was his hair.

"Oh, you're like one of these uptight Newport types who cries over the *Mayflower* and stuff like that."

"The *Mayflower* landed in Provincetown, Massachusetts," I corrected him.

"Right," he said casually. "Well, what do you need to know about this to sell it? I didn't donate it for someone to sell it. I just thought someone might like the look of it, put it on a table or something."

I put my hand on the bowl, ran my finger on the glaze carefully, and looked up at him.

"Well, you got a few unexpected middlemen. Do you mind if I ask where you got it? Did you get it in the Middle East? I've never really seen anything like it."

"It was a present when I was in Iraq on my third tour. I was there four times. And all those deployments, I had the same translator. He gave it to me. But then a few weeks ago, I heard he died, so I just decided I didn't want it around anymore."

"I'm sorry," I said. Iraq. It was from Iraq.

"Do you know anything else about it? Like when it was made? Was it something your translator had for a long time? Or something his family had?"

"I'm not sure. I didn't ask. Do you usually ask all kinds of questions when you get a present?"

My face must have gone red, because he smiled and shook his head. "Sorry, I just don't know."

"Did you know it has an inscription of some sort on the base? In Hebrew I think. Though it's hard to tell." I turned the bowl around for him to see.

"I think I noticed that at first and then forgot about it. It looks nice."

"Isn't it weird for a Muslim translator to own a bowl with Hebrew on it? Your translator was Muslim, right?"

"Yeah, he was, but like I said, I don't know anything about it. It was a gift, I accepted it, he died, I gave it away."

"Do you know what the Arabic writing says? Here on the inside."

"I do. He told me once. I think it's something like God heals the believers. It's really general. God heals all. I don't remember exactly."

"Okay, well, thanks for your help. At least I know it's from Iraq."

"If you can't end up selling it, I'd take it back."

I looked at him and looked at the bowl and said, "I'll keep that in mind."

Tyler placed it on a glass display case and put his brown suede gloves back on. He said goodbye, apologized for not being more helpful, and moved toward the door. Right before he opened it, he turned around and looked back at me.

"So, I'll see you again?"

"Me? I'm not in Newport for long. Just a month. Well, actually now, I'm just here for another twelve days. But yes, I would like that," I finally stammered out. "To see you again."

"I'll come by tomorrow then," he said and walked out the door.

# CHAPTER 7

Tyler came in the next day, just like he said he would. He came by in the morning to ask me if I would go out to dinner with him that night. William watched our interaction with interest.

"And that is?" he asked curiously when Tyler left. He had nodded a polite hello to William, but I had been too taken aback to introduce him.

"That's Tyler Ford. I told you about him. The bowl. The auction."

"That bowl led you to him? Lucky you. You can keep the ten dollars."

"Twenty," I corrected him.

"Keep the twenty then, Carolyn," said William, replacing a chair in the window display with a small end table.

"Can I also keep the bowl at home until we sell it?"

"You can keep it until you find out that it's valuable enough to sell. Then we'll sell it. I read a bit about the slant on the calligraphy last night and it was popular in the Middle East pre–fifteen hundreds. I'm not saying this bowl is definitely five hundred years old, but it could be."

"I think it's worth something, too," I said to William. "I'll figure it out. I promise."

I pulled on my coat and smiled. "I know nothing about him. Tyler Ford, the bowl owner."

"I'm sure that will all change soon."

And it did. It all changed that night.

Tyler came back to the store at seven, still wearing jeans and his serious, but not severe, expression.

"You know, I realized I don't have your number and I don't know your last name. I just knew that I wanted to see you again," he said as he helped me open the store's heavy door.

I told him both. He repeated my name as we walked outside, onto the icy sidewalk. Tyler drove an old black Toyota 4Runner with slightly oversize tires, and he walked over to the passenger's door to open it for me and help me in.

"Sorry, my car's a little—"

"Big?" I interrupted him as he closed his door. His car had not one but three Marine Corps stickers on the back window and what looked like a sporting goods store in the trunk.

"I was going to say old. And messy. I kind of live out of the thing. I wanted to clean it out before tonight but I couldn't leave early enough. I'm sorry."

"It's absolutely fine," I said as he started the car. It was absolutely fine. In high school, Alex drove a Porsche Carrera with a pristine beige interior. It was so clean you could lick the seats, which Alex had me do once in a fit of passion. But his car always seemed a little too sterile, a little too old for a kid in high school. This car was exactly what I thought Tyler Ford would drive.

He made his way through Newport's small, historic streets over to the Brick Alley Pub on Thames Street and parked right outside.

"Is this okay?" he asked when he opened the door for me and helped me out.

"This is great," I said, looking up at the familiar yellow and white striped awning. "I grew up coming here. It's fun."

Tyler followed my eyes up to the restaurant sign and I could tell he was hesitating on his choice.

"Maybe you'd like to go somewhere you haven't been a hundred times. Or when you were a kid. Somewhere nicer? I'm kind of a beer-and-burger guy but maybe you know someplace good. Like one of those places on the water?"

"Honestly, this is great. I like it here. Let's go in," I said, walking toward the door.

The thirty-minute wait that was typical at a Newport restaurant in summer was not a problem in early March and we sat down at a corner table against a wall full of military and sports memorabilia.

"Did you pick this table especially?" I asked, smiling.

"I come here a lot," he said, looking up from his menu. "Too much probably, but you know Newport. A lot of it's for tourists."

"You'd be surprised," I said, picking up my menu. "I could show you some things."

Tyler put his menu down and looked right at me when the waitress brought us our beers. "I have no doubt. You seem like a really smart girl, Carolyn. I'm glad you said yes to coming out with me."

We exchanged polite conversation over drinks, and I ignored the handfuls of women who stared directly at Tyler as soon as they walked into the restaurant. I had never been out with someone so alarmingly good-looking before and I sincerely hoped I was not acting the way some of the women in the place were. Plenty looked like they were about to deliver their underwear to him.

We finished our second round and I looked at Tyler, not

quite sure what to say. Tyler was quiet. But not in a way that bored me.

"You're from Newport, I'm from Wyoming," he said finally. "But not the pretty part with all the mountains. Like none of that *Brokeback Mountain* shit. I'm from the flat part. The eastern part."

"What's the town called?" I asked, slightly taken aback. I hadn't been on a date with a man who cursed in my face within the first twenty minutes, ever.

"Wheatland. Wheatland, Wyoming. Home of unemployed men and the women who love 'em."

"That's a nice name, Wheatland. It's lyrical," I said.

"Yeah, you wouldn't say that if you saw the town. I mean it looks nice and all. Not like Newport. Nothing like Newport. But it's got its own thing happening." He looked at me and laughed. "Okay, there's actually nothing going on there. But there are pretty nice bluffs. You know, the kind you'd see in an old western movie."

"I've never seen a western movie, I don't think."

He tipped his head back and I noticed just how defined his jaw was. He had very nice blue eyes, but it was the bottom of his face, the definition of his slightly square jaw, that really made him stand out.

"You've got to watch one. Just one at least. *Butch Cassidy and the Sundance Kid.*"

"With Robert Redford, right? I like him. Especially when he played Gatsby."

"Gatsby? Really? Why are all rich people obsessed with Gatsby? As soon as a person's got ten grand in their bank account they start talking about Gatsby."

I laughed and thought about how much I loved Gatsby. I hoped it had nothing to do with my bank account.

"Have you ever read it?"

"Yeah, sure, in high school." He leaned really close to my face until he was almost out of his chair. "I do know how to read, princess."

"I'm so glad," I said, not letting myself lean back. He stayed hovering in front of my face a beat longer than expected and then sat back down after I'd looked at every perfect inch of his face. I wanted to run my hands down the lines of his cheekbones. He may not have had time to clean his car, but he'd definitely shaved again.

The waitress brought out our cheeseburgers, calling Tyler by his first name, and between bites, I asked him about his childhood.

"What kind of stuff did you do there in Wheatland, Wyoming?"

"Drink and shoot things."

"That's what you did?"

"Sure. What did you do when you were a kid?"

"I was never very good at drinking," I said, pointing to my almost-full third beer.

"Then I'm not going to let you have a fourth drink," he said. He was already on his fourth.

"I can handle four beers," I replied. "But I've never fired a gun in my life."

"So you were one of those dorky girls."

He rolled up the sleeves of his white button-down shirt and I tried not to look at his thick forearms. There was a tattoo under the left one that I couldn't quite make out.

"Not really," I said in my defense. "I mean, I wasn't dorky, I don't think. It just wasn't like that in Newport. I went to a really tough high school and I wanted to be the smartest kid there. So I worked really hard. I had to get good grades. It wasn't a choice. My parents really care about that stuff."

"I was just teasing. But you'd look really cute with a PBR and a gun."

Before I could blush to a color more flattering to pigs than humans, Tyler started telling me more about where he grew up. It took a few beers, but our conversation had gained movement.

"My dad worked in an auto shop," he said. "My mom answers phones at a cattle ranch. That's about it. The house I grew up in was a piece of shit. It sold for twenty thousand dollars a few years ago and it took six months to get that."

I looked away, embarrassed that my first car cost more than that.

"What else do you want to know?"

"I don't know," I said. "Nothing, everything."

"Nothing, everything. Okay, I get it. Well, I'm Lutheran. Everyone there is Lutheran. I love my mama. Oh, and I do call her mama. I don't love my father."

"That's too bad, for your father."

"He doesn't deserve it," said Tyler, gripping the underside of the table with his calloused hands and leaning back farther in his chair. "So I guess it is too bad for him. It's also too bad that he sold my guitar to buy drugs when I was eleven. I'd mowed about two hundred lawns to buy it and then a month after I got it, he took it, traded it in, and spent the cash on booze and cocaine. I ignored him for a year but then he punched me in the face when I was twelve and it was hard to ignore that. He punched me so hard they had to reset my jaw. A few weeks later he was gone for good."

"I'm really sorry."

"Don't be. I was better off."

"Where did he go?"

"I don't know. I heard different things. Nebraska, Colorado. Who cares. Trust me, I'm never going looking for him and he's never come looking for me."

He finished the last of his fries and studied my face.

"You're very pretty," he said, and before I could get so embarrassed that I spent the rest of the night under the table, he said, "Do you like your father?"

"Sure I do. I love my father. We have nothing much in common and we're not very close, but he always wanted the best for me. Still does, I think. Just sometimes his idea of the best and my idea of the best aren't the same."

"Well, at least he cares. That's a good thing. The best life lesson I ever learned was you can't choose your father, but you can choose whether to talk to the son of a bitch or not."

"Wise words."

"Yeah, it sounds like you don't have to worry too much about it. That's a good thing. People should love you."

Tyler put his hand over mine on the table and looked at me, no trace of a smile on his face, his clear blue eyes unmoving. His hand was so big, mine was completely lost under his. It didn't move as I tried to flex my fingers. He didn't ask me if I cared, and he held my hand too hard for me to pull mine away.

"My dad was in the military, too," he said, looking up at the wall covered in military memorabilia, then finally letting go. He ran his fingers across my skin as he pulled his away. "But it wasn't like he did anything honorable. That was always something that got me about the military. You're enlisted for a day and all of a sudden you're doing something honorable, just because you've got a uniform. But not my dad. He got caught when he was eighteen stealing cars and the cops said he could go to prison or he could go to the army. He picked the army."

"Good choice."

"Yeah. Better than prison. I blame him for a lot, but not that. Probably the only good choice he ever made."

"What did he do in the army? Did he fight in Vietnam or the Gulf or anything?"

"Nah. He was stationed in Texas and he was in charge of handing out supplies. From what I can tell, he stole as much as he handed out. And then a few years into it, he overdosed on cocaine and was let go, but the VA gave him disability and all that crap. He was really good at rolling people. He was a drunk and a drug addict but I guess he was pretty charming. I look a lot like him."

He turned his face toward me and smiled for the first time all night.

"Think I'm charming?"

There was no one on earth whom Tyler Ford had spoken to who didn't think he was charming, that I was sure of.

"I think you're something. I don't know if it's charming exactly, but something."

The restaurant was getting pretty loud and we had to raise our voices to hear each other. I asked for a water and Tyler got another beer and laughed when I smacked my plastic cup against the neck of his IPA.

"We've got to teach you how to drink, Carolyn Everett. Go out with me at least one more time so we can work on that, okay?"

I smiled but didn't answer.

"So what happened to you? Why are you living in Newport in March? You don't look like the kind of girl who spends winters in Newport. Only summers."

"Well you're wrong there. You shouldn't be so quick to judge. I grew up here. I spent eighteen winters in a row in Newport."

"And then?"

"And then I left. But now, I'm back I guess. For a little while, anyway. Something happened to me in New York and I just don't want to be there right now. I'll go back when I'm ready."

"Nothing bad?" said Tyler, leaning in again. This time I could feel his breath on my face, could see his collarbones jutting out above his muscular chest. "Nothing I have to bust some guy's teeth over?"

"Nothing bad like that. Just me making a stupid decision. But at least I got to come home."

For all the wrong reasons, I let Tyler Ford into my apartment that night. He walked me to the door and when I unlocked it, he followed me in and I didn't object. It was stupid, and I knew it was. No one knew where I was, or who was with me. If he'd wanted to *Silence of the Lambs* me, he could have. But I let him in anyway.

"I don't have beer, but I have vodka," I said, moving toward the kitchen. He looked around the apartment and I explained that it was a short-term rental.

"I like it," he said. "Mind if I sit down?" he asked, motioning to the couch. I poured us both my famous concoction of vodka and tap water and he watched me walk around the kitchen. "You barely drink at dinner and now you'll have vodka. What's your secret, you only drink at home? Is that what the locals do?"

"I don't know. I guess I have been home a lot lately."

"No harm in that."

He unbuttoned his jacket and placed it on the couch, and for the first time since I had been with him, in the too bright lights of my apartment, I could really see his body, the way his biceps were almost bigger than his shoulders, how strong he was. He could have, physically, settled any score I had to settle in New York. But I wasn't the type to have any problems like that.

"Is that the bowl, there?" said Tyler, looking toward the bedroom at a wide bookcase, where the bowl sat on the top shelf.

"I brought it home last night. Verdict at the store is I should just keep it until we know more about it."

"That's a good verdict."

He motioned for me to sit next to him on the couch.

"Or you keep it until you give it back to me?"

I eyed him and his sly smile.

"I don't think that's going to happen."

"How much longer are you staying in Newport?" he asked, resting his glass on his knee. I could see it leaving a small ring of water on the dark denim.

"I've got about ten days left. Then I need to go back to New York."

"Why?" he asked. "Got a reason to run back so soon?"

"I don't know. I just told myself I would. I messed up, I gave myself a month to get over it, and then I'll try to fix it all again."

"I'd like to see you as much as you'll let me in the next ten days," he said. "Would you be okay with that?"

He put his glass on the coffee table, stood up, and before I could answer, he reached out his hand and pulled me up off the couch so I was standing in front of him. My head didn't even reach his shoulder. He walked us over to the wall by the front door and leaned against it. Still holding my hand, he pulled me close to him, put his other hand on my face, and kissed me, long, hard, perfectly. He pulled away and looked at me, ran his hands through my hair, to the back of my neck, and when he kissed me again, he grabbed me so tightly that my feet were barely on the ground. It wasn't just a kiss. It was a huge motion, some sort of physical wave that peaked with his mouth against mine, his tongue on my tongue, his body pressed hard against me. I put my hands on his arms, running them down his pressed white shirt, trying not to tremble. When he let go, I looked up at him and said, "You should go. Before I make any bad decisions, you should go."

"What sort of bad decisions are you planning to make?" he asked me before he kissed me again. He didn't move his hands from my neck but pulled me toward him again. He ran his hand down my shoulder, stopping just above my chest. "I love bad decisions."

"So I hear."

"Oh yeah? You seem like a girl who's smart enough not to believe what everyone else says."

"Sometimes people are right, though."

He took a step back and looked at me.

"Two weeks, you said?"

"Not even."

"Okay, then I'd like to take you out again tomorrow."

Not wanting to seem like a girl who was never asked out on dates by men who acted like Tyler Ford, even though that was true, I told him Sunday, walked him to the door, and touched my tingling lips, swollen from him biting them. I hoped Tyler was the best bad decision I ever made.

# CHAPTER 8

It had been two weeks since I'd emailed Max about the bowl and he still hadn't responded to me. Now that I had met Tyler, I desperately wanted the green and white bowl to be something valuable. I wanted to look up at him one night and say, "You'll never guess what I found out. . . ." Was there something about it that I wasn't seeing? Some signs pointed to it being a new piece, like the weight, but like William said, the intricacy of the design, the slant of the calligraphy, made me think otherwise. But I was not an expert and I still had no idea what the Hebrew writing on the bottom meant, nor did I have a confirmation on what Tyler pronounced the Arabic writing to be. I could have taken it to a mosque and a temple, but that seemed too dramatic. So as a child of academics, I decided to bring it to a bastion of learning.

Providence is not a pretty city. It is less than an hour away from Newport, but in beauty, it didn't belong in the same state. There were exceptions, and Brown University was one of them. I'd thought about applying to Brown when I was a senior, but it had always seemed a little too bohemian, the unpreppy, un-Ivy Ivy. Even now, the students walking across the quad had a good dose of hipster in their wardrobes. At Princeton, even before the term *hipster* invaded our lexicon, it was a dirty word. But now that I was older, I kind of liked the vibe of the place. It didn't seem like a school where people sold their souls to get into the right eating club.

The Joukowsky Institute for Archaeology and the Ancient World was on George Street, which ran straight across campus. Blair Bari, a professor of Egyptology, archaeology, and art history, had agreed to meet with me. I had sent him an email a thousand words long describing the backstory, begging for his help. He had written back, "Yes. Tomorrow. Ten a.m." That was the entire email. So he was a man of few words or polite phrases. He was still highly esteemed and making time to see me.

When I found Professor Bari's office, I knocked on the door and walked in after I heard his voice. He was sitting at a large wooden desk, which had bookshelves all around, and a granite relief fragment of a Nubian prisoner on one of them. He was wearing a polo and a sweater and a blazer and had the air-conditioning on. I didn't question his cooling methods and introduced myself.

"Carolyn Everett. I don't know you, do I?" he asked, taking off a pair of reading glasses. His black hair was thinning on the top but he had warm, inviting eyes. They were heavily wrinkled at his temples, showing years of squinting in the sun.

"You don't. I sincerely appreciate you taking the time to meet with me, especially since you don't know me."

"Well, your email was interesting," he said, folding his hands on his desk. "The Goodwill. I liked that part of the story the best. The Goodwill. I don't think I've ever put one toe inside the Goodwill. Is that where all the good artifacts can be found these days?"

"I don't think so. It's more like a needle-in-a-haystack situation over there except the haystack is a lot of discarded bric-a-brac and used clothing."

"Bric-a-brac. How fascinating." He looked up at me and waved me in. "Sit down, sit down, please."

I took a seat in the navy blue leather chair opposite his desk and put my bag on the floor.

"So you were at Christie's for many years, you said."

"Yes, I was," I said, crossing my legs under my wool skirt. "I was there for ten years, full-time for eight."

"I think I read an article about you last month. American furniture. Some sort of big bad Baltimore slipup?"

I froze. Of course this man had googled me. Why wouldn't he. He wasn't just going to let any old fool take up his office hours. Except I wasn't any old fool. I was a notorious young fool.

"Between you and me, the people over there have always scared the dickens out of me. So uptight!" he said jovially.

I tried unsuccessfully not to laugh. "They really are pretty uptight sometimes. But very smart and polished."

"Smart and polished, of course, of course. Not like the rest of us, who go digging on our hands and knees for the good stuff. We're barbaric!"

"I think you're just more adventurous," I offered.

"Well, you look like the adventurous type, Miss Everett. You have very interesting coloring. If I were a painter I would very much like to paint you. That smattering of freckles across your nose with those dark wide eyes and the flowing light hair. Very striking. You look Finnish. Are you Finnish?"

"Thank you for the nice compliment. I don't think I'm Finnish. Everett is derived from the Germanic Eberhard, I believe."

"Too bad. I love Finland. Wonderful fish." He lifted his fingers to his lips and smiled.

Perhaps I had picked the wrong professor at Brown. I wondered if he'd notice if I stood up and backed away slowly.

"Before I take a look at this vessel you've brought up, can you tell me about it? I'd like some background before I actually see it."

I should have told him to just read the ridiculously detailed email I'd sent him, but he had been kind enough not to throw me out of his office because of my Christie's history, so I told the story again, slowly.

"So this piece," he said when I was done, "went from an Iraqi translator to an American marine, to the naval base in Newport, to Goodwill, to an unsanctioned auction in Narragansett, to you." He pushed his chair back from his desk a little and looked at me.

"Not the most linear path, but that's it."

"And you doubt that it's more than fifty years old because . . ."

"I'm no expert, at all, which is why I contacted you, but I used to do appraisals at Christie's and occasionally I got to handle ceramics. I want the bowl to be worth something, like five figures. Part of me thinks it is. But every time I pick it up, I think it's too heavy to be old. It's in impeccable shape and the glaze is very even. The colors are not muted in areas as you'd expect them to be with ancient firing techniques, and the Arabic script inside isn't heavily stylized even though it has an interesting slant. The only thing that's very strange is that on the base of the bowl, there is writing in Hebrew. I was hoping you might tell me what it says. That and the Arabic in the middle. The previous owner told me it was something like 'God heals the believers.'"

"There's writing in Arabic in the bowl and Hebrew on the bottom of the bowl?" asked Blair, running his hands along his temples and thick black eyebrows.

"That's right."

"Well, now I'm itching to see it. Get it up here," he said, slapping his hand on top of his desk. I reached into my bag, pulled it out, and put it in front of him.

He turned it around a few times, picked it up and looked at the bottom, put his face almost inside of it to read the Arabic script, and then turned it around again.

"You're not too far off on the Arabic. It says *wa yashfi sudoora qawmin mumineena*, which means 'And God shall heal the breast of the believers.' It's from the Surah at-Tawbah, the ninth chapter of the Quran."

"A verse from the Quran—that's probably adorned pottery for centuries."

"Yes, definitely, at least from the seventh century, when the Quran was revealed to Muhammad, to today."

He turned the bowl around and looked at the bottom. "Do you know what this says?" he asked without looking up at me.

"I do not."

"This says 'first and the last.'"

"That's all it says?" I asked, leaning toward the desk.

"Yes, 'first and the last,' that's all."

"Do you have any idea what that could mean?"

"Well, if it were not etched on the bottom of a bowl with a clear passage from the Quran on it, I would think it was referring to Jesus Christ."

"As in Jesus is the first and the last."

"Right. King James Bible, Revelation 1:17: 'And when I saw him, I fell at his feet as dead. And he laid his right hand upon me, saying unto me, Fear not; I am the first and the last: I am he that liveth, and was dead; and behold, I am alive for evermore, Amen; and have the keys of hell and of death.'"

I had a decent knowledge of the Bible from school and church growing up, but I had never heard that passage.

"It's when John the Apostle was exiled to the island of Patmos," Blair explained. "Now some historians have rejected the notion that it was John the Apostle and believe it was a man referred to as John of Patmos. Either way, it's the unveiling of Jesus Christ to John."

I had stumbled upon a piece of pottery that combined all my weaknesses in art history. I spoke French, not Hebrew or Arabic. I had studied the Bible with the muted passion of a teenager. I certainly couldn't quote from Revelation like Blair.

"All this is an educated guess, you understand," he said, righting the bowl. "It's just when you see those words, 'the first and the last,' you have to think of Jesus Christ. There may be another Bible passage that refers to him as the first and the last, but that's by far the most well-known."

"But what is that doing on the bottom of a bowl that is adorned with a Quranic verse?"

"I have no idea. You said this belonged to a marine in Iraq. Maybe he was deeply religious and his etching it into the bottom was a small sign of protest against Islam."

I thought about Tyler's bedroom habits. The man was not deeply religious. And if he was, he was awfully good at hiding it. Plus, he said he was Lutheran. There was no way he could write in Hebrew.

"I don't think that's it. And what about the fact that it's written in Hebrew? The Book of Revelation is the New Testament. Most Jews don't subscribe to the New Testament."

"Most don't. A few do." He turned around and pulled a

book from his mahogany bookcase called *The Jewish Anno-
tated New Testament.* "It's not impossible."

"I haven't felt this confused in a long time."

"But isn't that what makes this line of work so interesting?"

"I suppose it is, yes."

"I've spent many years of my life looking at pieces that
some people wanted to just throw in a heap of garbage but
later revealed themselves to be much more."

Blair smiled at me and held the bowl in both his hands. "I
can see why you bought this. It's a very striking piece. The
vegetal motifs, the way they're painted, it's reminiscent of
Chinese porcelain but with a distinctive Muslim style. This
style grew in popularity in the Middle East during the Abbasid period. The ninth century."

"Do you think it's from the Abbasid period?" I asked
dubiously. William had said the same thing.

"You certainly don't; that's rather obvious," Blair said,
turning it around again.

"I would love it to be, but feel it. Doesn't the weight
bother you?"

Blair flicked the pot with his fingers and we both listened to the high-pitched sound that rang out when he did.

"The weight and that right there. From that sound alone
I don't think it's more than a hundred years old. The design
is in the style of the ninth century, one that stayed popular
for many centuries after, but the craftsmanship, it's not in
line with what we find from that period. If I had any doubt,
I would submit it for thermoluminescence testing. That
process is the most accurate. Heat an already fired piece and
test the amount of light that is emitted. You can also detect
restoration materials that way. But I'm ninety-nine percent
certain it's not worth our time."

"Ninety-nine?"

"Well, you can't ever be one hundred percent certain about anything, can you?"

"I guess not."

"This world was built on the wonderful notion of the gray area." He picked up the bowl again and handed it to me. "I wish it was worth millions. But pottery seldom is."

"I know, ceramics are so hard to identify. I'm glad it wasn't my field of expertise at Christie's. I'm afraid I would have made many more mistakes."

He looked at me as I stood up from the chair and reached across the desk to shake his hand.

"It could be some sort of encrypted message," he said, looking up at me. "It could be the doodling of a Jew for Jesus with a good pocketknife and it could be nothing at all. Maybe someone who spoke Hebrew decided it was the first and the last time they were going to hold a piece of Islamic pottery."

"Blair, don't keep going. You're just going to confuse me more."

"I'm sorry. And I'm sorry I couldn't be more helpful. I say put that nice bowl on your dining room table and enjoy it for what it is. Something lovely to look at."

"I'll take that advice. Thank you again for your time."

As I stood, Blair looked hesitant.

"You know what the most interesting takeaway from this entire conversation is?"

I shook my head no.

"That line. That biblical passage. It's from the Book of Revelation. Maybe it's a message about how this bowl will reveal something for the owner. Or maybe it was some code used in war. I know this sounds more like I'm talking about a war that happened before computers and cell phones and technology, but if you were trying to send a message that no one could download or copy, maybe this would be the way to do it."

"Do you really think it could be something like that?" I asked, looking at the bottom again.

"Maybe I'm just an old man who likes mysteries."

"It is interesting, though, the Book of Revelation of all the books."

"Like I said, that could be a stretch, too. But if it's not, then yes, it is interesting."

I thanked him again for his time.

When I got back to Newport, I stopped by a bookstore and bought both the Quran and the Bible. The shopkeeper probably thought I was having a religious awakening. With a mix of the Internet and my hard copies, I researched the phrase Blair had cited, "first and the last," and found it several times in Revelation. It was in the passage that Blair had recited rote and it was also in Revelation 22:13: "I am the Alpha and the Omega, the first and the last, the beginning and the end." It appeared again in Revelation 1:11: "Saying, I am Alpha and Omega, the first and the last: and, What thou seest, write in a book, and send it unto the seven churches which are in Asia." I understood why Blair immediately said the phrase was referring to Jesus. But Revelation was perhaps the most contested book in the Bible. Thomas Jefferson kept it out of the Jefferson Bible and many scholars wrote it off as hallucinatory prophecy.

I put the Bible down, realizing I hadn't held one in my hands since college, and shut my computer. I was making this bowl into the Rosetta Stone. Was it because, like William, I really thought there was something to it—or was I just enthralled with it because I now associated it with Tyler, who I was very quickly falling for?

After going out with him on Friday, Sunday, and Monday and kissing him standing up, lying down, and with my legs wrapped around his waist, I decided to call Alex. I needed to rip off a few shreds of honesty for Alex because what I was craving right now was to see Tyler every single day, and I wanted to do it with a clear conscience. I had asked Tyler on Sunday if he knew that the bottom of the bowl said "first and the last" in Hebrew and he gave me what felt like an honest no.

"You might find this surprising, but there aren't that many Jewish marines. And the few I knew were not man-handling my pottery. Also, we were in Iraq, not exactly Jewish Disney World."

I'd let out an almost-forced laugh and he didn't ask me how I knew what the base said. If my researching it bothered him, he didn't let on. And if he liked me doing it, he didn't give it his stamp of approval.

Before I got up the courage to call Alex, I drove down Ledge Road, where he had grown up and where his parents still lived. I knew the Blake house before I knew who lived in it because Newport was small enough that you had driven past every house worth remembering hundreds of times. It was a newer build, newer meaning 1915, but now had enough age on it that it fit right in. I remembered going there with Alex while we were at St. George's and liking it immediately. It had things like seashells in it and cookies made by his actual mother, and paintings by artists who weren't featured prominently in the Met. It was lived in and comfortable, but it was still a seven-million-dollar house. It had a wooden porch that jutted onto the thick green lawn and it was so close to the water that we had once tried to do a running leap from his living room window. Turns out it wasn't quite that close.

Alex was the youngest of four boys, though he was frequently asked if he was an only child, a question that both
annoyed and flattered him. All three of his brothers worked
in finance in New York and were very good at their rather
boring, high-profile jobs. Everyone expected Alex to follow suit, so he did. He was what Newport considered new
money, which meant his family hadn't started summering
there in the nineteenth century. In fact, his family only had
a normal amount of money until his father turned a small
family investment firm in North Carolina into a huge international investment firm in New York. He did so well
in the nineties that he put himself on the Forbes 500, for a
year anyway, in 1997. It was a year the family really enjoyed
bringing up and when Alex and I were in high school, that
particular issue of *Forbes* was glued to his nightstand. I
knew he'd done the same thing at Dartmouth. Alex's father,
Morris Blake, had had his last son when he was fifty-five. He
was semiretired when I first met him, happy to trade the office buildings of New York for Newport year-round. "I love
the North, and the more north the better. I grew up in the
Carolinas but southern money doesn't feel real," he had said
to me once. "You have to bring it up north for it to really
matter." His son, northern to the core, definitely agreed.

I had loved spending time with Alex in that house as we
went from teenagers acting like grown-ups to grown-ups
acting like teenagers. His parents hadn't spent their lives on
the water, but Alex more than made up for it. He looked and
acted exactly how a rich prep school kid from New England
was supposed to act. When we turned sixteen, and he had
the car and enough of an allowance to back it up, he got so
good at it that he even surprised himself. Alex Blake was
exactly the person I thought I'd start and end with.

I called Alex on Thursday night after work and caught

him as he was heading back to his apartment. The sounds of the city—the car horns, the sirens, the voices, people talking loudly to each other and into their phones as they walked past him—made me nostalgic for my old life. I used to love walking down the street with Alex, proud that he was so successful and that I worked for Christie's New York. I had wished for my old life every day that I'd been in Newport, until I'd met Tyler.

"Carolyn Everett," said Alex after he answered the phone. "I miss you."

"Do you?" I asked, trying not to sound surprised. Alex could be very sweet when he was in the mood to be.

"How is our hometown treating you?"

"You know, it's home, it's nice."

"Mmm, I couldn't live there now. Way too boring. What would I do, shuck oysters and become a docent?"

"There are a few other things to do. I haven't eaten an oyster or been to a mansion, besides the Dalbys', since I've been here."

"Well, you should, it's oyster season. So besides hanging out with Jane and that what's-his-name, what are you doing?"

"Carter. You know his name, Alex."

"Right. Carter. That's a fake name. It's a last name. So besides hanging out with them, what is it that you do up there?"

"I told you, I'm working at William Miller's."

"Oh, wait, you were serious? Didn't you do that in high school? What are you going to do next, get an internship?"

"I didn't call you just so my self-esteem could fall even lower."

"I know, I'm an ass," said Alex, laughing. "I'm sorry. I had a long day. I need a distraction. I need you. Why don't you come to the city for the weekend? We can eat out; see a play or something. I'll buy you presents. Whatever you want."

That sounded really nice. I missed swanky New York restaurants and going to the theater with Alex, who always bought us tickets right in the middle with perfect views, but I was already heading home in less than a week. And Alex. Could I really just run back to him and his nice-when-I-want-to-be ways?

"I don't think I can handle coming back to the city yet," I replied. "I planned to stay until March fifteenth and I'm going to stick to it."

"You can't handle the city or you can't handle seeing me? It's been a while since you've seen me."

"The city."

"Okay, then," he said. "But I feel obliged to say one thing. People don't wait for each other forever. I know I haven't exactly been perfect, but I've been here for you through all this mess you made. And I do love you. I know sometimes we break up and see other people and get back together and all that, and I'm sure it's a pain in the ass for you, but it's also just us, you know. And we've been us for a long time. I like us."

I liked us, too, some of the time.

"Anyway, we're both almost thirty now and you're going to get your career back on track and be the star that you are. So maybe it's time to be a little less flighty and a little more committed to each other."

Alex was the one who wanted this now? Alex? I had been subtly begging him to be exclusive for years, but all of a sudden, I leave and don't want to see him and he wants to sew me to his hip. It was always when you stopped caring.

"I'd like that. A lot," I said, though for the first time

since I had known Alex, my whole heart was not behind my statement.

"But not starting this weekend?"

"Right."

"Okay, Carolyn. It's just your job, you know. You'll get another one. But it would probably help if you left that crappy store, came back to New York, and looked for work. Something that pays you more than ten bucks an hour. What are you going to be, the girl who hangs out with the Dalbys and makes welfare wages? I think you've retired from living in their backyard."

Alex always knew how to hit me exactly where it would slice me open slowly. I had been happy growing up. I tried to be nice to everyone; I was smart and pleasant-looking and was friends with all the right people. But everyone also knew that the money my family once had was gone, and I wasn't a girl just like the Dalbys, I was the girl who slept in their carriage house. But not in boarding school. When I got to St. George's, it was the great equalizer, until we all went home for the summer.

I had walked around St. George's a few times since I'd been home, but I hadn't been able to stay long. The sentimental way it made me feel almost hurt, bringing back the emotion of a time when I thought everything was possible. When I thought I was going to marry Alex and be a big success. I was going to be *that* girl, and no one would remember who grew up on the edge of the ocean, and who grew up just behind it.

After three weeks in Newport, I was beginning to feel like me again. I didn't know exactly what that meant, but there was an element to it that I had lost when I moved to New York. Up here I wore my long hair in a braid. I had gained a few pounds from eating three meals a day and I didn't care if my sweaters were made in China. Even Jane, who was everything that all those New York girls wanted to be, was nothing like those New York girls, which is why she was in Newport, barefoot, with her husband, waiting for spring to come. Jane worked when she wanted to, and played when she was in the mood, but she never rubbed it in your face that she had the choice. She was good at being rich, and many people weren't.

I hung up the phone with Alex and wondered how I had put up with his yo-yoing since I was fourteen years old. I didn't want to be someone's safety blanket.

I called Jane's sister, Brittan, in New York to tell her about the conversation. You called Jane when you needed to feel better, but you called Brittan when you wanted to curse.

"So now he wants to marry you," she said, laughing.

"Yeah, I don't think marry, but be serious. More serious. I think it was his way of saying he was going to stop breaking up with me and cheating on me."

"That kid is really lucky he's so cute and that his dad is so minted. Because if not for those two qualities, he would have gotten beat up a lot."

"Yeah, deservedly."

"I don't know what to tell you, Carolyn," said Brittan. "If you think he'll change, really think he'll change, then go for it. But we grew up around men who were once Alex. You remember Anna Harbisher's dad? Yeah, he didn't change. Or Kate Van Stricklen's dad? Remember that Siberian model he married who was younger than her?"

"Serbian."

"Whatever, Carolyn. She was twenty."

"Yeah, I have my doubts," I admitted after Brittan finished listing every father we knew in Newport who had dumped their wives during some midlife crisis or another.

"It's socially acceptable polygamy," said Brittan. "That's why I'm never getting married."

"But everyone wants to marry you."

"Well, then it's a good thing I love to say no. And now I'm saying no to you. No Alex. Move on. Let someone else in your pants, for God's sake. He does not deserve your faithfulness."

"Well, I'd be more worried about it than I am, if I didn't have a bit of a distraction happening here."

"What? No way." I could hear Brittan getting up and closing her office door. I knew she would sit back down and turn in her dove gray leather chair to look at the expanse of Central Park twenty floors down.

"It's about time. Fuck Alex. Who is your distraction?"

"He's a marine actually. His name is Tyler Ford and he's nothing like anyone you or I have ever met. He's kind of amazing."

"Amazing? A marine? Does Jane know? Of course not. It's Jane."

"Not yet, but I need to talk about him with someone."

"Listen to you! We've been talking for thirty minutes and you wait until now to confess your scandal. I'm glad you chose me to dish to. I want to see all this for myself. I'm coming to Newport. Friday night. Tell Jane." Brittan paused and thought about it. "Never mind, I'll tell Jane."

And that was how I ended up at the Blue Hen again. I got to the bar early, to make sure Brittan didn't have to spend any time in there alone, and headed toward the back, but I was stopped by a smiling face.

"Do you remember me? Greg LaPorte."

"Sure I remember you," I said, smiling back. "Greg LaPorte. It's nice to see you. Thanks for helping me the other day."

"We told Ford about you. Did he find you?"

"Yeah, he did. I talked to him about the bowl. He seemed surprised that it was worth anything at all."

"I mean, there's a lot of chintz to buy over there. He probably thought it was just some piece of crap. Probably bought it from a kid for two bucks or something to get him to go away."

Greg walked me to the bar and bought me a beer.

"Remember when I told you I was a really nice guy?" he said, watching me drink.

"Yes, I do."

"Well, I'm still a really nice guy. I've probably only gotten nicer since you met me. I'm a captain in the United States Marine Corps, I love America, and I've got three sisters and a little brother who I never beat up. Wait, and look, here's a napkin on the floor that I'm going to pick up."

"No, gross!" I said, stopping him before he contracted hepatitis. "I believe you! You're a nice guy. Don't pick that up."

"Okay, good," said Greg, smiling. Greg was cute in a wholesome way, and he was definitely younger than me.

"So, let me guess one thing. You're dating Tyler Ford," he said as the band played Journey covers.

I didn't answer and Greg started to laugh. "Of course you are. They always do."

"Who is 'they'?" I asked, trying not to think of Tyler as some sort of Lothario who bedded every woman in town, swooning over his chiseled body and the stars and bars.

"You know, girls, pretty girls like you. They love Captain Ford."

"Oh yeah? But let me guess, things never get serious."

"Tyler Ford and girlfriends do not go together," said

Greg. "If they did, he wouldn't be Tyler Ford, and trust me, sweetheart, he really likes being Tyler Ford."

"Say Tyler Ford again," I said, laughing.

"No way. I'd rather say your name. Carolyn . . ."

"Everett."

"See, that's a better name. Carolyn Everett. That's pretty. Doesn't sound so much like the make of a truck."

"You're kinda charming, Greg."

"I told you, I was. You just have to listen."

"Right, now about the Tyler Ford girlfriend thing," I said after Greg watched me drink down half my beer. "He's really never had a girlfriend? I mean, maybe you haven't known him that long."

"Actually I have," said Greg. "And I know he hasn't had a girlfriend since Hannah."

"Hannah," I repeated. "Who is Hannah?"

"Wow," he said, laughing. "You really care."

"No! I don't. Not really, just a little."

"Hannah moved out of Newport. She was a teacher here. Art, I think. At St. George's."

"Oh. I went there."

"You did? Fancy place."

"Yeah, it's okay."

Greg slapped five with a couple of his friends who had just walked in and spotted us at the bar. I recognized one from the first night I met him.

"So was Hannah okay?" I asked after saying hi to his friends.

"Yeah, she was a nice girl. Things didn't end all that well with Ford, though. They usually don't."

"What Greg means is that he broke her nose and almost punched out her eye with his fist," said his friend who had been listening to our conversation and jumped right in.

"What?"

"Oh, it's Mason, by the way," said the friend, stuffing some chips in his mouth. He had very white teeth, more like a California coed than a gritty marine. "My name is Mason. And I remember you. You're the girl with the bowl, who is now in love with Tyler Ford. We warned you, babe. Don't fall in love with him."

"He's not really giving you the full story. Don't freak out yet," said Greg.

"You're, um, intimate with Ford, I take it," said Mason, grinning at me.

I didn't reply, which was the only answer he needed.

"Yeah, why am I even asking," he said, laughing. "It's fucking Ford. He can do whatever he wants. Lucky man. Where do you come in Tyler Ford's lineup? Let me think. Well, you're definitely after that chick with the fake rack from Providence who moved here for him and then he told her to move right on home. And you're after the Maple twins, who weren't really twins and there were actually four of them."

"Drop it, Mase," said Greg forcefully to his friend.

"He even charmed his way through the service. I mean, I'm not saying he's not a good marine," said Mason. "He is. He's tough as hell. He weighs like two ten. But he's a mustang and I doubt he would have gotten up there if he wasn't, you know, Tyler Ford."

"What's a mustang?" I asked, looking from Greg to Mason. I couldn't very well ask about Mason's other comments. So I stayed on that one.

"Oh, it just means you go from enlisted to officer," said Greg. "He wasn't commissioned, didn't go to college, he just got a little lucky." He moved farther from Mason and closer to me.

"No way," said Mason, watching us. "This shit is getting too complicated. I don't want to be a part of no love pentagon. I'm standing between you two. Plus," he said, inching closer to me, "if anyone is going to break her from Ford's clutches it's me. No one likes red hair, LaPorte." He moved right next to me and I smiled at Greg to assure him that plenty of girls in the world loved red buzz cuts.

"Ford was in a bar with Hannah last year. This bar actually, and this guy really started bothering her. Not a military guy, some fucking townie or someone. Some rich kid. It was July. You know, summer in Newport. All those sons of bitches come home. Anyway, you get it," Mason explained.

"So what happened with Hannah?"

"Well, like I said, this rich kid was really messing with her, and Ford found out about it, went crazy, and swung at him, but Hannah jumped toward him and he ended up punching her in the face. He broke her nose and knocked out four of her teeth and her eye was all bloody. I think he dislocated her jaw, too. Ford can fight, if you haven't already guessed. She never talked to him again after that. And when she figured out that he wasn't leaving Newport for a while, she did. Went to Hartford to teach at the university and never came back so that was it. Ford went back to being Ford, which meant all the single women, and I'm guessing the married ones, too, were a lot happier."

"That's fascinating."

"Okay, pretend you don't care. But just take this as your second warning."

I wondered what I would do if Tyler came in the bar that night. Would I ask him about Hannah? Would I pretend I didn't know? I had never had anyone warn me about a guy, and this was a guy who had broken his girlfriend's face.

As I was thinking about Tyler and his history of violence, I saw Brittan come in the door and made a beeline for her before anyone else could. By the time I got there, there was already a navy guy helping her with her coat.

"Forget everything I've ever said about this place," she announced as she hugged me. "This is awesome. These guys are crazy hot! I've never hung out with military guys before."

"Well, you're about to. Come on, my friends are at the bar. There, around the guy with red hair."

"Is that him? Tyler Ford?"

"No, Brit. Trust me, when you see Tyler Ford, you won't have to ask who he is. But I'm not sure if he's coming tonight."

Brittan glared at me. "You didn't ask him to come, did you."

"Well, not in so many words. It's new. I just want it to be him and me for a while, not him, me, half of base, and the beautiful Dalbys. We'll get there later."

"Before you come back to New York?"

I shrugged at the mention of my impending departure and didn't tell Brittan that I had done nothing to make my way back to New York.

"I'll meet him eventually," said Brittan with a sly smile. "By the way, this is for you." She pulled a folded note out of her pocket and gave it to me. It had my name on the front, written in small, slanted print. I opened it and read it. In even male handwriting was written,

*Just remember, you'll always have more fun with me.*

*—Ford.*

I looked up at Brittan and smiled. "Did Tyler give this to you?"

"No, some delivery boy. He looked like he was in the military, too, but really young, barely twenty. Not the type you would dump Alex for. He handed it to me when I got out of the car in the parking lot. Trust me, I knew he wasn't Tyler Ford. Pretty cute move, though. He wrote you a note. It's like sixth grade, but sexy."

It was sexy. I folded it again, put it in my pocket, and walked Brittan to the bar.

I saw every single one of Greg's friends' eyes light up as I walked over with Brittan and they all shook her hand with Christmas-morning-size grins when she said her name.

"Your friend is so pretty," Mason declared as he downed his fifth beer and watched Brittan walk out to the dance floor with Greg. "Fucking gorgeous. I've never seen anyone who looks like her. I mean, who's not in a magazine. Naked in a magazine. No, fuck that. She's prettier than those girls. She's amazing. Maybe I'll ask her to marry me tonight. Like in an hour, after we get better acquainted."

"She dated Tim Colby last year," I pointed out.

"The quarterback for the Jets?"

"Yeah, that one."

"Crap. Well, I better pull out my best dance moves then. Wait until she sees me do the tractor," he said, wiping his mouth and jumping up.

"Don't worry about him. He won't make too much of an ass of himself," said Greg when he got back to the bar.

"You kind of have red hair," I said, changing the subject.

"I know. Isn't it awesome. Growing up I was like, hell yes! God gave me red hair. This is going to make my life so much easier."

"Oh yeah?"

"Trust me. I was pretty happy when I joined the military and I got to shave it all off."

Mason was twirling Brittan in circles and screaming something about never-ending love, so I walked over and told him to go back to the bar and buy us drinks.

"I'll have a beer, she won't," I said, shooing him.

"I can't believe you're hanging out with these guys, Carolyn. They've probably all killed people!" She made a gun motion with her right hand and pointed it against my forehead. "Blammo. You seem to be very into murderers lately. Jane would not approve. Not me. I like ethical sportsmen."

"Let's take shots," I said with a grin. "Lots of shots." We wandered over to the bar and Brittan smacked her thin hand on the counter. Mason put his arm around her neck, blissfully.

"Hey, Mack, we want whiskey shots."

"The name's Justin, baby, but you can call me whatever." The bartender leaned over the bar so she could kiss him on the cheek and handed us our drinks. We drank them immediately and I felt my insides burning.

A few shots later, after Brittan had suggested we dance on the bar, "for our country," I told Mason we were leaving.

"You girls are drunk. We'll take you home."

"No way. I'm not getting in a car with a total stranger."

"I don't want to leave my car," said Brittan, looking at the parking lot.

"I'll drive your car," said Greg. "I barely drank. Mason will follow us and take me home."

Brittan looked at me, waiting for me to veto the idea.

"I spent most of the night with him. He barely drank," I concurred.

"Fine then. You better be able to drive, Ginger," she said, throwing the car keys his way. Mason took her arm and pulled her in front of us so we couldn't eavesdrop on their conversation.

"So you only checked the door and your phone about fifteen times looking for Ford. That's not too bad. Maybe your love is dying," said Greg.

"Did I?" I asked, embarrassed. "I'm sorry. That's pretty rude."

"That's okay, I've seen much worse. You're not the first of Tyler Ford's girls I've driven home."

"I am not one of Tyler Ford's girls."

"All right, then, you're not. Yet."

"Why don't you like him?" I asked as we walked slowly through the lot.

"Who says I don't like him?"

"You don't seem to. Did he ever do anything to make you not like him? I mean, don't you think he's a good guy?"

"Do I think Ford's a good guy? Absolutely not. I think he'll do anything to get laid and to maintain his reputation. He likes to be this tough guy. In Iraq he was the same way. But he doesn't have to try very hard, does he. He just looks like that."

Ahead of us Mason and Brittan were kissing while a car was flicking its headlights at them.

"So, where do you guys live?" asked Greg.

"I live downtown on Monument. But I'm obviously not letting you take Brittan home without me."

"Okay," said Greg, scanning the parking lot for a car that might be hers. He looked down at the keys and looked at me.

"Bentley?"

"It's her dad's," I said. "Don't worry, she won't murder you if you scratch it."

"Holy shit, I cannot drive someone's Bentley. Don't you have a Chevy or something we can drive instead?"

"Not here. It's fine, trust me. The Dalbys aren't really like that."

"Wait, Dalby? Like titan of industry, donated libraries and all that Dalby?"

"Yeah, that one. Brittan Dalby."

"Oh God. And if she's Brittan Dalby, then who are you?"

"I'm just her friend," I said, using a line I had uttered a thousand times before. Not a Dalby, just a friend.

"My car," said Brittan, pointing, when we had caught up with them.

Mason jumped into his Ford truck and started it up, waiting for us to get in Brittan's car and pull out.

"Isn't he drunk?" I asked, looking back at Mason's bright lights.

"Yeah, but who cares," said Greg. I gave him Brittan's address and he entertained us with war stories until we pulled onto Bellevue.

"I love this road," said Greg, taking advantage of how wide it was. When we pulled through the thick iron gate, past the fountain and tennis courts and into Brittan's driveway, Mason pulled right in behind us and jumped out of the car.

"Brittan, you live in a castle," Mason said.

"Not exactly," she said casually. "Have you ever been to the Mont St.-Michel?"

"Brittan, shut up," I said as Mason stared at her blankly with his wide black eyes.

She turned to walk away, but he took her hand and pulled her toward him. Greg and I turned around as they started making out on the hood of his truck.

"It's cold," said Greg, unbuttoning his jacket. He took it off and put it around my shoulders. It was so thick and warm, I instantly felt like I could spend the night outside.

"No," I said, reaching for it. "You can't stand out here without a coat on. It's like twenty-five degrees."

"I've felt much worse." He positioned his coat on my shoulders again.

"I know it's none of my business," he said, reaching his hand in his coat pocket. He didn't hold mine; he just curled his up and rested it next to mine. There was more than enough room. "I don't think you should be messing around with Tyler Ford. He really does have a hell of a reputation and you seem like too nice of a girl to get involved in all that. The thing with him is, it's not just all the girls. We got in a pretty bad fight once and he scared the shit out of me. He's pretty good at that. We overlapped when he was on his third tour." His voice drifted off and he turned and looked at the vast expanse of water hitting the cliff below us.

"What was the fight about?"

Greg paused for a few seconds. He looked like he was either trying to decide whether to tell me or trying to get his story straight.

"There was a rumor that some guys in his platoon were planning on selling military property. Guns, night-vision goggles, even these eight-hundred-dollar flashlights we all had. So I asked Ford about it."

"How'd that go?"

"Badly."

"Was anyone in his group, I mean platoon, was anyone ever caught doing that?"

"One guy was a few years later. He was selling assault rifles on eBay. But no one then."

"So not Tyler?"

"No. But there was still a lot of talk. He did four tours, you know. That can take a toll on a person. And when it's a person who was already hell-bent before, it's not a good thing."

"I appreciate the warning," I said, looking up at the sky.

It was a very clear night and you could see a handful of stars above us, shining through the cold.

"You appreciate the warning but you're not going to listen to it," he said finally, reaching for my right hand in his pocket.

"Did you hate it in Iraq? What was it like?" I asked, ignoring Greg's declaration.

"It was humbling and terrifying and empowering. Basically, take any emotion you've had and think of the extreme version. It was all those things, but every day, hour after hour." He held my hand a little tighter and I didn't pull away.

"How long were you there?"

"Seven months."

"Did you see a lot of people die?"

Greg looked at me like I was a five-year-old kid asking him why dogs couldn't talk.

"I know these questions sound ridiculous," I said, "but I'm genuinely interested and you're the first person in the military I felt like I could ask. My father is an architect. He never served. I don't have a brother. I have you."

"What about Ford? Why don't you ask him?"

"I don't know. You know him, he's not exactly approachable. He told me about his translator dying. The one he had on all four tours. But he said it so flatly, I just couldn't pry after that."

"Well, Ford's seen plenty of people die. A lot more than me." Greg tipped his chin and kissed the top of my head. A few seconds later he said, "Okay, Carolyn Everett. Do your thing. But just know I'm going to be watching out for you. Ford's just a person. I mean, everyone makes him out to be a bigger deal than everyone else, but you'll see. Then maybe you'll go out with me."

"I'd like that," I said, leaning my head against his chest. He kissed my hair again and didn't move his lips until I pulled away. I gave him back his coat and he whistled toward Mason.

"Hands off, Mason, we're going."

"Nah, man, she wants me to stay," Mason said between kisses.

"She doesn't," I said, walking over and pulling Brittan off the car and toward the door. I thanked them both for driving us home.

We fell into the Dalbys' entry and ran toward the living room laughing. As soon as we hit one of the couches and kicked off our boots a light switched on over the stairs and we stopped laughing, stared at each other, and laughed again.

"Could you two maybe shut up a little," said Carter, walking down the stairs. He was in a Yale T-shirt and flannel pajama pants. He sat down next to us and poured himself a scotch. "Where have you two been anyway? You seem nice and hammered."

"Oh, we are," said Brittan, reaching for the crystal scotch decanter near the couch. "And we're going to keep on drinking. Want some hooch?"

We both looked at each other, screamed, "Hooch!" and fell down laughing again.

Carter took back the decanter and refilled his glass. He handed his glass to me; I took a sip and gave it back. My face was totally numb from the alcohol and standing in the cold for twenty minutes. I looked at the Pissarro over Carter's head and it looked like it was drawn in crayon.

"Oh, what the hell. Cheers," he said, finishing the drink.

"So, where were you?" he asked, reaching for a remote control and turning up the heat in the living room.

"We were at . . ." We both looked at each other and screamed, "The Blue Hen!" through fits of laughter.

"You two are crazy," he said in his easy baritone. The man sounded like boarding school. "I mean, is there anyone in there besides sailors trying to get laid?"

"Yes," I said, standing up at attention. "There are marines trying to get laid!"

I fell back down and Brittan and I were bent over on the couch again, laughing until we couldn't breathe.

"Right," said Carter, finally laughing, too. "How did you get home? You should have called me."

"The sailors trying to get laid drove us," Brittan announced. "I should have slept with that one. He was in love with me. He asked me to marry him, Carter. A forever marriage. With swords!"

"Everyone asks you to marry them," said Carter. "Don't marry anyone. Not tonight," he said, winking at me. "I'm going to bed. You two going to sleep down here?" he asked. Brittan's eyes were already starting to close. He walked back upstairs to sleep next to Jane in what was, for many years, her parents' bedroom.

"I love you, Carolyn. I'm sorry you're unemployed," said Brittan, reaching for the blanket I had just brought her. "Poor tragic Carolyn. So smart yet working at the fish market."

I didn't correct her.

"It's okay," I said, wrapping the bottom of the blanket around her feet. "I had a lot of fun tonight. I haven't had this much fun since . . ." I stopped to think about it and by the time I had an answer, Brittan had passed out. She could have guessed the answer. I hadn't had that much fun since I was in college with Brittan and Jane. When all three of us had been there together and I hadn't cared about getting to work the next day. When I had no idea what my adult life would be like and the only pressure I had was getting good grades and getting boys to like me. Everything from that night, our laughter, the drive home, and drinking with Carter in the Dalbys' million-dollar living room, already felt like it had happened weeks ago, a mood we would never be able to create again.

## CHAPTER 9

As soon as I left the Dalbys' the next morning and walked up my creaky apartment stairs, I switched on my computer and found the number for the University of Hartford. What was bothering me about the Hannah story from last night was not what probably bothered most people, that Tyler had broken her nose with his fist, but what Mason had said: she had been an art teacher at St. George's. The only person Tyler had ever been serious about was an art lover. And now he'd found me. It could have been a coincidence, but in the light of day, it didn't feel like one.

I was connected to the main number at the University of Hartford and then connected again to the Hartford Art School.

"It's the weekend," said the operator, who sounded like a student. "You might just get voicemail." I assured her that that was okay and waited for the Art School's machine to prompt me for different extensions. Illustration, media arts, painting, drawing, printmaking, sculpture, digital art, and ceramics. Trying to figure out what I was listening for, I let the prerecorded message play the options again as I stood there, unable to make a move. When it played for a third time, I pushed eight for the last choice: ceramics.

The machine prompted me to choose from three different extensions; two were for associate professors and the third was for the ceramics technician, Hannah Lloyd. As soon as I heard her say her name after the verbal prompt had informed me of the extension, I hung up. I let the phone slip out of my hand and fall on the carpeted floor. Hannah was Hannah Lloyd, a potter and a good enough one to work at a major university.

I walked over to the bookshelf and took the bowl down and held it in my hand. Blair Bari didn't think it was worth anything, but could it have been glazed over? Repainted? I went to my desk and took out a medical magnifying headset that I had used when I was in appraisals at Christie's. The bowl was so smooth. There were no visible cracks, no chips; it was in near-perfect condition. I turned it around again and looked at the bottom, at the extremely faint small Hebrew letters. First and the last, that's what Blair Bari had said.

I grabbed my computer from the floor, opened it again, and quickly typed in the school's name and Hannah Lloyd. She came up under the art school's faculty page but, unlike the two professors, there was no picture and no bio. When I googled her, her name was too generic to show any decent results. But she had worked at St. George's. I could go there and ask other teachers about her, though that might get back to her. It felt safer to go to Hartford. To fake some sort of inquiry. I lay down on my bed holding the bowl and almost dropped it when my phone rang. I looked at the caller ID, which was blocked. My finger hesitated over the accept button and I pushed it on the fifth ring. But it wasn't Hannah.

"Carolyn, this is Nina Caine," said the voice I had come to associate with everything bad in the world.

"Nina?" I said slowly. Did she really have the gall to call me from a blocked number? Trick me into answering the phone?

"Don't get mad," she said immediately. "I heard you left New York and I just wanted to check on you, make sure you were doing okay."

"How did you know I left New York?" I asked suspiciously.

"Louise DeWitt told me. I spoke to her a few days ago and pressed her for information about you."

"I'm surprised she gave you any. She certainly hasn't contacted me."

Nina cleared her throat nervously. "Listen, I know that somehow with all that went on, you were a casualty. And I just want you to know I didn't mean for that to happen. I've known enough unemployed people in my life to never want to be the cause of someone's—"

"Firing? Demise? Undoing?" I chimed in. I kicked off my shoes and sat on the bed with my feet under me.

"I would never want to hurt anyone," Nina said, interrupting me. "I think that somehow, you got beat up in all of this."

"Well, we all know how the somehow happened," I said, throwing blame back in her face. "I'm okay now," I added flatly. "I left New York. I'm in Newport for a while."

"I'm glad you're getting some time to . . ." She thought better of it and changed her phrase. "Did you go home to see your family?" she asked.

"No, my family is not exactly that type. I went home because I am currently unemployable in my field in New York and I needed a break and some money. People know me here; they gave me a job."

"Well, home is always a good idea."

Neither of us spoke for a few seconds, and Nina finally said, "I'll just keep checking in on you then, if you don't mind."

"I don't mind," I replied, lying. But what could I say? "Yes, bitch, I mind; lose my number and go play in the river"? I was too well trained to say anything like that.

"You probably want me to hang up now, but I have some information about the table. Would you like me to tell you?"

No, I would like you to dangle it out in front of me like I'm a burro hopelessly chasing after a bendy carrot.

"That would be fine," I replied politely.

"Well, it's back with us in Baltimore. I'm looking at it actually. After the news came out about it in the *Sun*, Elizabeth, via Christie's, agreed to have it returned to us in Baltimore, no questions asked. I never even spoke to her about it and it didn't take more than ten days for us to get it. Isn't that fast? Ten days. It was driven here on a truck from New York and now it's in my living room, with nothing but a few hats on it."

Ten days wasn't just fast, it was suspiciously fast.

"Well, that seems appropriate," I replied.

"Yes it does. Anyway, I enjoy looking at it. Oh, and in two weeks I'm meeting with Elizabeth's lawyer in Washington, D.C., to sign some papers for Christie's."

"You let me know how it goes?" I asked.

"I'll call you after Washington," she said. "Also, and maybe I should have said this first, I spoke to the family that gave my grandmother the table in the first place. I mean to the surviving daughter. Her name is Rachel. She said to me, 'I don't remember very much about your grandmother, except that I loved her.'"

"Well, it's certainly all become very interesting," I replied.

"For me, too. It's strange that that table mattered to me so much. I don't know why I latched on to it like I did."

"Because it represented a time when you were really happy."

"Yes, probably."

"Your table, what happened, it's surprising, but you should know that Christie's, Sotheby's, and other major auction houses sometimes sell stolen goods," I told her. "That's a fact. We're not talking Van Gogh's *Poppy Flowers* stolen, something plucked from the wall of a well-known museum, but stolen all the same. It happens more often than you'd think, though it's often works from abroad. Stolen art makes an amazing amount of cash. In the world of criminal activities, looking at how much it grosses, looted art and artifacts are right behind drugs and arms sales. In Italy, about thirty thousand art thefts happen every year. In China, stolen art is believed to be their biggest illegal export. And sometimes those works end up on the auction block. Just last year, a painting by Renoir, *Madame Valtat*, was sold by Sotheby's for one-point-six million, though it was stolen from a collector in Japan in 2000. And it's not just Sotheby's. Christie's has done the same, many times over. Roman heads, Chinese relics. And there have been attempts to sell that were barely thwarted, like the sale of Russian army documents or several Nepalese paintings last year. Auction houses are meant to scrutinize provenance, but sometimes they knowingly sell fakes. They may be somewhat aware of the dubious provenance of a piece, but if there is no phone call, no documentation or anyone to stop them, then the sale goes through anyway."

"Really?" asked Nina. "Why?"

"Because it's money. And at the end of the day, it's a business all about money for people who love to spend it." I was supposed to be thinking about Elizabeth when I said that, but all I could think of now was Tyler.

I cleared my throat and looked at my lifeless apartment. "If you hadn't called, nothing would have happened. The sale would have gone through, and the buyer wouldn't have purchased a counterfeit, so what would Elizabeth have cared." I sat up a little and thought again about how it only took ten days for Elizabeth to return the table.

"I tell you this, and I'm pretty sure I'm right. Elizabeth knew what she was doing. That's why she requested that I come, not Louise. She said it was because she was friends with my grandmother, but now I doubt she even knew my grandmother. She was able to say all this stuff to me, make up a strong connection, because I don't know that much about my grandmother's life when she was in Baltimore. Why would I have questioned her for picking me? I was just thrilled to get the estate, and she knew I would be. I'm now sure that she would have sold us the estate even if I gave her a terrible deal, because she needed a hook to keep the top person away. So she found me. I was young, but had this big job. Elizabeth knew exactly how her husband got that table, and that's why she gave it back to you so fast. No fight, nothing."

"I think she knew, too," said Nina. "You can't be married to a man like that and have no idea of his affairs. Carolyn, I'm going to keep checking in on you," she said, more decisively this time.

"You don't have to check in on me, Nina," I said. I was not about to form a lasting friendship with the woman who had gotten me fired.

"I'll be in touch," she said, ignoring my last phrase.

As soon as I hung up, I dialed Tyler's number. He hadn't called me in two days. Maybe he was trying to lose me, but I was too invested to let that happen.

"It's you," he said when he answered. "I'm glad it's you." He sounded tired, like I had just woken him up.

"I got your note," I said. I reached for it on my night-stand and held it between my fingers as I said it.

"Well, good. I'm glad the old note trick still works. What are you doing today?" he asked. I rolled over on the bed, thrilled I didn't have to ask that question.

"I don't know, I was thinking about going to the Break-ers. I haven't been there since I've been back and I love it in winter."

"I've never been there."

"You've never been to the Breakers? How long have you lived here?"

"Four years. I've seen it a thousand times from the out-side. How can you miss it, it's the size of the sun."

"True, but you've never actually been inside?"

"I don't care about all that stuff. Mansions and rich people's lives—the Newport appeal. You can see those houses from the outside, and they look nice, I guess, but I don't know. Doesn't seem like the most inviting place in the world. And everyone who lived there is dead. It's strange, like visiting a huge mausoleum."

But I was beginning to think that Tyler Ford did care about the Newport appeal. Something about this place was keeping him here.

"But you're not going to visit Cornelius Vanderbilt," I implored. "It's a museum now. Anyone can go inside for twenty dollars."

"I can think of a lot of other things I would rather spend twenty dollars on. Like you. I would much rather spend twenty dollars on drinks for you. Or food. Or whatever you wanted."

"But what if what I wanted was to go to the Breakers with you?"

"Then I would spend twenty dollars on that."

We ended up at the Breakers on the first nonfreezing day of the year.

"It's forty-five degrees and it feels like spring," I said as we walked through the door.

"Yeah, I know. It's nine degrees back in Wyoming. My grandmother called to tell me. She likes to keep me real up-to-date on the weather."

"I like grandmothers. I don't have any left, but I like them."

"Do you? Well, you'd like mine. She worked in our church for forty-five years as the organist. She's not very good, but no one ever had the heart to let her know."

"At this point she probably doesn't need to know."

"Definitely not. I tell her plenty of other things, though. I write to her every week. Old habit from when I was deployed. If I don't, she worries."

I looked up at him and smiled. Tyler had written me a note, but I wouldn't have guessed he did something that sentimental every week. I loved it.

It was when we were walking up the stairs to the second floor of the Breakers, past the massive tapestry and below the stained-glass skylight by John La Farge, that Tyler said, "You were getting pretty close with Greg LaPorte last night." He didn't say it angrily; he said it almost in passing.

I walked ahead of Tyler on the stairs so he couldn't see my face when I responded. "I was with him at the Blue Hen. With a lot of friends. I wasn't getting close to him, not like that."

"Really?" he said. "I thought differently."

"Well then, you thought wrong," I said, hitting pause on our audio tour and turning toward the bedrooms. Who had told Tyler that I was out with Greg?

"I walked in there last night. I wanted to see you, but when I spotted you at the bar you looked . . . occupied," he said, turning into Gertrude Vanderbilt's light-filled bedroom. He still didn't sound mad. More like someone just making observations about a stranger.

"I wish I had known you were there," I said, for the first time not distracted by the beauty of the room. Growing up, Jane and I used to tear through the bedroom like it was our own.

"Did they tell you about Hannah?"

I paused to look out the window, toward the water. Hannah. Why was he bringing up Hannah? I thought about my early morning phone call. I hadn't even left a voicemail and I had been connected twice to her extension via an operator and prompts; there was no way she saw my number. "They mentioned her. They said she doesn't talk to you anymore," I replied. I felt the nerves in my voice.

"They said that." He walked away from the etching near the fireplace of Gertrude as a young woman so he would be next to me. "That's right. She doesn't. But it's probably for the best. She was a nice girl; she doesn't need to be hanging around me."

"Then why am I hanging around you?" I asked.

Tyler looked around the room, at the bed, the desk, and the view from Gertrude's windows and said, "One day I'd like to tell you my version of the story. It's probably a little bit closer to the truth."

And that was all Tyler said about Hannah and my night at the Blue Hen. He went right back to acting like himself, the stoic, very sexy man I was happy to be spending the day with.

"It's not that bad here after all," he said when we left the house. "It's all a little chickish downstairs, and walls made of platinum seems like a waste of cash, but it's not bad. Are you sure a dude designed this place?"

"Yeah. A famous dude," I said.

"Let's walk outside," he said, taking my hand again and leading me toward the garden. It was at that moment, with the confidence that he moved around the corners of the house, that I was sure Tyler had been to the Breakers before. Maybe several times. Probably with Hannah. But my suspicion, my certainty that he was now lying to me, didn't keep me from feeling drawn to him when he took my hand.

It was in the high forties by then and the sun was shining brightly on the dark water in front of us. We looked out at the beautiful blue line between ocean and sky.

"I absolutely love this place," I said, turning around to look at the house. "It's my favorite place in Newport. After the Dalbys' house."

Tyler didn't mention Brittan's role in his scheme last night, or how he knew who she was. He put his hands on my waist, then moved them up to my face and kissed me. Tyler wasn't a lips-barely-grazing kisser, he kissed you long and hard. "Follow me," he said, leading me to the end of the garden. A few people were on the Cliff Walk, and I tried to ignore them as he pulled me toward him.

"I need you," he said, pressing his body against mine.

I didn't reply and kissed him back.

"I'm sure hanging around with Greg and Mason you've heard plenty of stories about me. Some of them are probably true. But don't listen to what people tell you about Hannah. Or about me after Hannah. The thing is, and this is the truth, after Hannah, during Hannah, I never saw, barely spoke to, another girl until I met you. I'm sure you'll hear otherwise, but it's true. There was something about her. She really changed me. And I haven't looked at anyone since then."

"When did you and Hannah . . ." What was I supposed to say? When did Hannah leave you because you broke her face?

"July."

"And now it's March."

"That's right. Now it's March and I found you and I hope you don't end up being one of those girls who believe a bunch of crap circulated by guys who love talking about sex."

"Don't you love talking about sex?"

"No, I love having sex."

Before I could hit his shoulder, he kissed me again and led me across the Vanderbilts' backyard toward the bushes on the side of the house. He unbuttoned my coat and slid his hands under my sweater, onto my back. He moved them toward the waistband of my skirt all the way around, slowly. When he moved them down my skirt, I took a step back.

"I can't, Tyler. This place has cameras everywhere. I don't want to get arrested for public sex."

"That sounds fun," he said, pulling me back toward him.

"No, stop. It's the Breakers and we're outside."

He put his hands back inside my coat.

"There are many places in Newport where I'd love to take your clothes off. Not just this one. How about I take you somewhere where I definitely can't try anything."

"I can't possibly think where that would be."

"Good, let's go."

It only took us ten minutes to drive from the Breakers to the naval base, but I didn't think we were going in until Tyler showed his ID, and mine, to the guard at the gate.

"Base? No, we can't go here. I'm . . . I won't know what to do."

"We went to your sacred spot, right? How about we go

to my stomping grounds now. I wouldn't say it's exactly churchlike to me, but I've spent a lot of time here in the last couple of years."

"Fair enough."

"You're here with Tyler?" the security guard asked me. "You sure about that?"

"Yeah, I'm sure," I said, not feeling so sure.

"Because I would be happy to show you around myself. You don't have to endanger yourself with this guy."

"Thanks, but I'll be okay," I said, taking back my ID.

"Welcome aboard, then," said the guard.

"He's just joking," Tyler said, catching a glimpse of my tense face as we drove through the gate.

"Is he?"

"Of course he is. You really think he'd let me take you around on base if I was some cold-blooded killer of cute women from Rhode Island? The military has standards, you know. High standards. And I happen to far surpass every one of them."

I shivered, thinking about the way my body felt when his hands were on me at the Breakers.

For the first time since I had started seeing Tyler I was truly nervous. Maybe it was because of Hannah, or what Blair Bari had said, but I was panicking. I had the kind of nerves that I was so used to feeling at Christie's when something big was about to happen. But every time I had felt nervous at work, when sweat had rained down my body and my face had been covered in hives, something good had happened. The one auction when I had not had that reaction, the January auction, was my denouement. Maybe nerves were a good sign.

"I've never been on a military base before," I disclosed. "I'm tense."

"Why?" he said, laughing. "It's the safest place you could possibly be. Did you notice how hard it was to drive in?"

He had a point.

"It's Saturday. Base is a little emptier today, but I just want to take you to one place. If you think the view from the Breakers is nice, you'll really like this one. And you can't just buy a ticket; you've got to know some people. On the right night, it can be all yours."

We parked and walked along the water toward an open grassy area with a bench and flagpoles heavy with American and POW/MIA flags.

"I'd love to kiss you but like I said, I can't do that here. So you're safe."

"I like you like this," I said, leaning my head against his chest. "Restrained. You don't seem so much like Tyler Ford."

"I wish I didn't know what you meant by that, but I do," he said, smiling.

The crack of the flags and the ropes hitting the metal pole near us picked up as the wind started to change directions.

I looked over his shoulder from where we were sitting and saw four military jeeps roll by, all of the men in them staring at Tyler.

"Are you sure I'm allowed to be here?" I asked.

"Trust me. I have that on lock." ·

I tried to let everything I'd learned in the past few days disappear for a while and relaxed into his shoulder.

"I've never been out with someone I didn't really know," I said honestly. "I don't know much about you, and what I've heard isn't the best. But you're not like that when you're with me. Not yet."

"I think people talk about me because I'm too quiet for

their liking. Silence scares people. You don't tell them your life story, they get scared."

"You don't want to tell anyone your life story?"

"Nope." He looked down at my curious face. I knew I looked nervous. Louise had said I needed to work on my poker face and she was right.

He kissed me on the forehead and we sat in silence for a while enjoying the day until I finally said, "How about you tell me just a few things."

Tyler didn't protest, but he waited a while to say, "The thing about me is, expectations of failure were pretty high growing up. Somehow, despite everyone willing me to fail, I had a sense of pride, and to this day I don't really know where it came from. I always wanted to be someone more than people expected me to be, so I could come home and they might say, 'Look at you. You turned out okay after all.' Because, trust me, no one expected me to turn out okay."

"Why not?"

"I didn't try in school, at all, and I got into trouble a lot. All I really cared about was shooting things, playing football, drinking, and girls. Not in that order. And no one really noticed what I did. My dad was drunk, if he was around. He didn't care what my grades were or if I did anything after high school. No one even told me to graduate."

"So why did you?"

"I don't know. I knew if I left school I would really screw myself and the one thing I didn't want was to be dirt poor anymore. I won't admit this to many people but I really grew up poor. Ugly poor. We used to eat our cereal in a bowl of milk and then when we were done, we'd put our bowls back in the fridge and reuse the leftover milk the next day."

He looked down at me listening and said, "You didn't have to do that, I'm guessing."

I didn't answer.

"Trust me, I knew there was something better out there than struggling when I was with my family, stealing beer when I wasn't, and sleeping with girls who would turn into their mothers in ten years."

"That kind of sounds like a lot of America, though."

"Yeah, but it's not for me. Not even back then."

"Are you glad you joined the military? I mean, do you ever regret it?"

"Not for a second. I wouldn't have done well in college, not that I would have gotten in anyway."

"I think you're a lot smarter than you like to acknowledge."

"I'm smarter now," he said, taking my cold hands in his. His palms felt more calloused than usual. "But I left Wheatland eleven years ago."

"And you're never going back."

"That's for damn sure. I am never, ever going back."

"Show me a picture of you when you lived in Wheatland," I asked, turning my face toward his. I was hoping the wind was giving me a pretty blush, not making me look red and cold.

"Nah, you wouldn't have liked me then."

"But I like you now," I admitted.

"Good. Then just like me now."

He grabbed my face and I flinched a little from the surprise.

"Don't worry," he whispered as he kissed me until his afternoon stubble started to make my upper lip raw. "You don't need to be so scared of me."

Maybe I did need to be a little scared of him.

I didn't care that the wind was starting to rip through my clothes. Tyler was right: if you didn't look behind you, this spot was even prettier than the view from the Breakers.

"I had two older sisters," said Tyler, looking down at my face to see if I still wanted to listen. "One died when she was very young. Her name was Katie. I barely remember her. She was seven when a car right outside our house hit her, but I was only five. She had very straight hair, like you," he said, touching the end of my braid. "But dark. Your hair is so light. It almost has no color at all."

"Yeah, I don't look like my parents. They look more like you."

"Really? Your parents live here?"

"I thought this was you telling your life story."

"You could meet me halfway, though."

I sat up, lifted my head from his shoulder, and bent my neck a few times, to get the stiffness out.

"My parents don't live here," I said. "They live in Boston, which is fine by me. I really loved my grandmother more. She was more of a parent to me than either of my parents were, or are. But she died when I was thirteen. She lived with us until then and she taught me every good lesson I learned in life. She wanted me to be nothing like my parents and everything like her, which I guess in a way I am. I even look like her. My parents . . . it's not that they're bad people, they're just bad parents. And they don't really like people, besides each other. They prefer ideas. I was a mistake. But they're Catholic so there I came."

"They said you were a mistake?" asked Tyler, his voice rising slightly in protective surprise.

"No, of course not. But it's always been pretty obvious. My mom hadn't even graduated from college when she had me. That was not the plan. I don't know what the plan was, but that was not it. My father didn't marry who he was supposed to. My grandmother got back at him by living with him for thirteen years and then dying and not leaving him much of anything. Actually, she left me just a hair more than she left him, but that was so I could go to the right, very expensive schools. My father thought my grandmother would give him what remained, but instead she gave it to charity."

"Really? She just gave away all her money?"

"Really."

"Ever get mad about it?"

"No. Perplexed sometimes, but mad, no. It wasn't my money." That wasn't the whole version of the truth. It was a shred. Sometimes I got very mad. But I had enough self-discipline to never admit it.

"Do your parents know you're here and not in New York?"

"I haven't talked to my mother in a while, but my dad called the other day to tell me that I'm doing everything wrong. They think I'm crazy to be here and even nuttier to be working in an antique store for eight dollars an hour. They call it my 'latent rebellious phase.' I guess this is the closest I've ever come to anything like that. They're actually terrified that I'll just stay here and let this become my life instead of going back to New York to get my old life back. Or something even better. Not that I can think of much better; I had my dream job in New York. I really loved it."

Tyler looked down at me fidgeting on his shoulder. Just the thought of that job, of what I had, and I couldn't sit still.

"I'm sorry. I probably look pathetic. I'm still sad about the mistakes I made."

And with that, I told him everything. I told him about Christie's and Adam Tumlinson's collection and Elizabeth and Nina and the entire reason I ended up right back in the small town where I grew up.

From finding me at the store and from what I had told

him over the last few days, Tyler knew I worked in art and antiques, but saying the name Christie's, explaining I was there for ten years, implied a lot more expertise. If there were details he wasn't telling me about the green and white bowl, he might hesitate even more now. But I kept talking. It was one of those split-second decisions that your gut controls. Where you lock eyes with someone and your head and your heart race to dictate which way you'll go. As I looked up at Tyler, rested my weight against his body, felt his arms move around me, I knew my heart had won.

I recounted my last day at the auction house in January, how ashamed I had felt walking through Rockefeller Center that night, my persistent rage toward Elizabeth.

"I hate that woman, Tyler," I said, repeating her name. "I've never hated anyone before, but I hate her." He shifted his weight a few times and finally he stopped fidgeting and stood up to watch me as I told him the story.

He didn't kiss me, or comfort me, or chide me; he just looked down at me on the bench and said, "So Elizabeth Tumlinson is a bitch. You should try to let it go. Hate is a waste of time. Trust me."

Instead of answering, I just said, "Okay. I'm done. Your turn. Tell me something else." Tell me about Hannah. Tell me about the bowl.

"I've got a Silver Star," he said, with his sexiest grin plastered on for good measure. "I'm a bit of a hero."

"Oh yeah? Well, why did you go to Iraq so many times, hero?"

"I've thought about that a lot and I still don't have a good one-line answer. I should work on that. Maybe you can write me one."

"Try."

"Try . . ."

I sat there silently, slowly losing feeling in my fingers. I knew he wasn't going to bring up Hannah again.

"I guess a big part of me felt like I should. I was young and able-bodied and all that and I wanted to serve my country. One tour didn't do it, so I did four."

"What was the worst part about it?"

"The worst part about it? Definitely the lack of hot chicks."

"I'm sorry, did you say something?"

"Fine. Let's see, the worst part about it. Well, almost every moment, you're afraid you're going to die, but you're also afraid you'll never live that much again. When I joined the military, I first went to Quantico in Virginia and that was the farthest I had ever been from home, by a lot. I had never seen anything; I didn't know anything. I was from the smallest town you'd ever seen and it was whiter than a blizzard. I thought yarmulkes were what bald men wore to protect their heads from the sun. I thought the Freedom Riders were the Freedom Writers. You know, some black kids who sat around and wrote in their diaries about freedom. I had never met anyone Muslim. I don't think I had ever met anyone Jewish. A few Native Americans, a few black people. But very few. And then I left Virginia and went to Iraq and suddenly you're out there and you're next to everyone from everywhere and you've got a shit ton of guns strapped to you and you're totally sure you're doing the right thing because fighting for your country is the right thing to do. But then you remember what a dick you were like five minutes ago and since when did you sign up to become some hero."

"But you are some hero. They gave you a Silver Star. My guess is you didn't get it because you were crying under a rock."

Tyler shrugged, readjusted his arms, and let his cold left hand linger right above my heart.

"I got it for 'conspicuous gallantry and intrepidity in action against the enemy.' That's the official jargon anyway. There was a ceremony and all that back at Quantico. There was an American flag on a brass pole to my right and my commander talked about why he nominated me. He talked about me pulling guys out of harm's way. How I extracted five seriously wounded and mortally wounded marines from the wreckage with little regard for my own severe injuries or personal safety after an IED exploded and we came under heavy enemy fire from concealed positions. And when he was talking about it, all I could think about was how hot it had been that day. It felt like an afternoon where you could just drop dead even if someone didn't try to blow you up."

Tyler waited for me to interrupt him, and when I didn't, he paused for a few seconds and I imagined he was replaying the day in his head.

"Before they pin it on you, they publish your orders. Someone reads them aloud and says that the president of the United States awarded you your medal. 'Chief Warrant Officer Two Tyler Ford provided initial medical care to treat his teammates' multiple wounds. After the IED went off, Chief Warrant Officer Ford was targeted by snipers that killed four in his platoon. Chief Warrant Officer Ford's exemplary leadership and devotion to duty reflect great credit on the United States Marine Corps.' I remember it all, even the way my arm felt when I saluted, but at the time it didn't feel like I was there. I was just floating above it all, watching a stranger get a medal. It wasn't until I felt my commander's hand on my chest, pinning the medal on my uniform, that I dipped into the present for a few seconds."

"And how did it feel?"

Tyler looked down at me and let his lips rest on my forehead without kissing it.

"It felt okay."

"Just okay."

"I wish it meant more to me than it does. It sounds good, but I was so scared shitless during that whole ordeal in Iraq that I never felt like much of a hero. If I had done it and had been able to do it without worrying so much about my own ass, then I'd be prouder of it."

"But that's innate human behavior. You're supposed to be worried about dying."

"I was. I was always scared I was going to die during my first and second tours. By my third tour, death became less terrifying because I started seeing it more. I'd never seen a dead body and then all of a sudden I'm seeing dead kids. I'm seeing my friends die. It almost becomes familiar, and then you get less afraid of it. You matter less to yourself than before. Because why are you special? Why should they die and not you?"

"So you kept going back because you weren't afraid of war anymore?"

"Oh no, I was afraid of war. War is scary as shit. People act . . . sometimes you just look at them and you can't believe they're human, just like you. Same blood, skin, heart, insides. And sometimes you worry you're going to act like that, too. And sometimes you do."

Tyler took his arm back, away from my neck, and shrugged a few times to get some feeling back.

"Another reason I kept going is because I came back to Quantico and I was bored out of my skull. My second tour was the hardest and when I went back to Virginia I was pushing papers around my desk and doing crap work and dating girls who thought that gaining ten pounds was the worst thing that could ever happen to them. Everything seemed small. I'd gotten used to a bigger picture. Like did I give a shit if my fucking eggs were cage-free or not? Or why some chick I took to dinner had a gluten allergy? What is gluten? What the fuck is a gluten allergy? Why didn't anyone have one when I was growing up? It was like trying to fight with a nail clipper when you're used to a really big gun. So I went back."

"You curse so much, I think your sentences are twice as long because of it."

"Yeah, well, all those other words just get in the way of a good curse word."

Tyler winked at me. He knew I didn't care how he spoke. I just liked sitting there in his arms, liked hearing about his life, details I hoped he'd never told anyone before, even Hannah.

"But you've been in Newport since 2010."

"Like I said, the war ended. I didn't want to go back to Virginia, or go home, and then I had a chance to come here."

"And now your life feels small? Inconsequential?"

"Sometimes. But at least I'm living a small life right on the water. And you're helping. You are not a petty person."

"That's a compliment."

"It's supposed to be. You're intense. You're passionate. You're selfish and you're driven and I haven't met many girls like that. A few in the military. But they didn't look like you."

"I bet they would if they got to ditch the camo and slap on some mascara."

"Nah. Even normal people don't look like you."

"Thanks, Tyler. It's too bad you're so ugly. It must really be a hindrance for you."

"I get that a lot," he said, smiling. He looked down at me and put his hands in my coat. "Are you hungry? You must be. It's almost three and we haven't eaten."

"I am, actually. But where do you eat here? Do you have to hunt your own food?"

"That would be awesome, but no. There are some places to eat. But actually, you've probably had enough of all this. Why don't we go off base."

"Do you live here?" I asked after we walked to his car and he drove his 4Runner out the gates.

"No," he said. "I live off base in a town house. It's a lot like the Breakers. But bigger. More platinum on the walls. More servants."

I did not laugh.

On our way toward town after we grabbed food, Jane texted me and said that they were having surf and turf and that I had to come over for dinner. I texted her back that I was with Tyler, to which she answered, "Now you have to come. And so does he. See you at seven. I'm turning my phone off now so you can't say no."

"What are you doing tonight?" I asked as he turned the corner away from the water.

"What are *you* doing tonight?" he asked, looking over at me and putting his hand on mine.

"My best friend Jane just invited me over for dinner. Her husband will be there, too. He's a really larger-than-life kind of guy. You'll like him, I promise."

"Larger than life. Is that a compliment or a dig?"

"A little of both. You'll see. If you like big lives on a big stage, you'll like him. Trust me, Carter married Jane because that's exactly what he wanted."

The four times I had seen Tyler, I had managed to keep

some of my clothes on, but I knew that that was going to end soon. Tyler pulled into his neighborhood, so he could change before dinner. He lived in a complex of similar-looking white town houses near base.

"A lot of guys live here with their families," he explained as we walked up the drive. "I'm one of the only single officers here. It's a sad and lonely existence," he said, letting me in.

"I absolutely don't believe you. I bet you've had women propose to you."

"Only when intoxicated."

He grinned at me, showing off his lines of perfect white teeth. He caught me looking and held his smile for a beat longer.

"I'm twenty-nine, you know," he said, his face turning serious. "I can't keep living like this forever. I need a good girl to come save me one day."

"I'm twenty-nine, too," I said, refusing to look at him.

"Are you? You look younger. But come to think of it, you act much older."

"Well, thanks, I suppose," I said, walking inside. Alex used to say that about me and I hated it, but it felt important when Tyler said it. He'd been to Iraq, to war, four times; he seemed to need an old soul.

Tyler's apartment was very clean and he had the requisite leather sectional and huge TV and one picture framed on a bookshelf. It was of a young girl, which I guessed was his sister Katie. He caught me looking at it and said, "Don't worry, that's not my kid or anything. That's Katie."

"I know."

"I have lied about it before," he admitted. "But just to the girls who won't leave."

"You know, the way you talk about women is pretty disgusting."

"Is it?"

"Yes, it is."

I let my eyes scan his apartment again. I knew there wasn't going to be a picture of Hannah, but I looked anyway. I tried to make out the titles of a few books on his shelf. Most seemed professional. There were a few typical Dan Browns and Lee Childs and there was a King James Bible. I immediately thought about Blair Bari reciting the passage from the King James Bible and asking if the marine who owned the bowl had been religious.

"Are you religious?" I asked, trying my best to sound breezy.

Tyler followed my line of sight and saw the Bible.

"I'm not particularly. I'm probably your standard amount of religious. But my mother asked me to take a Bible with me to Iraq so I took a Bible. If you're going to war and your mama asks you to do something, you do it."

"Did you take that Bible?" I asked.

"That exact one."

I stood up and walked to the shelf and picked it up. It was not a Bible that had never been opened. It looked well read. I flipped to the back section and saw the Book of Revelation. Before I could flip farther, Tyler walked past me and I put it back on the shelf.

"Well, it must have been good luck," I said, running my hand down the binding. "You came back in one piece. Four times."

"Yes," he replied. "I'm thankful God made guns and armor."

Tyler walked toward the bedroom, took his shirt off, smiled at me, and turned around. I tried not to look. I really tried. But there were so many tan muscles screaming at me that it was impossible. Who had a tan in Rhode Island in March? And what man in my world ever had muscles like that? The men I knew had bank accounts with muscle. Jobs with muscle. But they didn't actually have muscles. Tyler was packed full of them. I couldn't take my eyes off his back. Then his arms, his chest. Was it fair of God to give him that many? Shouldn't he have passed around the wealth for other sex-starved, underemployed women to enjoy?

He opened his closet, thought better, and walked over to me, taking my coat off, then my sweater, and pulled me onto his bed.

"Take your shirt off. Let me look at you."

I was suddenly very aware of how thin I was. How pale I was in winter. Of how small my breasts were.

I lifted my silk shirt over my head and he looked at me, with an expression I hadn't seen before.

"You are perfect," he said before grabbing me, holding me against him, taking off my bra, and moving his mouth all over me.

I reached for his belt, and undid it as he groaned in my ear. When his pants were off, I saw that he had another tattoo on the back of his calf. He had two on his right shoulder, one on his forearm, and another in the middle of his shoulder blades. It was the first time we had taken off our clothes in the daylight together. I ran my hand over his shoulder, almost expecting it to feel different.

"Your body . . ."

Instead of answering, he transferred his weight on top of me and put his hand back where it had been that afternoon in the Breakers' garden. This time I didn't stop him. I didn't care about Hannah. I didn't care about everything Tyler was not telling me. Every single inch of my skin, of my insides, wanted him.

He moved his hand to the back of my head and pulled me in hard, grabbing my hair as he kissed me and bit my lip. He put his mouth on my breasts and stayed there until I started to moan.

"Are you okay?" he whispered in my ear.

I nodded yes.

He held my face in his left hand while he pulled down my tights and my skirt and fingered the waistband of my underwear before reaching down for me and moving his fingers inside me. He kept going, his entire body, two hundred pounds moving on top of me until I felt like I was floating toward the ceiling, moaning and ripping the skin from his neck in tiny scrapes with my nails.

My breathing quickened to a point where I felt like I was sprinting.

"No, I . . . ," I said as he put his mouth on my neck. But as soon as he was against me, I didn't care. I had never wanted anyone more. So what if I had only been out with him four times and hadn't known him for fifteen years. Why was I the way I was? I didn't need to be some monogamous turtle that never had any fun. I could be the kind of girl who slept with beautiful, mysterious men, even if everyone we knew in common warned me not to.

"Turn around," said Tyler as I released my arms from around his neck. He took out my braid, ran his hands through my hair, and looked at my body. I didn't turn around and he moved back from me so that I saw his entire body. Every muscle in his chest, in his stomach, his arms looked taut, used. His chest was moving with the force of his breath and then he put his hand under my stomach and turned me over slowly. He moved his hands on my back, then up to my arms, moving my hands until they were holding his bed frame. He put his over mine and had me grip the wooden slats. I could feel him on my bottom half, holding his weight slightly off me. I turned my head to say something but he ran his hand over my mouth.

"Don't say anything. Not now. Let me look at you," he said. I felt his eyes on me. I wanted to pull the sheets over my body, to hide myself from the afternoon sunlight pouring in through his window, but I knew that if I moved my hands, he would move them back.

A few seconds later, I felt his mouth on my back, and then his entire naked body lying on me. He moved against me, spreading my legs. I was about to say yes but before I could, he stood up and pulled the sheet on top of me.

"Not yet," he said, pulling on his underwear. "I told you, I'm not that guy anymore." He went into the bathroom and let me pull on my clothes. I spent the rest of the afternoon lying against him. Letting him take off my clothes again, but he didn't say a word about sex. And when we headed to Jane's that night, he didn't mention anything about our afternoon.

Like everything in Newport, it didn't take long to drive from near base to the Dalbys' on Bellevue. On one of the widest streets in town, we drove past the homes that had long been left by the families, donated to the Newport Historical Society for public consumption. The Elms, Rosecliff—the houses that were once filled with summer and money were now packed with tourists consuming tiny corners of a lifestyle that had faded out of fashion years ago. But the Dalbys hadn't lost their grip on it. The iron gate out front extended into a pair of gold-tipped double doors, one for entering and one for exiting. I didn't point my little house out to Tyler, instead telling him to drive past the fountain and the lawn tennis court, all perfectly illuminated with the last rays of the evening sun.

My house, which was intended to be and was first used as a carriage house, became a guesthouse in the early 1900s, before becoming the Everett house in the eighties. It had not been kept as a guesthouse after my parents left and now served as storage space for the gardeners. It was Newport's most glamorous shed. I opened the door once when I came home with the Dalbys for spring break my freshman year and had seen several green lawn mowers sitting in what had been our living room. It was worse than if they had just torn the building down.

Tyler looked nervous. He didn't seem like a man who could get nervous, the kind of guy who could take a gun in his face and not flinch, but I was sure he was. Something about his posture and the way he was talking a little too fast. I was suddenly sorry I had invited him. I should have had Jane meet us at a restaurant, or not at all. I shouldn't have broken us out of our little quiet, intimate world that we'd created in the last week.

"I probably should have told you, it's a pretty big house."

"This isn't a house. It's a museum."

I said his name and he repeated it. "It's strange to hear that. Tyler. Everyone calls me Ford."

"Should I call you Ford?" I asked as he parked the car.

"No, you can call me Tyler. But only you."

When we got out of the car he came to my side to help me out and looked down at what he was wearing. "Maybe I should have worn something else," he said of his jeans and boots. His blue shirt was perfectly pressed and tucked in.

"Jane will be in jeans," I promised, and when Jane came to the door, she was barefoot and in black jeans. I smiled, satisfied, and introduced her to Tyler.

"Carter's in Boston," she said apologetically. "I'm so sorry. He's going to be here in an hour or so, but Daddy needed him to do something in the Boston office, so he drove up. I hope you don't mind, Tyler. I promise you'll have male company soon."

"I think most men would commit a few crimes to be in my place," he said politely. "I can't think of better company. Carolyn said you're her best friend."

"Oh, I'm more than that," said Jane, smiling. "Carolyn grew up just right over there." Jane pointed toward the yard. "She probably spent more time in this house than I did. But of course she's too cool to stay with me now." I looked around the Dalby living room. At the Manet over the fireplace and at the couch we sat down on, tufted and stuffed like a sausage. And then I looked at Tyler. He was perfectly clean-shaven. He had the kind of face I imagined you had to shave three times a day to get it to feel like that. I bet if he wasn't in the Marines he would barely shave at all.

Jane did most of the talking as we waited for Carter, drinking wine and eating meats and cheeses that someone had put together on a marble platter earlier that afternoon. The Dalbys brought in a cook from New York every summer, as Florentine needed help handling the large number of people the family entertained in the warmer months, but now Jane had her here all year round.

It was just past nine when Carter walked into the house, delightfully yelling, "Honey, I'm home!" as he came through the door.

"We're in here, Carter!" Jane yelled back, making a face at both of us. "He's a brute, but you'll like him. He's a likable brute," said Jane.

"That's true," I agreed.

Tyler and I stood up with Jane as Carter came in the room. He put his hand on my shoulder and gave his wife a kiss. He then looked at Tyler, paused, and walked over to him. Jane and I waited for him to extend his hand, but he stood far enough away from Tyler that he didn't have to.

"I know you," said Carter, looking directly at Tyler, who was at least two inches taller than him.

"No, you don't," said Jane playfully. "This is Tyler Ford. Carolyn's friend. I told you they were coming to dinner. Marilynn cooked all that—"

"No, I know this guy," he said, turning his head toward his wife and interrupting her. He looked back at Tyler and took a step toward him. "I know you from the Blue Hen. You're the guy who punched that girl. The pretty girl. I was there that night."

Jane looked from Carter to Tyler, confused. "You two know each other?"

"No, we don't know each other," said Tyler stoically.

"I guess we don't know each other. Right. No, you're right," said Carter haughtily. "But I saw you that night. When was it, last July?" He leaned down toward the food on the coffee table, cut off some pâté, and put it in his mouth. Then he sat on the couch, crossed his ankle over his leg, and said, "I saw you punch that girl in the face. But you weren't going for her. She just got in the way, right? You were trying to hit someone else."

"That's right," said Tyler, not moving or raising his voice.

"Yeah. Well, that was my friend you were trying to kill."

That put it together for me. "Wait. Carter, why in hell were you at the Blue Hen?" I asked.

Jane looked at her husband suspiciously. Her Yalie husband who had chastised me and Brittan last week for putting a toe inside the unsanitary establishment.

"I was with Mike Fogg," Carter told Jane, putting his arms out on the back of the couch. His body language, his speech, everything about Carter at that moment was what I liked least about the very rich.

"Mike liked this girl who used to hang out there. I wing-manned for him that night and then this guy punched her in the face. He crushed her. Broke her nose. More. Didn't you break her jaw, too?" He looked up at Tyler, who was still standing in the middle of the room, unmoving.

"Mike Fogg was the guy who was hitting on Hannah?" I asked, starting to get upset. Mike Fogg just happened to be part of a hugely influential New England family. His uncle had even been mayor of Boston. They had two houses on Ocean Avenue, one that jutted out so far it looked like it owned the Rhode Island Sound.

"I certainly didn't know he was your friend at the time," said Tyler, walking toward the three of us. "Not that it would have made a difference. He should be in prison."

"Isn't it you who should be in prison?" said Carter. "Or did that nice girl decide not to press charges? Wonder what you had to do to make that happen. Play the war hero card? A little officer charming? She was pretty cute. Wouldn't be the worst way to get out of something."

"Are you kidding me, Carter!" Jane hissed angrily. She looked at me, concerned.

"Carter, you don't know anything about anything, so don't pretend you do. And please stop playing the pompous prep. It's appealing to nobody," I said angrily.

"I don't know anything?" said Carter, pointing at his chest. When he got going, Carter could really play the part. "Neither do you, Carolyn. Who the hell is this guy? I can tell you who. He's a military nobody who punched a girl in the face. A girl! You should have seen her. She was knocked out cold. Blood all over her face like in a boxing match. Pretty girl, too. Bet she never looked the same after that."

I stared at Tyler, panicked.

"I think you should go," said Jane, walking away from Carter, fuming. "I'm sorry," she said heading toward the door.

"No, it's my fault, Jane," said Tyler, turning to follow her. "I appreciate the hospitality. But your husband has his story wrong."

"So you didn't punch a girl in the face?" asked Jane, turning around.

"I did. Hannah Lloyd. She was my girlfriend at the time and I will never forgive myself for that. But that punch was meant for your friend. What's his name, Mike? Yeah, it was meant for him, and if he ever comes back here, I will beat his ass down. You can go ahead and tell him that."

"You're leaving with this guy, Carolyn?" said Carter, laughing. "Why don't you just stay right here."

"I'm sure he had a very good reason to try to hit Mike," I said quietly.

"Yeah, like he's some crazy military guy who had too much to fucking drink and likes to fight; that's a great reason. He's going to punch you in the face next. Stay in the house, Carolyn. Don't be a fucking groupie."

I looked at Tyler, desperate for him to explain what happened to Hannah, but all he said was, "Why don't you ask Mike? He knows well and good why I should destroy him and then do it again every day of his life. You just ask him."

He turned from me to Jane and said, "I'm sorry. I know how rude I'm being. I apologize."

He grabbed my hand and led me to his car. I waited until the door was closed to say, "You better tell me exactly what happened that night or I swear to God I will get out of this car right now and never talk to you again. Never. You embarrassed me! In front of my best friends."

"I know. I'm sorry," said Tyler, driving out of the gate and onto Bellevue so fast that his tires moaned on the turn.

"I don't live this way," I said, looking at the locked door.

He threw the gear into fourth and drove fifty-five around the turn. He drove expertly, away from Bellevue to Ocean Avenue past the new mansions, past the Foggs' two houses, and parked his car just past the beach club, by the national park. He rolled down his window and ran his hand against his short hair.

"I promised Hannah that I would never tell anyone what happened to her and I'm good on a promise, so I'm not going to say anything more about it. All I can say is, I would have killed that guy with my own hands for what happened to her and if anything like that happens to you, I will kill him."

My mind raced through scenarios but kept falling back on the same one.

"How well do you know that guy Mike?" asked Tyler, his hand gripping the steering wheel.

"I know him. He went to the same school as me," I said, thinking about the way Mike Fogg used to own St. George's when he was a senior there.

"I don't want you to ever be around him alone. Swear to me."

"I promise," I said, repeating it twice.

"Let's walk to the water. I can't breathe in here," said Tyler, opening the door and grabbing a blanket from the back. I heard him slam his door and scream and I didn't say anything. I wanted him to talk about Hannah. I needed to know everything. Who she was, where she was from, how long they were dating, how good she was at pottery, and how she was involved with the bowl that was tucked away in my house.

I looked out at the cold black water and shook my head. "I don't think so, Tyler. The rocks, they're so slippery and you're upset. We're upset. It's not the right time." Newport didn't have beaches the way Cape Cod or the Hamptons did. There were more rocks than sand and the water was dark and choppy, especially in the winter.

"I'll carry you," said Tyler, reaching down for me when we crossed the road.

We stayed at the beach for an hour, shivering in the night air. He told me a little bit about Hannah but he never mentioned where she was now or that she'd been an art teacher at St. George's. All he said was that she had been independent. Smart. And then everything had gone wrong.

I looked at my phone. I had three missed calls from Jane and one from Carter, but I didn't call them back. Right now I just wanted this; I wanted him. When he parked his 4Runner outside my apartment, I let myself out the door, even though I knew he was coming to my side to let me out. I met him halfway and said, "I really want you to come inside."

He looked at me with his signature expression, one that let absolutely no one figure out what he was thinking, and followed me in. I grabbed us two beers from my fridge and sat down next to him on the edge of my bed. "I'm sorry about Carter and Jane. I'll talk to them. It's just that Mike is a friend of theirs, a good friend. But I'll explain everything to them. They'll come around and Jane will apologize for Carter."

"I don't need an apology," said Tyler. "I need to kick that guy's ass until he's barely breathing. He doesn't come to Newport anymore, does he. I would know if he did."

"Mike Fogg only comes to Newport in the summer."

"Then I'll kill him this summer."

"Please don't do it around me."

"Seriously, Carolyn?" he said when he saw my face.

"I didn't mean it that way," I said apologetically. "I'm just a little shaken. That was the first time I've ever walked out of the Dalbys' house mad. It feels strange."

"You worship those people a little too much," said Tyler. "It's weird."

"Trust me, you would worship them, too, if you knew them. You met Jane for an hour. I've spent most of my life with her. I graduated top of my class at St. George's, but I worked my ass off to be there. I pretended I didn't. I snuck out of my dorm, went down to the beach, and drank just like everyone else. But most of the time I would spill the beer out of the can, because I knew that if I wanted to get the grades, I would have to keep working instead of passing out. My first year, I would study in the bathroom so my roommate wouldn't know how hard it was for me. Jane graduated top of her class, too, but she didn't try at all. Because everything is easy for her."

"Why don't you stop trying so hard for a while," he said, compassion starting to creep in between his criticism. I thought of myself standing up on my folding chair and cheering on Jane's graduation day as she walked elegantly in front of her St. George's class as valedictorian, like it was always meant to be for her.

"Life might be easier for you, too, if you just let it happen instead of trying to push and pull it in all these different directions," said Tyler, moving his face closer to mine. "I haven't known you very long, and I know I don't know you like that. I know you're pretty. I know I like you. And now I know a little more. Like how you're willing to suck up what you want to make other people happy. On our first date in that restaurant, I'm sure, now, that you didn't want to be on Thames Street in a place you used to go to as a kid. But you told me you liked it. And you had a good time, where some girls wouldn't be able to have a good time because everything wasn't going according to their premeditated plan. I know that you're the kind of girl who likes to be kissed for a long time and one who can look past someone's flaws. All you heard about me were terrible things, but you went out with me anyway. There have been girls I've been interested in who have been too afraid to go on a date with Tyler Ford. The womanizer. The guy who sent his only girlfriend to the ER. But you did. And you let me into your house and into your life and I hope you don't regret it. I doubt one of those stuck-up Dalby girls would have done that."

"You haven't met Brittan."

"I saw her."

He inched even closer to me and held my hand, not in a demeaning way, just in a way that meant he understood what it was like to be sick of your own personality. Maybe he was tired of being Tyler Ford, just like I was struggling with where I belonged in a part of the world dominated by women like Jane.

"So you grew up with those girls? Right on that property?"

"Yeah. In that smaller house we passed on the way in. Not like in a pup tent in their backyard. I was always thankful. I liked growing up in Newport. It was small and comfortable. Sometimes I look at that house and I'm surprised I got to live there. I'm still in shock."

"It's good to be in shock. Keeps you feeling alive. I never thought I would be an officer. I'm still in shock about that. I enlisted when I was eighteen. That's not the road to becoming an officer. But I was in Iraq so many times. I did decently. I got promoted to chief warrant officer, then limited duty officer, which made me a captain. Commissioned guys love reminding me that I'm still an enlisted piece of shit, but I'm pretty good at getting them to shut up. And I cared. You know some guys see the military as something to do. Don't know what to do with my life, I'll join the military. Can't go to college, I'll join the military. I guess that's why I'm still here. No one expected that. Over ten years as a marine now when everyone expected me to get thrown out or blown up."

"You're more than people think you are. Greg LaPorte told me you speak Arabic."

"Oh yeah? What's Greg LaPorte, your bosom friend?"

"No, just my regular friend. Do you really speak Arabic?"

"A little, just enough to buy liquor and porn. I was in Iraq four times."

"You're disgusting," I said, trying not to laugh. I was dead certain that Tyler spoke enough Arabic to buy much more than liquor and porn.

"So what do people in Wheatland think of you now?"

"I don't know. I haven't gone back in years. I've gotten pretty good at living here."

"So how good are you?" I asked, changing the pace of our conversation.

"How good am I? How good am I in bed? Oh, I'm really good," he said, laughing. "Haven't you heard the rumors?"

"Sure, but you told me not to believe the rumors. I bet you're lousy."

"Lousy!" he said, lunging my way and pushing me onto the bed.

"When you say the word, or even just half the word, hell, you can pantomime the word if you want, then you'll see how lousy I am."

"And what if I said the word right now?" I asked, sitting up. I pulled my shirt and sweater over my head and let them fall on the bed.

Tyler's face completely changed. I thought he would immediately rip off his clothes, but that wasn't his style. He pulled my half-naked body toward him so my head was in his lap, pulled my hair down, and started running his fingers through it. The long strands fell over my face and he picked me up in his arms, walked me to the other side of the bed, and laid me down, immediately getting on top of me. He put his hands on mine and put them inside his button-down shirt. He leaned into my ear and whispered, "You have no idea how much I want this."

I took my hands out from under his shirt and started to unbutton it. When I had done the first three, he propped himself on one arm, pulled it off over his head, and lay back on top of me, spreading my legs with his knee.

"Are you sure?" he asked as he unbuttoned the top of my skirt and lowered it down.

I nodded, unable to say anything, and he ran his hands over my skin, stopping at my nipples, listening to me moan. He relaxed his grip a little, leaned into me, and willed me to open my mouth a little wider. As I relaxed, he kept one hand on my breasts and moved the other one between my legs. He reached inside of me again, moving his fingers expertly, rhythmically until I was almost climaxing, and then he stopped.

"Not yet," he whispered, propping himself up again and telling me to take off his clothes. I undid his brown leather belt, his jeans, his gray boxer briefs. I looked at him hovering over me, almost a one-handed push-up, totally naked. I tried to move down the bed, to kiss his body, reach for him, put my mouth all over him, but he held both my hands down on the bed with one of his.

"I don't need that," he said. "I need to make you need me."

"I do need you," I said, moving my hips on the bed. I couldn't move my hands, but I could move my body closer to him. "I can't figure out why I need you, but I know I do. I feel like I'm begging you to love me."

He reached over to his jeans, pulled out a condom, and rolled it on. I looked at his body, huge over mine, and thought about what number I was. What number was I for Tyler Ford. Did it start with a one and end badly?

He leaned down over me again and whispered, "You're different, Carolyn. I swear to you. You are."

He let my hands go, told me to wrap them around his neck, and pushed himself into me. I let out a deep sigh, because it hurt, in the best way possible. I hadn't had sex in months and as soon as he started sliding inside me, his entire body against me, rubbing against my skin and then turning me over, I knew I had never had sex like that. I held on to his back, to the strong body that so many other girls had held on to, and I didn't care anymore. I let him push farther into me, run his hands hard down my arms, and then, much later, fall against me, resting on top of me.

The next morning, I extended my lease for another month.

# CHAPTER 10

On Monday morning I called William and told him I was going to be a couple of hours late.

"Playing hooky with your new boyfriend? I don't blame you," he said. "But you know I'll make you work late."

"I know. And you should. I'll stay as late as you want me to."

It was 8 A.M. and I now didn't need to be at the store until one. I put on the most nondescript outfit I could come up with—light blue jeans and a black cotton crewneck sweater with a gray peacoat—and got in my car. I pulled my hair back, wishing the color was a little less memorable. I hadn't washed it in two days and had added a few dabs of gel to try to darken the roots. I fixed my rearview mirror and started driving west on 138, over two bridges toward Ten Rod Road. When the road curved through a state park, I looked out at the cool, placid lake but put my eyes back on the road in time to see the sign for Hartford.

I had spoken to an operator at the art school on Sunday and told her I was a student who needed to finish a project with Hannah Lloyd. Hannah, she informed me, was not there on Sundays but would be firing pieces all day on Monday. I thanked her, declined to leave a message, and deleted the number from the memory on my phone.

The Hartford Art School was on the southern side of the university's campus, near the Hartford Golf Club. I first checked in on the main campus, showed them an old Christie's ID, and said I was there to do research. The bored student attendant gave me a visitor's pass that I was supposed to wear, but I dropped it in my bag as backup in case anyone asked. I got back in my car and drove to the Art School. I was ready to be nervous. When you're nervous all the time, you know which situations will bring on that flush of adrenaline, but it didn't happen. I walked into the Art School calmly and asked at reception for Hannah Lloyd.

"She's in the pottery studio," a pretty girl said. She had a pleasant accent that I couldn't place. "Do you know where that is?" she asked. I told her I did and headed to the second floor. I had studied a map of the campus the night before and knew exactly where to turn. I took five steps to the right when I got up the stairs, passing a few students holding blank canvases, and then through a double set of doors. The pottery studio was supposed to be the first door on my left, which it was. When I walked in, there was a woman at a desk in messy clothes, but she looked too young to be Hannah. I had no idea what Hannah looked like, but I knew she was old enough to work at a university. This couldn't be her.

"Excuse me," I said, doing my best to sound pleasant. "I'm looking for Hannah Lloyd."

The woman looked up from what she was doing and smiled at me. "You're looking for Hannah? She's firing right now. But I can get her for you. Is she expecting you?"

"I don't think so. Someone recommended I speak to her."

"No problem, I'll get her."

I relaxed my shoulders and tried to make my posture,

my entire demeanor, look as calm as possible. A few moments later, the younger student walked out with a woman who looked a few years older than me. Maybe thirty-one, thirty-two. She had on an old pair of jeans covered in clay and a fitted white T-shirt, which wasn't much better off. She was taller than me, a little heavier than I was, and very pretty. Her hair was long and dark and held back by just a few bobby pins. It curled in certain places and was straight in others, which somehow worked out to be very striking on her. As pretty as she was, it was hard not to notice a thin scar that ran around the bottom of her chin.

"Are you looking for me?" she said with a smile. "I'm Hannah Lloyd. I'm sorry, I'd shake your hand but I'm a total mess. Are you a student here?"

"No," I replied, smiling. "A friend of mine recommended that I see you."

"Oh, well, I'm afraid if you're not a student you can't use the kiln. Is that what you're here for? Sorry, I didn't catch your name."

"It's Katie; my name is Katie. But I'm not a student here." I didn't know what had possessed me to use Tyler's dead sister's name but it just came out and I couldn't take it back now.

"I work in an antique store in Newport, Rhode Island, and while this doesn't happen very often, we got a commission for a ceramic piece. It's a historical piece and we've been on a hunt for it and we absolutely can't find it. We thought it was in Boston but we came up empty-handed. The buyer is happy to have a copy instead, so we want to commission it for him, but we didn't know the right person to talk to. I started doing research and I came across this department and thought you might be interested."

I could tell Hannah was trying to keep smiling, but her

lips had dropped slightly. Maybe she could feel my lie. Or maybe my commission was making her think about something else.

"What sort of piece is it?" she asked flatly.

"It's hard to describe. It's a glazed bowl from the Middle East fashioned after Chinese porcelain, I think. It's not too big, just about a foot across. I meant to bring a picture with me, but I stupidly forgot it. If it's something you're interested in, I could come back later this week with the photo and you could let me know if you think you'd be able to copy it. Our buyer is willing to pay generously. The piece is something that he's very sentimental about."

I had stayed up for hours the night before deciding if I should say that the buyer was a man or a woman and had decided that I wanted to make Hannah squirm. So I said "him," and I could tell that just the pronoun had made her uncomfortable.

"Can I ask who the buyer is?" she said, still holding on to her faint smile, her upbeat attitude.

"I'm afraid he'd like to stay anonymous," I replied.

"I could be interested," she said, wiping her hands on her pants. "It's always flattering to get commissions. If you bring the picture in later this week, I'd be happy to look at it. To consider it."

"I'll definitely do that then," I said, smiling. "If you have any questions before that, you can call me at this number."

I pulled out the small white card that I'd bought at the craft store the day before. It was one of those that was meant to be put through the printer to make a place card for a wedding. It had scalloped edges and looked very feminine.

I took out a pen and wrote the name Katie, and under it the ten-digit number where she could reach me. I hadn't decided to do it until my pen had written the area code, but

I was glad I had. I put it in her hand and when she looked down at it, I knew it had registered with her. She'd immediately recognized Tyler Ford's number.

Hannah looked up at me and smiled. "Be sure to find me soon," she said.

I promised her I would.

# CHAPTER 11

I spent the night with Tyler on Monday and if Hannah had called him, he didn't show any sign that anything was wrong. He made love to me three times. He said all the things he'd said before. He was falling in love with me. He didn't say he was in love with me, but he kept saying that he was falling. If nothing went wrong, I knew he'd say it soon. Despite meeting Hannah and seeing her face when she saw Tyler's number, I could have said I love you to him that night and meant it.

The next morning, I woke up to my phone flashing and grabbed it before it woke up Tyler. It was Alex and I knew he had spoken to the Dalbys. Or maybe just to Carter.

Alex's voice was so filled with anger it almost shook the phone. I turned and looked at Tyler in bed next to me. He was still asleep, his blue eyes hidden. I'd picked up the phone so fast he must not have heard the ringer.

I moved quickly to the living room, slipped on my boots and a coat, and walked outside.

"You won't come home to me because of this guy, Carolyn? Who is he? Just some loser without an education who doesn't know his ass from his elbow? You're the smartest person I know. What do you even talk about?"

"A college education does not make a person smart, Alex," I said.

"Oh really?" he said, laughing haughtily at my statement. "I remember you saying that if you didn't get into Princeton you were going to be labeled a 'failure and ignoramus' by your peers. You said your mother was going to 'bronze you a dunce cap and force you to live with competitive mathematicians until you were reformed and sipping champagne at an Ivy.'" Did I say that? That seemed like an awfully complicated way to phrase a fear of failure.

"And now you've fallen in love with some undereducated marine who probably eats raccoon. That's awesome. Congratulations."

"Who said I'm in love with him? I just met him."

"You are in love with him. I've known you for fifteen years. It's obvious. You refused to come back to New York and you gushed about him to Jane and Brittan."

"They called you?"

"Carter called me. He said they're worried about you. According to Carter this guy is some sex fiend piece of shit who spends his time punching girls in the face. You think the Dalbys are just going to let you shack up with him? You know them. They care about you. But that's more than I can say for me. Good luck. Let me know what it feels like to get beat up by your boyfriend."

I heard the phone go dead and I opened the door and went back inside. Tyler was standing in the living room in his boxers.

"Everything okay?" he asked, picking up the blanket off the couch and wrapping me in it.

"Everything is more than okay," I said. And I wasn't lying.

"Don't go back to New York," he said, kissing the top

of my head. I rested it against his chest, his skin warm against me.

"I'm not going yet. But I can't stay forever and you're not going to, either. How many years do you have left in Newport?"

"Two, probably. I could stay longer."

"And if not, where are you going to go next?" I asked, turning around. I realized that I'd never asked Tyler how much longer he was staying in Newport. I knew he had been on base for four years, but I didn't know how much time he had left.

"I used to want to go back to the Middle East. I don't know now," he said, locking his eyes on mine. "There are guys over there as contractors," he said, then wrapped his arm around my shoulder. "Maybe it's time for me to try to make some money."

I stood on my toes, kissed his perfect face, and told him I was late for work. When Tyler was in the shower, I'd looked at his phone, which he didn't lock with a code. There were no calls from a Hartford number. He could have deleted it. But Hannah looked like a girl who thought things through. I didn't think she had called yet. She would wait until I came back to see her.

I was going to go back to see her. I didn't know when, but since Blair had told me the bowl wasn't worth testing for age and I'd learned about Hannah, I no longer thought I owned something that could make me and William five figures. I thought I owned a very convincing fake.

To keep life interesting, Hook had changed his auctions to Tuesday and Wednesday, since the population around the area was starting to swell with tourists. "You'll go to both," William had told me when I'd informed him of the change. "I heard he's going to shut everything down after this summer. The county sold the space again, so he must be itching to get everything gone. He's got a big storage unit in a more rural area, but I think he counts on the turnover, too. He sells some big things, all that furniture and those neon signs."

When I got to Narragansett, I parked my car in the small lot near the firehouse and saw Hook walking nearby.

"Hi, Hook. Looking for heiresses?" I said as he watched me get out of my little car.

"Yeah, where do you think Jane Dalby's hiding? I love that girl. She looks expensive."

"You know exactly where she lives. Everyone does. But you're not going to find her here."

"Who needs her when I have you?" he said, reaching for my hand. He kissed it and let out a laugh.

"You ever find out about that bowl?" he asked.

"Yeah, I did actually. Went to Goodwill a few weeks back. It's not so bad there. I bought a chessboard made of teeth."

"So what about that bowl? Worth anything?"

"Still not quite sure. I only half looked into it. Maybe a thousand," I lied.

"That's still a good return. I should have sold it for more. See, you come to Hook's, you get a deal."

"Sometimes you do. And sometimes you steal from drunk people."

Hook frowned at me and gave me a little shove toward the building.

"All right, enough yapping. Go inside, sit down on the bleachers, and buy something from me. Something expensive."

"I'll try," I said, heading inside. I took a seat on the cold metal bleachers. Every time I came back to Hook's I sat one row farther down, so I was getting closer and closer to the front, the rows where Hook yelled at you and the women swigged booze out of red Solo cups.

A few of the women who recognized me from the last couple of weeks smiled and said hello. There were more men in the room today, but the median age was still sixty-five. That was the thing with auctions. Even the small-time ones required some sort of disposable income.

I didn't buy anything that day. I bid on a small coffee table that had strong claw-and-ball feet, but I was outbid quickly and didn't think it was worth the $2,200 it went up to.

"Maybe you are a bit of a crook after all," I said to Hook as I walked out of there.

"Not my fault, darling. I started the bidding at two hundred. You can control certain things, but demand is not one of them."

"Lucky guy."

"You coming back next week? I'm getting used to seeing that pretty face of yours now. Gives me a real zip as I shout out those numbers."

"You're despicable," I said, walking out, but he knew I would be back the following week.

"Nothing today?" asked William when I walked into the store empty-handed that afternoon. "I don't want to rob you," I said, putting my bag down. "Everything went too high today; we would barely have broken even."

"There are days like that," said William, as he adjusted his bow tie. It had gardenias on it.

"For spring," he said when he caught me looking at him. "The season of innocence."

"I thought spring was for sex and bad judgment calls," I said, breaking his Victorian dream.

"And speaking of. Are you still seeing that good-looking marine who came in the other day? He was pretty dashing."

"I certainly am," I said with a grin.

"Then for you it is definitely not your age of innocence."

"William, that's what the first twenty-nine years of my life were. It's about time I shed that uptight person you used to know."

"I kind of liked her," said William, smiling at me as two women walked into the store.

I saw Tyler again that evening. It had become something of an unsaid rule that we spent every night together. A few days before, he had put his strong arms around me in the shower and whispered, "It's just you." That was the moment that I fully gave in.

When we were in bed, a few minutes before 1 A.M., Tyler looked around my apartment, void of all personal touches, pushed the sheets down so that his tan torso was totally uncovered, pointed toward the bookshelf, and said, "You should give that bowl back to me. I kind of miss it." Every tiny hair on my body stood straight up. I pulled the covers over me so he couldn't see my goose bumps. Hannah had called him. He wanted to take the bowl so that I couldn't bring it to her. He looked at it on the shelf, got up in his black boxers, and picked it up.

"You should regift it to me."

"No way," I said coolly. He had to know I went to see Hannah and that I suspected she had something to do with the bowl. That it was their bowl, not our bowl. Tyler was acting too relaxed, too deliberately calm. I tried to match it.

"I bought it. And now it reminds me of how I found you."

"How you found me?" he asked.

"My witch hunt for you. It was more like an information hunt but memorable all the same."

"Your mind fascinates me. I bet you're good at making cash."

"I'm good at making it for other people."

"What's the point, then?"

"I've always been more interested in everything that surrounds money than the actual money. I like the process."

"The people, the houses, the rooms full of furniture and gardens, cars, and boats and all that?"

"You're forgetting the art." I paused for a few seconds but he didn't say anything. "And the intellect and the big horrible personalities coupled with the few good ones. It always seemed more fun than a middle-of-the-road life. Plus I was used to it from growing up here. At arm's length, anyway."

"You'll give this back to me eventually," he said, putting it down and looking at it on the shelf.

I didn't say anything else, he didn't say anything, and a few minutes later I was letting him take off my clothes again, for the third time that night. When Alex and I had sex, it had been sex. It was good sex, but it was pretty much what I expected good sex to be. Tyler and I had amazing sex. I worried about my heart not being able to handle it, physically and emotionally. Every one of my senses teetered on the edge, in overload, in a pleasure spiral that I never wanted to end but could only handle for so many minutes. When Tyler was inside me, when his tongue was, his hands, I just gripped the sheets and everything I did, said, or thought seemed completely out of my control.

Tyler looked at my face as I glowed, always slightly embarrassed by what we had done, and kissed my forehead. "Why did you agree to go out with me?"

"Because everyone told me not to."

"Good reason. I think that's why a lot of girls say yes,

unfortunately. Or fortunately. That statement really depends on how much I like the girl."

"I thought you never really liked any of the girls except for Hannah." I wanted to say her name as much as possible. If he had a reason to be rattled, I wanted to see him try to hide it. "You just liked that they were pretty girls."

"But every man likes pretty girls," he replied, not reacting when I said her name.

"Right. 'Girls in Their Summer Dresses' and all that."

"Girls in their summer dresses. I like that expression. Is it an expression?"

"Sort of."

I had always hated that Irwin Shaw story. Was every guy really just a gorilla in heat waiting for girls to wear tiny swatches of thin fabric with straps in the summer? Tyler had been. Or maybe he still was. But this time, it was with me.


I had spent every single day with Tyler for six weeks and I hadn't gone back to see Hannah. I wanted to see if she would react without seeing the bowl, not even a picture. And even if she didn't react, I took an almost sick pleasure in thinking about how uncomfortable she was. I pictured her looking at that name, right above Tyler's number. She had to know that I knew. When I looked at the bowl now, I imagined her hands forming it. Maybe there had been others, sold for five figures to people who knew less about these things than me and Blair Bari.

I had my apartment on Fifty-Ninth Street rented out again. I had put two months more on my apartment in Newport. It was April and no one wanted it until June. That's when summer officially came to town, when the kites started to fly.

The last Saturday in April was a day you prayed would last well past the confines of twenty-four hours. A wisp of humidity had broken through the air, and suddenly everything smelled like life lived outside. When I woke up, with Tyler next to me, I had a text from Jane with a picture of her sailboat. I woke up Tyler and put the phone in his face.

"Jane's taking her boat out for the first time this spring. Brittan is up from New York and they want us to go sailing with them. You must sail; you've been in Newport for four years. We have to go. She has the most beautiful boat. It's a custom Sparkman and Stephens with a navy blue hull and it's basically just paradise on water. I haven't been on it in years."

"A day on a boat with you and the Dalbys," Tyler muttered in his sleepy voice. "Are you sure they don't want me to serve drinks or something?"

"Don't be an ass. They're nice. Even Carter can be. He's a little pompous since he married Jane, but he's just mad because she's still a Dalby and he's not."

"What's he?"

"Carter Lehmann."

"What's a Lehmann?"

"Not a Dalby."

"So Carter Not-a-Dalby is going to be there, too."

"We don't have to go. I just thought it could be fun. You might enjoy it. Seriously, her boat was on the cover of the *Robb Report*. It's beautiful."

"I'll enjoy it, because you'll enjoy it."

"Well then, let's try it. If it's terrible we can just swan-dive right off the side and swim home."

"All right. Tyler Ford boating with the Dalbys. I should send a letter to my mother."

I leaned over and kissed him. "I'll take lots of photos," I whispered, kissing him again.

We got in his car and drove toward the Goat Island Marina, where all the Dalby boats were kept.

"Why does Jane keep her boat out here?" Tyler asked as we drove straight over the water on Bolhouse Road.

"Deepwater facility. You should see their father's boat. It's not a dinghy."

"The charm of a dinghy is really underestimated."

"I'll take your word for it. Let's go on Jane's boat today and a dinghy next weekend and then we can compare."

"What?" said Tyler, seeing my smirk.

"The only problem is, I don't know anyone who owns a dinghy!"

"I'll steal one."

Not only did Hannah have to know that I knew; Tyler had to know, too.

"Oh good," I said. "That solves everything."

I rolled down the window and put my arm straight out, the wind keeping it cold and taut. I wasn't going to say anything until he did. Or until Hannah did. I imagined their conversations, Hannah calling him, telling him what I'd done, a card with his number and his dead sister's name on it. She'd ask why I'd scribbled those things down, come to see her in the first place, and maybe he'd have an answer for her. I imagined him saying in his deep, even voice, "I think she knows." But what was it that I knew? That the bowl wasn't an antique, but looked alarmingly close? Tyler knew more about it than he was telling me, and it had to be because of Hannah. He was in my apartment all the time. He could have taken it, could have demanded it back, but it just continued to sit there, untouched, on my cheap shelf.

I looked out at the rows of beautiful white sails giving

a little in the breeze. "We used to sail all the time growing up," I said, raising my voice so he could hear me over the wind. "Even our school had this monthlong sailing program. That's really what I missed the most when I was in New York. The Hudson looks like toilet water compared to the Rhode Island Sound."

I looked at him in his thin white T-shirt. The back was so sheer that you could see the outline of his tattoos through it.

"I bet you're very good on a boat."

"I can get by."

"Get by?"

"Yeah, I'm decent. I like the water. But I grew up in Wyoming and then spent all that time in the desert. The water still surprises me."

"We're up here!" Jane's voice rang across the dock as we walked toward her. I looked up at her standing on the boat in white shorts and a dark green cashmere sweater. "It's freezing! Tyler, wear more clothes. You're going to love it!"

I grinned at Tyler, grabbed his hand, and pulled him toward the dock. "Never listen to a woman who tells you to wear more clothes," I said as we walked. "She's clearly never seen you naked."

Carter came over and greeted us as we kicked off our shoes and made our way up.

"Hey, man, good to have you. Sorry about the other night. Try not to punch anyone today."

"I'll do my best," said Tyler, walking past Carter and giving Jane a hug.

"Jane ask you to be nice to him?"

"Of course she did. How am I doing?"

"Badly."

I gave Carter a kiss on the cheek, waved to Jane, and walked down to the bow, where Brittan was standing in white jeans and a navy sailing jacket. She looked like an advertisement for living well.

"So you brought your prizefighter. I can't wait to meet him. When is he going to beat up Carter?"

"Maybe later."

Brittan looked down the boat at Jane and Tyler talking while Carter sailed out of the harbor.

"Good God, is that him?" Brittan lowered her sunglasses and looked at Tyler in his khakis and thin shirt. "You don't mess around. Lose a job, gain a supermodel? Doesn't seem like that bad a trade."

Tyler must have felt us watching him. He excused himself from Jane and came over to us. I introduced him to Brittan, who gave her coolest hello, the kind she gave to people when she wanted them to talk about her later.

"So you're the mysterious Tyler Ford. It's just a pleasure to meet you."

"A pleasure? I think you're lying," he said, putting out his hand to shake hers.

"A handshake, how quaint," said Brittan. She was wearing three gold bangles, just like her sister. I remembered when Jane had started wearing her bracelets in high school and I asked her about them. She had said, "Because four would be too many and two would be too few," like it was the most obvious thing in the world.

"So, Tyler, sail often?" asked Brittan, sitting down and picking up a book.

"He lives on a naval base, Brit," I said, sitting down next to her.

"But he's a marine. You're a marine, right?" she asked, looking up at him.

"I am a marine."

"Good. I think I like marines better. This is the first time in my life I've ever given the topic any thought at all, but I have a hunch I do."

"Go with it," said Tyler.

"Jane said you've been over to the house, but it didn't exactly go . . . swimmingly?"

"Swimmingly, aptly put," I said, looking out at the water.

"Turns out Carter is friends with someone I would like to beat the shit out of," said Tyler, looking down at us reclining in front of him.

"So I heard. Mike Fogg. He's a bastard and I never liked him anyway." She leaned over to her side, stretched out her long legs, and propped herself on her elbow. Jane and Carter were out of earshot, expertly steering the boat out of the harbor. I could see the southern stretch of Aquidneck Island quickly moving out of view.

"He cried once in high school in front of me, if it makes you feel any better, Tyler."

"That does make me feel better," said Tyler, laughing. "What did you do?"

"I punched him."

"Really?"

"No, but I should have in hindsight. Don't worry, Tyler. He'll just end up marrying some boring girl and living a very plain life with too much alcohol and monotonous sex. I'm sure you don't suffer from any of those curses."

"I definitely don't."

Jane walked over to us then, sitting down next to Brittan and letting out a big happy yawn.

"What a perfect day to be out. I love this stupid boat."

"This is a very beautiful boat," said Tyler, finally sitting down, too, and taking my hand.

"Let's sail to Naushon Island!" Brittan called out to Carter, who put his hand to his ear like he couldn't hear her.

"Oh, that bastard can hear me. He just wants company. I'm not moving."

"I just sat down! Go help him, Brittan," said Jane, leaning in toward her sister.

"Eventually. I don't feel like standing. Plus, you'll get up again soon, Janey. You're the nice one."

"So if you're the nice one and you're the—"

"Less nice one," Brittan offered. "Though I'm awfully witty. Everyone says so. Jane's the good one; I'm the deviant. But that's the way it's supposed to be because I'm just heaps younger than her."

"Three years, smart-ass," said Jane in her best bored voice.

"Like I said, heaps."

"Okay. Then what's Carolyn?"

"The smart one," Jane and Brittan said in unison.

"Ha-ha," I said, looking up at the sky. There were a few thin white lines slowly fading that had been left from a plane.

"She really is," said Jane.

"I know she is," said Tyler. I refused to look at him. At that moment, I didn't want to know how much he knew.

"She'll ignore you if you say it, just like she's doing now, but she graduated first in her class at Princeton. First. Do you know how hard that is?"

Tyler propped himself up on his hands and listened.

"And she was hired by Christie's way before she graduated. She didn't have to finish with a perfect GPA, she already had a dream job lined up, but she did anyway."

"And look at me now. I make a hair above minimum wage, I haven't talked to my parents in months, and my apartment smells like dead people."

"But you're happy," said Brittan, lifting her glass. "I can tell you are."

"Maybe a little."

"So Carolyn's the smart one and what are you, Tyler?" asked Brittan.

"Well, if you're asking Carter, I'm the violent one."

"Not funny," said Jane. "Men are ridiculous."

"How many people have you killed?" asked Brittan coolly. "Five? Ten?" Brittan was very good at coming off cool, like a Hitchcock blonde without the hair color.

"More."

"How do you sleep at night?"

"Soundly," he said before kissing me.

Tyler stood up, grabbed his bathing suit from my bag, and walked away from us, slightly behind the sail. He took off all his clothes with his back to us, his tan body kissed perfectly by the flooding midday sun. He reached down and pulled on his bathing suit.

Brittan sat up to watch, then lowered her aviators again and shook her head at me.

"Jesus. Who cares who he killed. His body is superhuman."

"It all makes sense now. Carolyn is painfully shallow. Who knew," said Jane.

"It's not just the way he looks."

"Oh, stop trying, Carolyn. It just seems sad when you do. He's gorgeous. He looks like a G.I. Joe. We get it. You like sex. It's only normal."

Tyler walked back over to us, acting like he'd just been in the corner reading Bible passages.

"Anyone want to swim?" he asked our group.

"Obviously not," said Jane, wrapping a cashmere shawl around her cashmere sweater. "The water is fifty-two degrees. I refuse."

Tyler looked at me and Brittan.

"No way," said Brittan, zipping her jacket to her chin. "Carolyn's a good swimmer. She'll do it."

"It's too cold," I said, looking out at the water. "It even looks cold."

"But what if it was a dare," said Tyler, pulling me to my feet. "Then you'd do it. You're the smart one, and the smart one always says yes to a dare."

"I think you're thinking of the drunk one. The drunk one always says yes to a dare."

"Can I offer you a cocktail?" said Jane innocently. "Gimlet? Martini, flaming shot?"

"Fine. Fine. I hate all of you," I said, grabbing my bikini and going below to change.

"Slow this thing down and come back and get us," I said to Carter as I walked topside.

"Are you idiots swimming?"

"It's what idiots love to do," I answered back.

Jane met me as I walked back to the bow.

"You're jumping off a moving sailboat in April because someone dares you. I like it. In fact, I like you with him. You seem light."

"I'm happy, Jane. I don't know how to explain it but I am."

"You don't need to. I get it. Is this, him, better than Alex?"

"Who's Alex?"

I took Tyler's hand when we moved over the guardrail.

"You two look like a postcard for bad decisions," said Brittan, watching us with a camera in hand. She snapped a photo of us holding on to the side of the boat with our toes.

"Ready?" asked Tyler. "You're up for a little adventure, right?"

"I think Carter actually sped this thing up," I answered.

I ignored his words and let my body tense up with the thought of the water. "Oh who cares, let's just jump!" I yelled, pitching myself off the boat with Tyler's hand firmly in mine.

The cold water hit me like a fist. I struggled to catch my breath and as soon as my lungs filled again, I turned around and screamed. Immediately, I felt Tyler's hands around me.

"It's glacial! I hate you!"

"But you should always jump if someone says jump."

"Who gave you that crappy advice?" I said, pulling my hand away so I could tread water.

"My father. See, everything else he ever said to me was bad advice. That phrase, I actually took with me."

"You should have been a paratrooper. They would have loved you in the air force."

He swam back over to me, kissed me, and did a few strong strokes before dunking his head under and slapping his palm on the water.

"Feels pretty good, right?"

"Refreshing!" I screamed as he swam circles around me.

My teeth were going to start chattering soon, which Tyler must have noticed, because he glided my way underwater, put one arm around my waist, and kept us afloat with the other.

"I love you, Carolyn," he said, looking me right in the eyes as he pushed my wet hair out of my face. "No matter what happens, I love you."

He had said it.

"I love you, too. A lot. Too much."

"Too much? Who ever told you there was a limit?"

He kissed me hard, the way a person should be kissed, and said it again.

We looked up to see the boat coming back around for

us, Jane throwing the buoy so we could move quickly back
toward the ladder.

Tyler helped me up by not so subtly pushing my butt
vertically and we collapsed on the deck with towels and let
the sun dry us.

"Why do you have so many muscles, Tyler?" asked Brittan with her eyes closed when we'd finally dried off.

"Because God loves me. Why do you have so much
money, Brittan?"

"Because God loved my great-great-great-grandfather."

"None of you are amusing," said Carter, sitting up and
taking off his sunglasses. "Tyler, go help Jane with the boat.
Prove your salt."

Tyler kissed my head, grabbed his towel and a beer, and
walked toward Jane.

"You can't just boss everyone around, Carter. It gets
very old," said Brittan by the time Tyler was out of earshot.

"So, is this like showing him how the other half lives or
something, Carolyn? Want to put a fire under his ass so he
makes something of his life?" Carter asked.

"I'm not that sadistic."

"Sure you are. You're a plotter. You always have been."

"You've only known me for six years. Don't make such
sweeping statements."

Carter poured himself a swig of cognac and lit a cigar.

"That smells like old fat men," said Brittan, pinching her
nose. Her brown hair was flying everywhere but she didn't
bother to tie it back.

"A smell I'm sure you're more than familiar with, Brit,"
he said, blowing the smoke in our direction.

"It's odd that you like to dismiss Tyler being in the military," Brittan said to Carter in response. "He has a Silver
Star for valor. He was telling us about it."

"Of course he was! What else does he have to talk about. You know the military is a bunch of crap, right? I mean, they have to convince all these young suckers that they're going to be instant heroes when they come home or they would never go. If they thought they were going to come back and still be nobodies, but with the added bonus of PTSD and some holes in their skulls, no one would go. No one. It would be an army of one."

"Aren't you glad we have a military?" asked Brittan. "You want terrorists to just shuffle step onto our shores and toss a bunch of A-bombs around?"

"I'm thrilled we have a military. I'm just not thrilled it's on our boat."

"And all this time I thought this was Jane's boat," I said, lancing Carter with his most detested dig.

"I think he intimidates you a little, Carter," said Brittan, smiling. I could tell her eyes were shining, even though she still had her sunglasses on.

"Why, because he looks like some muscle-head with bad tattoos who grew up sniffing paint out west?"

"I think they're pretty good tattoos, don't you, Brit?" I asked.

"They're very good. Like Rembrandts on skin."

"You two are monsters," said Carter, laughing.

"Oh, Carter. Go take a long swim south, would you?" said Brittan, rolling over onto her stomach.

"I think I'll stay right here. I like watching that buffoon sail." He puffed on his cigar and let it ash right onto the deck.

Brittan turned her head and watched Jane and Tyler for a few moments.

"You're just mad because he can sail. He lives on a naval base. What did you expect. For him to hang himself from the line?"

"Maybe," said Carter, laughing. "Fine, you wenches. I give, I give. Carolyn, date an abusive pauper. Brittan, go get gang-raped by football players. You two do whatever you want. I'll just stay here and live the good life with Jane. You two can tell me all about what prison's like every Thanksgiving."

Carter stood up and walked away from us, toward his wife.

"I hate that he's amusing, don't you?"

"It's his worst quality. Makes it hard to loathe him."

"I like Tyler, you know," said Brittan, rising up on her elbows. "He's actually very elegant for someone who grew up on some dirt road in Wyoming and likes bar fights."

"Isn't he though."

"He is. He's surprisingly elegant. Probably because he's so good-looking. He's almost too good-looking. Makes you think he made some pact with the devil or something."

"People probably think the same thing about you."

"But I'm a girl. It's different with girls. We're expected to be pretty. His looks are a little . . ." She looked at Jane, who looked happy laughing at something Tyler said.

"A little jarring," said Brittan.

We drank away most of the afternoon with Tyler, leaving the sailing up to Carter and Jane.

"I'm going to marry that cute friend of Greg LaPorte's. Do you know him, Tyler? Mason something or other," said Brittan.

"You're going to marry Mason Dekker," said Tyler without breaking his poker face.

"Yes. But don't give him my number. I'm just going to surprise him one day."

"He'll say yes."

"I know. But it might have to be a second marriage. He seems more like second-marriage material."

"What am I, then?" Tyler asked Brittan.

"Oh, you're definitely affair material, not marriage. But some girls like their whole lives to feel like affairs, so you'll be just fine."

Two days later, the water temperature had gone up five degrees and spring had finally settled in Newport. Tourists were visiting the tennis club, the Vanderbilt Grace hotel was full, and there was a line to get into the Breakers. I smelled the ocean air, lifted toward me. I smelled promise, newness as I walked to work. It was warm enough to open the front window at William Miller's store and I pulled the heavy wooden frames up and anchored them with solid brass hooks.

The world and all its sounds were being let in, so before I saw them, I heard them. They had those types of voices. The ones that were distinctively male. Not the kind of voices you would hear from fathers at a children's soccer game or the ones that spoke sweetly when they had women around them; they were the voices of men who were used to speaking with men. Men like them. And when they came in to speak with me, I didn't grip the table. I didn't hold my breath. I knew, with Tyler, that I was waiting for something to drop. I just didn't want it to be so soon.

## CHAPTER 12

There were two of them. Both in their forties—one early, one late—with short hair and tough-guy airs of importance. They were wearing suits and frowns. The younger one, with a smaller build, only a few inches taller than me, asked for me first. Before he introduced himself, told me what they wanted, why they came looking for me at the store, I knew I would hear the words *Tyler Ford*.

Tyler did not toe the line; he shot the line. Two months ago, I would have stayed away from him, even as attractive as he was. But after Elizabeth, after Christie's and Nina and my big life mess, I wasn't so careful.

"Are you Carolyn Everett?" the younger man asked after the door had closed behind him. He had a few acne marks on his cheeks, which were overshadowed by the prominence of his cheekbones. They looked like right triangles sewn into his skin.

"Carolyn Everett. Yes, I am," I said, flipping a small end table back over and standing up to meet them. My thighs hurt from being bent for too long while I teetered on the balls of my feet. I had been polishing the table that morning for William, who was on a buying trip in Boston.

"We're sorry to bother you at work, but we were hoping

to talk to you about something. And someone. Do you have a few minutes?"

My heart started to pound and my head was full of pressure. I needed to close my eyes for a few seconds, to right myself. It was Tyler. I knew it, but I didn't say it. My asking before they asked me would help nothing at all. I waited for them to say Tyler's name, but all they said was mine.

The three of us sat at the back table. It was glass, built in Venice, and used to hold my books when I worked there in college. We used it for client paperwork now, but I always thought of it as the table I grew up with, the one that took me from studying art, to knowing art, to selling it.

"I'm Josh Wallace and this is Brian Van Ness. We're with NCIS, the Naval Criminal Investigative Service at Naval Station Newport."

I looked from one to the other and said, "Okay."

"We have a few questions about something you own. It's a relic of some sort, a bowl." They knew about Tyler and Hannah. I exhaled quietly and put my hands on the table.

The shorter one, Josh, took a printed picture out of his bag and put it on the table. It was a picture of Tyler's bowl. My bowl. The one that was sitting in strips of muslin in my desk drawer a few feet behind us.

"Where did you get this?" I asked both of them. "I've never seen this photo."

"Yes," said Brian, taking out another. "We're aware of that."

"Can you tell us everything you know about this item?" Josh asked. "Starting with where you bought it, why you bought it? Where it is now. Just every detail you know. And if you have it here, we'd like to see it."

"Why?" I had no idea about military protocol. Did they have the same power as the regular police? Did I have to answer them? Should I call a lawyer? Could I make them leave?

"We have reason to believe it was stolen."

"But it wasn't stolen," I said, looking at the picture. "I bought it."

"Not stolen by you, stolen by Marine Captain Tyler Ford. We think it could be an Iraqi object, an antiquity that was smuggled to the United States during the war."

There was no way. Blair Bari had said so. It wasn't old. It was made in the last one hundred years.

"And why would you think that?" I said. The picture in front of me was almost blurry.

"We have some information about it that leads us to believe it is," said Josh. "So what we need you to do is tell us everything about that object, starting with where you got it, why you got it, and what you did with it."

"I'm not exactly sure what you want me to say," I said, trying my best to be vague.

"Where did you get the bowl?" asked Brian.

"Where did I get it? I bought it at a local auction run by Hook Durant in Narragansett for twenty dollars."

"And where did Mr. Durant get it?" asked Josh, writing notes.

"He got it at a Goodwill. The only one in the state. It's in North Kingstown."

"And why did you want to buy it?"

"Because I wanted to lap milk out of it."

They both glared at me. Brian opened his mouth to talk but I cut him off with an apology.

"I bought it because I wanted to sell it. That's my job. I looked into it, made an inquiry to Max Sebastian, who is the chairman of the Middle East and India department at Sotheby's. He's the best in the world and who you go to ask questions about Middle Eastern pottery. He never got back to me, so I spoke to Blair Bari, a professor of Islamic art and history at Brown, and he didn't make anything of it, so I decided to hold on to it because it's nice. It's a pretty piece of pottery."

"Where is it now?"

I could lie. I'd lied plenty. Not to cops, but to buyers, sellers, dealers, colleagues. I was a good liar. So I did.

"It's not here."

"Does Tyler Ford have it?" asked Josh. He had a slight South Boston accent, which was unbecoming when he was trying to sound polite. He was one of those people who should just resign themselves to always sounding tough and rude.

"No, I have it," I admitted. "But it's not here."

"Is it in your apartment?" said Josh. "The one on Memorial Boulevard."

"I'm not even going to ask why you know where I live," I said, standing up from the table. "Is this going to take much longer?"

"Absolutely."

I walked over to get a bottle of water from our small fridge and didn't offer any to either man.

"Captain Greg LaPorte, you know him?" asked Brian, looking down at his notes.

That was the question that threw me. I must have showed it, too, because Brian asked me again. "LaPorte. Instructor at Mardet. Tell us about your relationship."

I didn't say anything and finally Brian said, "Listen. It's not a choice right now. Don't lie to cops and don't lie to us. I know you're not stupid enough to do that."

I already had.

"I know him, not well. We met in February when I

moved back to Newport. As far as I know, he brought the bowl to Goodwill along with a bunch of other stuff. What other stuff, I'm not sure. Hook Durant bought it and he sold it at auction to me. Now I'm trying to figure out what to do with it."

"Let us look at it, then."

"It's not here, I told you that."

"When can we see it?"

I shrugged and looked at the wall.

"I don't know what kind of person you are," said Brian, looking around the room, "but you strike me as someone who cares a lot about these kinds of things. About antiques and looting and the smuggling of goods for profit. You look like a woman who cares about all that."

"You worked at Christie's? The auction house," said Josh, taking notes. "But you got fired. Made a big mistake. Something that was stolen." He looked up at me but I refused to meet his gaze. "Must have been pretty devastating for you. Is that why you moved home? You're from here, right? Smart girl. Went to that nice boarding school on Purgatory Road. That's a rich kids' school. Vanderbilts and Astors. Then you went to Princeton."

"Yes, all that's right. You know that's right. Why are you asking?"

"We're not asking. We're just kind of surprised we're here."

"Well, that makes three of us."

"This doesn't have to happen again if you tell us everything today, drive home, get the bowl, and let us bring it in."

"It probably will, though. Happen again, that is. Because you look like you're in the mood to lie to us," said Brian.

"So keep going about the bowl. What happened after you bought it at Hook Durant's auction?" Josh asked.

"I tried to find out more about it. I wanted to sell it. Like you said, I used to work at Christie's. I know a lot more about art and antiques than most people. But I didn't know much about the bowl except that I thought it was beautiful and a few things about it made me think it was older. But after studying it for a while, I changed my mind. I decided it was made in the last hundred years or so. I still think it is. And when I asked around I didn't find out anything that would make me think otherwise. I gave up on selling it for now."

"You just gave up?"

"Sure. I asked two people who are widely regarded as experts. I didn't hear back from one; the other said it was made recently, so I didn't think I could turn much of a profit."

"But someone who worked at Christie's must have really loaded buyers. Quiet people who would pay big money under the table for something valuable."

"Are you insinuating that I know something about that piece that I'm not telling you? Because if I did, I would have sold it, here, in this store. I bought it while working for the owner, William Miller, with his money. I would have sold it while working for him, too, and turned a profit for him."

"You don't get a cut of profits?"

"I do. I get fifty percent of commission any time it's over two hundred dollars."

"Fifty, that's a lot. So you and Mr. Miller could be scheming to do some deal with it. Why sell it from the store when William can use your connections to sell it on the black market?"

"I had no intention to do that. I don't sell anything illegally. Like you said, until January, I worked for Christie's. I had, and have, no plans to sell that bowl because I don't think it's worth anything. I think someone gave you a bad tip." I argued for a living, convinced people to see things my way, to sell things, buy things, get attached to pieces, cut off their attachments, but this was out of my comfort zone. I wanted to get up. To walk outside and feel spring on my face, but they were not leaving.

"Why do you think that bowl is so valuable?" I asked.

"Why do you think it's not?"

"Well, for one, because it's in really good shape. I could go into more detail, but I'm sure it's too inside baseball for you."

"Try us."

"Fine. To start with, the bowl is heavy. Most new pieces are heavy; most old ones are not. And for its size, a foot in diameter, it's very heavy. Also the resonance sounds high. When you hit an older piece—gently, a bit of a flick with your fingers—it makes a deep, dull sound. This one sounded higher than I thought it should. Also the glaze, the encrustation, was very even, a sign of a newer piece. Older pieces aren't so uniform, because they were crudely fired. And the color. There are two tones of green used, but they are even. There aren't noticeable changes in the color of the glaze. If it were older, there would be. This is not my field of expertise, but I'm sure I know more than your average NCIS agent. No offense."

"Right," said Brian, making a mark on his notepad and flipping it closed before I could see it.

"It's not like I've done petrographic analysis—I'm not an archaeologist and I didn't think it warranted sending it to one—but that's my best guess. If I had thought it was worth looking into further, I would have."

"And your relationship with Tyler," said Josh. "You're intimate with him. You're—"

"You're fucking him," Brian interrupted.

"Excuse me?"

"We know you are, so just say you are."

"I'm pretty sure you can't talk to me like that."

"I'm pretty sure we can."

"Tyler Ford from Mardet," said Josh, taking the questioning away from Brian. "You two are very close. You're dating."

"I know him, yes."

"You're dating. He's your boyfriend."

"I doubt the nature of our relationship is important."

"It's very important."

"Do you know about that trouble he got in last year? What was her name, Brian?"

"Hannah."

"Right, right, Hannah Lloyd. She was some St. George's girl, too. He must only take the rich ones seriously. The kind of guy who likes money. Doesn't come from money, but likes to keep it around somehow. From girls, or maybe from something else, like selling stolen art."

They knew about Hannah. It had taken me about five minutes to figure out that Hannah also happened to work in a pottery studio. But if they knew anything apart from what Tyler had done to her, they didn't say so.

I looked at Josh coldly and he smiled at me.

"So, Hannah. You know about her?"

I folded my hands and looked up at them sternly.

"Never met her in my life."

"Right, well, maybe you two should get together. Talk about yachts and diamonds. Compare notes about Tyler."

"I think we can end this conversation. That's really all I have to say to you. I don't know what else I can tell you."

I stood up and they both stood up and looked around the store.

"We're not done, but we'll come back tomorrow morning to get that bowl from you," said Brian. "You seem . . . tired, but we'll expect you to have it tomorrow. Thanks for your time."

"You know," said Josh, pausing at the door. "I know you're an expert from Christie's and all that. You're one of those real smart girls. But this, this might have been worth looking into after all."

I waited until their car had disappeared down the street, then I left, deserted the shop, slammed the door behind me, and tore down Spring Street toward the base and Tyler's apartment. Because it was the middle of the day, it took me only eleven minutes to drive there. I parked my car badly, ran out, and pounded on his white wooden door. No one came. I rang the bell, but still nothing. I took my phone out of my jacket pocket and called him twice in a row. Both times it rang and went to voicemail. I texted him. I didn't know what to write and settled on "Find me now. Right now." I walked around to the back of Tyler's place and saw that his car wasn't parked there. There were no lights in his house and the lid was off the recycling bin, like it hadn't been put back on from the night before. I walked back toward my car, started it, and drove to town. I opened all the windows and banged the radio off. My chest was so tight that I untucked and unbuttoned as much of my shirt as I could while holding on to some semblance of decency. Just forty-eight hours ago, I had been sailing through the air, holding Tyler's hand, falling into the cold water, exchanging our first "I love yous."

When I got to Bellevue and through Jane's gates, I was hyperventilating. And when Jane opened the door, I was just panting.

"I can't—I can't breathe," I said, trying my best to regulate my gasps.

"Sit down. Right now. Hold your breath, count to ten, and then let it out again. Do it five times. Slowly. Slower."

We sat like that for five minutes until my muscles started to relax. I put my hands over my forehead, turned away from the gates, and looked at Jane.

"You're fine now. You're fine," she said, smoothing my hair.

"I'm not fine," I said softly. "I'm so far from fine, Jane."

"Why? What happened?"

"It's Tyler. Two NCIS agents came to the store today. They think . . . I mean, I think they think that the bowl that connected us, that bowl I told you about, was stolen from Iraq."

"What! NCIS? The naval crime unit? You spoke to them? To whom? To agents?"

I nodded yes. My panic for Jane was real, but it wasn't just Tyler I was worried about. It was Hannah, and me. That bowl could not be old. They had to be wrong.

"When did this happen?"

"Just now. A few minutes ago. Two agents, stationed on base as part of their NCIS unit, came to the store and started asking me questions. They said they knew everything. That I fucked Tyler Ford. They actually said that. 'We know you're fucking Tyler Ford.' They asked if I was going to sell it privately to a buyer on the black market."

"This is really bad, Carolyn. Were you, I mean, did you have plans to do that?"

"Jane! Haven't you known me since birth? You think I'm involved in art crime?"

"No, I don't. Of course not. But what do they know? I mean, what information do they have to even want to come to the store? They're clearly in the middle of some full-blown investigation!"

"That's the thing. I don't really know. They were making me talk more than they were talking. But they had pictures. When I first bought the bowl, I thought it could be worth a lot of money. I wanted it to be. So I took pictures of it, from every angle, just like we do at Christie's or at William's, of any object we're intending to sell, and I sent them to Max Sebastian at Sotheby's."

I didn't need to explain to Jane who Max Sebastian was. Her family knew every important person in the auction industry and they all scrambled to know the Dalbys.

"Really? Straight to Max?"

"I wanted an answer about Middle Eastern art, so I emailed Max because he's the best. But I never heard back from him. I sent him the pictures in February; it's April, and not a word. I also took it to Brown but Blair Bari, the prof there, said it wasn't worth looking into. Not an antiquity, he said."

"But these guys from NCIS think it is. And they had the pictures?"

"Not the pictures I sent to Max. They had other pictures. Ones I had never seen before."

"Where did they get them?"

"I have no idea. The only person who has been in my apartment since I bought the bowl was Tyler."

"Do you really think it's worthless?"

"At this point I don't know. Now I'm second-guessing every decision I've ever made. Islamic art is probably what I'm worst at. I never studied it in college and never dealt much with it at Christie's. There were a few things that made me hope it was an older piece: the sophistication of the design, the style of the glaze, and the fact that there is a very faint etching on the bottom of the base. A few Hebrew letters that read 'First and the last.' I thought Max would be able to help me with that, but like I said, he never wrote back. And you know Max, he's a seller. He wants every good piece he can get for Sotheby's, so if he thought it was anything, he would have responded."

"I think war trophies and looting happened more than people care to acknowledge. I remember reading something about soldiers taking gold-plated AK-47s from a palace and trying to get them home to Georgia."

"That's embarrassing. Of all the things to steal."

"I know, but it definitely could have happened before with Iraqi and Afghani antiquities. Soldiers stealing stuff. Maybe even Tyler. How old was he when he went to Iraq?"

"He was eighteen. Just out of high school."

"And when was he first deployed?"

"Eleven or twelve years ago, since he's twenty-nine now. 2002, 2003."

"The National Museum was raided in two thousand three, remember? It was looted."

"Of course I remember. That was the first thing that came to mind, but Tyler Ford? You met him. He is not an art thief. He's like . . ."

"He's like what? You don't really know him. I mean, you know him a little now, but maybe he was a very different person eleven years ago. What were you like eleven years ago?"

"The same. Jane, I was exactly the same. I'm sorry, I just don't see Tyler Ford as some art-thieving mastermind. Not to belittle his intelligence, but I don't see it."

Jane looked at me with a worried frown. "The last thing I'm going to say is this: I don't know how much you read about the raid of that museum—we were pretty young when it happened—but I don't think the people involved were like, the head of the Met and art history professors at Princeton. So maybe don't discount that dramatic theory just yet."

She had no idea.

When we stood up and went inside the house, Carter took one look at my face and simply said, "I told you."

"You told me what, Carter?"

"I told you to stay away from that guy. That's why you're here, aren't you? And upset like this. It's something about him."

"Yes, Carter. You're so smart. It is something about him. You must feel very proud of yourself."

"You shouldn't have been associating with any of those guys. Any of those base guys. You belong here, in this house, or you belong in New York in your old apartment, not living in some squat house hanging around with guys who picked the army over unemployment."

"The army is an entirely different military branch, Carter! What is wrong with you? Why do you know so little about this? Are you secretly Canadian or something?"

"Canadian? Have you gone fucking insane? I don't know about the military because I don't jerk off to guys in uniform like you suddenly do. Are you hearing me, Carolyn? All that Christie's crap screwed up your brain. And now you're just rebelling. So what happened? Whose ass do I have to kick?"

Jane looked at me and I just told my story again. When I said the word *NCIS* Carter's face tightened. "This is real classy, Carolyn. Keep this up and the world's your oyster."

"Shut up! Both of you. I can't even handle this," said Jane, standing up. "Carter, just go. Go drive around, go to Boston."

"Fine. Goodbye, Carolyn. I'm sure the lesbians will love you in prison."

Carter walked out the door, letting in the sunshine, and didn't bother to close it.

Jane looked at the door and didn't walk over to shut it. We both knew there were big iron gates protecting Jane's perfect multimillion-dollar world against the outside.

"This sounds really bad, Carolyn," she said, pouring us a glass of scotch to share. Jane and I always shared drinks. When we were teenagers, we always swore that when we were old alcoholics, we'd share one very large glass, so we might as well start now.

"I know it does. But that piece. I swear to God I still don't think it's a precious Middle Eastern antiquity. There's something wrong about it."

"Maybe it was glazed over."

"Maybe. But it's more than just the glaze. I've sat through those auctions before in London. I've seen all the catalogues. And I used to handle some of it when I first got to Christie's and worked in appraisals. It just doesn't fit the norm."

"What about Max Sebastian from Sotheby's? Could he have set off some sort of alarm about it but bypassed you?"

"I don't know. You've met him. I'd be surprised. He's not an ethical choirboy when it comes to stolen goods. There was once a big mess with the sale of Nok terra-cotta heads from Nigeria at a London gallery. They were all stolen by grave robbers and brought to the U.K. on cargo planes. He owned the gallery, he knew how they were obtained, and he was going to let them sell anyway. The sale was stopped and his hands somehow remained clean, but lesson learned. Max is not the type to tip off the cops."

"But they're not really the cops."

"They're *worse*. Tyler could get a dismissal because of them if this is what they're alluding to, or fines. Jail time."

"How do you know?"

"I googled it."

"Oh, goody, well then, it's gospel."

Jane took the drink out of my hands and finished it.

"Have you talked to anyone else but those two agents?"

"No. I've talked to no one. Tyler wasn't home and he didn't answer his phone. I called on repeat. Ten times. I'm too scared to go to base and ask for him."

"Do you want to stay here for a while?"

"I do, but I don't think I should. I don't want these NCIS guys to think I'm hiding under the cloak of privilege. They're coming back to the store tomorrow to see the bowl. And I guess I have to give it to them. I can't just refuse, can I?"

"No, you can't. They know you have it somehow, so you have to give it to them. Or cooperate, as they say. But they're not after you; they just asked you some questions. They don't care where you stay."

No, they probably didn't, but I wanted to be exactly where Tyler would expect me to be.

"I'm sorry to bother you with this, Jane," I said, standing up to leave. "Apologize to Carter for me. And try to keep him from getting involved."

I smiled at her and walked out the open front door. The long walk to the gate felt good and I looked out toward the east, to the little house that used to be mine. I could see myself, running in the yard with Brittan and Jane, cradled in a world of ease.

I walked slowly back up Bellevue toward my apartment. I tried Tyler again. This time, when I called, his phone was off. Before, it had rung and then went to voicemail; now it was just dead. I called again. Same thing. I thought about calling Hannah, but the agents hadn't even placed her at the University of Hartford. I started running. I had forgotten my jacket at Jane's and now I was stunned cold in my T-shirt and jeans, running past rows of houses that had been built for very genteel people. Carter was wrong. I didn't belong in the Dalby house and my New York apartment felt like something that suited my former, untainted self. I belonged somewhere in the middle, a gray area I'd been fighting to avoid my entire life.

When I got closer to my apartment I saw someone standing outside, but I knew it wasn't Tyler. It was Greg LaPorte. As soon as I saw him I stopped moving. He was in a white button-down shirt tucked into pressed khakis and he looked very calm. Annoyingly calm. He turned and looked at me and started walking my way. I stood where I was, wanting him to run toward me, but he just sauntered.

He looked at my face, my worry, and tried to take my hand. "They talked to you. I thought it would happen today."

"Greg. Jesus. Why didn't you tell me anything first?" I put my head on his chest without thinking about it and started to cry.

"I'm sorry, Carolyn. I'm sorry. I wanted to, but that's not exactly protocol. Don't worry, this isn't about you. It's about Ford and you're just a small part of all of this. You're not in any trouble."

"A small part of what? I still have no idea what's happening to Tyler."

"Let's take a walk," Greg said, starting to move away from my apartment. "I don't want to talk about it here and I'm not going to ask to come into your house right now. You would be right to say no."

I looked at him helplessly. He nodded at his car, the burnt orange Jeep Wrangler that the man at Goodwill had first told me about, and I got in. We drove in silence, first back to William's, where he got out and checked the door of the store to make sure I had locked it when I ran out, and then to Ruggles Avenue. We parked by the water, got out of the car, and headed toward the Cliff Walk. Part of it was closed to tourists because of storm damage, but everyone who lived in Newport ignored the thin rope and warning sign the town had strung up. Greg helped me climb under it and toward the rocks. This part of the walk had never been paved, and now that it was closed, it was almost secluded. I jumped to a big, slick gray boulder overlooking the ocean, one of the area's best surfing spots when it was open, and sat down. I didn't care if my shoes got wet or if I slipped and cut my hands. I wanted to feel something. Greg sat next to me and tried to take my hand, but I pulled it away from him, looked out to the water, and said, "Tell me everything you know."

He put his freckled hands in his lap and laced his fingers together. They looked dry and cracked.

"It was something you said that night at Brittan's when we were standing outside her house and it was so cold. You were shivering. Brittan was with Mason and it was just us. Remember, we walked around to the side, past the tennis court, so we could see the water."

He looked at me for some sort of emotional response but I didn't say anything. The wind was blowing hard and I was freezing, but this time, I was not going to let Greg attempt to put a jacket around me in some feigned gentlemanly fashion.

"That night, you asked me if I had known a lot of people who died in the war. I remember it really well because you asked very genuinely. Some people ask because they want to see if you're all messed up from PTSD, or they just like all the gruesome crap, but you asked like it mattered. And I was going to answer, but you said that you'd tried asking Ford. That he wouldn't tell you."

"He wouldn't."

"But you said that Ford told you his translator had died. The translator he'd had on all four tours."

I looked at Greg, my face confirming what he said.

"We shared a translator on my only tour in Iraq, his third. His name is Hassan al-Bayati. You said Tyler claimed he'd been his translator four times, which he was. I checked. But he's not dead. He lives in Baghdad. I still keep in touch with him here and there. He's waiting to get a special immigrant visa with the Iraqi Refugee Assistance Project. People have tried to kill him, because he worked with us, but Hassan's not dead. As soon as you said it, I knew Ford was lying to you."

Funny, that was around the time I knew that Ford was lying to me, too.

"Another person would have thought, no big deal, just a lie about someone I don't even know. But I know Ford. I thought he was lying to me in Iraq about selling military weapons but I could never prove it."

"So what? So that nothing incident has prompted you to investigate every statement he makes?"

"He lied to me then, Carolyn! He took out a loaded Beretta and held it in front of my face. He's a lying sack of shit. I knew it then, but I couldn't prove it until now. And you helped me. He stole that bowl. He didn't get it from a translator."

For the first time since I'd lived in Newport, the water looked menacing. The blue sky seemed too low, like it was moving down, quickly, toward me, and Greg's presence was suffocating.

"Are you sure about the translator being alive?"

"Absolutely. I spoke to him yesterday."

"But Tyler said—"

"Ford must have been caught off guard by your question.

And it was a believable answer if you didn't serve with him in Iraq, or know about his fucked-up behavior there, or bother to check out his story. I'm the only one from base who was with him over there on his third tour. Good lie, just bad luck."

"But what's the bad luck? If that bowl wasn't a gift from his translator, which it could have been, then where did it come from?"

"Well, that's what I wondered when you said that."

"But why didn't you ask me? You know I worked for Christie's."

"Because you already said everything you knew. That night we met at the Blue Hen you said you thought it was worth something, but you didn't know what. That's why you wanted to meet Ford, right? So you could figure out where it came from, figure out how much it was worth. After that you were intending to sell it. Just get some info and make a couple thousand bucks. You just hadn't counted on Ford being Ford."

"I wasn't counting on anything. I just wanted to sell it. I had emailed Max Sebastian. He's the—"

"World's leading expert on Arabic antiquities."

"Yeah. Why do you know that?"

"I know him from Quantico. He taught a class on Middle Eastern history while I was on base, before my deployment. I don't know him well, but I knew him well enough to contact him. I sent him pictures of the bowl."

"*You're* the one who took those pictures?"

"I took a few pictures of my Goodwill donation. Goodwill sells some of their best things online, to draw national buyers. I thought the bowl had potential for a bigger sale. I've been working with them for a long time. It's a good cause."

"But there were several pictures! There was one of the bottom, too."

"Like I said, I thought they could sell it online. They can make a lot of money that way. I was trying to help them. I wasn't trying to help someone like you make money."

"But you didn't even recognize it when I showed it to you at the Blue Hen. You didn't even remember giving it to Goodwill!"

"Well, I remember now."

I looked at him, thinking about him kissing my head outside Jane and Brittan's house, and shuddered. "Greg. You're a captain in the United States Marine Corps. You teach at a Marine aviation school, you do charity work. You're a smart guy. Why do you care about this?"

"What you said bothered me. I'm not a fan. I think Ford's a cocky son of a bitch, and yes, I like you, so there's that. You know that. But ever since what happened in Iraq in 2005, I knew he was a liar and a thief. But no one else saw it. To everyone else he was Tyler Ford, a total hotshot, and a dick to women, but one of the most loyal guys out there. Don't piss him off and he'll always have your back. Piss him off, and he'll still have your back. Well, that reputation is bullshit."

I didn't answer. I dug my hands into the rocks until one of my nails bent.

"In the Marines, well, in every branch of military, there's something called a general order—there was one in Iraq and one in Afghanistan. It covers conduct and prohibits members of the military from looting, stealing, taking trophies of war, all that crap. I mean, you can't just go abroad and rape and pillage. If I'm right about the bowl, which I am, this is what will first happen to him. Ford will get an article ninety-two for breaking general order article one-B, which prohibits the taking or retaining of public or private property of an enemy or former enemy. He might get an article one-twenty-one, too, for larceny and wrongful appropriation."

Greg still didn't know about Hannah. He was frothing at the mouth with details, so excited to steamroll Tyler. If he'd known about Hannah, he would have told me. I could not be wrong about her. Greg was wrong. He had to be. The bowl may not have ended up in Goodwill because Tyler's translator died—but the end of his relationship with Hannah was a death of a different kind.

I moved my shoes against the rocks and listened to them slide on the rough surface. "So say he does get these charges placed against him. Then what?" I asked without looking at Greg's arrogant face.

"Then he could get court-martialed. Maybe he could get a plea deal, but probably not. He won't go into pretrial confinement; that really only happens if the guy is suicidal or a flight risk or is going to cause great harm to other people."

"Will I be able to talk to him?"

"Yes, definitely. Even though you're a witness now. Pretrial confinement is usually reserved for big crimes. And preventing the subject from talking to witnesses usually happens in domestic abuse cases only. Murder. The heavy stuff."

"Still, he's going to have to go to court because of this thing that *you* brought to Goodwill."

"I only brought it to Goodwill because he left it in the Goodwill boxes we have on base. Maybe he didn't think anyone would notice him doing it, or that it would get bought by an art dealer who used to work at Christie's, but the world doesn't always work out in your favor, does it."

"I can't understand why, if you say he stole it and that he

knew it was worth something, he would donate it to Good-will. That makes absolutely no sense."

"Maybe he wanted to get rid of it without destroying it. Maybe it was hot. Maybe someone knew he had it. I don't know."

"Okay, so let's say it is hot. You're forgetting that I have it now. He's let me just keep it on a bookshelf in my bed-room?"

"Did he ever try to get it back?"

"No. Not once." But that was another lie. He had asked for it back repeatedly. "Let's say the whole translator thing was a lie and he does get reprimanded."

"Reprimanded? He's not going to a time-out. He could be dismissed. Officers don't get dishonorably discharged; that's just in movies. But the likelihood of him being dis-missed, that could happen. He could get fined, six figures, per offense, and up to ten years in prison."

Everything was just suspicion right now, Greg's hunch.

"I'm sorry to be the one to tell you that your golden boy isn't so golden, Carolyn."

I was positive that Greg had practiced that line in advance.

"Does Tyler know anything about this yet? I can't get in touch with him. I've tried, I keep trying, I can't find him."

"NCIS investigations always start with witnesses and then move on to the subject. I reported it, they talked to me, then you, I don't know who else. When they're done building a case, and if they have enough to build a case, then they'll talk to Tyler. If he's not talking to you now, then he must have been contacted."

"Why did NCIS bite on this? Why do they believe you?"

"Someone I spoke to thinks the bowl was looted from the National Museum of Iraq in 2003. Tyler was part of one of the first units deployed in April. His unit was closest to the museum when it was looted between April tenth and April twelfth. Now it's in his girlfriend's bedroom. It doesn't look good."

I wanted to scream, I wanted to shake Greg until he changed his mind, said it was all a lie.

"Who thinks that? Max Sebastian?"

"I don't think I'm at liberty to say. It doesn't really matter at this point. You have to give it to them. I told them you had it."

"Of course you did; you're such a virtuous guy."

Greg stood up and walked over to me, but I stopped him.

"No Americans were involved in the looting, Greg. Everyone said that. There have been books written about it."

"Maybe they're wrong."

"Really? Eleven years of experts looking into the theft are wrong? It was actually masterminded by some eighteen-year-old American marine from Wyoming with a high school education? You think that kid orchestrated one of the most devastating raids of priceless artifacts in history?"

"I didn't say he was the mastermind. Involved."

"You're wrong. That's like assuming the shoeshine boy at the White House assassinated Kennedy."

"Wow, for being in love with Ford, you sure don't give him much credit. Maybe he's smarter than you think he is. Or than I think he is, for that matter."

I stood up and looked at Greg, sitting calmly next to me. "Stay away from me, Greg," I said, my voice full of anger. "I mean it."

Greg didn't follow me down the rocks. I could feel his eyes on me, watching me to make sure I didn't fall.

The agents came back to see me the next day and I gave them the bowl, reminding them that legally, as far as I knew, I owned it. They didn't say a thing about Hannah working in a pottery studio. I didn't understand how they were missing that link, but I wasn't going to bring it up. The only thing I felt sure of in all of this was that Hannah Lloyd was not a coincidence.

Two days passed without a word from Tyler or Greg. I told William what had happened and he told me to keep coming to work, living my life, rebuilding what I had come to Newport to rebuild. But it wasn't possible now. Every hour that drifted by without Tyler, or the promise that I'd see him, felt like ticking off minutes of nothingness. I would wake up at night and expect him to be next to me, to throw a reassuring arm around me, to make love to me, but instead I slept with fear. It had only been two months, and I was very aware of the time frame, but I was a goner. All I cared about was Tyler.

"No one is going to tell you what's happening," said Jane when I spent my third night without Tyler, next to her instead of alone. Carter was ignoring me to the best of his abilities, but Jane was there, just like she always was.

Another day went by and still nothing. I went to his empty house. I called his phone. I contacted the agents who wouldn't return my calls and I drove to a base that refused to let me past the gates.

It was early May, but the weather was still cool and thick clouds hung over the town, holding back a storm that refused to break through. I piled on sweaters, kept my head down, and tried not to lose myself. It had been five days since I'd talked to Tyler. After a day of work, while William went to Hook Durant's for me, I took the free tourist bus that ran around the historic downtown in spring and summer, ignored the scenery, the swell of sightseers, and let my heavy eyes close. When I got home, I fell asleep for an hour, holding my phone. When I groggily came to, I tried Tyler again, but the phone never even rang.

# CHAPTER 13

M ax Sebastian is in Newport."

"Say that again."

"Max Sebastian is here, in Newport, today."

"How do you know that? Did you see him?" I put down the Pennsylvania Dutch stool I had been polishing, with far too much vigor, for the last hour.

"He called Jane. He wanted to meet with her while he was here. He's always trying to get her to sell her grandmother's Muhammad Haravi watercolor, which she'll never do. She declined Max's invitation and wasn't sure if she should tell you or not. She thought you might get too upset. So while she thought about it, I decided to come here and tell you. I know how disturbed you are by all this and I'm aware that I haven't been your, shall we say, strongest ally lately."

I looked up at Carter standing in the doorway of William's store.

Max Sebastian was here. After my attempts to contact him he was now in Newport and not because of me.

"It has to be for Tyler's bowl. I'm sure he's the one who came up with all the National Museum of Iraq garbage."

"That's what we immediately thought when he called Jane this morning."

"This morning when?" I looked at my watch. It was almost four o'clock. Max Sebastian could have come and gone.

"Around ten."

"What do you know about how NCIS works?" I asked Carter. "Do they have their own art crime team? Could they do any testing on the bowl? Date testing?"

"I have no idea. But that could be why Max is here. He's the best, right? Maybe they brought him in to authenticate."

Carter left the store after I thanked him and when he closed the door I thought about Greg. Max was definitely the someone he spoke to who thought it was looted from the National Museum of Iraq. No one knew the inventory of the National Museum better than Max. He probably had a firmer grasp on what the museum had than many people who worked there.

I had to find him before he left Newport. I tried Greg's phone, but it was off. I called the main number for Mardet and they said Greg was teaching for the next thirty minutes. I screamed to William, who was in the back doing inventory, that I was leaving and drove the route I had spent far too much time breaking speed limits on, toward the base.

When I got to the main gates I asked the guard to contact Greg LaPorte.

"He's teaching at Mardet today. Did you try reaching him personally?"

"I have," I said, knowing full well that they were not going to let me on base if I wasn't someone's guest.

"I think his phone is off and I have to see him, urgently. Could you leave a message and ask him to meet me here?" I asked.

I must have looked desperate because the guard called in

and then told me to turn my car around and wait a few feet from base for Greg.

"You can't be in this area and you can't go on base without him. Just stay in my view and I'll send him to you," said the guard. I thanked him, did a U-turn, and parked my car illegally about ten yards from security. The only thing I could count on in this mess was Greg coming to see me when I needed him.

It was beautiful enough outside to roll down the windows, but I kept them up. I turned the radio off and sat there, staring ahead, in silence. How long had it been since Tyler and I had been on base, telling each other just enough to start falling in love? I thought back. It had only been two months. And in the short time before and after I had found him, I'd become infatuated with him, been afraid of him, fallen in love with him, believed in him, questioned him, and been disappointed and abandoned by him. I didn't know which of those emotions was strongest now. Maybe fear.

I was overwhelmed with that fear when Greg came to see me, and because my windows were up, I didn't hear him approaching the car. He knocked on the glass and I screamed. I looked to the left and saw him still wearing the placid expression that I wanted to slap off when he told me about Tyler on the Cliff Walk.

I rolled down the window and told him to get in the car.

"Where are we going?" he said with an impish grin.

"We're going to drive." I headed south toward town on Farewell Street and let Greg smile like a marionette for the first five minutes. I didn't know where to go so I turned onto Thames, passing the Blue Hen, and taking a left up Mill to Spring. I parked in front of Trinity Church and let go of the steering wheel.

"Max Sebastian is in Newport," I said, turning my head

toward him and shutting off the ignition. "Can't imagine you know anything about that."

"I know everything about that, but you said you never wanted to see me again."

"I remember what I said!" I screamed. "Obviously, I remember. But my current disdain for you is muted by the fact that you know a lot that I don't. I'm not sure why that's the case, but it is."

"Because I'm on base. And also, I don't have blinders on in regards to what Ford's done."

I hated the way Greg talked about Tyler. His superiority seeped out of him.

"Have those detectives talked to you again?" I asked.

"Just once." Greg looked at me without a shred of guilt and said, "You may have pieced together by now that the person who believes that Tyler's bowl was stolen from the National Museum in Iraq was Max Sebastian."

I raised my eyebrows, too fuming to answer. Tyler's bowl. That's probably what Greg had been calling it to everyone who would listen. Say it enough and the world would start to believe him.

"When I reached out to Max, he didn't say anything about the fact that you'd emailed him," Greg said. "I didn't know that until you told me when we were on the Walk. Max was very responsive and we had a few back-and-forths right away." He spoke like Max was some old prep school buddy instead of an instructor he barely knew at Quantico.

"The detail that I've been wanting to tell you all day, but was afraid to because of our memorable last encounter, is that we, Max and I, spoke to NCIS together this morning. That bowl, the one you have, or had, Max was able to confirm that it was once in the National Museum of Iraq."

I didn't buy it. There was no way that Tyler was ever in

possession of something from the National Museum of Iraq. It was impossible. Greg may have been giving it his stamp of approval, but I was not, even with Max involved.

"I don't believe you."

"It doesn't matter what you believe now. Max confirmed it. He was in touch with the head of the museum, who sent a fax of their file. They have pictures of the bowl in their records. It was acquired by the museum on March twenty-fifth, 2003. It was never fully inspected but it was logged into their system. They have the record stating that they acquired it."

Greg was smug. He was trying to come off as caring, helpful, the good cop to Tyler's callous criminal, but it wasn't working. He was too proud of what he'd done, catching Tyler in a lie and getting marvelous Max all the way to Newport. I didn't want to know the rest. I turned away from Greg and looked at the church next to me. It was where John and Jackie Kennedy had married. I remembered walking past it when I was young and dreaming about Jackie's fairy-tale day. Then when I got older I found out that Jack was already cheating on her and that she had to stand in a receiving line for three hours. The truth lost a lot of its luster with age.

"Why was it never inspected?" I asked Greg. I knew the answer, but I had to hear him say it for it to become real.

"It was stolen from the museum during the looting a few weeks later."

"So let me try to understand something." I put my hands in my lap and squeezed one with the other. "I contact Max Sebastian, nothing happens. You contact Max Sebastian and suddenly this bowl was part of the collection of the National Museum of Iraq and it was looted during the war. Don't you find that a little odd? It's not like we contacted him months apart. It had to be a matter of weeks."

"Maybe he didn't pay any attention to it until two people contacted him about the same object. That was probably enough to get him to start looking."

"You who has all the answers. Tell me one thing. Where has Tyler been through all this? Because he is certainly not with me."

"He's on base. I don't think he's left since it started. I've seen him a few times, but we haven't spoken."

"Because he would spit in your face."

"He's a little more reserved than you are."

"Oh yeah? That's not what everyone told me. Weren't you and your friends warning me every chance you got? Worried that I'd be the next Hannah Lloyd."

Hannah. Greg still hadn't said anything about Hannah. NCIS had to have pieced together that Hannah was a potter. They couldn't be missing that very important link. If they were talking to witnesses, their reach must have gone beyond me and Greg.

I rolled down the windows and let the voices and laughter from the tourists walking from Thames Street to Bellevue move through the car. I wanted so badly to be one of them, just a girl without a care in the world who went to Newport simply to vacation.

"I want to see Max," I said firmly. "You know he's here; you must know where he is."

"He's not in Newport."

"Then where in the hell is he, Greg? You're his sudden soul mate. Tell me where he is."

"He's in Providence for the day. He's doing something called a TL test on the bowl."

I turned to Greg, feeling my face flush.

"Max Sebastian is doing a thermoluminescence test? You cannot be serious."

"I am. Thermoluminescence, is that a TL test? He specifically said TL test."

"Yes, that's the most definitive test you can do to date-stamp pottery. But why is he bothering! The museum in Iraq may not have had the opportunity to properly test it themselves but if it's even three hundred years old, it wouldn't be worth half a million. Max never goes to this much trouble for a single object. It's not even from an important estate!"

"But it's a crime. It will be in all the papers. Three years after Operation Iraqi Freedom ends, eleven years after the museum was raided, objects that were looted are still turning up and in the hands of marines in the United States. Max probably wants the press."

Of course he did. Max would glue himself to a camera lens if he could with his overly done Cambridge accent and Dunhill suits. But to go to the trouble of TL testing? Blair Bari hadn't even considered it. He handled it for a matter of minutes and ruled it out. The difference was that Max now knew it had been in the museum, because Max had access and connections that no one else had. It seemed that was all it took.

"Will they really be able to date it?" asked Greg.

"Definitely. It's one of the only methods that can get you in a hundred-year window. TL is just the light that some minerals emit when they're heated following irradiation. It's all about light. If you compare the light output that the bowl, or whatever you're testing, produces and compare it to commonly known doses of radiation produced naturally by the object, you can tell how much radiation the piece has absorbed. When the piece was originally fired, it would have been stripped from all its TL. So TL at zero. You then have to measure the accumulated dose and break it down per year. You drill out a tiny part. But it's really small, like five millimeters, and they'll do it from the base."

I looked at Greg, repulsed by the satisfied expression on his face, and watched him stand up to leave. "I'll try to connect you with Max. Drop me back at base and I'll call you as soon as I hear anything. He's not leaving tonight."

But Max did leave that night. Greg called me to tell me that he hadn't heard from Max that evening and didn't the following day, either.

I woke up early the next day. It was a perfect mid-May morning in New England. No humidity, all sunshine, and everyone in town trying to figure out how they could spend the day outside. It was the weather you boasted about if you were from the Northeast. The good weather made me panic. It was like the world was tumbling peacefully forward while I'd stopped following. It had been eight days since I'd seen Tyler. I was overwhelmed with thoughts that all started with "If he really loved me . . ." but I knew it wasn't fair. He could have been told not to contact me. But what seemed more likely was that he didn't want to contact me.

I took out the pictures of the bowl that I had sent Max and laid them on the floor again. I sat there and willed some sort of new thoughts, for some marking on the thing to expose its story, but I still saw nothing. I had meant to ask Greg if Max had said anything about the words on the bottom, but I'd been too taken aback by the fact that Max was bothering to TL-test it at all.

I'd tried calling Max again. I'd tried to contact him four times yesterday, hoping he might take my calls because of Greg, but still nothing. No response to any attempts I made from phone messages, to emails, and even one relayed by an assistant. Max Sebastian did not want me involved.

I thought about him in Newport and why he bothered

to come in the first place. If he'd gone back to London, that meant that he'd finished TL testing. I knew getting the results from the military was a reach, so I called Blair Bari. TL testing was a process, and not a cheap one. If Brown had done it for Max, he could have been involved.

The phone rang three times before Blair's voice came on the line. I said my name in the rushed, nervous tone I'd gotten used to using that week and he responded warmly.

"You are calling about Max Sebastian."

"Of course I am. Were you involved at all with his TL test of the bowl?"

"I could have been."

Yes, and I could have been born with a tail. Blair Bari was supposed to be the voice of reason in this. My confidant.

"Can you tell me anything about it?"

"I'd like to, Carolyn. I would. But this is all part of an ongoing NCIS investigation. I can't just take you through everything step by step, now, can I?"

Of course he couldn't. I was just hoping he would.

"What if you took me through it in a complicated way?"

"What if I promised you that you would be hearing something soon?"

"Then I'd probably sleep on my front stoop."

"You're lucky it's spring."

After my nothing conversation with Blair, I decided to go to Hook's auction that afternoon. I had tried to be helpful in the store but William likened me to a nervous zoo animal with rabies.

"You're going to froth on something. Please leave," he said, trying to lace his concern with humor. I knew I looked terrible, I was acting disastrously, and all through it William did his best to carry on like everything was pleasant.

I wanted to stop by Tyler's again, to pound on his door and

call his name like I had done every day in a row for a week, but it was getting too embarrassing. He didn't want to see me.

Hook's was exactly like it had been every week that I'd attended. This time, the only difference was that the Merlot was a dark purple, almost the color of eggplant skin. When I came in, Hook brought me a glass and I tipped it back and drank it. My sophisticated Christie's-trained eye was doing nothing for me. My instinct about Hannah was totally off the mark. I might as well just down enough to see double; then I'd feel like I was getting a good deal.

I passed on Hook's first five lots of the day.

"Lot six now, ladies and gentleman, lot six, for the real lover of American furniture, is a Hugh Finlay chair. It was originally part of a set of six, but we've just got the one for you today. We'll let you go find the other five, but you can have this one, right here, right now. This is a museum-worthy piece, ladies and gentleman. The best of the best. You want to impress all your friends for the Newport summer season, you better buy this chair and put it right in the middle of your living room. Now let's start this bidding!"

Hook had a Hugh Finlay chair. I had no idea how he had gotten it, but I knew I had to have it. I grabbed my phone and texted William. "Hook has a Hugh Finlay chair. Maple and cane, painted and gilded. Curved crest tablet. Near-perfect condition. Can I bid?"

"Do not go over seventy-five thousand," he wrote back. "Authentic . . . give me a percentage."

"One hundred," I wrote back. I knew the chair. The set had originally been in the summer home of the founder of the *Baltimore Sun*. Four were at the Museum of Modern Art in New York. One was at the High Museum in Atlanta. I knew we could sell it for over a hundred thousand.

A few of the men readied their paddles but I already knew none of them was going to win.

"Who's got fifty thousand for me, starting at fifty thousand . . . Carolyn Everett! Welcome back to the show, princess."

The bidding went up to $65,000 and I was the one bringing every bid up. I'd sell my firstborn to have that thing.

"Seventy thousand who's got seventy thousand against this Newport brat, come on now someone take it from her. Let's see it in the crowd now seventy thousand."

A man in Nantucket red pants bit on the bid and I went straight for seventy-one thousand. The seventy-thousand bid dropped out and Hook winked at me as he lifted the tusk he used for a gavel and said, "Sold to my favorite gal . . . of the day, Carolyn Everett."

I stayed at Hook's until the end of the auction, buying two Chinese ginger jars and a piano stool. Afterward, I asked him to help me put everything in William's car. I, for a few moments, owned a Hugh Finlay.

"Where did you get this chair?" I asked. "I could sell this to a museum, you know."

"Oh yeah?" he said with mischief in his voice.

"But you know that," I replied. "Fine, I won't ask you how you got it. I'm just very happy you sold it."

"You been keeping busy?" he said as he walked backward, holding the chair with me. "You don't look yourself. Thin and jumpy."

"I know. I'm not myself. I'm about three steps from disaster but I'll keep it together. This right here is helping a lot."

"Let me know what I can do," said Hook without prying. He loaded my trunk and left before I closed the door. The chair's feet were sticking out a little too far and I pushed it in a few more inches so they wouldn't hit the glass when I shut it. It was heavier than I thought it would be. I braced myself with my back leg and lifted it a little higher, pulling the legs up. And then I saw it. There was a note taped to the bottom of the seat of the chair. I pulled it off carefully and opened it. On a small white piece of thick paper it said, in small black slanted letters,

*Carolyn. I'm sorry. Soon . . .*
                                        *—Ford.*

## CHAPTER 14

He knew I would buy it. The Hugh Finlay. Of course he knew. Or was he there? Had Tyler's eyes been on me this entire time? When I was with Greg, entering the Dalbys' house or repeatedly knocking on his door, calling him from the street—could he have been watching me? I stood motionless in the parking lot. Tyler had not abandoned me. I shut the trunk, got into the car, and locked the doors. *Soon.* I needed soon to happen immediately.

When I got back into town, I passed Carter walking down by the water. I slowed the car down and called his name.

"Carolyn, look at you sane enough to drive. Park the car. I'm about to take my boat out around the harbor. Thirty minutes. Come with me. It's right here." He pointed behind him to the dock that was closest to town.

I parked the car a few feet away in a wide space and walked slowly to him. I took my sweater off and tied it around my waist, letting the sun hit my shoulders. Suddenly everything felt better. Tyler was near me and soon he would be with me. I could feel his presence.

"Did Jane tell you about this thing?" said Carter, kicking off his Sperrys when we got to the dock.

"No," I said, looking up at the beautiful sailboat. The

Dalbys only had sailboats. They would never own yachts. They, as a family, held on to their east coast blue blood the way southerners held fast to accents.

"I love your boat, Carter!" I yelled out as he hopped on and gave me a hand.

"I do, too. I bought it, you know. Not Jane. Makes it even better."

I smiled, looking up at the white sails, jetting out so beautifully against the sky.

"That does make it better. It's wonderful. Even better than Jane's."

It was smaller than Jane's, but I liked the intimacy. It felt like a very polished version of normalcy instead of Newport grandeur.

"I'm going under the bridge out for a couple miles and then back," said Carter, jibing the boat north. "There's something off with the mainstay, according to Jane. And you know Jane, she knows best. I wanted to check it today."

I kicked off my shoes and offered Carter a hand, but he told me to relax and keep him company.

"You want to talk about it?" he asked as we coasted under the bridge.

"Not at all!" I shouted back. This was the first time I'd felt like I wasn't about to have a stroke since NCIS had come to my door.

"Can I just ask about Max?"

"I missed him. He was here and I missed him."

"Why was he here?"

To ruin my life.

"I don't know," I said, smiling.

Carter let me leave it there and we moved past Gould Island, up toward Prudence Island.

"I appreciate this, Carter," I said when he moved away

from the sails. "I really do. I wish I could stay here indefinitely."

"No you don't. You have too much to do."

"I know. But let's pretend I don't."

When we got off the boat I thanked Carter again for sticking out his olive branch and drove back to William's. I polished, I rearranged, I dusted, I catalogued, I logged, I updated the site, I changed the front window display, and at ten minutes to six, right before close, I opened the front door to Brian Van Ness, the officer from NCIS who had grilled me before.

"I'm glad you're here," he said as he walked in without being invited inside. He was alone.

"You mind if I sit at that table?" He pointed to the glass table where we had sat before.

"Do you want to let me know why you're here first?" I asked, trying not to get upset.

"Why don't you invite me to sit down and then I'll let you know."

I gestured rudely toward the table.

"First of all, I know you've been trying to contact us. I'm sorry we couldn't be in better touch."

I didn't respond.

"Secondly, have you had any contact with Tyler since we talked to you?"

"Not a word. Nothing. The second you spoke to me, he vanished. Was that your doing? Did you tell him he couldn't talk to me?" I needed him to confirm. It had to be because of them.

"He was pretty upset over everything. He's got a reputation on base, a real stoic thing going, but he showed a lot of anger over what was happening to him the past couple of days."

"Anger or emotion?"

"A little of both. It's understandable. Accused of possession of stolen goods, breaking several military codes, laundering."

"Laundering? What are you talking about?"

"Donating the bowl to Goodwill. Make it pass through a few hands, come up again after it makes its way through different channels, possibly in a different state. By the time you have it back, it has lost its stigma. It's just another one of those instances where a five-dollar bowl sells for several million. You know, those things happen."

"They happen, but not because of laundering. They happen because people don't know what they have."

"But all signs pointed to Tyler knowing what he had."

"And the museum? Was there really a record of that bowl?" My hands were sweating, sticking to each other. Why did these NCIS agents just walk into the store? Act like they had authority over me, speak to me whenever they wanted to. I thought of Tyler's note, of him close to me, looking after me, and tried not to panic.

"How do you know there was a record?" asked Brian.

I hadn't meant to blurt that out. Greg. He would know Greg had told me.

I shrugged.

"I'll ignore that and tell you like you don't know. Yes, there is a record of that piece at the National Museum of Iraq. It was brought in right before the museum was looted, and two weeks after it got there, it was stolen. But the American military was in no way involved in the theft."

"Until Tyler."

"I didn't say that."

"What did you say?"

"That it looked bad. Tyler ditched the bowl in the middle of the night in some Goodwill pile and you, a girl he's sleeping with, has it in her apartment. Then the museum's photos of the bowl. That same bowl. All of that is enough for a front-page *New York Times* story. It wrote itself."

"So did it?" I asked, my voice broken. Was this what Tyler had meant by soon?

Brian reached down into a leather bag he had with him. He put the bowl on the table in front of me and I lowered my face onto the glass table, trying not to cry.

"Like you said, this bowl isn't an antiquity. It was made in the last ten years."

I was crying now. My tears fell on the table around me, dripping, salty, near my mouth. Brian let me stay like that until I collected myself and sat up and dried my face.

"I didn't mean to react like this. I've been thinking the worst. I thought I got it wrong."

"Tyler Ford is not getting court-martialed, no charges are being pressed, and I can give this"—he pushed the bowl slightly forward—"back to you."

I looked at it on the table, sitting there, like nothing had happened to it. It had gone from Tyler to Goodwill to Hook's to me to NCIS and back, and it still looked beautiful, like a bowl that should be put on a shelf and left alone. I didn't want to touch it yet. I just looked at it sitting between us, and wondered how I had become entangled in all this, just by buying something that I thought looked nice at a nothing auction.

I wiped my face again and pushed my hair back in place.

"The TL testing. Were you there for it?"

"I'm not asking how you know about this. You haven't said any of this."

"Fine, I haven't said any of it. But can you tell me about the TL testing? I want to know if that happened."

"It did. Max Sebastian from Sotheby's was the lead on it with an archaeologist and an Egyptologist from the Joukowsky Institute."

"Was Blair Bari one of them?"

"Blair Bari, no. I don't remember meeting him."

"And the results?"

"Like I said, it's only ten years old, they believe. Made within the decade."

I had been right. Greg and Max and NCIS had been wrong and all of this with Tyler, all of it had happened for some piece made ten years ago. I couldn't believe it.

Brian stood up, leaving the bowl behind on the table for me. My twenty-dollar bowl was no longer a stolen half-million-dollar bowl. It was back to being my twenty-dollar memory.

"I'm sure Tyler will come find you now," said Brian, heading for the door. "He probably just wanted to keep you out of it."

I told him I hoped so. As soon as Brian left, I planned to bound out the door and find Tyler myself. All the anger that I'd felt toward him was being chipped away because he had done absolutely nothing wrong.

"There's just one thing I haven't been able to drop. But it's not my job to care about it anymore, so I'm going to stop caring, but I am still going to ask you," said Brian.

"What's that?"

"That bowl." He pointed to my bowl on the table. "It's new, right? Fired and glazed just ten years ago. But it looks exactly like the one that the museum has on file, the Arabic phrase, the pattern, the size, it's identical."

"Did the museum record say anything about the underside of the base? The Hebrew writing?"

"It didn't. I don't think. I don't remember seeing that in

the pictures Max had the museum fax over. But everything else, like I said, the colors and that intricate pattern and even that line from the Quran, all the same. So how could that happen? Did someone have the real object and just throw together a copy in the last couple of years for fun?"

"Could have been," I said. "Did the documentation say where the bowl had come from?"

"A dig. An archaeological dig in Jaffa."

"In Jaffa?" I said surprised. "But that's in Israel."

"Right. I looked that up and saw that."

"Why would it have been donated to the National Museum of Iraq?"

"I don't know. It's not our jurisdiction to look into that. We're only concerned with military crimes. The bowl in Tyler's possession, previously in his possession, was not stolen, so the rest doesn't matter to us. But that just bothered me, personally. You know, the copy."

"There could have been a picture if it came from a dig site. Someone could have admired it and copied it, the way countless people try to repaint the *Mona Lisa* because it's a challenge. They don't necessarily try to pass it off as the real thing."

"I'll take that as an explanation. Between you and me, I like Tyler Ford. I wouldn't have liked to see him on the wrong side of all this." Brian smiled contently. We walked through the store and I shut the door behind him.

Tyler's bowl. Now I could call it that. Now I wanted to call it that. I walked back to the table and looked at it. I didn't want to touch it yet. I knew that as soon as I picked it up I would never want to put it down. I put my hand inside and ran it over the glaze, the even greens, the vanilla cream white. I had always loved furniture because of its size. It was heavy and substantial. Sturdy. Something you could live with and didn't have to frame and hang away from dirty hands. But I loved the lines of this bowl. Its perfect roundness, the slanted Arabic script. I finally put both my hands on the sides and picked it up. I held it in the air in front of me and as soon as it was level to my eyes, I almost dropped it. It slipped from in between my hands and I barely caught it with my left. I screamed out for no one to hear me. But I still had it. I held it up again and then transferred it from one hand to the other. I sat back down at the glass table and put my head on the surface again. It was still wet from my tears of joy. Now I could add fresh ones. This was not Tyler's bowl.

## CHAPTER 15

I hesitated and then dialed three out of the ten numbers I needed for the phone to ring and hung up again. I shook out my nervous hand, stretched it like a guitar player before a concert, and sat back down at the table. I was sitting on time I didn't have. I crossed my legs, picked up the phone again, entered the number, and waited for the phone to ring. An operator answered quickly. She had a pleasant voice, a college student's voice.

"I'd like to be transferred to Hannah Lloyd, please," I said, trying to make my tone sound smooth, normal.

"She's in the pottery studio, but I can get her if you like. Can I tell her who's calling?"

"Tell her it's Katie, with a commission for the bowl we talked about. She'll know me."

I was put on hold for a few minutes, and when a voice came back on the line, it was the same girl who answered.

"She's in the middle of firing but she said she'll call you back in ten minutes. Can you leave a number?"

I gave her my number and put my phone on the table next to the bowl. I picked the bowl up again and felt the weight of it.

That had always been my concern with Tyler's bowl,

the weight. It was heavy. Substantial. Nothing like the older Middle Eastern pottery I had ever touched. I took out my photos of the bowl and compared every inch to the one in front of me, but there were no differences that I could see. It was only the weight. I knew for TL testing you had to core out a five-millimeter piece to sample, but that was not going to make a difference.

How could Brian not have felt it? I thought about how much I had held that bowl since I had bought it. I had carried it in my bag with me around Newport when I went to meet Greg. I had felt its weight on my body; I knew how much it pulled on my shoulder when I walked. I had turned it over to be photographed, moved it from shelf to shelf. At this point I knew it almost the way a potter who threw it would have known it. And I understood why Brian hadn't felt the difference. It was too subtle to tell if you weren't very familiar with both.

Both. Because there had to be two.

My phone rang and I jumped and hit my knee on the bottom of the table, just like I had that January day in Baltimore when I had been at the Rusty Scupper with Nina and her brother. I grabbed it, pushed accept, and before I could say hello, I heard Hannah's voice.

"What's your real name?" she asked me immediately.

"Carolyn Everett."

"How do you know Ford?"

"I'm dating him."

There was silence after that. I could hear the faint sounds of students or other teachers behind her but she remained quiet.

"Are you still interested in that commission?" she said.

I hesitated. She was in public. Maybe still in the building where I had gone to see her.

"I am. I'm very interested. I'd like to talk to you about it."

"You're in Newport?"

"That's right, but I can go anywhere."

"Let's meet in the middle. What's in the middle of Hartford and Newport?"

I thought of the scenery along Route 165. Right on the state line there was a pond. I used to go swimming there sometimes when I was younger.

"Do you know Beach Pond? Route 165 cuts right through it. It's not a busy road."

"I know it."

"If you turn right off the road, a left for me, there's a small parking area that leads up to hiking trails and you can access the water right there. It's always empty except in the height of summer. There's a no-swimming sign nailed into a tree. It's old-looking; you can't miss it. I'll meet you right under it."

"I'll be there in two hours," she said, then hung up the phone.

Two hours. It only took forty-five minutes to drive there from Newport but I wanted to leave immediately. I went to the back of the store and got one of William's thick foam packing boxes and cut out enough in the middle with a box cutter to fit the bowl. My days of throwing it in my purse were over.

I taped around the middle of the foam with packing tape and then thought better of it and ripped it off. I didn't want it to be difficult to remove. Nothing to make Hannah more nervous. Or me. Instead, I put the foam box inside a grocery bag, one of the thick ones with a large square bottom that you took to pastry shops. I ran outside to my car and found a beach towel on the floor of the passenger's side. It was lapis blue and slightly torn at one edge. I folded it and put it on top of the bag. I walked back into the store and looked at one of the grandfather clocks, ticking rhythmically. An hour and thirty minutes until Hannah. I put on a green cashmere sweater that Jane had lent me, wrote William a note, left it on the glass table, and started my drive toward Connecticut.

The roads into Connecticut from Rhode Island were not highways. They crossed right over the hum of Interstate 95 and stayed completely removed from the soulless drive to New York. The streets were full of New England charm: farmhouses set back from the road, tiny antique stores, a few slightly dilapidated barns. And when the winding suddenly stopped, you rolled down a hill and came upon Beach Pond, right on the Connecticut–Rhode Island line, edging slightly farther into Connecticut. Away from the parking lot and nature trails, houses flanked the swollen side of the lake, their docks peeking into the water. I saw it in the distance and flicked on my left-turn signal even though there was no one behind me, no one in front. I pulled into the gravel area with a few non-outlined parking spaces and turned off my ignition. It was an afternoon of gray-blue skies. Right overhead, the blue was spotless, but if I looked west over Connecticut, I could see spring rain starting to roll in. I hoped it held until the evening. I walked onto the beach and took my shoes off. I still had forty minutes until Hannah was due to arrive. I dipped my toes in the cold water and let it climb up my ankles and then my calves, right to my knees. I hadn't put my feet in the water since I'd jumped in with Tyler. Our dare. Our "I love yous."

I moved toward the road as I heard a car and saw a white Volkswagen slow down as it approached the turnoff. I walked out of the water, not bothering to wipe my feet, put my boat shoes back on, and headed to the parking lot. Hannah parked next to my car and I stayed rigid on the beach as I watched her get out of her hatchback and turn around to look at me.

"I just need to get something from the car," I said, pointing to my backseat. She nodded and watched me as I opened the side door, reached in, and got the shopping bag. I slung it on my shoulder and walked toward her. She was leaning against her trunk. Her long dark hair was up in a thick ponytail and this time, she wasn't wearing clothes covered in clay.

"We can sit on the beach if you like," I said, pointing to where I had been when she pulled up.

"That's fine," she said, following. Hannah was a few inches taller than me and was dressed like someone who didn't care too much about clothes but always looked nice despite it. She walked with me onto the sand and I put my oversize towel out and sat on it. She kicked off her gray sandals and joined me.

"Why did you say your name was Katie?" she asked, looking at the bag and then looking back at me.

"Because of Tyler's sister. I thought you'd recognize the name and frankly, I wanted to make you nervous."

I could see that it had worked.

"What's in that bag?" she said, motioning cautiously with her head.

"A bowl. Would you like to see it?"

"No." She looked at the glassy water, which was beautiful, despite being next to the road. "It's a shame you can't swim here anymore. I used to come here when I was younger."

"I did, too. I used to love to swim here. It's a lot calmer than the Newport water. Are you from Rhode Island, too?"

"I'm from Hartford. I moved to Newport for a job."

I didn't bring up St. George's. I wasn't sure why but I

didn't want Hannah to know I had gone there. I looked at her face, and the scar on her chin was much more noticeable from this short distance. It went around the bottom and up the sides a little, like where the elastic from a child's paper party hat would leave a mark.

"Do you mind if I ask you a few questions?" I said, not knowing what I was going to ask her.

"Oh, stop being so phony polite. Why are all you Newport girls like that? Just talk. It's not opening night. That's why I came, right? Because you want to ask me questions. Prying personal questions about the commission."

"There is no commission."

"No shit."

I pulled one of my legs under me, adjusted my white shorts, and didn't answer. I wanted to take the bowl out. I wanted to see her face when she saw it.

"I got a call last week," she said, not looking at me. "Which is the only reason I'm here." Her head seemed turned permanently toward the water. "It was someone from NCIS."

My heartbeat doubled. I had no idea that NCIS had called her.

"Brian Van Ness? Josh Wallace?" I offered.

"The second one. Josh Wallace. He left a message at school for me."

"Did you ever talk to him?"

"No. He called and said he had some questions about Ford and I called him back but then he never returned my call, so I figured all their questions were answered. But it still scared me. It was almost worse because they didn't call me back. They called you too, right? That's how you found me?"

"No, I found you because someone told me you taught art at St. George's. I just kind of pieced it together from that. But NCIS did contact me."

"Was it about Ford? Is he in trouble?"

"I don't know exactly. I don't think so. They stopped contacting me so they seemed to have dropped their investigation about his possible wrongdoing. But I haven't seen him in nine days, so I don't know all the details."

She sat up and wiped the sand off her palms before putting them on the towel, slightly behind her.

"Did all their questions get answered?"

"Yes, they did."

"But you have different ones."

"I think I know something that NCIS doesn't."

"I don't have to talk to you, though," she said, stating the obvious. "Who are you even to come to my school and throw Tyler Ford's phone number in my face?"

"I don't remember throwing it, but you're right, I'm no one. I'm just a girl who works in an antique store in Newport. But I used to work at Christie's."

That last word caused her to turn and face me.

"You worked at Christie's, the auction house? Why don't you work there anymore?"

"I got fired."

She turned away from me again. It was then that I noticed that her nose, which might have been naturally thin and small, now looked almost too thin and small, like it had been redone when there was nothing much left to remake it with.

"You got fired from Christie's and now you're in Newport dating Tyler Ford. Not the typical resume." She paused and changed directions.

"Does he know you know me? I mean, that you contacted me?"

Hannah had never called Tyler to tell him. Or she was just trying to catch me off guard.

"Not that I'm aware of," I said. "Unless he's following me."

"He might be," said Hannah. "That's definitely his style. He's . . . intense." The clouds had started to thicken above us and I reached for the edge of the towel and wrapped it up around my bare legs.

"Did everybody tell you what happened to me, when you started dating Ford?"

"Everybody did."

"That's nice of them. Don't end up the next Hannah Lloyd, right?"

"Something like that. I should also tell you that I know Mike Fogg," I admitted.

She turned to me and focused on my face until we were staring at each other.

"I don't talk about Mike Fogg. You bring up his name again, and I leave. Okay?"

"I'm sorry. He's not a friend. I just wanted to be honest."

"Yeah, well, the truth isn't worth it sometimes."

We sat silently next to each other for a few moments, two women trying to size up each other's agenda.

I sat in the stillness and tried to take in the tenor of Hannah. The way Tyler kept his promise of silence to her, coupled with her reaction just now, I knew Mike had done the unthinkable. Hannah was just one who wanted to keep it quiet, wanted to bury it, and Mike was still in New York, living his fortunate life, planning to come back and summer in Newport. Instead, we were all chasing Tyler.

"Can I ask you one thing about that night at the Blue Hen and then I will drop it?" I asked Hannah. "I don't think I can have the conversation you and I need to have without asking you this question."

"Try me."

"Did Tyler mean to hit you that night or was it an accident?"

"Do you think he's the kind of person who would do that? Punch his girlfriend in the face? Because if any part of you thinks that, you don't know him very well."

"So it was an accident."

"Of course it was an accident. I shouldn't have been there, but he was in one of his moods where he'll do anything to right a situation as much as he can. I thought he could kill Mike. I seriously did. He might have if I hadn't jumped in."

"Did you worry he might hit you?"

"I wasn't worried about anything right then except what would happen to Ford if he attacked Mike. How far he would go. I never thought it was going to end up like it did. Me being the one knocked out cold, waking up in the hospital unable to move my mouth."

"You left after that."

Hannah was fidgeting with her jeans, rolling and unrolling the bottom of her left cuff as she spoke. Her face was flushed and I understood then how Tyler could have been in love with her. When she let her guard down, she came off very soft, very pretty.

"Things changed; you can understand why. I grew a little afraid of him. Not because I thought he would hit me, but because he's a lot of person. He can be hard to deal with. And there was so much pressure from the town, my whole world. You hear the way people still talk about him. I was in the hospital. My face was shattered. Everyone told me to never speak to him again and I didn't, but they didn't know the circumstances. They thought Ford was violent on top of everything else they already thought. But that's not really the truth. I just couldn't bear everyone knowing. It happened the Saturday before the Fourth of July, and I haven't seen much of him since."

"Doesn't he know where you are? You're less than two hours away."

"Sure. He tried to come and see me all summer. He called hundreds of times, but I refused. And Ford, he'll be Ford, but he won't push that limit. He could feel what I needed, and for a while, it wasn't him."

"And you haven't seen him since then?"

"I did, just twice though."

"Twice. Why twice? Recently?"

"Open that," she said, pointing at the bag next to me, "and I'll tell you."

I looked at her for a long while before reaching for the bag. I wanted to give her time to change her mind, to tell me to leave her alone, but she didn't say anything else. She just watched me watching her until the heaviness of her expression turned my confidence to awkwardness. I looked behind us to make sure there wasn't anyone around and took out the foam box. I took off the top and let her see the bowl.

"Can I take it out of this?" she said, pointing to my makeshift packaging.

Part of me was afraid she would break it. Shatter it and throw the shards in the pond so I could never do anything with it. That was the problem with art. It was so easy to ruin. I hesitantly nodded yes and she reached her hands down and took the bowl out delicately, by both sides of the rim. She turned it around and looked at the words carved in the bottom, then she ran her fingers around the circumference of the base and up along the sides. She turned it over and looked at the glaze, holding it up slightly to see it in different light. Finally, she put it back in the box, just like I had packed it.

"Is it yours?" I asked, trying to contain myself.

"It's definitely not mine."

I looked at her, her hand still on the bowl like it was something she had owned for decades. It had to be hers.

"But you've seen it before."

She picked it up again and transferred it from one hand to the other.

"Do you know what the words in Hebrew on the base say?" I asked her.

"Of course I do. 'First and the last.'"

She'd made it. I knew she had.

"How do you know that?" I asked.

A car flew past us, speeding toward Connecticut, and we both jumped at the sound of the motor tearing through the silence. It pulled over on the side of the road about a hundred yards in front of us and we both watched it, frozen. A middle-aged woman in the New England uniform of a navy and white striped sweater and khakis got out, took a picture of the swelling side of the lake with her phone, and got back in. Neither of us moved until the car was out of sight.

"I never thought I'd be in this position," said Hannah finally. She took both her hands and ran them through her hair, her elastic stopping their movement. "That phone call from NCIS stunned me."

"It surprises me that they didn't call you back."

"Well, they didn't."

"They took this bowl from me when they came to talk to me at the store. They thought it could be stolen. There is a bowl exactly like this in the National Museum of Iraq. They thought this could be it."

I watched Hannah's pretty face turn icy. She looked down, her thick eyelashes fluttering.

"They said that? There's a bowl that looks like this in the National Museum of Iraq?"

"You didn't know that?" I asked.

"I had no idea. Is it still there?"

"No," I replied, trying my best to gauge her reaction. "It was stolen during the Iraq War. It's been missing since 2003."

I could tell that what I'd said had upset Hannah. She was very nervous. Her heart-shaped face was flushed and everything about her body suddenly felt restless.

"And what did NCIS tell you about this bowl?" she asked, touching it again with her fingertips."

"They said it was a copy. Not the original. They even TL-tested it. Do you know what TL—"

"Of course I do," she said, interrupting me. "I'm sure I know a lot more about ceramics than you do."

I was sure she did, too. Especially how to throw and glaze pottery so well that it could be confused for an antiquity.

"They had an expert from Sotheby's, Max Sebastian, fly in from London to do the test at Brown. He's the one who alerted them that it could be the real thing. I had reached out to him and so had someone else from Newport. He did the TL testing. You know how expensive that procedure is. But they did it. Max and the NCIS guys concluded it was new. Made recently."

"TL testing is not always accurate."

"No, but in this case I think it was."

Hannah looked at me, still not offering an admission.

"Did you make this bowl?" I said, taking it out of the box and holding it.

She reached for it again and I let her take it out of my lap. I looked at her, her pretty face, her faint scar, the determination in her body language. We heard thunder in the distance but the storm still felt miles away.

I asked her again if she made it.

"Yes, I did," she finally said curtly. "I made it in the exact same studio at Hartford where you came to see me."

She had just confirmed what I'd thought since I'd called her voicemail. It was just that I had the wrong bowl. Now I had to figure out why.

"When did you make it?" I asked, watching her turn it over in her lap.

"January. Right after the new year."

"January. Are you sure? But I only bought it in February. And Tyler said—"

"Let's not get into 'Tyler said' yet."

She didn't want to talk about Tyler. I was sure this conversation was impossible to have without him in it.

"Why did you make it?" I asked, studying her.

"Why? Because Ford asked me to."

I didn't want to know anymore. She'd said the phrase that had halted me in good decision making since I had come home. Ford. He had asked Hannah to make it. It was definitely not a gift from a translator; a girl he was once very attached to made it for him. Maybe still was.

"Why did he say he wanted it?"

Hannah looked down at the bowl again, like if she didn't keep checking on it, it would disappear.

"Around October, after trying to see me all summer, he stopped contacting me, stopped trying, and it was just silence between us. Nothing. Like we had never happened. Which is how I wanted it. Or thought I wanted it. But when he called me in December and I saw his number on my phone, I couldn't resist. He gets under your skin." She looked at me with a flicker of animosity. "But I don't have to tell you that, do I. You know him." Hannah brushed her thick brown hair out of her eyes and shifted her position on the towel. "I answered the phone and instead of the flood of apologies I thought I was going to hear, he said he had a big favor to ask me and could he come to Hartford to see me on a weekend."

"A weekend in December."

"Yes, early December. He asked, I said yes, and we ended up in the pottery studio completely alone—"

"There was no one else there?"

"Right. That's what alone means." She glared at me for interrupting and kept talking. "We didn't talk about what happened in July. He just touched my face, the scar on my chin, my nose, sat down, put his head in my lap, and cried."

I didn't want to feel the jealousy that flooded me as she explained. I wanted to feel sympathy, understanding, even a renewed force to keep questioning Hannah, but all I felt was envy. She had had Tyler's head in her lap; she had seen him cry. That, more than anything, was what I wanted. Tyler laughing, crying, screaming. I had seen him angry before but it was always tempered by his consummate self-control. That measure, his internal metronome, is what made him Tyler Ford. It was also what made me think, even when he was revealing his heart, that he was hiding something. I wanted the something. I wanted all of him.

"After that I felt—and you know why—an overwhelming amount of guilt," Hannah admitted. "So when he asked me for a favor, I said yes."

"And the favor was to copy this bowl," I said, pointing to the one in her hands. "Or not that one, but one he had?"

"That's right."

"What was the story behind it? Did he give you a reason that he wanted it done?"

"Not really," she said, reaching for the hem of her boyfriend jeans again. "He said it was important and that it didn't have to be exactly the same, just as good as I could make it. I didn't ask him any questions. I thought maybe it belonged to a friend of his from the war and he wanted one, too. Ford was never very open about his time in Iraq. I didn't want to pry."

"So how good did you make the copy?"

"Perfectly," said Hannah, looking down at it in her hands. "I majored in ceramics at the University of Hartford a decade ago. I studied pottery in Egypt for two years after school. There's nothing I know better."

"And Tyler knew that about you?"

"Of course. We were together for a year. What do you think, we barely introduced ourselves?"

Hannah was also proving to be an expert at slicing my confidence away.

"He asked you to just make him one."

"Yes! That's what I told you. He asked, and I did. It took me a little while to get the glaze perfect. I had to distress it slightly. And the pattern, that was very hard to copy."

I didn't understand why Hannah had been committed to making a perfect copy if it wasn't intended as a forgery. I felt like she was lying, but also that NCIS had made her very nervous. Maybe too nervous to lie.

"How do you distress it?" I asked, wishing I had more than a sophomoric knowledge of pottery.

"It's pretty straightforward. First you fire it twice. Once before glazing, once after. Then you use a coarse-grit sanding block, followed by a fine sandpaper. After all that you leave it in the sunlight during the day and under a heat lamp at night for a few weeks. It also helps if you dip it in urine."

Our brown eyes locked, but she didn't confirm if she'd gone to that extreme.

"You did all that, just so Tyler Ford could have a copy of a nice bowl to place on a shelf? Forgive me, but I'm having a very difficult time believing you. Doesn't that seem like an awful lot of trouble to go through for someone to have a keepsake?"

"It doesn't matter what you think. I did it that way. He wanted that bowl, I cared about him, so I made him that bowl. I didn't ask questions. He's a marine who works at a flight school. What did I think he was going to do? Sell it at Christie's? I thought he just wanted something nice. Something he was sentimental about. Ford hasn't had that many nice things in his life. I thought he deserved it."

"But what about the bowl he showed you? The one he wanted you to copy. Did he say that it was a gift from his translator?"

"No. Was it?"

"I don't know. That's one version of the story. Did he leave you the bowl to copy?"

"Yes. I had it for almost a month. It took me a while to make a replica. It's a very complicated pattern."

"And what did you think of the bowl you had? You who knows so much about this stuff. Did you think it was old? An antiquity? Did you think it could be stolen?"

"Stolen, definitely not," she said without pausing.

"But you didn't know that there was a bowl in the National Museum of Iraq that looked exactly like the one you had in your hands."

"No, I didn't know that, but I did know Ford. I never considered that it was stolen."

Hannah seemed far too smart to have never considered that possibility, but I dropped it. She had clearly found the answer she was sticking to.

"What about the age. Did you think it was an antique?"

"At first I didn't. It was in such perfect condition."

"But then . . ."

"Like I said, I studied the glaze. It looked—in the right light—it looked mellow. And there was slight, very slight, crackling and crazing. But that was it on the glaze. I didn't think it could be very old until I studied the base. It showed its age."

"I don't remember that it did."

Hannah shrugged and stood up from the towel. She stretched her arms over her head, leaned from side to side, and sat back down. "These conversations should never be had on a beach."

"They should never be had at all, but I don't think we have much of a choice now."

"Since that day we met, I've been thinking about whether I would tell you all this if the chance came up," said Hannah, leaning back on her hands again. "If you came back."

"Why did you decide to?"

"Because you did come back, and because now I'm scared. That phone call. I'm worried that they'll call again. I don't want to talk to them. So instead, I'm talking to you. You can deal with it." She did not sound scared, but she struck me as a girl who never went too far into the white and black of life.

"When was the bowl in the National Museum of Iraq made? I mean, the one that used to be there," she asked.

"I'm not sure. It wasn't fully entered into their records."

Hannah didn't reply. She crossed one leg over the other and stared out at the water, as if the solution she was hoping for was hiding somewhere in that shallow pond.

"Do you think the bowl that Tyler gave you to copy could have been several hundred years old? Museum-worthy?"

She turned to look at me, her eyes emotionless. "I don't."

"Is it even in the realm of possibility?"

"I'd be very surprised."

I shifted my legs again, which were freezing now that we'd lost the sun to thick clouds.

"I just don't understand why you tried to make it so close to what he gave you. Maybe you can explain that to me again, because if anyone ever asks you, that's what they're going to wonder. The way you describe it, it sounds like you were trying to make a forgery."

"But I wasn't!" She sat up straight and wiped her sandy hand onto her lap. "I swear to you, I never intended to make a forgery. I didn't know the thing he gave me was worth anything. I still don't. I just wanted to do a good job because it seemed to matter to Ford. I hadn't seen him since July; there was a lot of emotion tied to it. This was just a small way for me to show him that even from out here, I was still in his life. I cared. I still do." She looked at me to see the reaction I refused to give her.

"So you copied it," I said coolly.

"Yes, I copied it. A copy. Not a forgery." She shook her head and put her fingers on her temples. "It's going to rain, I can feel it," she said, starting to rub her forehead. "What could happen to me if they decide I forged something?"

"I don't think they ever would. Like you said, you had no idea that one existed at the National Museum of Iraq. You never had intent to deceive. You just took a commission. That's a good point, actually. Did Tyler ever pay you?"

"Do you call him Tyler to his face?" asked Hannah.

"Yes, I've never called him anything else."

"That's surprising. He always hated that name," she said dismissively. "Everyone calls him Ford." She lay down on her back and closed her eyes. "No, he never paid me."

"Then it was just a favor for a friend. I don't think you should be worried about getting in trouble even if something did come out of all this. Something with Tyler."

"It's very strange to hear you say that. Tyler. You're probably the first girl who ever got away with calling him that. He must like you."

She opened her eyes, sat up, and then stood. By her body language, I could tell that our conversation was over. I stood up, too, shook as much of the sand off the towel as I could, folded it, and held it against my chest. I bent down, moved my shoes, and slipped them on my cold feet.

"I appreciate your honesty," I said finally. "You're right. You didn't have to tell me anything."

"You were going to find out soon enough."

"I don't think I would have." I started heading to the area where our cars were parked and Hannah followed. "I appreciate your time. I'll be in touch if anything happens."

"Please don't be unless you have to be," she replied.

"Okay. Then good luck. I hope we don't have to speak again."

I reached into my bag, where the bowl sat safely packed in the Styrofoam box, my car keys right on top. I put everything in the backseat, making sure the bag was secure, and reached for the driver's side door. Hannah was doing the same but she looked up at me before getting into her Volkswagen.

"Do you promise you'll try to keep my name out of this if it ever becomes something?"

"I do. I promise," I replied, surprised. She stepped slightly away from her car door, closed it, and leaned against it.

"Then I'll tell you one more thing. But if anyone ever asks me in an official capacity, I plan on denying it."

I nodded in understanding.

"I added something to the original bowl. The one that Ford brought me to copy. The one that, you seem to think, could have been from that museum in Iraq."

She looked at me like I should have known what she was alluding to. Me with my big education and my big career, but I had no idea.

"I added a fake base to the bowl he gave me. I created an exact likeness and then added it to the original base so that the foot rim is almost flush with the new base. That's the only obvious difference between the two bowls, though I must have done a good job because you didn't notice."

"No, I didn't."

"But the most important part of that base is that in between the real base and the fake base is a thick circle of marble."

I went over Hannah's words carefully. I didn't know what to say next. My mouth felt dry, thinking about all the days I turned that first bowl, the Goodwill bowl, over and over in my hands. I finally was able to open my mouth and all I said was "the weight."

"Yes, the marble, it made it a lot heavier. It also meant you never saw that bowl's original base. That's why you didn't think it was old. The weight was wrong and the base looked new because I covered the old one."

"You put a fake base on the bowl?"

"Yes."

"But you never thought it was an antiquity. Worth anything."

"I didn't think it was worth all that much. It's pottery."

"But just in case it was, and just in case he was asking you to copy it with fraudulent intent, you wanted to cover Tyler's ass by making both of them look new, your copy and the one he gave you."

"I never said that. And if anyone asks me, I won't say that."

"But that's exactly what you did."

"I told you I knew a lot about TL testing. More than you." She did know more than me. But both of us knew that TL testing was always done from the base unless forgery was suspected; that way the glaze stayed intact. If there were grave concerns about authenticity, a very small piece had to be cored from the side of the piece to TL-test, which would damage it. From what I had gathered from my few hours spent with Hannah, she was good enough not to have anyone suspect a fake.

"Ceramic forgers put old bottoms on new bowls to turn a big profit. You put a new bottom on an old bowl," I said.

"A reverse forgery. That makes me sound even more innocent."

I didn't reply. All I could think about was Max Sebastian and his TL test at Brown.

She opened her car door again and put her hand on the door to get in. "Try not to fuck him over," she said, turning her head toward me. "He's a decent guy underneath every-thing."

"What about you? Aren't you worried about you?"

"Of course I am, but like you said, I didn't even know about the National Museum in Iraq. There's no crime there. I was just copying a bowl that I thought was some cheap keepsake. It was just a favor for a friend."

"And the new base you put on that cheap keepsake?"

"Artistic license. I thought it looked dirty. I wanted to freshen it up."

"A convenient explanation."

"Carolyn, for the record, I don't think Ford was doing anything wrong."

She might have believed that, but I no longer did.

## CHAPTER 16

I t was an hour before I made it back to downtown Newport. I drove straight to Tyler's. I wanted him to be
there, but as soon as I pulled up in front, I knew he wasn't.
Everything around his town house had an undisturbed
stillness to it, like even the mailman hadn't dared to walk up
the path. I tried the front door, pounding on it, ringing the
doorbell, but no one came. I walked around back and did the
same thing, but still silence. I opened the screen door and
rested my hand on the doorknob. As soon as I put a little
weight on it, it turned. The back door was unlocked. I tried
the knob again, but it moved just like before. Had Tyler been
home? Was he home now?

I hit it with my fist again and called his name, but no
one came. I turned the handle for a third time and pushed
the door open with my hip. The hinge creaked slightly as I
walked in but the house was completely quiet. Behind me, I
could hear the faint shouts of children playing somewhere in
the neighborhood. I stood motionless in the kitchen, looking
around. There were no dishes in the sink, no mail on the
counter, nothing to indicate when someone had last been
home. I wanted to scream his name again, but now that I was
inside I was afraid to. I took a few steps into the living and

dining room. Everything was immaculate. I could see vac-
uum cleaner lines on the beige rug and it looked like no one
had walked on it since it had been cleaned. I moved carefully
into the guest bedroom downstairs. The bed was made and
the desk had a few letters on it. I walked over and looked at
the date they were stamped. They were from two weeks ago.

Tyler's bedroom was on the second floor and I hesitated
at the bottom of the stairs, feeling like a criminal. I thought
about the last few times I had been over to the house looking for him. I was sure that the back door had been locked.
Positive. I closed my eyes and thought about the first day
I had come searching for him, when NCIS had been to the
gallery and I hadn't yet spoken to the Dalbys or to Greg. I
had turned the doorknob back and forth, I was sure of it. He
had to have been inside since then, but there was no noticeable sign that he had. I climbed the stairs to the bedroom
and the first thing I noticed was that his window, the one
closest to his bed, was fully open. I was sure I had looked up
to the second floor the last time I was there, and hadn't seen
it open, but now I wasn't so sure. The house wasn't that
cold. If it had been open for nine days, it would be cooler
inside. Our nights in May were still in the forties. I looked
at his bed, his navy blue comforter pulled perfectly over it.
I wanted to lie down, to remember what it felt like the first
time my body had fallen horizontally on it and he had lain
down on top of me.

I opened the top drawer of his dresser, but everything
looked totally normal. Boxers folded, socks paired. Nothing
seemed out of character except that it was a house that had,
by what I could tell, been empty for nine days and was now
unlocked.

I ran my hand against the edge of his bedspread and
went back to smooth it out when I saw the crease I had left.

When I went back downstairs I looked around the living room again. I didn't know what I was looking for besides Tyler himself. Some sign that he was okay or that he had been home, but I didn't have either. I saw the picture of Katie, just where it had always been, and close to it was the Bible I had looked at after I had spoken to Blair Bari. I walked over to it and examined the spine. The leather-bound King James Bible. I was afraid to touch it. It was from his mother. He'd taken it to Iraq. It felt sacred—too sacred for a stranger's hands.

I ran my finger very gently down the spine and thought about how Tyler had put me in this situation. If he had come to see me in the last nine days, done something besides leave me a note via the Finlay chair at Hook's, then I wouldn't be here. Feeling a small burst of anger, I took the book down from the shelf and as soon as I opened it, a picture fell out onto the beige rug. I leaned down and picked it up, trying not to smudge it. It was a family photo taken in a field in what I imagined was Wyoming. There was Tyler in his military uniform with his mother and his older sister. His mother had blue eyes and dark hair, deep wrinkles around her eyes, and was tall like him, but his sister had brown eyes and lighter hair. She was very pretty. Not as attractive as Tyler, but beautiful in a more innocent, made-in-the-Heartland way. They stood, with Tyler in the middle, against a white fence. I put the photo back inside the cover, feeling like I was leaving dirty fingerprints and traces of guilt all over it.

I didn't know what I would do if he came in. Apologize when I should have been screaming and I didn't want to be in that position. I held the Bible in my hand, sure not to drop the picture again, and flipped back to Revelation. I moved slowly to the sections until I found 1:17: "And when

I saw him, I fell at his feet as dead. And he laid his right hand upon me, saying unto me, Fear not; I am the first and the last: I am he that liveth, and was dead; and behold, I am alive for evermore, Amen; and have the keys of hell and of death." In Tyler's Bible, in unsteady blue ink, the phrase "I am the first and the last" was underlined. I looked at it for a few moments, then quickly flipped through other sections to see if he had underlined anything else, but that was all. Just that passage in Revelation, the same one Blair Bari had spoken to me about when I showed him the bowl. With numb hands, I placed the Bible back on the shelf, made sure it was flush with the other books, rushed to the back door, and let myself out.

I put in a few hours at William's store that evening, staying late just like I promised.

"Your punishment is inventory," he said, handing me a flashlight. He straightened his navy blue blazer, undid his bow tie, and walked out the front door, locking it behind him.

I didn't mind staying late that night. I had so much to think about after what Hannah had said and what I'd seen at his house. I needed to talk to Tyler. I could do nothing until I spoke to him and until then, all I could do was replay Hannah's words in my overloaded mind. She had made a fake base. Not only a fake base, but a weighted fake base. Few potters, I imagined, had ever been tasked with making an old bowl look new, but she had taken that upon herself. Or had he asked her to do it?

Marble and a fake ceramic bottom with the same words in Hebrew. I thought about the words and the way she had said, "Of course I do," when I asked if she knew what they were. I had never seen the pictures of the bowl from the museum's archives, but maybe the words were different, or not there at all. But then I thought about Max. If there had been a discrepancy on that detail he would not have flown in.

I took all these parts and tried to make them a whole as I sat on the floor in the back of the store, logging in what William had bought on a trip to Boston. There was a small table that reminded me a little of the Hugh Finlay stenciled pier table from Baltimore. I thought about that day sitting on the floor of Elizabeth's sprawling Texas home with Nicole. My career was booming. I had just sold the most expensive piece of American furniture in history and I was poised to help acquire the country's best private collection of American-made furniture before flying home to a perfect New York life. I missed walking in the park and the energy pumping from the city every season. I missed all the parties and events I used to attend because of Christie's. And most of all, I missed the challenge of the job. I loved William's but the chase was different when you were doing it for an antique store. Until recently. I sat and inspected and typed things in a spreadsheet and thought about everything that made New York perfect, until I admitted to myself that it hadn't been perfect. My nerves, after a decade at Christie's, had been shattered. Alex treated me like a call girl he could always run back to, and I was so consumed by work that the New York life I dreamed about was still out of my reach. I didn't have anything there outside of Christie's.

I turned over the table that looked like the one from Elizabeth's and examined the base. I thought about Hannah's base, the false one she had created. What I couldn't figure out was why *that* bowl. Why replicate something that, at best, was worth half a million dollars when there were so many other, far more expensive works out there? The Sacred Vase of Warka, a five-thousand-year-old piece found in the thirties in southern Iraq by German Assyriol-

ogists, had been stolen from the Iraqi museum. It was dated
to 3000 B.C. and worth a fortune on the black market. Ten
thousand other pieces were missing, and I was sure several
thousand of those were worth more than the green and
white bowl. Tyler's bowl. There were also items that were
much smaller and easier to smuggle that were stolen from
the basement storeroom, including glass bottles, cylinder
seals, and jewelry. Things so small that you could put them
in your pockets and get on an airplane. That bowl, why
Hannah was copying *that* particular object, didn't make
sense.

I had read a lot about the robbery at the museum in
the last nine days. Mobs of thieves had looted the building
between April 10 and 12, 2003. American troops had been
criticized for not guarding it, and the higher-ups had been
under even harsher judgment for not ordering it to be
protected, but many troops who were on the ground said
that their first job was protecting life, not art. I understood
that. Some global press didn't, but most of us would protect a human over a vase. Even a very valuable vase. But it
was devastation. One of the world's oldest civilizations was
stripped of its cultural heritage. Or as I and many others
saw it, our collective cultural heritage. A recent article I had
read, recent but still three years old, talked about 632 pieces
from the museum being returned from the United States.
Six hundred and thirty-two was nowhere close to the ten
thousand that were missing. I imagined a majority of the
pieces were in the United States. We were the largest art
market in the world with a huge collector base.

In the last thirty minutes I hadn't logged anything for
William. I was still staring at the legs of the pier table like
I was waiting for them to wiggle. I clicked open the Excel
spreadsheet I was working on and wrote, "far left inside

leg, minor scratches," and then flipped the table back over. When I raised my head, I realized that there was someone at the door. The motion sensor light we kept over it had turned on and even from the back of the storage room I could see it. I stood up and walked to the main room and through the glass I could just make out his face, his blue eyes, his revealing expression. He lifted his hand to knock but pulled it away when he saw me emerge from the back room. By the time I got to the door, unlocked it, and opened it, I was crying. He came in the store and put his arms around me. He was wearing the same thin white shirt he wore on the boat that day with the Dalbys. It smelled clean against my face. I let him pull me closer to him, his arms firmly around me, and I cried uncontrollably, the kind of crying you're surprised your body can sustain for more than a few seconds. Everything about Tyler seemed bigger. His muscles felt thicker, his eyes wider, his presence more palpable. The part he played in my life had gone from starring role to all-encompassing.

"I said soon," he whispered into my ear as I flooded his shirt with tears. He ran his strong hands through my hair, down my cheeks, across my lips. I didn't move my head. I said, "I hate you," over and over again until he held me an arm's distance away and said, "You can't. I won't let you."

That was enough to turn my elation at seeing him into anger. All the veins in his arms seemed to be jumping out of his flesh. I may have been in love with him but right now I hated every inch of that skin.

"You do not get to do this!" I screamed, pulling away. I walked past him and closed the door to the store, sensing how my voice was going to travel into the street very quickly. "You do not get to be the one who comes to me, just like that, when *you're* ready, when *you* want to. Nine days without one word from you! How dare you. You are a selfish bastard."

"I'm sorry. I didn't want to get you involved any more than you already were."

"You're sorry? Oh, well, thank you. Everything is fine now! One 'I'm sorry' and the world can go on turning. You're acting like this is nothing, Tyler! Nothing! Like this is a dentist's appointment!"

"I'm not acting like anything," he said, walking toward me. "I needed a couple of days to sort out a few things." He pressed my arms to my sides and pulled me toward him, so close that I could feel his heart beat.

"Oh. A few things. What did you need to do? Update your Netflix queue? Maybe pick some fantasy baseball team? Or did you have to, say, cover your tracks because you're an art smuggler? Is that what you had to do? Did you have to, I don't know, destroy evidence? Or see how you could pin the entire thing on me? Maybe tell NCIS that I wanted to sell a stolen piece of chintz on the black market to my billionaire buddies? But wait! There's the kicker! Because it's not a piece of chintz, is it. Since February, I happened to have something worth a couple of hundred thousand dollars on my bookshelf in my mold-infested apartment. But why would you tell me that? Not because you're in love with me! Remember that speech, Tyler! It wasn't very long ago, was it? 'You should always jump when someone says jump.' Well, let me tell you how much I regret jumping. I should have never, never gone looking for you!"

"You're worried," he said, leaning down to kiss me. I pulled away before he could, so hard that his fingers left marks on my arm. He rested his hands on his slightly faded jeans, the ones he had been wearing the first night he walked into the store, when he had changed everything for me.

"Worried? Worried? Oh no. Not at all. Why should *I* be worried! It's just a day at the fair to have military police come to my door and seize my property. And then everyone I know tells me you're a worthless piece of shit. Why would that cause me any worry? And to just blow another hole in it, you disappear! I haven't seen you in nine days. Nine fucking days! I've been going crazy. I can't sleep, I'm a zombie at work. William thinks I'm about to hang myself with some antique militia rope. I've been searching the town for you, and for what?! You haven't been home, you don't answer your phone. You abandoned me!"

"But you don't hate me. You're going to still love me through all this because I need you to."

Tyler's voice was steady, and smooth, his thin shirt tight around his upper back and shoulders. He looked settled, not like he'd been distressed or hiding out on base, panicking. I looked at him and hated the way his hair was cut so close to his head, detested the translucent blue of his eyes, the way his muscles flexed even when he wasn't moving, and I hated him for wearing the last shirt I had seen him in, like no time had elapsed at all, like nothing had changed.

"Why should I love you!" I screamed. "I loathe you. I loathe the very thought of you. It's *you* who is not in love with me. Is this how someone acts when they're in love? You are selfish. You are selfish to a point of embarrassment. You should be ashamed of yourself."

"I am ashamed of myself. I'm very ashamed of myself," he said, moving closer to me again. "I have been for years. That's been part of the problem. Do you think I would have become this guy, Tyler Ford, Newport's inglorious bastard, if I thought I was a real great guy?" Even then, with that admission, his voice didn't rise, gliding toward me, unshakable.

"So tell me something about what's happening, Tyler," I said, trying to calm myself down. I was starting to choke on my own tears. "Who are you? Who the fuck are you? You're supposed to be this asshole Newport playboy who sleeps with every girl under forty with slightly symmetrical features and scares the crap out of people and for a few short weeks, you end up being the best guy I've ever known. Then you turn out to be the best guy I thought I knew. You paint yourself to be this nobody from nowhere who never went to college and drank his way through high school. You make fun of this quirky little obsession I have with antiques and then you are the reason I'm getting harassed by NCIS—over what? Over an antiquity! Or not an antiquity. Is it a copy? Is it real? Or are you just fucking all of us over? I don't know what you are anymore. Right now I think you're a liar."

"I am a liar," said Tyler, coming even closer to me.

"How much do you know about art?"

"Not that much."

"How much do you know about the art of the Middle East?"

"More."

"How much do you know about theft?"

"A lot."

I sat down on a chair and wiped my eyes on the sleeve of my white shirt. It was one that I used to wear all the time at Christie's, spun so thick that the sleeves wouldn't fray for the next hundred years.

"I know about Hannah," I said. "I saw her yesterday."

"Yeah," said Tyler sitting on the end of an Italian Rococo sofa that was next to me. "I know. She called me."

"Oh really? You answer her calls? Because you haven't picked mine up in nine days. Are you sure it's me you love?"

"I'm sure." He didn't reach out for me or move from his chair; he just looked at me. I wanted his voice to rise, I wanted him to scream with me, but he was still and even, his body language irritatingly composed.

"What did she tell you?" I demanded.

"She told me that you were very smart. That you had, at two different times, owned the bowl I gave her to copy and the bowl she made me. And she asked me what I had done."

I wiped my face on my sleeve again and tried to keep my voice from breaking. "I don't care what you told Hannah. I don't want you to talk to Hannah. I want you to tell me what you did."

"Well, it's a long story."

"Really, it's a long fucking story? How perfectly swell. How about you start telling it right now, immediately, from the beginning."

"After I tell you everything, someone is going to be arrested."

"You?"

"Maybe."

"Hannah?"

"No."

"Fine, who. Who is going to be arrested?"

"Max Sebastian."

I felt my body go cold. Tyler knew Max.

"Max Sebastian? Do you know Max Sebastian?" I said, my voice rising in equal parts of surprise and anger.

"I do. I've known him since 2003, when he came to Quantico to teach a class on Middle Eastern history."

"You have got to be kidding me."

"I'm not. I'm not kidding, I'm not lying and I'm not keeping anything from you from this point on, so listen."

I crossed my legs, glared at him, and listened. Max

Sebastian was British. He had a very big job at Sotheby's. What the hell was he doing at Quantico all the time? Greg had met him and so had Tyler.

"I got to know Max pretty well during his first visit to base. I liked him. He was the first British person I had ever met and even without the accent, I'd never met anyone like him. He was refined, well dressed, well spoken, well everything. One night, right before I was being deployed, he asked me to go out drinking. We got along pretty well and he asked if I wanted to see New York. I'd never been there before and he offered to take me, to pay for the trip. Other people had gone home to say goodbye to parents, friends, but I figured it was one of those God-bless-America kind of moments and I went. It was in New York that he asked me if I would be interested in making money while I was in Iraq. I asked him what kind of money and he said, pretty good money."

"What is pretty good money to an eighteen-year-old from Wyoming?"

"Four hundred thousand dollars."

"Four hundred thousand dollars. That's good money to anyone."

"Yes, it is. And it was very good money to me then."

"What did he ask you to do?"

"Well, I thought that he was going to ask me to kill someone. I really did. I was eighteen, I'd watched a lot of movies."

"But he didn't . . ."

"No. He asked me to meet someone while I was in Iraq and to bring something back for him. He knew which unit I was in. He knew that I worked with supply helicopters. I was the perfect middleman for him. I was young, too stupid to question what I was doing, and could get through a lot of security easily."

"What did he ask you to bring back?"

"He didn't tell me then. He said it was nothing illegal. No weapons, no drugs."

"Not illegal. That's bullshit. There's a lot more that's illegal than just weapons and drugs."

"Right, but it made me less worried." Tyler cleared his throat and looked at me watching him in a total panic. I knew what he was going to say next. I watched him shift his weight on the sofa. He was too big for the piece and looked out of place in the store, and suddenly, in my life.

"I won't bore you with every detail, but I became a middleman for Max. He had orders from collectors in the U.S. and the U.K. Specific objects from the museum that they wanted. He had people inside the museum, he had runners from the museum to base, and then he had people on base to bring everything back to the U.S."

Tyler sat back uncomfortably, as if telling this story, out loud, maybe for the first time in his life, had stiffened him, pulled a little more of his youth away from him.

"You're saying that Max Sebastian, the world's leading expert on Middle Eastern antiquities, is a thief."

"No. A thief is someone who steals cell phones in the subway. Max Sebastian is the head of the biggest ancient art theft ring in the world."

I thought about the two bowls. The one Tyler had given to Goodwill and the copy that Hannah made. Had Max even done TL testing on the bowl that NCIS took from me? Did he have the fake that Hannah made? Had he switched them? How did he know that I had the original? I asked Tyler and he said, "I'll get to that."

"Is this all true? Max Sebastian? He's in his fifties. He's so posh—"

"Yeah, and he's a fucking criminal." Tyler's voice rose for the first time that evening.

I twisted my hands in my lap and looked up at him, thinking about the way he looked at me the first day we met.

"That bowl, the one I bought from Hook's auction, that was the real bowl. The one from the National Museum."

"Yes, it was."

"But you were never in the museum?"

"No, I never even got close. A man, whose real name I never knew, gave it to me, along with several other things. I hid them for the rest of my deployment and six months later, I brought it all home in medical equipment bags. I met one of Max's guys in New York, gave him everything, and he gave me money, in cash, and deposited it in several different bank accounts."

"What did you do with the money?"

"I spent some."

"Some. What did you do with the rest?"

"Guess."

"I'm guessing your mother no longer lives in a twenty-thousand-dollar house."

"She doesn't."

"Do you know how illegal that is?"

"Of course. But I didn't understand the bigger picture for a long time."

"And now you do." His calmness was choking me. The way his blue eyes bore into me, his unemotional delivery, his sex appeal that was ever present, I wanted to push it all away. He didn't deserve it.

"I'd like to think I do," he replied. "But back then, I didn't. I really was a kid who wanted a challenge and money. At that age, I needed to be challenged. I had a lot to prove."

"War wasn't enough for you? Because the Marine Corps really does it for most people. But not you, right? You're Tyler fucking Ford. You can't just go to war; you decide to be part of a major international art smuggling ring, too. What a beautiful challenge." I gripped the arms of the chair I was sitting in until my hands hurt. I let go and slammed them on my lap. "There was an amnesty program, Tyler!" I yelled. "Do you understand that? The museum had an amnesty program. You could have turned it in! Or had an Iraqi turn it in for you. There would never have been criminal charges. Nothing. You could have reported Max. Been a hero who helped save the museum instead of being part of the looting. But no. And now, what could happen?"

"A lot has already happened."

"Oh, well, I know what's happened to me! That much I know. And I know what I figured out from your stupidity, or Hannah's stupidity, even Max's. But I've got a few holes, so why don't you go ahead and fill me in." I crossed my arms. My emotions had been running erratically but for now, they'd screeched to a halt somewhere in the realm of furious.

"I'll tell you as much as I know, but there was a lot I never knew."

"I'll take what you've got." Tyler reached for my hand, trying to remind me of our intimacy, but I refused to let him touch me. He leaned back on the couch and waited until I looked at him.

"When I brought everything back to one of Max's . . . associates in New York, he took it—"

"How much was there?"

"A lot. Carolyn, sit there, listen, ask me questions later."

"Because you're controlling this show."

"Yes, right now, I'm controlling this show. And though

you probably think differently, I wasn't controlling that show. Until now."

I looked at Tyler, the outline of his Marine Corps tattoos coming up from under his shirt. I thought about his Silver Star, how he would never have gotten it if they knew. Maybe he would have only done one tour. Maybe he wouldn't even have completed it.

"I gave everything to a man in New York. We met in a hotel room. We both carried plain black luggage, we switched it, I had my money, that was it. Except that he told me to keep that bowl."

"The bowl? The green and white bowl."

"Yes. He told me to keep it because there was a money problem with the buyer and he didn't want it on him because it was stolen."

"But he wanted you to keep it. How ethical."

"I think I made it pretty clear that Max Sebastian and everyone he works with are about as unethical as you can get. The man, again, whose real name I never knew, threw some more money my way, and I agreed to keep it until he told me he needed it."

"So you never knew these other men's real names but you knew Max. The top of the top."

"Yeah, I did. He's smart enough to know that someone like me would not have responded well to one of his circle. People I usually dealt with were not the Max Sebastian type. And I, and whoever else he had in the American military, were essential to his plan. He needed to get things back to New York and he was smart enough to know how much could be found by customs agents when badly concealed."

"Did anyone ever ask for the bowl?"

"Not for years. Not until last December."

"December! Last December? That's when you asked Hannah to make you a copy."

"Right. Somewhere between 2003 and last December, I grew up. What I'd done was getting to me and I didn't want to be a part of it anymore. I couldn't fulfill the agreement I made eleven years ago. I think what attracted me to Hannah in the first place, besides the obvious, was that she loved this stuff. I'd never really thought about it before her. Even when I brought it all back from Iraq, I didn't think of it as anything but a bunch of old junk from a museum that had the fingerprints of Saddam Hussein's regime all over it. My opinion of all that changed because of Hannah."

My throat felt like it was closing as I heard him repeat her name. I abhorred that she was a part of this.

"But why did you have to get her involved?" I asked, fighting back the current of jealousy.

"Because I needed her to be. I couldn't do what I wanted to do without Hannah. By that time, I knew a lot about forgery. If she didn't think she had an original, she was not forging anything. I even told her not to make the copy very good."

"But she made it perfectly."

"Yeah, she did. And I knew she would."

"Did the original bowl, the one from the museum, the one I had on my crappy bookshelf, have the Hebrew writing on the bottom?"

"Yes. Exactly the same as you know it to be."

"Did you know that she put a fake base on the original? A new base on an old piece."

"I did. I never told her I felt a difference, but I had that bowl for eleven years. I knew it pretty well. I figured out what she was doing, trying to save my ass if things got messy with TL testing, and it was a pretty good idea, so I kept it on."

"Did you send it back to Max when his person asked for it back?" Tyler looked at me with a hint of mischief in his eyes, the same expression he'd had that day on the boat.

"I didn't. A different guy. Again, someone who used a fake name and who I only spoke to on the phone asked me to leave it for him in a designated place in New York. But I didn't leave him the real one, I left him Hannah's."

"And the real one you dropped in the Goodwill box on base that Greg LaPorte set up."

"Right."

"Because . . ."

"Because I wanted it to get back to the museum. But I couldn't do it. I needed it to get laundered a little. Turn over, exchange hands, then eventually get back there."

"Who was supposed to buy it?"

"Someone, anyone but you."

"Not me? Oh, I get it, Tyler," I said, standing up rigidly. His cool blue expression felt like knives on my skin.

"So I messed it all up for you. I bought it, me who knows a little too much about all this stuff. And even worse, I kept it." It was right then that I realized why Tyler had asked me out that night we had first met. He didn't just fall over from love at first sight. He had to.

I said as much through fresh tears and collapsed on a chair. He stood up and tried to bend down toward me but I put my hand out to stop him. "Don't you dare. Do not touch me right now. Do not even come close to me," I said. "You had it all figured out, you were going to make good on your youthful idiocy, but I got in the way. I brought what you were trying to get rid of right back to you. So what did you decide to do, Tyler? Fuck me? Seduce me so that I forgot all about it and you could realign things like you'd intended them to be in the first place? Is that why you kept trying to get the bowl back from me? I wouldn't give it to you, though. And why? Because I stupidly, so stupidly, fell in love with you. But it wasn't even you! It was just some character you were pretending to be. You know what, Tyler? Everything anyone has ever said about you is true. They thought you weren't going to amount to anything and look at you now. You're even worse than they thought you'd be."

He didn't respond and I didn't feel bad for saying it. He knew, and I knew, it was true.

"You and me, it started for the wrong reasons. I admit that," he said forcefully. "I needed to keep tabs on you. But after that day on base, after the Breakers, everything changed. I didn't care about my plan anymore, or anything. I just wanted to make things right and move the fuck on."

"And how were you going to make things right? How!" I screamed. My throat hurt from tears and anger. My shirt was stained and my face was burning.

"I had sent Max the copy. He was going to notice it was a copy eventually because he's Max Sebastian, but it was so good that it would buy me a little time, enough for me to get the original back from you and to the museum. But then, you sent him those pictures in February so he figured it all out a little faster."

"Bad luck, right?"

"Pretty bad."

"Greg LaPorte also sent him pictures."

"Yeah, I know. So he figured out who you were and where you lived and how you were connected to me through Greg and then he came to Newport to test the bowl."

"And what do you think he did?"

"I know what he did. He brought the bowl he had, the

one Hannah made, and that's the one he tested. That he could even core from the side, not the base, in front of NCIS and the results would say it was a copy. He showed those results to NCIS and then switched the bowls. They gave you back Hannah's bowl and he took the real one from you."

"But the real one has a fake bottom."

"Yeah, he's not a football coach, Carolyn. He's the very best. I'm sure he tested under the glaze and then he probably removed the bottom and got it to the buyer. That's why he contacted me for it in December. His sale, I don't know the details but he wanted it back fast. He must have finally gotten his money."

"But you could have sent the real one back and gotten away with everything. Why the hell would you do what you did? The switch? Getting Hannah involved? Dropping it in that box on base, telling me everything? You yourself admitted that Max would eventually know you were trying to fuck him over. Why are you doing this?"

"I don't know. I guess I just had my come-to-Jesus moment, Carolyn. I spent a long time being Max Sebastian's yes-man, then I got to prove my salt, put a wrinkle in his plan with Hannah's bowl. Now I've had my retribution, grown the fuck up, and I need to wipe my plate clean."

"Clean?"

"Fine. Cleanish. I wanted to control everything."

He smoothed his thin shirt over his body, pulling it so close that I could see muscle and skin. He looked down at me, his light eyes focusing on my flushed face.

"If this was going to move, I wanted to be the one to move it because, look, it's eleven years later and I still got away with it."

"You say that like you're proud!"

"I am a little proud. And I promised you I wouldn't lie.

So yes, Carolyn, I'm proud of myself. That I, some dumb-ass kid from nowhere, could do what I did."

"Smuggle? How hard is it to smuggle?"

"Pretty damn hard."

"That's disgusting."

"Disgusting or not, it is what it is. But now everything is different and I'm ready for the gig to be up."

"So what the hell have you been doing for the last nine days? Getting ready to have Max Sebastian out you?"

"No. I've been trying to deal with this without getting you involved."

"Well, that was an epic fail, Tyler. You've put me in a hell of a position. Why would you ever do this to me?"

"It wasn't supposed to be you. Like I said, you weren't supposed to buy that bowl. But I'm glad you did."

Tyler sat down and moved closer to the end of the sofa, stretching his legs so they almost touched my feet. I pulled mine in and sat back on my chair.

"So now what. You admit everything and get court-martialed and dismissed? Are you ready for that?"

"I wouldn't have switched it to begin with if I wasn't ready for consequences."

"What about losing me? Are you ready for that consequence?"

"That's the only one I couldn't face."

"What about Hannah?"

"What about her."

"You're still in love with her!"

I didn't know what I was more upset about: his lies, his backhanded duplicity, or how much he needed Hannah.

"I am not in love with her. I swear to you," he countered, his voice letting through as much tenderness as Tyler knew how. "I'm not. I care about her very much. I'll always, for many reasons, be tied to her, want the best for her, but I'm not in love with her. I'm in love with you."

"You screwed Hannah and now you're screwing me. What am I supposed to do with all this, Tyler? What!"

He stood up again and this time I let him walk closer to me. He lifted me from the chair and put his arms around me.

"I despise you," I said, holding on to his arms.

"You love me," he said, kissing my face. He repeated it until I kissed him back.

I wanted to tell him I didn't. I wanted to look at him straight in those blue, glassy eyes and tell him he meant nothing to me. That I could walk out of that room and never again have my heart beat with him in mind. But we both would have known I was lying.

"What's going to happen now?" I said, gripping his white shirt with my hands. I wanted to rip it to shreds, to pound on his chest with my fists, to berate him for being such an idiot, but all I did was stand there and cry. "Tell me what's going to happen now. Tell me."

"I don't know, Carolyn. I guess that depends on what you do."

# CHAPTER 17

I didn't leave the store until half an hour after Tyler was gone. I walked outside and the same motion light that had startled me two hours ago turned on again. I locked the store and texted Jane that I was on the way to her house. She wrote back that she wasn't home, but she would be momentarily. I told her I'd drive slow, but instead I walked fast. By the time I got to Bellevue, my tears had dried up and all I could think about was how many times I had driven up and down the street with Tyler.

Jane opened the front door before I rang the doorbell, and for the first time in my adult life, I realized just how enormous her house was. As I looked up at it, instead of marveling at it, it bothered me.

"What's wrong? A lot is wrong. I can tell. You have a face full of storm clouds," said Jane, giving me a hug. She was wearing cashmere. Jane always wore cashmere until the end of May, and then she switched to linen.

"I can't talk about it, Jane," I said trying not to flood her with more than she ever needed to know. "I just need you to be the friend who can distract me."

"I can be that friend," she said, pointing to the living room. "What do you want to do? It's a little late but do you want to eat? Do you want to walk? Or maybe drive? Swim? Drink?"

"Swim and drink."

"Fine. Swim and drink. I'll get us bathing suits."

She walked upstairs and I sat and stared at the Manet on the living room wall. The Dalbys had paid $32 million for it at a Christie's auction in London in 2010. It had been part of a huge sale with a Picasso blue-period painting and one of Monet's water lilies, which surprisingly went unsold. I had asked Mrs. Dalby why she went for the Manet instead of the Monet and she'd said, "If I want to look at a water lily, I'll just build a pond. No matter what I do, I can't look at the real Édouard Manet." I found it to be as good an argument as any.

Jane handed me a plain black bikini and we walked through the living room, a study, and the sunroom before opening a door to the pool.

We changed and dove in and I lay on my back and let the water fill my ears. Jane did a few laps, but I just floated. I was so angry at Tyler that I didn't know what to do with my anger besides let it boil through me. Everything hurt. My brain felt slow, my arteries clogged, my muscles ripped. I tried to take a deep breath but the oxygen felt stuck in my neck. I had two choices. I could do nothing and see if Max did anything. Or I could tell NCIS everything I knew and put it in someone else's hands. The thought of both made me sick.

Jane lifted herself out of the pool, walked over to the antique beverage cart, and poured me a neat whiskey. She handed me a half-full glass and got back in.

"Here, don't drown," she said, resuming her laps. We stayed like that for half an hour, Jane swimming, really swimming, even though it was almost two in the morning, and me lapping whiskey, refilling the glass, and letting my brain be washed over with Tyler.

When Jane gave up on her laps and swam toward me to see how I was doing, I was very drunk. She swam to the wall and stretched her arms out on either side of her, her three gold bracelets dinging together every time she moved her arm.

"Can you take those off? I just can't hear that right now," I said, staring accusingly at her wrist.

"But I never take them off."

I knew she didn't but all of a sudden I wanted her to. I needed something to hate right then, so I hated them.

"It's just the jingling. It's rattling my rattled nerves. They sound like tin cans."

Jane raised her eyebrows at the suggestion that she was wearing tin and lowered her arm underwater.

"Thank you," I said, knowing full well that in a few minutes I'd hear them again, a constant reminder of her charmed life. There, standing in someone else's pool, I was feeling very sorry for myself. There were moments at Christie's when I felt like I would one day get somewhere close to where I wanted to be. Nothing up to Dalby standards, but something that met mine. There wasn't huge money to be had working at Christie's, but if I got high enough, I knew I'd be able to stretch it out into something. Especially if I left and worked as a dealer.

"You're not going to tell me what's going on?" said Jane as I poured the rest of my second glass of whiskey down my throat.

"No."

"You're going to sit in the pool and drink whiskey."

"Absolutely."

"Fine. I don't want to be around you, then."

She got out of the pool and grabbed a towel, shaking it out vigorously, her three bracelets clinking together, not like tin cans, but like champagne glasses on New Year's Eve.

"Those bracelets sound like golden handcuffs right now," I said, not turning to face her.

Jane continued to shake her towel and said, "I don't know when you became a mean drunk, but it's about as becoming on you as a woman with a mustache."

She walked out of the room, her towel tight around her body, and I screamed out an apology just as the glass door banged shut behind her.

I fell asleep, in the bathing suit with two towels wrapped around myself, on one of the lounge chairs by the pool. I woke up the next morning feeling like my head was in a vise. The bathing suit was still somewhere between wet and dry and my entire body felt like a mix of whiskey and swamp. I passed a clock on the way to the pool bathroom. It was eleven. I was two hours late for work, horribly hungover, and my face hurt from all the crying I did the night before. I would go to work. I would give myself the day. And that evening, I would go to Tyler's and decide what to do. William didn't say anything except "I see you've decided to work the night shift" when I walked in. I apologized, promised him I'd work until eight, and hoped that I smelled more like chlorine than alcohol.

By eight that evening, I was dragging. I was wearing a mix of what I'd worn the day before and another one of Jane's cashmere sweaters that had been in the bottom drawer of my desk. I left the store and locked the door under the motion light. Tyler's words kept sprinting through my brain. I had to be the one to decide. I'd thought about him sober, drunk, crying, stoic, naked, clothed, sweet, mean. And every time I did, I thought about my last day at Christie's, talking to Nina on the phone, getting kicked out of my office, blackballed from my career. I'd called Tyler selfish, but really, I was about to do something very selfish. I could not make the same mistake just a few months after what happened at Christie's. If I didn't say anything, and it all came out and I was part of it, I would never work in art again. Not legally. But Tyler—I needed him to come out of this, too. If I came forward, he could get dismissed; everyone had said that, even him. I knew that would kill him. He'd been in the Marine Corps for eleven years. It had taken him out of a three-thousand-person town in Wyoming and shown him the world. It had given him eyes, and without it, I didn't know what he would do.

I walked back to the glass table and laid my head on the cool top just like I'd done when I found out I had the wrong bowl. Someone had to save Tyler Ford, but it couldn't be me. I bit my top lip and called the number I had for the NCIS agent I'd spoken to twice now, Brian Van Ness. He answered after two rings and I explained why I needed to see him.

"Should I meet you at the antique store?" he asked.

"Definitely not."

"Want to meet at the Blue Hen?"

"You're kidding."

"Yes, I'm kidding. How about that meat restaurant on America's Cup Ave."

"Smoke House."

"Yeah, that one. I'll met you at the bar in, what, twenty minutes?"

"I'll be there in five."

I was there in four. And by the time I was sitting at the bar I wanted to take back everything I had just said to Brian on the phone. What was I doing? I should have just let fate dictate.

When Brian came, I explained my regret and he nodded.

"But you can't take it back now. And you know you're doing the right thing."

"Am I? How many tours did Tyler do? Four. And now what? He serves his country and I fuck him over?"

"You're not. He fucked himself over. And he's delivering you to give the message. It's kind of a chickenshit move, if you want my opinion."

"He already put himself in the position to fail."

"Yeah, I got that from what you said on the phone." He cleared his throat and looked at me. "I stopped by Tyler's house on the way to meet you but he wasn't home."

"That seems to be a trend lately."

"When he wasn't home, I turned around and looked for him a little on base, but he wasn't there, either. Have you called him since you two talked last night?"

"No, I was going to tonight. I want to tell him what I'm doing, that I talked to you, but after the fact."

"Can you try to call him now? I just want to see if he will pick up if he sees your number. He didn't answer my call. It went to voicemail."

I took my phone out of my bag and tried his number. My call didn't go through, either. I didn't even get voicemail.

"Nothing. Not even a message."

"No voicemail?"

I shook my head no.

"Fine."

I waved to the bartender for another drink and Brian asked me to tell him everything I had told him on the phone again.

"Did Tyler say if he worked with anyone else from the military? It seems unlikely that Max would only recruit him to be involved in this."

"He didn't say."

"And what about this other bowl? The fake one, the copy. Where did he get it?"

This was when I had to lie. I put my glass down, looked at Brian, and said, "I don't know. But I know it's fake."

"You don't know."

"I don't know," I said a little louder.

"You do know that all we have to pin Max Sebastian right now is your word that he's the head of a huge black-market antiquities smuggling ring."

"What's wrong with my word?"

"It would help a lot more if we had Tyler's."

"But when you talk to Tyler, he'll get court-martialed."

"Definitely. That we have enough for. With everything you've said, if he admits to it, then we do."

"You think he'll tell you something different than I'm telling you right now?"

"Possibly. But I have to find him first."

"Well, then I don't know why I'm still here. I told you everything I know. So go to London. Deal with Max. Arrest him." I finished the drink quickly to numb my escalating nerves.

"You don't get it, do you. Max is not my problem. Tyler is my problem. This is NCIS. Military law, military crimes conducted by members of the military. Max is, I'm guessing, not a member of the armed forces?"

"He's fifty-something and British."

"Right. I'll talk to the Newport police. Actually, we'll talk to the Newport police. But tomorrow, when you haven't been drinking. Now that I say that, stop drinking. Here, have this." He pushed his water glass toward me and watched me down the whole thing. "I'll meet you at the Newport police station on Broadway at ten A.M. tomorrow. Can you do that?"

"Of course," I said, hiccupping.

"Fine. Switch to water."

The next morning when I met Brian, I was there with a clear head and clean clothes. Brian waved me over to him before we walked in the door.

"You look better."

"I feel a little better."

"That's not going to last long. I found Tyler. Well, kind of."

"How can you kind of find someone?"

"When did you say Tyler told you all of this?"

"Late the night before last. The night before I spoke to you."

"Did he ask you to wait twenty-four hours before you spoke to anyone?"

"Of course not. He didn't ask me to talk to anyone. He didn't ask me to do anything. I'm sure he would be incredibly pissed off if he knew I did."

Brian paused and looked away from me.

"He knows you pretty well?"

"I'd go with very well."

"He knew you'd talk, then, but he also knew you'd wait to do it. You're not much of a rash decision maker, are you? Kind of a slow boil?"

"I guess so. What are you trying to say?"

"Tyler's in Turkey. Or at least he landed in Turkey last night. He took a flight from Boston to Istanbul. He knew you were going to talk to me. But I think he also knew you wouldn't do it immediately. If he thought you'd do it right after you left him, he wouldn't have gotten on that long of a plane ride."

I stared at Brian for a long time before saying anything. Tyler knew I was going to report him. I was, despite everything I had always hoped to the contrary, predictable. And that night, I'd told him he'd turned out worse than anyone thought, worse than every cliché about him. And now he was gone. That's what he'd been doing during the nine days he'd disappeared. He'd been getting ready to run.

"What's in Turkey?" I asked in a low, tired voice.

"I have no idea," said Brian. "But he just made things a lot worse for himself. If Max is what you say he is, Tyler could have confirmed that, gotten a deal. Now he looks really bad. And he's also a deserter."

"A deserter? He's been gone for twenty-four hours and he's already a deserter?"

Brian pointed to the door of the police station. "Let's just assume he's on vacation, okay? We need to get through the rest of this."

The rest of it did not go well. I told the head of the Newport police criminal investigation unit, Captain Jeff Ambrose, everything I knew and that was all I was able to do. When I asked Brian what would happen next, he shook his head and said, "I'll be in touch. Captain Ambrose might be in touch. Until then, just keep living your life."

## CHAPTER 18

It wasn't until a month later that I heard from Captain Jeff Ambrose with the Newport police. It was almost mid-June and the town was swelling with tourists and the boats that cut through the water for the America's Cup qualifying races. The town looked perfect, but my Newport was desolate. I had given the Dalbys, Carter, and William very thin versions of the real story. I hadn't heard from Tyler. I hadn't been able to get back on Jane's boat even with the perfect summer weather. I didn't think I'd ever get on it again.

"Do you want me to sell it?" she'd asked after I'd declined for the fourth time. I'd shaken my head no and said, "I think I'll take up windsurfing instead."

The day Captain Ambrose called was one of the days I'd declined Jane's invitation, but I had stayed on the harbor. I couldn't get on the boat, but I could watch it from the shore, the white sails cutting through the wind. I could picture Carter and Jane in her white shorts and thick linen sweaters, her gold bracelets not bothering anyone. But all I could hear when I looked at that boat was Tyler's voice daring me into something with him. "You always have to jump if someone tells you to jump." I had definitely jumped.

"I've got a question for you," said Captain Ambrose over the phone.

"Yes, what is it?" I said, looking at the boats cross the water in front of me. I had lost sight of Jane's dark blue boat. It was gone, in the water at the point that I liked best, when the shore was just out of view and you knew everything was still close by but you felt lost at sea.

"We've had someone in London paying attention to Max Sebastian. I told you that, I believe?"

"You didn't."

"Well, we do. We didn't think there would be any interest, but I guess he's kind of a big deal over there."

"Has anything happened?"

"I can't really go into the details. We've been watching him for a few weeks now and there hasn't been anything worth calling about but today he booked a plane ticket to Houston. Do you know anything about that? Or have any guesses?"

My heart dropped.

"Houston, Texas? Are you sure?" I asked, my voice rising like the tide.

"Definitely. Tomorrow at nine A.M. Any idea why Mr. British would be going to Houston? There's a Sotheby's consultant in Houston but that doesn't seem to fit. Would he be going there for work?"

Houston. I hadn't talked about Texas since January.

"I don't know," I said, stretching out the last word. "I have a weird hunch but it's a very far-fetched one. Can you give me a few hours to look into it before I tell you about it? I need to look at an auction record."

"Yeah, okay. He doesn't fly before tomorrow morning, but call me sooner rather than later if you think it's anything."

I promised him I would and then dialed a number that I hadn't used in six months.

Nicole picked up her phone on the first ring. I realized as soon as she said hello that I missed her. I was still mad at her, but I missed her more.

"Nicole, I imagine you're still banned from talking to me, but I could really use a favor," I said quickly.

"Oh, hello, Aunt Irene. How are things in Maine?"

"Fine. I'm Aunt Irene and you can't say anything because I'm guessing you share an office with someone new. Someone who is far more boring than me."

"Rain! How devastating," said Nicole. She sounded far too convincing. She had probably spent half her time having fake conversations when I was in that office.

"I would be forever indebted to you if you could send me Adam Tumlinson's auction record. The whole thing, every department, from his first bid to his last. Could you do that for me? I know it's a huge ask but it will help me immensely. I can't explain now, but—"

"No explanation needed. You should go to your favorite hotel in town. The one you told me about all those times. I think they have just the remedy for the bad weather at the bar. Why don't you go there in an hour or two?"

"Fine, fine. Castle Hill Inn in an hour or two. Thank you so much, Nicole."

"Let's say two. Lots of love, Aunt Irene. Keep in touch."

Maybe it was because she knew she'd been deplorable and owed me a favor, but as soon as Nicole hung up the phone I forgave her for forgetting I had a heartbeat all these months.

The Castle Hill Inn was the most charming hotel in Newport. If you liked luxury you stayed there. If you liked something quaint you stayed there. And if you were broke, you didn't even come for lunch. I walked up the familiar stairs and went to the concierge, who knew me well.

"I think someone faxed something here for me," I said.

"Just let me check, Ms. Everett. It's nice to see you back at the hotel."

The Castle Hill Inn was one of the places where if you grew up in Newport, you knew everyone who worked there, and everyone who worked there knew you, especially if you were best friends with the Dalbys and their money.

"Here you are," he said, reaching out and handing me a very thick manila envelope. "Can I help you with anything else?"

"That's all. Thank you very much." I walked out the front door of the gray storybook property and onto the wraparound porch that overlooked the water and rocks. I walked halfway down the big grass hill and sat alone in a slightly weathered white Adirondack chair. There was no one near me and even the people far away didn't seem to notice me. They were too busy absorbing old New England through their pores. I unhooked the string loop of the envelope and placed the pages on my lap, gripping them tightly so they didn't fold or fly away with the wind.

Line by line, I went through the nearly fifty-page document that Nicole had faxed over. It was full of Adam's buying and selling records for decades. He had died last year but he'd been buying from Christie's since the fifties. American furniture, American painting, American photography. The man was more patriotic than Nathan Hale. It wasn't until 1988 that I saw something that wasn't American. That year, he not only bought Sargent's portrait of Mademoiselle Suzanne Poirson but three pieces from a Middle East auction, including a jar from the late twelfth century. I looked carefully at the entry, "Stone-paste painted in black

under turquoise glaze H: 31.1 W: 21.6 cm Raqqa, Syria."
Holding my breath, I put the papers back into the manila
folder, shoved the folder into my bag without sealing the
top, and called Captain Jeff Ambrose back at the Newport
police station.

"It's Carolyn Everett. I know why he's going to Houston."

"Can we meet? I can come to William Miller's."

"I'm not that close right now. I'm at the Castle Hill Inn.
Can you come here?"

"You do your prying at very tony establishments."

"Well, this is Newport. It's hard not to. I'm on the main
lawn; you can't miss me."

I couldn't sit still as I waited for Captain Ambrose to
appear. I walked down to the water. I walked toward the
private cottages and when I couldn't walk anymore, I went
to the bar, lapped up a Maker's Mark on the rocks, and
headed back outside. Five minutes later, I saw him walking
down the hill, looking for me. He turned my way after a few
seconds and waited for me to reach him.

"How about here," he said, pointing to two Adirondack
chairs together. "This is a very nice place, isn't it," he added,
taking in the view.

"It is." I opened the folder. I knew already what he was
going to say after I explained about Elizabeth. He'd say I
had a hunch and a hunch wasn't enough to do anything. But
I would try.

"What is all that?" he asked, looking at the thick stack
of paper in my lap.

"These are buying records from Christie's, fifty years of
buying records, sales all to the same person, Mr. Adam R.
Tumlinson. Have you ever heard that name?"

"I haven't. Who is he?" He was peering at the sales
figures.

"Was he. He died last year. Before that, he was an important art collector, mostly American art, furniture, portraiture, militaria, but he had a few other interests, too. I asked Christie's to send me his buying record because I wanted to see if he had ever bought Islamic art, especially pottery."

"And has he?"

"He did in 1988. He bought a significant piece from Syria." I flipped to the page where I had underlined the entry and showed him.

"Three hundred and seventy-five thousand dollars," Jeff read out loud. "That's not chump change."

"Well, for Adam Tumlinson that was chump change. I haven't finished going through this record, but I will and I was hoping you might be able to get his records from Sotheby's, too. I don't have anyone who—"

"You don't have a mole in there who can send them to you."

"This is art. Not Stalingrad. But yes, I don't know anyone who would send them to me."

"I'll see what I can do. We don't have anything on Max Sebastian right now except your story, so—"

"And you think my story is false?" I protested. "Tyler Ford flew to Turkey! He disappeared. You think that's because we had a bad breakup and he needed a *hamam?* I'm right about this, I know it."

I shifted in my wooden chair and looked back toward the hotel. It had a large turret covered in gray shake shingles that made the property look a little more whimsical than most in the area.

"I worked with Adam Tumlinson's wife, Elizabeth, on my last sale at Christie's," I explained. "We sold the couple's storied American furniture collection. One of the pieces in it, a table, was contested after it was sold and returned to a family in Baltimore. Several people said it was stolen and that's why it was given back so quickly without legal involvement or an attempt on Elizabeth's part to save face. You don't just return a table that sold for two hundred and sixty thousand dollars because of one thin accusation. I am sure she knew she owned stolen goods and I'm sure she didn't care."

"Fine," said Jeff, making a note. "Anything else?"

"In the papers, there was talk about certain people Adam worked with. Corrupt dealers. It's hard to find them now that he's dead, but there's been a hum about it since January. A source told the *Baltimore Sun* that since Adam started collecting in the fifties, he'd been paying people off to acquire items that weren't exactly for sale."

"So they'd steal them."

"That's what I gathered."

"You left Christie's after you worked with Elizabeth? Isn't that what you said?" asked Jeff, making more notes.

"Yes. I was fired because of her sale. I didn't notice what I should have about the table."

"And this wouldn't be some vendetta you're carrying for the outcome of that sale."

"Vendetta? Certainly not. This is me trying not to make the same mistake twice."

"But you said Adam is dead. If Max is going to Texas, then who is he going to see? Elizabeth?"

"Exactly. Max is going to see Elizabeth Tumlinson."

Jeff kicked his legs out straight in front of him and leaned back in the chair. "I would like to believe you."

"But you don't."

"I mostly don't. A little part of me thinks it could be something."

"You also have to consider the actual sale of her collection in the first place," I pointed out. "We're not talking a trestle table and a few Queen Anne chairs. She had the best collection of American furniture in the world and all of a sudden she wanted to sell it, all of it, and fast. Why? She's not dying, her kids aren't trying to steal from her, her interests haven't changed. Why did she need that money, eight figures, all of a sudden? Maybe it was to create a diversion."

"Who else are the big collectors of Middle Eastern pottery in Texas?" asked Jeff, writing down my theory.

"I'm not sure." I tried to think back to my early days at Christie's when I was in sales and appraisals. Who was there in Texas? "I can only think of two right now. Afif Adil, he's Saudi Arabian and works in oil down there, and Jill and Hadi Basir. She's Texan, he's from the UAE. He works in oil, too. I remember them in the New York office. I've met all three before, but I can't think of anyone else."

"You haven't gone through all the records and we don't know what the Tumlinsons' buying habits were at Sotheby's, but it doesn't look like they bought much from the Middle East, right?"

"No, I don't think much."

"And there are probably many other art collectors in the state of Texas who have bought something, just one or a few pieces, from the Middle East from Christie's or Sotheby's."

"Sure. It's a big state. But we're not talking photography or modern art here. This is Middle Eastern pottery. There are fewer buyers. Plus, those sales are always in London, not New York."

"How is Elizabeth Tumlinson any more of a suspect than anyone else who collects that kind of art in Texas?"

"I don't know," I said, crossing my ankle over my knee. "Because none of those other collectors have lied to me."

"Can I take this?" said Captain Ambrose, looking down at the folder in my hand.

I handed it to him and we both stood up.

"I'll look into it," he said, holding the envelope out slightly at me.

"But you think nothing will come of it."

"Probably not. But I'll still look into it."

I didn't tell him that even I thought I was putting pieces in a row that fit together too easily. Still, it was possible.

I watched hours of bad TV that night. Reality TV, old TV, even an infomercial for scrambled egg molds. When my phone rang at 8 P.M., I jumped. It was the detective from the Newport police.

"Carolyn, nothing at Sotheby's. Adam Tumlinson never bought one piece or painting or anything from the Middle East department. Never even attended one of their auctions in London," said Jeff.

"Really, that's too bad. Maybe I'm wrong. You can't do anything about Texas anyway, can you?"

"How strong is your hunch?"

"I recognize that it's a stretch, but I just think there's a reason Adam never went to Sotheby's Middle East auctions and only to Christie's. If you're working with someone on shady deals, you don't ever want to be associated with them, even legitimately. I think they kept a professional distance on purpose."

"And you really think Max is flying to Houston to sell this bowl to Elizabeth."

"I really do think that, yes. What time does his flight get into Houston?"

"He leaves London at nine A.M. It's a ten-hour flight and London is six hours ahead, so if there are no delays, he'll land in Texas at one P.M. Maybe we should see if London will alert someone at the airport, look for it in his luggage when he goes through security."

"Not worth it. Max Sebastian is not that stupid. He clearly had a buyer in the U.S., which is why he had an American marine bring it back here. He got it back in Newport, and he definitely hasn't taken it out of the country. I bet the bowl is already in Houston or someone will bring it there."

"You're probably right. That is, if he's planning on selling it in Houston, but we don't know that."

"No, we don't." I stopped to think about Elizabeth. It didn't make perfect sense when I explained it to Jeff, but it did if you knew Elizabeth. She was artful. Her deceit had been executed with precision during the auction, and even in this case, Max was the one who was slipping, not her.

"What if you just had someone watching her house in the afternoon tomorrow? Just in case Max does go there."

"Because you have a hunch."

"Yes, exactly."

"I seriously doubt I can make that happen. It's outside of my jurisdiction and it's not a lead, it's a guess."

I didn't reply but I knew he could imagine my pleading face.

"Fine. Give me her address just in case. I've reported it to the FBI's art crime team, which is how London began to move. They have a keen interest in cases like this. They might follow up, but remember, this isn't exactly the Gardner heist."

I recited Elizabeth's address and phone number from memory.

I didn't sleep that night. I bit my nails until there wasn't anything to bite. I opened all my windows so I could convince myself that I wasn't suffocating. I checked prices on plane tickets to Houston and had to remind myself that I couldn't exactly place Max Sebastian under citizen's arrest if I was right. When the sun started to rise, I drove to Sachuest Point, to the beach close to where I'd gone to school, and watched the day break. I'd been doing it a lot lately, thinking about Tyler. Greg had tried to contact me once to talk about him, but I hadn't answered. I'd avoided going anywhere I might see Greg and if I saw a flicker of red in anyone's hair, I went quickly the other way. I knew what he would say, his boastful face, his dismissal of Tyler. I couldn't bear to have that conversation. I knew I couldn't talk to him, didn't know when I'd see him, but I wished then that I at least knew where Tyler was watching the sun rise.

I stayed on the beach all day. I looked on as tourists put up big colorful umbrellas and lathered their children in sunscreen. I watched a group of girls point toward the school and I wondered if they were getting ready to go to St. George's in the fall. I put my feet in the water and let the cold seep into me. After 2 P.M., 1 P.M. Texas time, I kept my phone ringer turned on as high as it could go and checked it every five minutes. At 8 P.M., I watched the sun set. I'd been on and around the beach for fourteen hours. I hadn't eaten, my face felt burnt, and I hadn't heard from Jeff. I turned my ringer down, put my phone in my bag, and drove home.

Four days later, I finally got a phone call. It wasn't from Captain Ambrose with Newport police or Brian Van Ness with NCIS. It was from a man named Ryan Barton, from the FBI art crime team.

"Do you want the bottom line or do you want all the details?" he asked immediately. He had one of those hard voices where the intonation almost never changed.

"I want both. Start with the bottom line and then give me the details if that's okay."

"Bottom line. Adam Tumlinson was a huge crook. Max Sebastian is an even bigger crook."

"And Tyler Ford?"

"Tyler Ford is a small- to medium-size crook. But more than anything, he was a kid being very stupid. Actually, I should tell you all this in person. I'm in Newport. Would you like to meet? There's a coffee shop next to the police station on Broadway. Do you know it?"

"Do I know it? This is my town." I hung up the phone and for the first time since Tyler had left Newport, it did feel like my town again.

I nearly killed three pedestrians getting to Broadway, and when I parked and ran out, a man in his late forties with a thick build and a bald head was sitting by the window with two coffees. He handed me one when I came in and then introduced himself.

"I know a lot about you. Probably an unfair amount, so forgive me when I talk to you like we've met before."

"I'll do my best."

"Let's walk," he said, motioning outside with his head. I followed Ryan onto the sidewalk and we headed away from town.

"Did you arrest Max Sebastian? Was he at Elizabeth's?" I asked immediately.

"It's a complicated story, but one that's going to be in the news in a couple of days, so I wanted you to hear it from me first."

I looked at him like he was about to tell me that the moon landings were staged.

"I have to ask, how could you have guessed that Max was going to Elizabeth's? Did you really guess or did you have a tip?"

"So he did go there?"

"Yes. He went there. The bowl was taken from him right outside her gate and he was brought in for questioning. So how did you know?"

"I didn't know exactly. It was a mix of things. It was a hunch first. When Captain Ambrose from the Newport Police Department said Max was going to Houston, I immediately thought of Elizabeth because she's very rich, not very ethical, and could be working on a new collection. But right after I met Jeff a few days ago, I thought of something else. I had mentioned Elizabeth's name to Tyler a few months ago and I still remember the way he shifted his weight, fidgeted, and stood up when I said it. There was almost recognition. I didn't sense it then, but now that I look back on it, there was."

"The name Noah Kulik. Does that mean anything to you?"

"No. I've never heard that name."

"He was a marine, too. He served around the same time Tyler did but they don't seem to know each other. Or if Noah knew Tyler, he's not talking."

"You spoke to him already? Did Max name him?"

"Of course. Him and everyone else on earth. He's trying pretty hard to get a deal."

"Will he get a deal?"

"I doubt it."

We turned the corner and stood single file as a group of tourists passed us with shopping bags.

"So when are you going to tell me everything?"

"Everything, I can't tell you everything. It's a surprisingly, or maybe not so surprisingly, complicated story. How is your knowledge of the Crusades?"

I looked at him with wide eyes and stopped on the sidewalk.

"The Crusades? You can't be serious."

He nodded.

"My knowledge of the Crusades is rusty."

"Then this will be even more complicated. Bear with me."

He pointed to a side street that gave onto Easton Pond and we walked toward the water. We slowed down and he looked at me, my expectant face, and started to explain the last ninety-six hours.

"In the mid-nineties, Adam Tumlinson purchased a letter from Max Sebastian—on the black market, not through Sotheby's. This letter, which Elizabeth is in possession of and which she claims she only recently found, is extremely rare and very old. It's from the twelfth century and was written by Maimonides. Does that name register with you at all?"

"Vaguely. Jewish philosopher and scholar of some sort."

"Right. He was a little more than that, but that's fine for now. Anyway, in this letter, which is in Hebrew, Maimonides is telling a story of working as a personal doctor for Salah al-Din Abu 'l-Muzaffer Yusuf ibn Ayyub ibn Shadi, or just Saladin to you and me, the first sultan of Egypt and Syria."

"Wait, this was a real letter, penned by Maimonides?"

"Yes, we actually have it now."

"That must have cost millions. I wonder how Max even got that."

"I don't know," he said, pointing to a bench near the water that was now empty. I nodded and we walked forward.

"In the letter, Maimonides specifically writes about Saladin ordering him to bring fruit—specifically plums and pears—and snow to his enemy, Richard the Lionheart, also known as Richard the First of England, to give him relief from fever."

"Richard the First. You cannot be serious."

"It gets better. Listen."

I shut my mouth and let him continue. After another sentence I interrupted him again.

"I'm sorry but are you saying that at the end of the twelfth century a famous Jewish doctor was working for Saladin, a Sunni Muslim, as his personal physician?"

"Yes. The letter is from 1192. The Jews and the Muslims got along okay back then."

"Fine. So Saladin ordered his doctor to bring Richard the Lionheart—King of England and Crusader—fruit and snow. You know, I actually remember that from studying the Crusades in college. That's a very famous 'give peace a chance' moment. And Saladin was following the Quran. Richard was sick, not a fair fight and all that."

"I think it's worded slightly differently in the Quran," said Ryan, smiling.

"I'm paraphrasing. So in this letter Maimonides explains that he was the one who brought the provisions to Richard?"

"Exactly. He was the one who did, and he also took the opportunity to spy on how many men and how much supplies Richard still had, but that's not relevant to this story. What is relevant is that Maimonides wrote in the letter that before he delivered everything to Richard, he carved the base of one of the bowls with the words 'First and the Last,' which is the end of the fourth principle of faith—Maimonides's Thirteen Principles of Faith, which I'm sure you've heard of. They're still a pillar of Judaism today."

"The fourth principle of faith? You mean, that line is not from the Bible? From the Book of Revelation? I thought it was, Blair Bari, a professor at Brown, did, and so did Tyler. I saw that passage underlined in blue pen in his personal King James Bible."

"It's a common way to refer to God, but it's not from the Bible in this case. Maimonides wrote that it was a reference to the fourth principle from his Thirteen Principles of Faith: 'I believe with perfect faith that the Creator, Blessed be His Name, is the first and the last.'"

I had gone, in six months, from my Americentric existence to discussing the Crusades with an FBI agent in Newport. Life felt almost unrecognizable.

"So that bowl, the one that I had in my bag as I walked around a dive bar in Newport, and that had a fake bottom added to it, was the bowl that Maimonides delivered to Richard the Lionheart on behalf of Saladin in 1192."

"That's exactly what I'm saying."

"Holy shit."

Ryan laughed loudly and looked at me, sitting by the water on a beautiful day in June leveled by my shock.

"Yeah, holy shit. There's more holy shit, too."

"Wait, do you think Tyler knew any of this?"

"Tyler Ford? No way. I don't think anyone who worked with Max in the Middle East knew about this or they might have kept it and sold it themselves. Without that history, it's just an old clay bowl. What did you think it was worth?"

"When I knew it was in the museum? Four hundred, five hundred thousand."

"Yeah, not anymore."

"But how could it be in such perfect shape? It's over eight hundred years old."

"I'll get to that. Let me backtrack. This letter that we found perfectly states what this bowl is. In it Maimonides describes the passage from the Quran—'And God shall heal the breast of the believers'—painted inside the bowl in Arabic in deep green script and writes that he etched part of his fourth principle into the base in Hebrew. He describes carving it in with a medical knife that he had used as a court physician in Egypt. He wrote not only of the health of Richard the Lionheart but how the king of England had previously invited Maimonides to be his personal physician, an invitation that he declined. Maimonides had been a leading physician in Saladin's court since 1185 and was extremely respected in his profession. In the letter, Maimonides also perfectly details the appearance and beauty of the bowl: the green pattern, the off-white background, the fine brush detailing, the vegetal motifs. According to Max, after buying that letter, Adam Tumlinson wanted him to find the bowl."

"And Max did."

"He did but it took eight years. The letter was bought in 1995 and the bowl was discovered in 2003. January 2003."

"The same year that the museum was looted."

"Right. The bowl was found in a private home. It had been—supposedly, this could all be bullshit—but supposedly it had never been in a museum, always in private hands with the family, the descendants of Maimonides. Richard and Saladin reached an agreement in 1192 and Saladin died in March 1193. It's unclear how the bowl made its way back to Maimonides, but it could have been returned to him before Richard left for Europe. Max Sebastian or his people in the Middle East were able to obtain it in Jaffa, in Israel."

"Jaffa, that's where Richard the First was in 1192, right? The Battle of Jaffa."

"Yes, you're not that rusty on the Crusades after all. The bowl was found there and Max had arrangements to have it brought to the United States, but it didn't work out like he planned. Before it could be brought here, it somehow ended up in the collection of the National Museum of Iraq."

"But how? From Jaffa to Iraq? That makes no sense."

"Does any of this make sense? It sounds like a deal gone wrong. There were so many trades for money, objects for money, art for money, money for arms. Something slipped and instead of going to the States, it went to the museum."

"But Adam knew that it went there?"

"No, Adam didn't, Max did. And that's when he hired someone inside the museum to get it from the collection before it got archived. It was going to happen before the war, but when the war broke out in March 2003, everyone could sense the museum was going to be looted; it was a perfect opportunity. From what we know, Max already had people in place to loot the museum, on a timeline he dictated, so it was an easy add for him. The fact that the bowl went to the museum actually made it even easier for him to obtain. The bowl, along with thousands of other artifacts, was taken. Some of that was by petty thieves, but we think a huge number of those thefts were arranged by Max for American and European buyers. Tyler and many others helped bring everything back to the United States and Great Britain."

"Okay, but then why didn't the bowl go to Adam?"

"We're not perfectly clear on that yet but we think it's money. Adam didn't pay him in full."

"So the bowl never went to Adam?"

"No. But eleven years later, Elizabeth, Adam's wife, was going to finish the deal."

"But Max gave it to Tyler to hold until he was sure he had a buyer."

"Max is giving a different story on that, saying Tyler insisted he keep it, but that sounds like crap, too. I think, like you said, he didn't want to take it out of the U.S. And he definitely didn't want it in London, where it could be associated with him. So it stayed with Tyler. Probably at Quantico, maybe at home in Wyoming, I don't know where it was when he was deployed again, but it was in the U.S. until it got to Newport."

"And then I bought it."

"Yes, you bought it in February, but the wheels were in motion for the sale well before that. In December, Max contacted Tyler because Elizabeth Tumlinson had found Maimonides's letter and the translation and correspondence from her husband where he talked about acquiring the bowl and how much money he had spent. Elizabeth discovered the letter, in one of her husband's many safe-deposit boxes, before she ever contacted Christie's about selling her furniture collection. Then she waited a suitable period to make sure the sale looked promising. A month before it was set to go in New York, when the press was giving it love and saying it would bring in forty million, and you all had already given her a big chunk of the guarantee, then she promised Max his money. Several million. And that was on top of what Adam Tumlinson had already paid."

"How much money had Adam spent?"

"Five million."

"You have got to be kidding me."

"No, but I bet it's worth much more than that now, don't you think?" asked Ryan.

"It's worth whatever someone is willing to spend on history." From my experience, that could go to eight figures.

"She wanted the bowl and she was set to pay the rest of the money to get it."

"Wait, more money? How much was that?"

"I'm not sure. But more."

"So then Max contacted Tyler to get it back in New York?"

"Yes, exactly, but like you told Captain Ambrose, Tyler gave him the wrong bowl. He gave him a fake."

"Which Max realized when I contacted him with pictures of the real one."

"You and then Greg LaPorte, whom he linked to Tyler. You he couldn't connect. He didn't know you were living in Newport. With Greg, he knew."

"How did you get him to admit to all of this?" I asked, very surprised.

"Torture."

"What?"

"I'm kidding. We just used what we had from Tyler, via you. If you act like you know everything, they fill in the blanks."

"Max filled in the blanks?"

"The ones in Savile Row always break down first."

"Did he switch the bowls in Providence?"

"Yes."

"And what about the other bowl? The copy?"

"The one Hannah Lloyd made?"

I stared at him with desperate eyes. Of course they had found out about Hannah.

"Don't worry. We don't care so much about that," Ryan assured me.

I nodded nervously and let him keep going.

"You still have that bowl, we know that. But we have the one that matters. In the last four days, the false bottom was removed to reveal the original bottom, which was in fact identical, just not in great shape. Elizabeth has given us access to her husband's papers and Max has been fired from Sotheby's and is waiting arraignment. The bowl will eventually find its way back to the National Museum of Iraq, and—"

"And Tyler Ford?"

"And Tyler is nowhere to be found and now has official deserter status with the Marine Corps."

"But Tyler was never inside the National Museum of Iraq?"

"No. Definitely not."

"And what about the other guy, the one you mentioned who didn't know Tyler. Was he ever inside?"

"Noah. Noah Kulik. No, from what we have gathered, and this investigation is by no means complete, he was also a middleman like Tyler."

I shook my head and looked out at the lily pads floating by the shore.

"It's funny about you and Elizabeth," said Ryan. "How you worked with her before and she dicked you over. It's almost like you planned it."

"Trust me. I didn't."

"I know. But isn't the world strange. This woman kicks you in the teeth and a few months later, you do it right back. Only you do it a lot fucking harder."

# CHAPTER 19

It was June 29 when news outlets picked up the story about Max and Tyler and Adam and Elizabeth Tumlinson. Unlike the one about Elizabeth's American furniture collection, this story was worthy of a major news feature in the Sunday edition *New York Times* and every other paper in America. I called Nina and told her to be sure to buy a newspaper or seven. I wouldn't tell her why, I just told her to call me back. She did, but it had just been screams for the first two minutes.

After I had spent a solid twenty-four hours talking about what had happened with Jane and Carter and Brittan, my phone rang from a New York number.

"Carolyn Everett? This is Alan Buckmaster from Sotheby's, head of private sales Americas. I don't think we've ever met and I hope you don't mind me calling. Your former colleague, Nicole Grant, was kind enough to give me your number and assure me that I wouldn't be disturbing you."

"You're not disturbing me at all," I said. It was definitely about Max. They wanted to talk to me. I knew they would call. But everything I knew about Max was already out.

I spoke to Alan for thirty minutes, saying everything I'm sure he had already read. Then I offered to forward him the original email I had sent to Max and he gladly accepted. When I was about to hang up, Alan asked me what I was doing in Newport.

"I work at a little antique store. It's called William Miller's Antiques. You should stop by if you're ever in the area."

"You should go back to New York," he offered. "You might not have been able to get a job before, but you will now. Don't you miss New York?"

"I've been thinking about it. Coming back."

"Then you should. I think you've earned it. Call me when you do. I'd like to buy you a drink."

Three weeks later, my New York apartment was empty and I had paid an extra month to my landlord in Newport to leave early.

"You can't go," said Jane with tears in her eyes when I told her I was leaving for New York in five days. "I've gotten so used to having you here, and with you here, Brittan comes home more, and everything is just perfect. Now you have to go and ruin it by going back to New York."

"I don't think things were perfect when I was here, do you?"

"Maybe perfect is a stretch, but I've had worse years. You brought a very needed wind of excitement up here and it changed the course for everyone, especially you."

"Especially Tyler."

"Yes, but from what you've told me, he set things in motion for himself before you got here. You just got in the way. But everyone likes it when you're in the way."

"You're going to go to Boston in September anyway."

"I would have stayed if you stayed. But now, I guess I will go."

"You really saved me from myself, Jane. I love you for it."

"No, you did it all. I just provided the sound track." She

shook her wrist, letting her bracelets ding against each other, and gave me a hug. The only other people I said goodbye to before leaving were Carter, Hook, and William. William said I owed him $10 million for the bowl and he gave me a bowler hat to show there were no hard feelings. Hook said he was going to scout Goodwills every single day.

I got to New York the evening of July 26. My apartment didn't smell like me. I'd had it cleaned two days before I came home but four hours of bleach hadn't been enough to scrub out the odor of the tenant I had never met. I looked at the chair by the window. It had been fixed. There was a note on it from the renter and a thank-you for giving them such a good deal on the place. "I hope you don't mind, I had this restored. I really enjoyed sitting in it and hope you do, too."

I sat down and ran my hands over the arms. I would enjoy sitting in it this time, even more than I had when I'd first bought it and imagined my life very differently.

I didn't have a job yet, but just knowing I could have a job was enough for now.

That night, before I went to bed, I called Greg LaPorte. I hadn't wanted to see him in person before I left Newport, but now that I was safely in New York, he deserved a phone call.

"Just don't say 'I told you so,'" I said when he answered.
"Please?"
"No way."
"Can you just say, 'Greg, you were right'?"
"How about I just say this: Greg, you're a nice guy. You're a much nicer guy than Tyler Ford."
"I'll take it for now. I guess that's all I deserve really. I didn't guess all of it. That whole part about the Crusades and Maimonides, Saladin and Richard the First."
"I can't believe you missed that."

"I know, fail. I really like that story. And so does every-one else. The Jew, the Christian, and the Muslim happy together. I heard they're selling the film rights."

"Seriously?"

"No. But can't you see it happening?"

"I hope not."

"Yeah, then it definitely will."

I kicked off my shoes and stretched out on my bed. Somewhere near my window, someone was screaming. I knew the park, with all of its summer runners and cyclists, was just a few blocks to the west. Just a few blocks past that in one direction was Sotheby's, in the other direction, Christie's. This time, I wouldn't make any mistakes, and if I did, I wouldn't let them knock me all the way up to Newport.

"Is it all roses in New York? Top of the Rock and all that?" asked Greg.

"How exactly do you think people live in New York?"

"Well. Very well."

I turned toward my window and admired my bad view. After all those months away, it hadn't gotten better. But I didn't mind.

"I do love this town," I admitted.

"I hope you grow out of that."

"I might. I miss the Newport water every day."

"You've only been gone for a day, you said."

"Then I've missed it for a day."

"I'll let you go, Carolyn. But with the risk of sounding uncreative, I'll just repeat myself. When you get sick of chasing Tyler Ford, I'll be waiting for you."

"He's a deserter, remember? Flew back to the Middle East? Never said goodbye to me? Left me to do his cleaning up for him. I am done chasing him."

"I don't believe you."

"But you should."

"Yes, and you should be telling the truth. Good luck with everything. I hope you come see me in Newport."

The truth that Greg knew, and that I knew, was I would always be in love with Tyler. He was furtive and deceitful, but he was solid. He seemed, from the beginning, to be made up of what real American men should be made up of, and that included miles of flaws. But I liked his flaws: his closed-book personality, the way his eyes were unreadable, and that just when you expected him to say one thing, he surprised you with something else. From the moment we met, Tyler took my hand and pulled me into a world that I forgot existed. One where people struggled to make ends meet, where men went to war and never came back, where children shivered at the idea of ending up in their home- towns, and where people loved blindly and completely. Not everyone on earth sprang to life on Bellevue Avenue, and now that I knew Tyler, I was glad. All my life I had been looking at Alex, at the Dalbys, and holding them up as the radiance to chase after. I learned to trail them, at times surpass them, and wrote myself a resume that shined with privilege. I took every leap I could to stay in their moneyed world, their gilded age, but when I met Tyler, I took a step out and I knew I'd never find my stride with them again. In some essential way, he was better than all of us, better than I would ever be, better than the rest.

The next evening, when I got home from dinner with the head of the Vollinger Gallery, where it looked like I had a chance of getting a job, I picked up my mail from the box downstairs and put it on the breakfast counter. I flicked a Christie's auction catalogue aside, wondering why I was still on their list, and went through the rest quickly. My hand stopped on a basic white business envelope. It was plain, but my name and address were written on the front in Tyler Ford's now-familiar small, slanted handwriting. There was no postage on it, no markings showing that it had made its way through a sorting facility. The return address was simply "Top of the Rock." I ripped it open with my teeth and two thin pieces of paper fell on the ground. One was a note with a line in Tyler's small print; the other was a plane ticket to Turkey. The note, written in black pen, read,

*Come with me.*

I put it on the counter and let it stare up at me. An hour later, I ripped it up and put the pieces back in the envelope. He would come back. One day when I was walking alone along the Hudson, or through the crowded, ringing streets of Midtown, or home in Newport, floating on the water with the sound of wide, white sails cracking sharply in the wind, I knew he would reappear, just as he did the day I was near my breaking point without him. After all this, he was still Tyler Ford, and I hoped he always would be.

# ACKNOWLEDGMENTS

My heartfelt thanks to . . .

My editor at Atria, Sarah Cantin. You are nothing short of spectacular. Your insights, your humor, and your talent as an editor and wordsmith are what made this book. I hope there are many, many more lovely sailboats, summer days, and cashmere sweaters to create in our future. Thank you for your brilliance and thank you for being so darn fun.

Bridget Wagner Matzie, my agent extraordinaire. You not only championed this project from day one, but helped me take it from "art crime and a really hot guy" to a story with depth. You're one of the smartest and most dynamic in the business and I'm beyond grateful for everything you do.

Judith Curr, Greer Hendricks, Tom Pitoniak, Carla Benton, and all the other gifted minds at Atria. Your vision, creativity, and support are so appreciated and I'm thrilled to call Atria home.

Jarrod Stuard, thank you for sharing your expertise on the complex legal proceedings of the military and for your patience and invaluable editorial input. You helped give depth to many characters in this book.

Colette Loll with Art Fraud Insights. You've got the best Room of One's Own in Georgetown, and from it, you're producing great things. A thousand thank-yous for educating not only me, but all of us art lovers, on the world of fakes and forgeries, and the art of deception.

Elsa, your extensive knowledge of the glamorous auction world shaped this book. We're talking from-a-puddle-to-a-pentagon shaped it. Thank you. You've been rocking my literary life since day one.

My wonderful family. Mom, you are, and always have been, my biggest cheerleader, and in two languages at that. I'm indebted. Dad, thank you for discussing those light subjects, like the Crusades, with me, and being a never-ending source of inspiration. Ken, your dedication to everything you do raises the bar.

Craig Fischer, my incredible husband. Thank you for inspiring so much of this book, for making every day that much better, and for marrying me. I promise we're going to live an electrifying life together.

Georgia Bobley, my twin sister in all things books, boarding school, nautical outfits, tomfoolery, Internet stalking, and never, ever, acting our age. Thank you for exploring Newport with me, for being my partner in the world's best two-person book club and for just being lovely you. My life is so much better because you're in it.

Amy Cenicola, Mary-Alice Farina, Lauren Roche-Garland, Julia Seufert, Anna Timbie. Thank you for being the best friends a girl could ask for. You helped me walk down the world's longest aisle, chez Edith Wharton, and you support me in everything (sane) that I do. Lucky, lucky me.

# THE PRICE
## *of*
# INHERITANCE

# KARIN TANABE

*A Readers Club Guide*

# Questions and Topics for Discussion

1. Discuss the ways Carolyn is shaped by her family. How does she follow in her parents' footsteps, and how does she react against their choices?

2. Consider the novel's epigraph. Did you notice it before you began reading, and if so, did you find it shaped your understanding of the novel? If not, how does it affect the way you consider the book retrospectively? Who in the novel do you think this quote could most closely apply to? And do you agree with Wilde?

3. Tanabe often uses clothing to give us insight into the personalities of her characters. Pick a few individuals from the novel and examine what you infer about them based on the descriptions of what they wear.

4. Ostensibly, Tyler and Carolyn are from completely different walks of life. In what ways are they actually quite similar? Beyond their apparent physical attraction, why do you think they are drawn to each other?

5. When she first meets Hannah, why does Carolyn give her Tyler's phone number instead of her own? What is she trying to gain from that action?

6. Consider how the themes of ownership and theft are explored within the novel. When it comes to stealing, who is the most reprehensible character?

7. Nina tries to build a relationship with Carolyn after she plays a major role in her undoing. Do you think Carolyn was too unforgiving toward Nina? Do you think either Nina or Carolyn acted selfishly?

8. How are wealth and the wealthy depicted in the book? Why do you think Tanabe chose to have Carolyn grow up adjacent to such affluence, and have her family be "formerly" affluent?

9. Discuss the ways the military and Newport's old-money society are juxtaposed within the novel.

10. Do you think Greg acted honorably when he voiced his suspicions about Tyler or were his actions self-serving? Do you think he cared about the raid on the museum or was he simply interested in Carolyn?

11. Why do you believe Carolyn cares about "old things" in the way that she does? What is it about antiques that captures her imagination? Do you share this fascination to any degree? Why or why not?

12. Though Hannah's relationship with Tyler ended badly, she still chose to help him do something she suspected was illegal. What other legal and moral boundaries do Hannah, Tyler, and Carolyn cross when they follow their hearts?

13. After years of being "on again and off again," Alex seems to finally want to commit to Carolyn once she has left New York. "It was always when you stopped caring," she remarks. Have you had this experience before? Did you agree with Carolyn's choice to walk away from Alex?

14. "I was going to be *that* girl, and no one would remember who grew up on the edge of the ocean, and who grew up just behind it." How does Carolyn's sense of herself evolve over the course of the narrative? How has she changed by the novel's end?

15. Which of the characters did you feel ultimately knew Carolyn best?

## Enhance Your Book Club

1. If you haven't already, read Tanabe's first novel, *The List*, and discuss it as a group. Compare and contrast the protagonists of each book. In particular, you might consider how these two books depict power and influence—for example, who holds power in each book, and how is it gained or lost?

2. Many of Christie's auctions are streamed live on their website, at https://www.christies.com/livebidding. Consider watching one as a group.

3. Imagine you are casting the film version of *The Price of Inheritance*. Who would play Carolyn and Tyler? The Dalby sisters? Alex and Hannah?

4. The raid on the National Museum of Iraq took place in 2003 and the FBI is still searching for thousands of stolen artifacts and works of art. Take a look at the FBI's Top Ten Art Crimes list (http://www.fbi.gov/about-us/investigate/vc_majorthefts/arttheft) to learn more about "stealing history."

5. The historical figures Maimonides, Saladin, and King Richard I are at the heart of the mystery of the book. Read more about these three famous men and how their lives were connected during the Crusades.

6. Tanabe has her characters visit many Newport landmarks built during the Gilded Age, such as the Breakers and the Bellevue Avenue Historic District. Read more about the families who built them, including the Vanderbilts and Astors.

7. Tanabe modeled the Dalby mansion, "Morning Star," after a real house on Bellevue Avenue, known as "Miramar." Read more about the private home and the Widener family, who commissioned it as a summer house (in fact, two of the Wideners never saw the mansion, as they lost their lives in the *Titanic*).

8. Several art theft stories inspired the author, including the films *The Thomas Crown Affair* and *The Red Violin*. Consider watching one of these films as a group.

9. Consider taking a trip to a museum to look at ceramics from the Middle East, or browse a collection online. The Metropolitan Museum of Art, Freer and Sackler Galleries at the Smithsonian, Sackler

Museum at Harvard University, Detroit Institute of Arts, and Los Angeles County Museum of Art all have noted collections.

10. Many of the characters in the book are passionate about collecting or working with American furniture. If money were no object, what types of art or artifacts would you collect?

11. Finding a famous work of art at Goodwill has happened before. Read about the Salvador Dalí sketch discovered at a Goodwill in Washington state or the Giovanni Battista Torriglia painting that was discovered at a Virginia Goodwill.

## Further Reading

For a detailed account of the raid of the National Museum of Iraq by a man who was on the ground and helped recover stolen objects, take a look at *Thieves of Baghdad: One Marine's Passion for Ancient Civilizations and the Journey to Recover the World's Greatest Stolen Treasures* by Colonel Matthew Bogdanos.

*Seven Days in the Art World* by Sarah Thornton gives an expert and amusing look at the contemporary art world, including Christie's auctions.

Thomas Asbridge's *The Crusades: The Authoritative History of the War for the Holy Land* is an accessible read that delves into the fight for the Holy Land between 1095 and 1291, with a strong focus on King Richard I and Saladin.